PR... ...N

...S ...

"Cynthia Ede... ...KEN is what romantic suspense is supposed to be—fast, furious, and very sexy!"
Karen Rose, *New York Times* bestselling author.

"Sexy, mysterious, and full of heart-pounding suspense!"
Laura Kaye, *New York Times* bestselling author

"I dare you not to love a Cynthia Eden book!"
Larissa Ione, *New York Times* bestselling author

"Fast-paced, smart, sexy and emotionally wrenching—everything I love about a Cynthia Eden book!"
HelenKay Dimon

"Cynthia Eden writes smart, sexy and gripping suspense. Hang on tight while she takes you on a wild ride."
Cindy Gerard, *New York Times* bestselling author

CALGARY PUBLIC LIBRARY

JAN   2017

By Cynthia Eden

The LOST series
TORN
SHATTERED
TWISTED
BROKEN

ATTENTION: ORGANIZATIONS AND CORPORATIONS
HarperCollins books may be purchased for educational, business, or sales promotional use. For information, please e-mail the Special Markets Department at SPsales@harpercollins.com.

CYNTHIA EDEN

TORN

AVONBOOKS

An Imprint of HarperCollinsPublishers

This is a work of fiction. Names, characters, places, and incidents are products of the author's imagination or are used fictitiously and are not to be construed as real. Any resemblance to actual events, locales, organizations, or persons, living or dead, is entirely coincidental.

AVON BOOKS
An Imprint of HarperCollins*Publishers*
195 Broadway
New York, New York 10007

Copyright © 2016 by Cindy Roussos
Excerpt from *Taken* copyright © 2016 by Cindy Roussos
ISBN 978-0-06-243740-2
www.avonromance.com

All rights reserved. No part of this book may be used or reproduced in any manner whatsoever without written permission, except in the case of brief quotations embodied in critical articles and reviews. For information address Avon Books, an Imprint of HarperCollins Publishers.

First Avon Books mass market printing: June 2016

Avon Trademark Reg. U.S. Pat. Off. and in Other Countries, Marca Registrada, Hecho en U.S.A.
Avon, Avon Books, and the Avon logo are trademarks of HarperCollins Publishers.
HarperCollins® is a registered trademark of HarperCollins Publishers.

Printed in the U.S.A.

10 9 8 7 6 5 4 3 2 1

If you purchased this book without a cover, you should be aware that this book is stolen property. It was reported as "unsold and destroyed" to the publisher, and neither the author nor the publisher has received any payment for this "stripped book."

*I want to dedicate this book to my readers—
you are so wonderful! Thank you for your
support, your emails, your Facebook notes,
your Tweets—thank you for everything!! And
I hope you're ready to get LOST again . . .*

ACKNOWLEDGMENTS

FIRST, I MUST SAY "THANK YOU" TO THE WONDERful Avon staff—working with you is a pleasure. Thank you so much for the support that you have given to the LOST series!

I had an absolute blast researching this book—my stay on Jekyll Island was particularly memorable (ghost tour, Driftwood Beach, a night sighting of turtles trekking to the ocean). And, no, there weren't any deranged killers on Jekyll . . . just gorgeous views. Thank you to the people of Jekyll for such a fabulous welcome and for sharing the beautiful island with me.

I have loved writing the LOST series, and I hope that readers are enjoying the tales! More books are coming—and more twisted villains are waiting.

PROLOGUE

KENNEDY LANE'S SNEAKERED FEET POUNDED over the pavement. Her breath heaved in and out and her heart raced as she ran. The trees passed her in a blur. Her ear buds were snugly in place, blasting out a hard and fast beat that pumped her up. The music played and her gaze stayed locked on the trail in front of her.

Only two more miles to go. Two more . . .

She jogged faster. Her pace was on target. She'd do great in the upcoming race this—

He stepped from behind a tree. A tall, thick oak tree. She didn't have time to avoid him. Didn't even have time to stop as his arm flew out. His arm—powerful and strong—caught her right along the throat as she literally ran into him.

Kennedy flew back. Fell. Slammed right into the hard dirt trail.

Then she looked up, glaring as the man stepped fully into the old path.

And her glare froze.

He shouldn't be here. She yanked out her ear buds.

"What the hell was that?" She rose and brushed the dirt off her legs and then dusted off her palms. Her throat ached where his arm had hit her. The jerk had nearly strangled her. "You can't do some crap like that to me—"

Sunlight glinted off the object he held in his right hand, and her words stilled as she realized just what he gripped so tightly. *A knife.*

Kennedy backed up a step.

"Did you think we were done?" he asked her, shaking his head. "Just because *you* said we were through?"

"Wh-Why do you have the knife?" But Kennedy knew. She could tell by that sick, twisted expression on his face. And to think she'd once thought he was so handsome. So perfect.

He wasn't perfect any longer.

You have to get out of here. No other joggers were out on that trail. No one was close enough to hear her screams.

So she wouldn't waste her breath on a scream.

He glanced down at the knife, almost as if he were surprised to see it in his grasp. And when he looked down, Kennedy seized that moment. She turned and ran. She pumped her tired legs faster and faster and—

He tackled her. The impact was so hard that her whole body shuddered when she hit the earth. Then he flipped her over and before she could fight him put the knife to her throat.

"Sweetheart . . ." He smiled at her. "I'm not here to kill you."

Liar. She could see her death in his eyes.

"I'm just here to love you . . . and you're going to love me."

She didn't. She wouldn't. No matter what he did.

"We're going to be together you and I," he promised her softly, "for a very, very long time."

CHAPTER ONE

"FIVE YEARS AGO A WOMAN NAMED KENNEDY Lane went for an early morning jog and she never returned home." Gabe Spencer stood at the head of the conference table and spoke in a quiet, emotionless voice. "She was a twenty-two-year-old college student living in Savannah, Georgia. The authorities searched extensively for her, but they were never able to locate Kennedy—or to develop any leads in what was considered an abduction case."

Beneath the conference table Victoria Palmer nervously rubbed her palms against her jean-clad legs. Another case. Maybe this was what she needed. Lately, she'd started to feel as if she were about to jump out of her skin. Her nightmares were getting worse, and she needed some sort of escape—desperately.

"Kennedy's boyfriend—Lucas Branson—is the one who first alerted authorities to her disappearance," Gabe continued in his tough, no-nonsense voice. Gabe . . . he was the one who'd brought their team together, the mastermind behind LOST.

The Last Option Search Team.

And that was exactly what their little group was . . .

the last option for so many families. When cases went cold, when the cops gave up, families turned to LOST for help.

"Kennedy didn't turn up for their date, and Lucas became nervous. He went to her place, found no sign of her, and when she still hadn't shown up the next morning, he called the cops."

Victoria reached for the manila file in front of her. All the LOST agents had a manila file, just like hers. Gabe believed in being thorough, so she was sure every detail of Kennedy's abduction would be spread out for the group to review in their manila files.

"Branson came to me this morning," Gabe added. "So as of . . ." he glanced down at his watch, " . . . three hours ago, LOST is officially on this case."

Across the table, Wade Monroe gave a low whistle. That sound drew Victoria's attention, and she found him gazing at the handouts in the file.

"Five years . . . and not a single lead? No blood, no DNA trace evidence, *nothing*?" Wade's dark brows rose as he looked over at Gabe. "Seems like she just vanished from the face of the earth."

Gabe nodded, and, for a moment, sadness flashed in his bright blue gaze. Victoria knew that the cases were always personal for Gabe—the ex-SEAL had started LOST when his sister vanished. He'd found Amy—too late—and become desperate to try and help others.

You can't help everyone, though. You can't save every lost soul.

Sometimes, you couldn't even save yourself.

Victoria's heart pounded a bit faster. Lately, she'd started to think that she might be past the point of saving. *Joining LOST was a mistake. I should've stayed away.*

She should have stayed locked away, all safe and sound, in the labs at Stanford. Instead . . .

"Victoria, I want you heading out to Savannah."

She nearly fell out of her chair when she heard Gabe give that order.

And suddenly everyone's eyes were on her. Victoria schooled her expression as quickly as she could and her hand lifted as she made a quick show of adjusting her glasses, not that they needed adjusting. They hardly ever did, but the tactic often bought her precious time when she was nervous. "But there's not a body to study . . ." She almost flinched at her own words. *Talk about sounding cold.* Jeez, but she always felt like she said or did the wrong thing. "I mean . . ." Victoria cleared her throat. "If there aren't any remains for me to go over, I'm not sure how helpful I'll be with this case."

The dead were her domain. Mostly because she didn't know how to handle the living. A forensic anthropologist by trade, she'd been behind the safety of an Ivory Tower when Gabe had convinced her to join LOST.

And, lately, it was a decision that she regretted.

"You'll be plenty helpful," Gabe murmured, then inclined his head toward Wade. "You and Wade will be teamed up together on this case."

No, no, oh, please . . . no.

Wade flashed her a wide smile, one that instantly sent a flicker of heat surging through Victoria's veins.

Wade Monroe was trouble—trouble that she couldn't quite handle right then. Handsome, dangerous, and more than ready to play dirty on any case—yes, that was

Wade, all right. He was a threat to her, she knew it. Wade was an ex-cop, an ex-*homicide* detective, and while the guy was great at following up on leads and building comradery with local law enforcement personnel . . .

He made her nervous.

We're friends. We've been friends since day one. So why do I suddenly feel so different around him?

Maybe because their last two big cases had sent them both into a life-or-death panic? Maybe because the memories had unlocked in her mind and they just wouldn't stop?

She felt different around everyone now. It was harder to keep her mask in place, but Wade—handsome, sexy Wade—was the one who made her feel most on edge. She had to constantly watch herself with him.

And, lately, she'd felt *him* watching her, too much.

Victoria cleared her throat. "I'm not sure I'm the best agent to accompany him."

Wade's golden eyes narrowed. Such an unusual color. Beautiful and . . . intense.

"Why not?" It was Gabe who spoke. "Victoria . . ." And his voice softened as he added, "It's time for you to get back in the field."

Her gaze shot around the table and desperation gripped her heart. There was sympathy on the faces that stared back at her. Sympathy and, God forbid, *pity.* She hated the pity.

Dean Bannon sat to her right. An ex–FBI agent, Dean had seen plenty of horrors—up-close and personal. He was tough as nails, and *he* wouldn't ever balk at taking a field case.

Neither would Sarah Jacobs. The profiler was to

Victoria's right. Sarah, the woman who could get into any killer's head without the slightest hesitation—she wouldn't be running scared.

Just me.

"This is a good case for you," Gabe assured her. "And Kennedy needs you."

Kennedy. Right. The woman who was missing. The woman who was probably dead. A woman who wouldn't be coming home.

I'm supposed to help the dead. I'm supposed to give them their justice. Didn't Kennedy deserve justice?

Yes . . .

So Victoria balled up her shaking hands and nodded briskly. "What time do we leave?"

"Seven A.M. tomorrow," Gabe told her, and approval gleamed in his eyes. "Be packed and ready to go."

And that was an order. Right.

"You'll take the private plane to Savannah, and then you'll have an SUV rental waiting for you," Gabe added. "Don't worry. My assistant will take care of all the details."

Not worry? Right. She excelled at worrying.

The team members filed out—not that those assembled were the only agents at LOST. The organization was growing by leaps and bounds these days, and she knew that Gabe was even talking about opening a second office, maybe one along the West Coast. Currently, LOST was in a high-rise located in downtown Atlanta. But if Gabe really had his eye on expansion, she knew a second office wouldn't be a dream for much longer.

What Gabe wanted, he got.

Victoria grabbed her manila file and hurried toward the door. Sarah was lingering there, and, even though Victoria considered the woman her friend, the *last* thing she wanted was for Sarah to start poking around in her head. Sarah was a perfect profiler—

I just don't want her profiling me.

Because maybe, just maybe . . . Sarah might stumble upon all of those dark spots that she tried so hard to hide from the rest of the world. Once, she'd thought that Sarah might be like her. That she might understand just how hollow she was on the inside.

But the last case had changed that idea. Sarah had fallen in love, she'd battled her demons, and even made peace with her past.

Sort of, anyway . . . if facing off against your serial killer dad counted as making peace. Because Sarah *had* faced him—she'd gone up against the infamous Murphy Jacobs and come out alive . . . and stronger.

Murphy the Monster. The serial killer had escaped from jail. Most folks thought he was dead, killed in the fire that had lit up New Orleans on their last case. But . . . Victoria wasn't so sure. A guy like Murphy would be smart enough to cheat death. And at the scene of the deadly inferno that *most* believe had killed Murphy . . . *I thought I heard him humming . . . humming as he slipped away.*

Did Sarah worry that her father was still out there? Victoria didn't know for sure. What she *did* know . . .

I'd never want to face off against my father again. So it's a good thing he's under six feet of dirt.

"Viki," Sarah began, her voice hitching just a little, "we should talk—"

Victoria forced herself to smile. "Definitely. We *definitely* have to do that. How about as soon as I get back from this case? Because, wow . . ." She glanced down at her watch. A move she'd totally stolen from Gabe. "I have got to hurry home and pack if I'm going to be ready by seven A.M." *Such a lie.* She always kept a bag ready and packed. An old habit. "But as soon as I get back . . ."

Worry flickered in Sarah's dark eyes.

She hurried away from her—okay, she pretty much ran down the hall toward the elevator. She wasn't going to waste time stopping by her office. If she did, someone else might snag her. She was getting out of there. She'd review the file, get her bag, and be at the airport—ready to board LOST's private plane—just in time for that seven A.M. departure.

She jumped in the elevator and jabbed the button to close the doors. She had to get out of that place. It was so hard to breathe and as those doors slid closed—

A body bag, zipped up around me. No air. Can't breathe. I'm—

"Viki?" A man's hand flew through the elevator doors, activating the sensors and sending the doors flying back open. His deep, dark voice also vanished the nightmare that had tried to swirl around her.

Not a nightmare, though. Not really. Just a memory.

As the doors opened fully, Victoria squared her shoulders and pasted a false smile on her face.

Wade frowned back at her.

Wade . . . big, strong, dangerous Wade. He'd made

her feel nervous from the moment they met—*he still does.*

He stepped inside the elevator. "You leaving for the day?"

"Yes." Her voice came out too high. She cleared her throat.

"Me, too. Guess we'd better both get packed and ready." He pushed the button for the bottom floor. The doors closed. They started to descend and—

And he hit the button to stop the elevator.

"What are you doing?" Victoria demanded. "You can't just—"

"Stop the elevator?" One dark brow rose. "Sure I can." His head cocked to the right. Wade was wearing jeans and a T-shirt. He was often casual, usually pulling off one of those rough and tough I-don't-give-a-damn-vibes as he stalked around the office. She wished she could not give a damn, too.

He had his laptop bag slung over one shoulder, and she was sure that his case files were inside that bag, too. His arms were crossed over his chest as he studied her.

Victoria found herself backing up. In such a small space, retreat was pretty hard, but she still made a rather valiant effort.

His jaw hardened. "You don't need to be scared of me. You should know that by now."

Right. Dammit, she *did* know that. Victoria stopped retreating.

"What's going on?" Wade's voice softened. "And don't say nothing, because it's obvious that something is happening with you. You hardly talk to anyone lately.

You didn't want to go out into the field. Hell, you used to beg Gabe to send you out, but now—"

"That was before." She hated the brittle sound of her own voice. "Before a twisted SOB kidnapped me, drugged me, stuffed me into a body bag, and then decided it would be ever so much fun to use his knife on me." That case—it had changed everything for her.

His golden eyes darkened as he moved closer to her. Her shoulder bumped into the elevator's back wall, a mirrored wall. She hated mirrors. Hated looking into them because she was always afraid of what she'd see staring back at her.

My father's daughter . . . ?

Wade's hands rose, and for a moment real fear pulsed through her because she thought he was going to touch her, but . . .

He didn't. His hands flattened on either side of her head and she eased out a quick breath.

When Wade touched her, her heart raced too fast. Her skin heated.

His touch makes me want him so badly. She'd thought the attraction was just on her side, but lately Wade had been staring at her with a gaze that seemed to burn.

Just like he was staring at her right now.

"I wish it had been me," he gritted out. "I'm so sorry you went through that hell."

Oh, Wade. You don't know what hell is. I've been there more times than I can count. But that man who'd taken her . . . he'd forced her to see her past once more. He'd opened Pandora's box, and she couldn't seem to close it, no matter what she did.

"Have you talked to someone?" Wade asked. While

he hadn't touched her, his body was still intimately close.

"Gabe set me up to see a counselor." Like she hadn't talked to one of those before—and hated the whole experience. She wasn't the soul-baring type. "He says I'm totally fine." Actually, the guy hadn't said anything of the sort, and Victoria had only visited him twice. Sharing just wasn't her thing.

"He wants you in the field so that you can get past your fear." Wade's gaze searched hers. "But if you aren't ready . . ."

"I am." She nodded briskly. "I'm more than ready."

His lips firmed. "You don't have to lie to me."

Yes, yes, I do. I have to lie to everyone. But she couldn't very well tell him that.

I just need to get some control back. No, maybe what she needed was to lose that control, for just a little while. That had helped her in the past. It would help again.

Her shoulders relaxed as the plan blossomed in her mind. And, after a few moments, her left hand lifted. She was the one to touch Wade as she lightly skimmed her fingers over his cheek. "Don't worry about me. I'm fine."

His nostrils flared. "You don't even see the threat, do you?"

There was no threat. Not with him. He was her friend, nothing more. Nothing less. So she was attracted to him. So—

"You're playing with fire." A muscle jerked in his jaw. "And you don't even know it."

Maybe I like the fire. "Start the elevator," Victoria

told him softly. "Seven A.M. is going to be here too soon, and I have a lot to do tonight." More than she'd realized. Her hand slid away from him.

Slowly, Wade backed away. He reached out and pushed the button to start the elevator once more.

Her breath eased out on a sigh of relief.

"You know," Wade murmured, "partners are supposed to trust each other."

"Is that what we are? Partners?"

"On this case."

She'd never had a partner before.

"But . . ." Wade continued, voice thoughtful. "I think you're holding back on me. Keeping secrets."

I am. The doors opened. She slanted a quick glance his way. "Maybe when you tell me your secrets," Victoria said, "then I'll share mine." And she nearly ran from the elevator. "See you tomorrow." She didn't look back but could feel his gaze on her.

You'll never know my secrets. Because she never let anyone get close enough to know them. That was one of her rules.

FOLLOWING YOUR PARTNER wasn't standard procedure, not at LOST, not at any damn place. But at ten o'clock that night Wade found himself sticking to the shadows as he followed Victoria Palmer—*Dr. Victoria Palmer*—into one of the wildest clubs in Atlanta. *Wild Jokers.*

It wasn't Victoria's kind of place. He knew that. Hell, he'd bet his life on it. He'd been worried about her—a nagging worry that wouldn't leave him alone—and found himself heading to her building.

He'd arrived just as she left and . . .

I followed her.

Because something had been different. Not just *one* thing. Her pants had been traded in for a short skirt. A form-fitting top hugged her breasts. Her long, dark red hair wasn't pulled back in a ponytail or in one of her usual long braids. Instead, her thick hair flowed loosely over her shoulders.

And her glasses—the glasses that he always found sexy—were gone.

She almost looked like another woman. She was sure acting like one, too.

She strode into the club as if she owned the place. The bouncer let her sweep right past the snaking line. Wade had to give the guy fifty bucks just so he could cut through and follow her.

And once inside . . . the music was pumping. Roaring. Bodies were pressed together in a giant blur on the dance floor. The drinks were flowing, voices were rising, and Wade was pretty sure people were having sex in the corners.

Having sex. Getting high. Doing anything they wanted.

This isn't her place. Victoria didn't belong in Wild Jokers.

She had started working for LOST right around the time he'd come aboard. She was smart—crazy, wicked smart—and the woman always seemed to be bubbling with energy. He'd noticed that she didn't like to be still very much—she was a mover, a thinker, a doer.

She was friendly at the office but she didn't flirt.

Not with him, not with any of the LOST staff. Just business, that was Victoria. Killer hot, just business Victoria.

She'd been putting up Keep Away signals from day one, so he'd stayed back.

Even if her body was wonderfully curved. Even if her gorgeous hair was sexy and thick. Even if he sometimes looked into her green eyes and almost forgot what he'd been about to say.

Just business.

Victoria Palmer was a beautiful woman, but one who tried to downplay her looks. A futile effort since there was no hiding her smooth skin, her high cheekbones, and her full, sensual lips.

Maybe he thought about her too much.

There's no maybe about it.

Especially lately. Their last few cases had taken deadly turns, and he'd started to see her in a whole new light.

Just not this light.

This place . . . this scene . . .

Victoria sauntered up to the bar. She ordered a drink. When the martini glass with the bright green liquid was placed in front of her, she made quick work of downing the drink.

She must definitely be in the mood to let off some steam. And if that was her goal . . . *I can help.*

But some bozo had already moved in on her. A big blond guy with hands that immediately reached out and settled around Victoria's waist.

Wade lunged forward. Victoria didn't like to be touched. He knew that. He'd seen the way she shut down when someone touched her, so he made sure to keep his hands off and—

She didn't shove the guy away. She turned back to him. Smiled. And put her hand on his chest.

Wade froze.

Some asshole bumped into him, and he snarled at the guy. The music rose around him—harder, sharper— and Victoria was laughing as she stared up at the blond stranger.

What in the hell?

Wade shook his head. Victoria was out for a hookup. That much was obvious. And he was standing there, glaring at her. He needed to get his shit together. This was none of his business. They might be partners, but if she found out that he was there . . .

Clenching his back teeth, Wade whirled away. Victoria was a grown woman. More than capable of looking after herself. He strode toward the exit.

But something is wrong. I've seen pain in her eyes lately. Pain that she tries to hide from everyone else.

He stilled. His gaze cut to the left. Yeah, that was a woman nearly having sex up against the wall. This club was all about the fast hookups. Strangers in the dark. He knew because . . .

I've been here before.

Wade looked back over his shoulder, but Victoria was gone. So was the blond guy. Real alarm shot through Wade as his gaze flew over the packed dance floor.

He didn't see Victoria, not anywhere.

Wade started searching the shadows. It had just been a moment. Where the hell was she? He rushed up to the bar and slammed his hands down on the bar top.

A bored-looking bartender glanced his way. The guy was sporting what looked like a freshly styled Mohawk.

"The sexy redhead in the short skirt," Wade bit out. "Where did she go?"

The bartender jerked his thumb over his shoulder. "Headed out the back door."

Wade shoved away from the bar and hurried toward the door.

"I don't think they want to be bothered!" the bartender yelled after him.

Screw that. Victoria couldn't just run off into the night with some stranger. Considering the business they were in, she *knew* just how dangerous that behavior could be.

He shoved open the back door and it bounced against the brick wall. More shadows waited for him. Shadows and stench—it reeked out there, smelling of old booze and cigarettes. It was *not* Victoria's scene. She was fine wine. She was flowers. She was seduction.

And he still wasn't seeing her. Wade rushed forward. He turned to the right, saw the narrow alley and the couple locked in a hard embrace.

The man had the woman up against the wall. Her hands were on his shoulders and—

"Victoria." Her name tore from Wade before he could get enough control back to stop himself.

The man whirled to face him. Same big blond guy. And, apparently, he was a guy who liked to fight—because he whirled and lunged at Wade with his fists clenched.

"Stop!" Victoria cried. He'd know her voice anywhere.

She'd been making out with that jerk.

Wade glared at the guy. It was too dark for him to see the man's expression clearly. They were close to the same height and build, but Wade didn't doubt he'd be able to take the creep down.

"You need to get the hell out of here," the man told him. His voice was a low growl.

"Actually," Wade fired right back, "I will be leaving. With Victoria."

The fellow cursed. "The hell you—"

"Easy, Flynn. I know. He's my . . . partner at work." Victoria pushed between them. Her hand slid across Wade's chest, and heat singed him. "Why are you here?" she asked him.

I followed you. I've got some issues. More than some. "Maybe I'm here for the same reason you are," he said instead. "A fast fuck in the dark."

She flinched. Then said, very clearly and flatly, "We were kissing, not fucking . . . in case you couldn't tell the difference."

Oh, hell. He hadn't meant to hurt her. *Jealousy makes me such an ass.* Hurting Victoria was the last thing he ever wanted to do. His voice softened as he said, "It's time for us to go home, Victoria." And yeah, he emphasized the *us* because he wasn't leaving without her.

"Vik . . ." The other man rolled back his shoulders. *Vik . . .* Wade realized that the blond man wasn't a stranger to Victoria. There was too much intimacy in his voice. "Who is this joker? And do you want me to kick his ass?"

I'd like to see you try. What had she called the guy? Flynn? Freaking Flynn. He hated the man.

"I told you, he's my partner at work. And . . . Wade's a friend, too," Victoria said. "Sorry, Flynn, but I have to go." Her right hand was on Wade's chest but her left was on Flynn's, and Wade really wanted her to stop touching the guy. "Go back inside. I'm all right with him, really."

The blond guy's hand rose. Slid over her cheek. "You know where I am. When you need me, find me. I'll always come when you call."

She doesn't need you.

And then he just . . . walked away. Just left Victoria in the alley.

Victoria didn't speak for a few moments. She did pull her hand away from Wade. They stood there, Victoria in front of him, her body so close, her scent—light lavender—rising over the smell of that stale alcohol. Wade tried to figure out what to say to her. He tried to find the words that would smooth over this mess that was developing between them.

"What are you doing?" she finally asked him.

He had no clue. Making an ass of himself? Yeah. Because when he'd seen Victoria with that jerk, jealousy had burned through him and he'd lost the ability to have a sane thought.

"Wade, please, answer me. Why are you here?" Victoria pressed.

He really wished he could see her eyes in the dark. Victoria's green eyes could shine with so many emotions. "Why are *you* here?" Wade asked her. "I know you aren't into bars like this. I've heard you say before that these places aren't your kind of scene."

Victoria just shook her head and started walking away from him. "I'll see you tomorrow," she muttered.

No, she was going to see him right then. He was tired of feeling as if Victoria didn't see him. *I don't like her looking through me.* He caught her wrist. "You know how dangerous it can be to hook up with strangers." At LOST they'd seen—firsthand—what death and horror could follow when you trusted the wrong person. The rest of the world might walk around with blinders on, but they didn't. They *couldn't.*

"Maybe I was in the mood for some danger."

Her voice was so low he had to strain to hear it, and then he shook his head, hard, even as his fingers tightened around her wrist. "That's not you." But Victoria had been changing. Ever since that damn attack. Ever since . . . *I nearly lost her.*

And he hadn't even realized how important she was to him, not until then. Victoria and her sharp mind. Her slow smile. Her sexy glasses.

He hadn't realized it . . . not until he'd seen her covered in blood.

I won't lose her. Not to some psycho killer. Not to some random stranger.

"Maybe you don't know me nearly as well as you thought," she said.

For some reason, her words pissed him off. "Actually, I think I know you better than you realize." He'd worked intimately close with her—and intimate was the key word. He'd spent too many hours with her. Fantasized about her. Realized that the one thing he wanted—

Was right there.

"I'm taking you home," Wade said.

"Oh, Wade . . ." Victoria sighed his name. "I don't need protecting. I'm an adult. I can take care of myself."

"And I'm your *friend*." That had been her word choice. "So let me just give you a ride home, okay?" Because he needed to get her out of that alley. Away from that club.

Before the blond bozo came back. Freaking Flynn.

"I haven't stopped you from sleeping with anyone," Victoria said.

Yeah, baby, you have. Maybe she didn't get just how drastically his life had changed since her abduction. Maybe it was time that he stopped playing it cool. Stopped giving her *time* and started acting.

"Let's go," Wade said. He tugged on her wrist.

Victoria sighed again but she didn't argue. They headed out of the alley and then dodged cars as they hurried across the street. His motorcycle was waiting, and he jumped on the bike and revved up the engine.

"At least you don't have to take a cab back home," he told her as she climbed on behind him.

Her hands curled around his waist.

"You'll need to hold on tighter," Wade told her as his hands rolled around the handlebars. "A whole lot tighter . . . and come closer." Because she was trying to distance herself. That wasn't going to work. He intended to eliminate all the barriers between them.

Victoria wouldn't be able to hold any of herself back.

He felt her inch forward, and a hard smile curved his lips.

If Victoria was in the mood for danger, she wasn't

going to be taking a walk on the wild side with a stranger. If she wanted passion, if she wanted hot sex, she didn't need to go looking for it at some club.

He shot away from the corner and they raced down the street.

If she wanted danger and passion . . . *then I'll damn well give it to her.*

CHAPTER TWO

H ER LEGS WERE TREMBLING WHEN VICTORIA climbed off Wade's motorcycle. He'd parked underneath the streetlight at the corner of her building, and when she glanced at him—

He looks furious.

As if he had the right to be angry. He'd totally screwed up her night. All her careful plans had gone straight down the drain because of him. And now tension was coursing through her blood. Her body was too tight and aching, and her control had never been so close to splintering.

"Thanks for the ride home," she told him. *Not.* "I'll see you in the morning." She turned away from him and hurried up the steps of her building.

"Not that easy . . ."

She glanced back over her shoulder. He was *following* her. Looking all tall, dark, and deadly as he strode away from his beast of a motorcycle. If he hadn't been her partner, if he hadn't been a *friend,* he would have made for a perfect lover. The kind that she usually took when the need got to be too much for her.

But he's Wade. Not some guy that she could forget

the next day. She'd see him, again and again. And Victoria had one rule when it came to her lovers—*no ties*. No emotions.

Not ever. Wade wouldn't understand that rule.

She'd seen how dangerous love could be. *Love* had ripped apart her family. Love had sent her father into a killing fury.

She looked back up at her building. Safety was a few feet away. She nodded to her doorman and hurried inside. The marble gleamed beneath her feet and—

Wade was behind her. The doorman had just let him come right in. Probably because he'd seen Wade before and knew they were friends. Only she didn't feel friendly at that moment.

The alcohol had lowered her inhibitions far too much. She probably should have just stopped with one drink, but a second one—for courage—had seemed like a great idea at the time.

She jabbed the button on the elevator. Wade came up behind her. She could practically feel the heat from his body reaching out to wrap around her. "I'm home, safe and sound," Victoria said as the elevator doors opened. She stepped inside and turned to face him. "You can go now."

But he shook his head. He walked into the elevator, and she had to step back. "We aren't done," Wade told her, his voice a bit rough.

She knew he was used to getting what he wanted. She'd known that from the first week of working with him. But . . . *what does he want from me?*

His gaze slid toward the control panel.

"Don't even think it," Victoria warned him as she

leaned forward and swiped her security card over that panel. The last thing she wanted was to play another round of stop-the-elevator with him. Very resolutely, she hit the button for her floor.

His lips curved, just the faintest bit. "I don't have to stop it this time. I'm sure we'll have plenty of privacy at your place for our little chat." He rolled back his shoulders. "We need to clear the air. It'll be good, for both of us."

She seriously doubted that. They didn't speak again until the elevator stopped on the top floor, and then he was the one to back away. He motioned for her to head out, and she pretty much jumped out of that elevator. She hurried past him and nearly ran down the hallway. Victoria was the only resident who lived on the top floor. A penthouse. Expensive as all hell, but totally worth it— both for the view and the privacy. In order to get to this floor, a special key card was required in the elevator.

The lush carpeting swallowed their footsteps as they headed for her door. She fumbled a bit with the lock but seconds later they were inside. Victoria shut the door behind them and sealed them into her home.

She tossed her keys onto the small table in the foyer. She didn't bother flipping on the lights. The large, floor-to-ceiling windows in her den let in plenty of illumination, courtesy of the Atlanta skyline. She headed toward those windows and stared out at the city. Usually the view soothed her.

Not tonight.

She waited for him to speak first.

"You want me to apologize, don't you?" Wade said as he came to stand near her.

Victoria risked a quick glance at him. His gaze wasn't on her. It was on the city. The lights.

She followed his stare. *This view is why I sank all of my savings into this place. Because I can stand here, look out at the rest of the world and feel safe. No one is around me. I'm free up here.*

Free, but not alone—not right then. She cleared her throat. "An apology would be a good start." She turned to face him. "Just because we're partners on this case, that doesn't give you any rights in my life. You don't get to control what I do or who I do it with." No one did. "So if I want to go out, hook up with some hot guy and forget the rest of the world—"

He turned toward her. "Why not me?"

Her mouth fell open a bit.

"Why not hook up with me? If it's sex you want, come to me." He moved even closer. She stiffened her knees and refused to back up. "You know the attraction is there between us."

Victoria wasn't going to pretend that she didn't feel that hot lick of heat when they were close. "I think you're attracted to most women." She'd seen the way he flirted—too many times. "You said you knew me? Well, guess what? I know you, too."

He shook his head. "You were right before. I don't think we know each other nearly as well as we both believed." He lifted his hand.

She tensed.

"I don't want you to do that," he said, voice thickening. "You let *him* touch you. Why not me?"

Because the man at the club hadn't mattered. *Her* rules. Always, hers. Flynn played the game she wanted.

No commitment, just fun. He was easy to deal with. Easy to understand.

She didn't think there was anything easy about Wade at all.

Wade's fingers curled around her chin and he tilted her head up.

"I'm not looking for some kind of commitment," Victoria blurted. Commitment was the *last* thing she wanted. Ever. "I don't want ties, Wade."

"And you think you'd have them with me?"

"We work together, we—"

He kissed her.

She'd wondered before how he would kiss. If he'd be careful at first, if he'd try to woo her with sensual skill.

She hadn't considered that he'd just . . . *take*.

There was no tentativeness in his kiss. No hesitation at all. Her lips were open, so were his, and he claimed her mouth with a hot, hungry savagery. His tongue slid over the curve of her mouth. He thrust it past her lips, and her heart slammed into her ribs.

Maybe she should have pushed him away. She didn't. Instead, her hands rose and locked around his shoulders. She pulled him closer. She opened her mouth wider. He wasn't the only one going to take.

Earlier that night, fear and sadness had twisted inside of her. She'd left LOST as fast as she could. She'd gone home. She'd read over those terrible files on Kennedy Lane.

She's dead. I know she is. Another one gone.

And it had been too much. She'd needed to escape. To put the dead behind her and feel alive again.

But Wade had stopped that plan. Wade—handsome,

sexy Wade. Wade—the man kissing her as if he wanted to devour her right then and there. And she . . .

Maybe I want to be devoured.

His mouth slowly pulled from hers, but he didn't let her go. She didn't let him go, either. Victoria realized that she'd never just kissed a man before—and ignited.

Not until Wade.

"Been wanting to do that for a while," he admitted.

Then you should have done it.

"You don't have to go to some bar," Wade said gruffly. "And find a stranger to give you what you need."

He had no clue what she needed.

"I'm right here, Viki. I can give you everything that you want."

Oh, but those words were tempting.

But Wade . . . Wade wasn't a onetime thrill. She wouldn't be able to walk away from him and go on with her life. She'd see him every day, and how was she supposed to handle that? Her fingers flexed on his shoulders. "I told you . . ."

"You didn't want ties. Fine with me. I'll take what you want to give."

Those words . . . she didn't understand him, not at all. "Just what are you offering?"

"Consider me your partner, with benefits."

Her eyes widened. *No, he had not just said—*

Wade pulled away from her. "Think about it."

Her hands fell to her sides.

"See you in the morning." Then he headed for the door.

Wait—now *he was leaving?* When she could still taste him? When her body was aching? When she just wanted to drag him into her bedroom and forget everything else? *Now?*

She didn't want to think about his offer. If she thought about things, she'd change her mind. She'd see how wrong this was. How wrong *all* of it was.

Partner, with benefits.

Her breath came a bit faster. Yes, yes, this was wrong. In so many ways. It was— "Stay," she said.

He turned back toward her. She saw the glint of hard lust burning in his gaze. That hot fire should have made her hesitate. It didn't.

It just made her hurry toward him. When he was just a few feet away, she stopped. Her heart was racing hard enough to shake her chest, but she tried to school her expression as she gazed up at him. "No promises. No ties." They could just take the pleasure and walk away, right? They were both adults. Smart, capable. They could do this. He seemed to understand and actually be cool with her rules.

"I'll give you what you need," Wade promised her.

Right then, *he* was what she needed. Even when she was kissing Flynn she'd been on edge. And when Wade called her name in the club, her first thought had been . . .

Yes. Him! She hadn't been angry that he was in the alley. She'd been glad to see him. Even if he had screwed up her plans.

And, maybe . . . maybe he was the answer that she'd been looking for. There was no risk with him—she knew Wade was one of the good guys. He wouldn't hurt her. So they'd take each other. They'd let their desire go, and . . .

No ties.

She offered her hand to him. Wade's gaze dropped to her fingers. His lips tightened but he took her hand. She felt the press of his calluses against her. "Then I guess we have a deal," Victoria said. She licked her lips, nervous now and—

He kissed her again, and the desire she felt flared even more within her. "Damn right," Wade rasped against her mouth, "we do."

And Victoria knew there would be no going back.

HER HIGH HEELS wobbled a bit on the broken sidewalk. Melissa Hastings put her hand on the brick wall, steadying herself. She'd definitely had too much to drink.

Time to call it a night.

She sucked in a slow, deep breath and tried to fight the nausea rolling through her stomach. She didn't usually get sick when she drank, but tonight . . . tonight was different.

Tonight she'd had way too much because she'd been celebrating.

I'm free.

Finally. He wouldn't be holding her back any longer. She'd be able to do exactly what she wanted, *when* she wanted.

Freedom was heady. Freedom was hot. Freedom was . . .

Making my head swim.

Her hair slid over her face as she lowered her head. She'd go catch a cab and head back to her apartment. She'd sleep this off and be as good as new tomorrow.

Better than new.

I'm free.

After another bracing breath, she lifted her head. Her hair slid over her shoulders and—

He was there.

Standing in the shadows, just a few feet away.

"Are you feeling all right?" His voice carried easily to her.

And, no, she wasn't feeling all right. She was actually even dizzier and her tongue had started to feel thick in her mouth. That wasn't normal. She'd been drunk before and hadn't felt this way. *What is wrong with me?*

"You probably should have been more careful," he said as he stepped forward, "with what you drank."

"Y-You . . ." Her breath choked out as fear snaked through her. He shouldn't be there.

"Did you think we were done?" he asked her softly as he continued to close in on her. "Just because *you* said we were through?" His deep voice seemed to wrap around her. A sexy, seductive voice.

A voice that belonged to a very dangerous man.

She glanced over her shoulder. The club wasn't so far away. There were plenty of people right there. She was perfectly safe, even if she was beginning to feel sick as all hell. She turned her stare back to him.

He'd stopped a few feet away, but with the light behind him, shadows covered his face. He had a tall, powerful form. *A great body.* She'd thought that the first time she'd seen him. And, sure, she'd been aware of his danger—he had that sexy, bad boy edge. She'd wanted him.

He'd wanted her.

Now I want to get away from him.

"Stay away from me," Melissa said as she backed up a step. "I told you—"

"Are you afraid of me?"

Yes.

Something glinted in the darkness. Her heart thudded even faster. Oh, dear God, did he have a knife? No, no, surely he didn't. That was crazy.

Wasn't it?

But then he stepped forward, and that glint vanished. "I'm not here to hurt you."

The dizziness was getting worse. She put her hand to her forehead.

"Oh, Melissa . . ." He sighed out her name. "Don't you know better than to leave your glass unattended?"

She . . . she *had* . . . but just for a moment. One dance. And her friends had been at the bar, right next to her glass. Her roommate Jim had been there. Jim always looked out for her. The drink had been safe.

Hadn't it?

Her knees started to buckle, but he was there to catch her.

"You put . . . something in my drink . . . ?" Now her nausea and dizziness made sense. He'd drugged her drink. Maybe roofied her. *So scream, Melissa!* A voice in her head cried out. *Scream! People are right there.*

She opened her mouth.

And felt the sharp prick of a knife beneath her chin.

I did see a knife, glinting in the dark.

"I'm not here to hurt you, sweetheart. I just want to make you happy."

A tear slid down her cheek.

"So don't scream. Just relax. In a few more moments you'll be far away, with me."

Melissa didn't want to be with him. She'd broken it off. They were done.

"Sorry!" She heard his voice boom out. She blinked and tried to see what was happening. "My girlfriend had a little too much to drink." His arm was wrapped around her. "I'll make sure she gets home okay."

He was talking to someone else. Her eyes narrowed as she turned her head. One of the bouncers from the club was walking toward them. She had a chance—

The knife pricked her skin. Could the bouncer see it?

"Say a word to him," he said softly, "and I *will* hurt you, so very badly."

She didn't speak.

"Don't worry!" he called out to the bouncer. "I'll take good care of my girl."

She wasn't his girl.

The bouncer's footsteps shuffled away.

Her eyes began to drift closed. She couldn't hold them open any longer.

"That was so good," he said. "Now don't worry. I'll take care of you. Just like I said. Such good care . . ."

WADE CLENCHED HIS hands into fists and fought to hold onto his control. They were in Victoria's bedroom. He was near the bed. She was in the doorway.

Holy hell, this was happening. Victoria was about to be *his*. Finally.

She stared at him and then lifted her fingers and turned off the lights.

"You don't have to do that," he said. His voice

sounded rough and a bit ragged, but when a wet dream came to life, how else was he supposed to talk? "I want to see you." *All of you.*

He heard the rustle of clothing, and, with the city skyline drifting through her bedroom blinds, he could just make out her sensual form as she pulled her shirt over her head. "You don't want to see my scars," Victoria said. "It's better this way."

Screw that. He knew she'd been attacked by that bastard with a knife while they were in Louisiana. And her scars—they weren't a turnoff. Nothing about her was. Not to him.

There was more faint rustling and then . . . then Victoria was walking toward him. He could hear the soft sound of her footfalls. When she touched him, when she pressed her body to his, he realized that she was totally naked.

"You're wearing too many clothes," she told him. "If this is going to work, you need to get naked."

"Oh, it's going to work," he muttered. *Provided my control stays in place.* She had no idea just how badly he wanted her. He got that now. She'd understand soon enough.

But he didn't strip. Not yet. Instead, he put his hands on her shoulders. Such smooth, soft skin, and then, slowly, his fingers skimmed down her body. Over her arms. Across to her breasts. He loved her breasts, so round and full. He could feel the nipples—tight, aroused—pushing against his fingers, and he had to tease them. Stroke them.

"Wade . . ."

And on down his fingers went as the two of them

stood in the near-dark. Over her stomach. Over the faint line of a scar that he could feel. His fingers lingered there, caressing softly, wishing that he could take away her pain.

"Don't—"

His fingers moved away at her sharp cry. He'd come back to her scars later. He'd show her that every single inch of her body was perfect to him.

Down, down his fingers went. Her legs were parted and his hand slid toward her sex. Soft. Hot. And when he thrust his fingers inside—

Her hands clamped around his arms and she held on tight.

"I can't wait to be in you," he rasped.

"Then don't wait." Her hips rocked against his hand. "Don't make *me* wait."

She was wet. For him. Turned on already.

He slid his fingers over her sex. He liked to touch her. Liked to explore every bit of her and hear the hitch of her breath. His cock shoved against the front of his jeans. The zipper was probably imprinted on him, and he didn't even give a damn. He enjoyed touching her far too much to stop.

Would she climax for him this way? It would be so much better if she came now, then he could go in, drive deep, get her to erupt for him—

"Strip," Victoria told him as her short nails bit into his arms. "Now, Wade, *now*."

He liked the need in her voice. The sensual demand.

She pulled away from him and climbed onto the bed.

Wade stripped. Threw his shirt across the room. He

ditched his shoes and socks and lowered himself onto the mattress. His hand curled around her hip and he leaned over her. He wanted her mouth beneath his, he wanted—

"You don't have to seduce me," Victoria whispered. "I'm ready now."

Good to know. But he'd been fantasizing about her like mad for the last few weeks, and he wasn't about to screw this up. *She won't ever think of freaking Flynn again.* So he kissed her. Deep and hard, and he savored her. His hands stroked her body as he explored every single inch of her.

First her mouth. Then her neck. He pressed his mouth to her throat, right over the frantic beat of her pulse. He licked her and used the light edge of his teeth on her tender skin. She moaned for him then, so he did it again, harder.

He kissed her breasts. He *loved* the taste of her. Sweet. So sweet. She arched up against him when he licked her nipples. She whispered out his name.

And he kept exploring. He spread her legs wide and put his mouth on her.

This wasn't going to be some fast hookup in the dark. By the time they were done, he'd own her body.

Just as she'd own his.

When she tried to pull away from his mouth, he put his hands on her hips, held her close, and he tasted her. He got a little drunk on her—a *lot* drunk as he stroked and licked and she came against his mouth.

She yelled out his name and he rose above her, still licking his lips. Still tasting her.

He grabbed for the condom in his wallet, and he was damn grateful the thing was there. He shoved his jeans away. Put on the condom.

My control is gone.

He'd just needed her to come first, come before he let that last thread break. *She had to enjoy it, she had to enjoy me . . .*

Because they weren't going to be together just one time. Oh, no, he had plans for her . . .

"*Now,* Wade," Victoria said, her voice so sexy he knew he'd be hearing it in his head every time he closed his eyes.

He positioned his cock at the entrance to her body. He caught her hands, threaded her fingers with his, then pushed her hands back against the pillows, pinning them there even as he thrust deep into her. And after one thrust—

Wade nearly lost his mind.

Better than good . . . better than in his dreams.

Her legs locked around him. She took him in deeper. She moaned for him, and he thrust even harder into her. The bed shook beneath him, and her sex—so tight and hot and freaking mind-blowing . . .

She was slick from her climax. But when she called out his name, when her body tensed beneath his, he knew the pleasure was hitting her again. As her sex squeezed him, Wade's own release barreled into him. The climax drove through his whole body, hollowing him out as he sank into her.

Hot. Dirty. Wild.

His breath heaved out of his chest.

Hell, yes, they'd be doing that *again*.

He kissed her. *We'll be doing this all night long . . .*

"WADE."

He stirred when he heard her voice, and a smile started to curve his lips.

"Wade, you need to go."

His smile stilled. His eyes opened. He had to blink quickly against the harsh glare of the overhead light.

Victoria stood near the bed, a white terry-cloth robe wrapped around her. Her eyes seemed so wide and deep as she gazed at him. "You should go now."

He glanced toward the clock on her nightstand. Nearly three A.M. They'd stopped their last round less than an hour ago. He must have fallen asleep . . .

"We have to be on the plane at seven, remember?"

He remembered.

He also realized Victoria was kicking his ass out of her bed. He rose, taking his time, and she immediately backed away. At that retreat, he stilled.

Was she still scared of him? After what they'd just done?

He took a minute, then rolled back his shoulders. He could smell her all around him. That sweet, heady scent of lavender, and he was still aroused.

Tonight hadn't satisfied him. It had only made him want more.

The question was . . . did she feel the same way?

Not if she's kicking me out.

He put on his jeans. Dressed in silence. He could feel her eyes on him and he knew she had to see his arousal. When he looked up at her, Victoria's cheeks were flushed.

Holding her gaze, he closed in on her.

Victoria backed up a step.

His eyes narrowed at that retreat. She was supposed to trust him. *Not* retreat.

His hand lifted and—sure the hell enough—she gave a little flinch. After everything . . . no. His hand sank beneath the weight of her hair and he brought his mouth down on hers. He kissed her slowly, taking his time and enjoying her mouth. Then he pulled back and said, "I like touching you."

"Wade . . . *no ties.*"

That had been her rule, not his.

He smiled and let her go. If he could, he'd tie her to him in a thousand different ways.

But he could be patient. He could play the game, for now.

So he turned away from her and headed toward the front of her penthouse. When he reached her door, he glanced back over his shoulder. Victoria had followed him.

"Two questions . . ." His voice was a little harder than he would have liked. But he didn't understand this game between them, not fully, not yet.

Victoria nodded.

"Question one . . . do you often go out and look for a stranger in the dark?" Because if she did, he'd have a whole lot of asses to kick.

"Not . . . often."

His back teeth clenched.

"And I wasn't . . . wasn't looking for a fuck, not like you said. I was kissing him. I—I don't know what else—"

She stopped.

He didn't want to think of anything *else*.

Very slowly, Wade exhaled. "Question two . . . when you feel the need to let go again . . . when you want to climax until you scream . . . will you come to me?"

Silence.

Hell—

"No ties?" Victoria asked. "No strings? Partners, with benefits?"

He nodded.

"Then . . . yes."

That was what he needed to know.

For now.

"See you on the plane," Wade told her, and then left. He didn't let himself look back, because if he did, he didn't think he'd be able to leave.

VICTORIA LOCKED THE door behind Wade. She set her alarm and crawled back into the bed—a bed that smelled of him.

She swiped at the stupid tears on her cheeks.

The sex had been *amazing*. Toe-curling, can't-catch-my-breath fantastic. But it should have only been sex. Nothing more. Nothing less.

Instead, she'd fallen asleep in his arms. She'd let down her guard and enjoyed being held by him. She'd awoken and hadn't been scared. She'd awoken and thought—

He's with me.

But she had to keep him from getting too close. He couldn't learn her secrets. And he could *not* break through the wall that she kept around herself.

Sex was one thing.

Secrets . . . trust . . . no, there were some lines that she would *never* cross. Not even with him.

SHE DIDN'T SLEEP well the rest of the night. Mostly because she kept thinking about Wade. Thinking far too much about him.

So at six A.M. she had her bag and rushed out of her building. She'd already called a cab to take her to the airport. She intended to play things very cool with Wade. She could do casual. Maybe. Hopefully.

She could—

"Victoria?"

At the familiar voice, she turned her head. Flynn Marshall was jogging toward her, clad only in a pair of loose shorts. Sweat covered his muscled chest.

Right. He runs. Just like clockwork when he's in town.

That was how they met. She'd been on her way to work. Flynn was jogging right by her—they'd nearly collided.

Then she'd seen him again, at Wild Jokers. He bought her an apology drink.

Now, Flynn barely seemed winded as he closed in. He put his hands on his hips and his gaze swept over her. "I was hoping I might see you today."

Uh, okay.

"I was worried," he added. "I went back to that alley about ten minutes later and you were gone."

Were her cheeks turning red? She thought they might be. "Wade took me back home."

His blue eyes narrowed. "The work . . . partner."

She'd been clear with Flynn. No strings. And they'd had sex once. Just once . . . "Right. My work partner."

His gaze slid to her bag. "Another mysterious trip?"

"Just business as usual." He was a pharmacy rep, so she knew Flynn took plenty of trips out of town himself.

"Maybe we can get together when you come back." His ear buds dangled loosely around his neck.

She hesitated. *Wade and I have a deal.* "I don't think that's such a good idea."

His eyelids flickered. "Because of the partner?"

A cab pulled up at the corner. Her cab.

"Because of the partner," Victoria agreed. Then she shook her head. "No, no, it's because of me. I'm sorry, Flynn. I—"

His smile was sad. "You never led me on, Vik. I knew where I stood with you." He nodded. "I'd hoped that you knew where you stood with me, too."

The cab driver had exited the vehicle.

"Stay safe," Flynn murmured. Then he was gone, running off at a steady pace.

I never felt the same with him.

The cabbie took her bag. Victoria murmured her thanks and climbed into the vehicle.

I never felt the same attraction with Flynn. Not like I do with Wade. When Wade touches me . . . it's not fear that makes me tense.

It was need. Desire.

Deal or no deal, she wouldn't have been meeting Flynn when she got back to town.

Because now she knew what it was like to want someone so badly that nothing else mattered. And that kind of desire . . . it was dangerous.

CHAPTER THREE

"T HIS IS WHERE SHE DISAPPEARED," LUCAS BRAN-
son said as he put his hands on his hips and
paused in the middle of the running trail—
Jupiter Trail. The sunlight glinted off his sunglasses.
"Or at least, this is where the cops found her ear buds.
She always ran with those things in, said it helped her
to get in the zone . . ." He trailed away, then shook his
dark head.

Victoria glanced around the area. They were in a park
on the outskirts of Savannah, and the mid-afternoon
sunlight flickered down through the trees. The dirt path
snaked through the trees—a *lot* of trees. Enough trees
to provide the perfect cover for someone who might
be waiting to attack. Birds chirped happily from the
shelter of those trees.

"We have Kennedy's case files," Wade said as he
paced toward a tall oak tree. "There have been no
ransom demands, no phone calls . . . no contact at all
from Kennedy or her abductor in five years."

Did Lucas understand just how bad that was? A
ransom demand at least meant the victim *might* be
alive. You could get a proof of life with a ransom

demand. You could work with the abductor. But when a perp took a victim, and the family or friends never heard so much as a whisper . . .

That means the perp never intended to let his victim go.

"There was nothing," Lucas said, and sadness flashed across his face. "I even offered a ten-thousand-dollar reward, hoping someone would come forward and tell me what had happened to her, but no one seemed to remember anything." His hands lifted, then fell. "She was here one moment and gone the next. If it hadn't been for those ear buds, hell, I don't even know that the cops would have believed she was ever out on this trail." He pulled off his sunglasses and shoved them into his shirt pocket.

"Her hair was found on the ear buds," Victoria said. She'd read that bit of info in Kennedy's files. And the hair had been compared by forensics to the hair at Kennedy's home—in her brush. The cops had proved that Kennedy was in the park, but then she'd disappeared.

"Yeah, that was when they finally started to believe me." Lucas sounded angry now, anger reflected in the hardness of his blue gaze. "But that was over forty-eight hours after she disappeared. And I know, *now,* that the first forty-eight hours are the most important. That's when you have the best chance of finding the missing, right?"

Victoria met Wade's gaze.

"That's what they say on TV," Lucas muttered. "If you don't find them in that first forty-eight hours, the chance of the person coming home alive . . . it goes down so damn far."

There was such pain in his voice. It pulled at her. She didn't quite know how to handle the victims—not the living ones, anyway. That was why she spent so much of her time with the dead. *They* talked to her. She found evidence on them. She could recreate their last moments. Piece together what happened to them.

Track their killers.

Yes, it was the dead that helped her. The living . . . she just hurt for them.

At that moment, she was hurting for Lucas. "TV isn't always reality," she heard herself say.

Hope flashed in his eyes.

Oh, crap. I don't want him to expect a miracle. Yes, they were in Savannah to help find Kennedy, but after five years—*five years!*—the chance of finding her alive . . .

It was astronomically low. Surely Lucas understood that?

Wade cleared his throat. He crossed to Victoria's side, but when he spoke, his attention was on Lucas. "You told the police that Kennedy didn't have any enemies."

"Everyone loved her." Lucas's chin lifted. "Maybe that was the problem. She was so beautiful. She'd enter a room, and the men would take one look and want her. She was just that kind of woman, you know? You saw her, and you wanted her."

Wade tilted his head to the side. "I'm sorry, but I have to ask you this . . . was Kennedy involved with anyone else? Were you two exclusive?"

"I was going to marry her."

Wade's expression remained neutral as he said, "If

we're going to do this right, you should know, we have to dig deep into Kennedy's life. If she had secrets, we *will* uncover them. So if there's something that you know—now is the time to share it."

Actually, Victoria thought, five years ago would have been the time to share it.

"Were you exclusive?" Wade pushed. "Or was Kennedy involved with anyone else?"

Lucas's gaze fell to the ground. "There were a few times . . . I—I thought she might be cheating. There were just . . . marks on her. Marks that I hadn't put there."

Now Victoria was curious. "Marks?"

Lucas's jaw locked. "Faint bruises on her hips. Redness near her . . . her breasts. Marks that a lover would leave."

"And you're sure that *you* didn't leave the marks?" Wade wanted to know.

"She said they were nothing." Lucas's gaze turned distant. "That she'd just bumped into something or that her clothes had chaffed her during her last workout. I was always the jealous type—she knew that. And she just laughed and told me that I didn't have anything to worry about." He ran his hand over his face. "I never saw her with anyone else. I never found any trace of the guy after she vanished, so I thought—I thought I *was* just being jealous."

Wade was silent.

In the distance, Victoria heard the sharp cry of a bird.

They'd been out there for a while, and they hadn't encountered any other people. The spot was so isolated. So perfect for an abduction.

"Her routine was the same, every day?" Wade asked.

Victoria was just letting him run with his questions. That was Wade's thing. As a former homicide detective, he always seemed to know just what to ask the witnesses and family members.

She figured he could handle the living.

She'd stick with the dead.

Only I wish we could find Kennedy alive. She wished that sometimes the good guys would win and the monsters in the dark wouldn't claim so many victims.

"Every single day," Lucas rasped, "she'd run three miles. She said it helped her clear her head. Same path, same time. Kennedy liked her schedules."

But a schedule like that could prove dangerous. It was too easy to follow someone else's patterns. Too easy to watch and find those weak moments.

Victoria glanced around once more.

Too easy to find those isolated spots.

It was far better for people to vary their routines—to try different trails. Different times. Because you never knew . . .

Just who might be watching.

"I need closure," Lucas suddenly said. Her gaze slid back to him. She tried to study him objectively—a handsome man, fit, in his late twenties. He seemed guileless, as his emotions flashed easily on his face and in his eyes. He was the one who'd contacted LOST. He was the one who'd never given up on Kennedy, but . . .

"Closure?" Victoria repeated carefully.

"I've found someone else." His cheeks flushed. "And I love her. We want to get married . . ."

Now she got the picture. "But you think you can't

move on, not until you know for certain what happened to Kennedy?"

His Adam's apple bobbed. "What if she's still out there, hoping that I'll find her? Waiting for me?" And the guilt was there, creeping into his voice. "And I'm here . . . with someone else? Planning a new life? A life that—" He broke off, but he didn't have to say the words.

Victoria understood. *A life that should have been hers.*

"We'll do our best," Wade said. "But as Gabe told you, we can't guarantee that we'll find Kennedy. We'll reexamine the case, look at it with fresh eyes, but if there isn't anything to discover . . ." He shook his head a bit sadly. "You have to realize that Kennedy may never come home. You may never get the closure that you seek."

"And that's the hardest part," Lucas said as his lips curved down. "Not knowing. Is she dead? Is she alive? Did some sick bastard take her from me? Or did she . . . did she just choose to vanish? That's what some of the cops thought, you see. That the ear buds weren't proof she'd been taken. They said she could've just dropped them. That she could've just decided she didn't want marriage or a life with me." He shrugged. "So she just vanished. Without any of the clothes in her closet. Without her money. Without anything." His laughter was bitter. "That was such bullshit. I *know* she didn't leave me. Kennedy wouldn't have done that. I *knew* her."

Silence.

Lucas's phone began to ring. He pulled it from his

pocket and glanced down at the screen. "It's Connie. I'm sorry, I have to take this . . ." He turned and paced a few feet away.

Victoria focused on Wade. "I'm guessing Connie is the new lady in his life."

Wade's considering gaze was on the other man. "I think he knows that Kennedy was cheating on him. He didn't believe her excuses. There was another guy." Now his stare turned to her. "We need to find that other man."

"You think he took Kennedy?"

"I think some men can't let go of a woman." His gaze darkened as he stared at her.

Her breath came a little faster. "You mean Lucas," she whispered. Five years—and he still hadn't let Kennedy go, not fully. But was that love? If he was holding on because he wanted to help her, because—

"He's lying to us." Wade's soft voice barely reached her ears. "I don't trust him."

What? He didn't trust the man who'd hired them? That made zero sense to her. Why would Lucas hire them if he was hiding something?

But she didn't get to question Wade because Lucas was closing in. He'd put the phone back in his pocket and was striding toward them. "Sorry," he murmured. "Connie wants to set up the appointment with the caterer."

Wade's brows climbed. "A caterer . . . for your wedding?"

The flush on Lucas's cheeks deepened. "Connie doesn't understand. She thinks that Kennedy is gone, but I . . . I have to be sure."

Now Wade whistled. "Does your fiancée know that you hired us?"

Lucas shook his head.

Wade seemed to absorb that new piece of info. Then he said, "Do you usually keep secrets from the women you're planning to marry?"

Lucas glanced away. "Only when I think those secrets might hurt them . . ."

Wade was silent for a beat of time, then said, "Thanks for the information this morning. Dr. Palmer and I will keep you updated on anything we find, but should you need to contact us—"

"I've got your numbers," Lucas said quickly.

"And we're staying in town," Victoria added, rattling off the name of the B&B that LOST had booked for them. "If you think of anything else that might be able to help our case, please let us know."

Lucas nodded. "I—I will. And thank you. Thank you for coming here." His gaze turned distant. "Thank you for looking for my Kennedy."

Sympathy stirred within Victoria because she could hear the pain in his voice, but when she cut a quick glance at Wade, she saw him staring at Lucas with . . .

Suspicion.

"Why would he lie to us?" Victoria demanded.

Wade had wondered when she'd ask that question. They'd left Lucas behind—less than an hour ago—and were now on the campus of Worthington University. Kennedy had been a senior at Worthington when she vanished. He wanted to talk with some of the professors she'd had, see if they remembered anything about her.

"Wade." Victoria sounded annoyed. She reached out, locking her hand around his wrist. "Answer me. Why would he lie?"

He looked down at her hand. She'd touched him. That was a good step. Maybe. "He's already keeping secrets from the woman he's about to marry. Doesn't that tell you anything about the guy?"

"He *hired* us!" They were just beneath the bell tower and no one else was around. "That tells me he wants to find Kennedy. He wants to get closure—just like he said."

Closure was one thing. Lies were another. "He knows she was screwing around on him, Viki."

"Because of a few marks?" She pulled away and motioned dismissively with her hand. "Maybe those were just from her workout, maybe—"

He laughed. He couldn't help it.

She glared at him. Victoria pushed up her glasses. Did she know that the glasses made her eyes look even darker? Sexier? Probably not.

Her hair was up in a ponytail again today. He knew she meant the style to be no-nonsense, but it just accentuated her high cheekbones and the elegant curves of her face. She didn't have to ditch the glasses and let her hair down to be hot to him.

She kind of . . . just was.

"Wade . . ."

She was also back to sounding annoyed with him.

His hand lifted. She tensed. *Still not past that, are we?* One day, she wouldn't tense when he reached for her.

Keeping his eyes on hers, he slowly pushed back the

collar of her shirt. His fingers brushed over her soft skin, right along the base of her neck. "There's a big difference," he told her softly, "between the mark that comes from clothes rubbing against you and the mark that a lover makes."

Her lips parted.

His fingers stroked over the faint mark he'd left on her skin. "I can look at this and tell it was made from my mouth."

She backed away from him.

"And I'm betting," he said, as his hand dropped to his side, "that when Lucas Branson saw the marks on Kennedy's body, he knew another man had left them."

She touched her neck. "I didn't even notice it!"

Now she looked horrified.

His lips twitched. "Don't worry. Your shirt covers it. No one else will know." *Just me and you, baby.* "But if you had another lover . . ." *And that thought sure as hell pisses me off.* ". . . he'd notice. He'd notice any marks left by my mouth or by my hands."

"Her hips," Victoria said. "He said there were marks on her hips."

Wade nodded. "If she had bruising on her hips, it could have come from a lover holding tight during an, um, delicate moment."

"And *that's* why you believe he was lying. You think he had to know about the other man."

"I believe he knew of him, but I don't think Lucas knows *who* the guy was." That was where they came in. "Another lover could be the key to finding her."

She paced away from him, to stand in the shadow of the tower. "You're good at reading people."

"I've had to be, in my job."

"But are you ever wrong? Do they ever fool you?" She turned back toward him. "Is there anyone that you just can't figure out?"

"Yes." He waited a beat. "You."

Her gaze quickly cut away from him. She sure seemed to be paying a whole lot of attention to that bell tower.

But he wasn't done. "You've got so many secrets surrounding you. Other people at LOST, they think that Sarah is the one with the dark past . . ."

"Her dad *is* a serial killer," Victoria pointed out. "One who is still out there, and no one knows what he is doing or if he'll strike again."

That thought had kept him up plenty. He knew exactly how dangerous Murphy Jacobs was. The guy hadn't earned the name of Murphy the Monster for nothing.

"And I think everyone at LOST has a dark past," she continued quickly. "Isn't that why we take the cases we do? Why we do the job?"

Maybe. Or maybe there was more to it.

Maybe some of them were trying to atone for the sins of the past.

I know I am.

"So you believe," Victoria said, her gaze seemingly still on the tower, "that Lucas Branson is a liar, but not a killer?" She sighed and looked over her shoulder at him. "You don't think he killed Kennedy, do you?"

Killed her, then waited five years and hired them to find her? No, that didn't make sense to him. "I just want to find out what else he's holding back." And until he

did, Wade intended to tread very carefully around the
other man.

Victoria turned to fully face him. "To know him, we
have to know Kennedy." She straightened her shoulders. "And not just the bare facts. We already know
those. At the time of her disappearance, Kennedy was
twenty-two years old, majoring in psychology. She was
an avid runner, she worked as a waitress at a club just
off-campus, and she was planning to marry Lucas."
She tapped her chin in a considering manner. "On the
surface, she seemed to have a perfect life." The wind
pulled a lock of Victoria's hair free from her ponytail.
"I've always thought the perfect lives were the ones
that held the most jagged pieces."

Now that was interesting. "You don't believe in perfection?"

"No. Not in perfection. Not in happy endings." Her
lips flattened. "I spend far too much time with the dead
for that."

And she was far too comfortable with them.

But he didn't say that. Instead, Wade looked over to
the right, focusing his gaze on the Life Sciences building. "I think it's about time for the good doctor to see
us now," he murmured.

Because they had an appointment in five minutes
with Dr. Troy North. Dr. North was the acting head
of the psychology department *and* he'd been Kennedy's advisor when she was a student at Worthington. If
anyone on campus could tell them about Kennedy, he
should be their key.

Victoria nodded curtly and turned to hurry down the

steps that would take them away from the clock tower and toward the Life Sciences building. A little research had shown them that the psychology department was housed in that seemingly massive building. Wade followed her, and after a while he couldn't stop himself from saying, "We aren't going to talk about it, are we?"

She froze. So did he. It was either freeze or barrel into her.

"Wade . . ." Her spine was stiff. So was her whole body.

He didn't want her nervous, but he did want answers. "Just making sure I understand the rules."

She looked back at him. *So lovely.* But her eyes were filled with a sadness that he hated. Did she even realize that he could see her pain? "I think the rules are clear," Victoria said, then turned away and kept walking.

He didn't follow, not immediately. *I'm going to change the rules, baby. I'll be changing everything.*

Because one night with her wasn't nearly enough for him. Yes, he'd marked her.

But she'd marked him, too. A mark that cut deep.

"KENNEDY LANE?" DR. TROY North leaned back in his leather chair. He exhaled on a rough sigh. "Now that's a name that I haven't heard in years."

Victoria perched on the edge of her seat. Wade was right beside her on the long, rather uncomfortable couch. Only he didn't perch so much as sprawl. *Dominate the space.* He appeared completely at ease and in control, but then, Wade had probably done hundreds of interviews just like this one.

I don't know why he wanted me in the field.

Usually, Wade just called her in when she was supposed to examine the dead or work in the lab to study evidence. *Not* to interview witnesses.

Not that Dr. North was a witness—not exactly.

Her gaze darted to the wall behind him—and all of his diplomas. A bachelor's degree in psychology, a master's degree, both from Northwestern University. A Ph.D. from Harvard. He had certainly spent a lot of time studying the inner workings of the human mind.

He was like Sarah, she thought. Only a much harsher, male version. When he looked at her—and the man *kept* glancing her way—Victoria had the uncomfortable feeling he was trying to peer into her head. Or her soul.

"Northwestern," she murmured. "I've heard it's a great school. I have a . . . friend who attended." Though she didn't think that Flynn Marshall really qualified as a friend. "Did you enjoy your time there?"

Dr. North seemed caught off-guard by her question, and that was exactly what she wanted. "I— Yes, I learned a great deal there. It was at Northwestern when I realized just how very interesting the human mind could be. Our motivations. Our desires. Our compulsions."

The way he said those words . . . it was just creepy.

"Dr. North . . ." Wade began, his voice flat and calm. "What, exactly, was your relationship with Kennedy?"

The doctor blinked. He had green eyes—a light, almost icy shade. "I was her advisor. I helped her pick her classes each semester and I guided her research." His stare became a bit distant. "She had enormous potential." He rose from his chair and moved to a framed photograph on the wall. "She was our student of the year," he said as he tapped the frame with his knuckles. "Such potential," he murmured.

Victoria's eyes narrowed as she rose and moved closer to the photograph. It depicted Dr. North handing Kennedy Lane a plaque. She had a smile that stretched from ear to ear.

So did Dr. North.

"You two were close," Victoria said as her gaze cut toward him.

One of his shoulders lifted and fell in a careless shrug. "I suppose we were."

She didn't think there was any "suppose" about it. The doctor was tall, fit, maybe in his late thirties or early forties. He was also attractive, in a somewhat cold, hard way.

His blond hair was cut very precisely, falling away from his high forehead. His suit was top-of-the-line and his shoes gleamed as if they'd been freshly polished.

He felt like old money. Power. But there was something else about him . . .

"Are you close with all your students?" Wade asked. He hadn't moved from his position on the couch. He still looked way too comfortable. Way too casual.

She knew his pose was a lie.

"I try to be," Dr. North said as he headed back around his desk. He didn't sit, though. He crossed his arms over his chest and said, "I want to guide them. Help them."

"And you . . . *helped* . . . Kennedy?" Wade studied him with a neutral expression.

"Kennedy needed very little help. She was incredibly

driven. She was going places. I'd written her a letter of recommendation for graduate school just before—" He broke off. "Well, before she went missing." Then he shook his head. "I don't understand . . . why are you all looking for Kennedy now?" And he reached forward, picking up the card that Wade had handed him when they first entered his office. It was a card Dr. North had only given a cursory glance before placing it on his desk earlier. "Last Option Search Team?" He peered over at Wade. "That's what your questions are about? You're still searching for her? After all this time?"

"We've been hired to look into her disappearance." Wade rose to his feet and closed in on his prey. "As I said when I arrived, Dr. Palmer and I have just a few questions."

"About Kennedy . . ." Dr. North said.

"Actually . . ." Wade smiled at him. It wasn't an overly friendly smile. "Our questions are about *you* and Kennedy."

The other man blinked. He even took a step back.

Victoria eyed him with more interest. She really enjoyed watching Wade work.

"Were you intimately involved with Kennedy Lane?" Wade queried.

"I . . . I was her *advisor*!"

"Were you sleeping with her?"

Dr. North sucked in a sharp breath. "I don't have to answer that question."

"Well, that kind of *is* an answer." Wade ran his fingers over the edge of the desk. "You say her name like it's some kind of caress. You keep her picture on your wall—"

"Because she won a prestigious award from the school!"

"Psychology student of the year. I got that." Wade glanced toward the wall. "So why aren't any other winners up there? Why just her? I mean, surely, in five years, there *have* been other winners."

Dr. North didn't answer.

"I'll tell you why . . ." Wade said with an inclination of his head. "Because you were involved with her. I think you were lovers."

Dr. North didn't flush. Instead, he went almost deathly pale.

"You were," Wade pushed. "Weren't you?"

Well, well, Wade certainly worked fast. In town for just a few hours, and he already knew the identity of Kennedy's secret lover.

Victoria had to admit it, she was impressed. Wade was good. So good that she thought she might learn a few things from his interview techniques. *So this is what fieldwork is really like.*

"One time," Dr. North finally rasped. "We slept together once."

Wade shook his head, and she could see the disgust on his face. "You never mentioned that fact to the cops, did you? You kept it secret."

"I would have lost my job! I'm not supposed to have a sexual relationship with a student! I had to keep silent, I—"

"You didn't want to look guilty," Wade charged. "*That's* why you didn't say a word. You didn't want to be labeled suspect number one because the woman you'd been sleeping with vanished. A woman who could have destroyed your career if she said the wrong word to the wrong person."

That sure sounded like a motive to Victoria.

Dr. North yanked a hand through his hair. *Not so perfect now.* "It's not what you think! I had nothing to do with her disappearance! Nothing!"

Wade didn't look convinced. Victoria understood his suspicion.

"She wasn't going to marry him," Dr. North suddenly announced. "She was breaking it off with Lucas. She told me that. Kennedy wanted grad school. She didn't want to settle down with that kid—she had plans."

Now this was interesting. Victoria crept closer to him.

"She had plans," Dr. North said again, shaking his head. "So many plans . . ." His sigh was sad. And then . . . then he turned his stare on Victoria.

And his gaze sharpened. "I'm sorry," he murmured as his eyes seemed to bore into her. "But I just realized . . . I think we've met before."

What? "No, no, I don't think we have." Her denial was adamant. She would've remembered him.

But he cocked his head to the side as he studied her. "*Doctor . . . ?* Are you also a doctor of psychology?"

A brittle laugh escaped Victoria at that question. "Hardly. I'm a forensic anthropologist." She was also an M.D., though she didn't think it was relevant for him to know that information.

He stared blankly at her.

Wade straightened to his full height and moved his body just a bit, positioning himself between Dr. North and Victoria. "She's a doctor of the dead."

"The . . . dead?"

"Yeah, buddy, that's what I said." Wade definitely sounded annoyed. "Now, how about we keep talking about *Kennedy*. You remember *her,* right? The woman you just admitted sleeping with? The woman who had such plans—"

"But I—" Dr. North seemed to be floundering. And he'd moved so that he could stare directly at Victoria once more. "I know we've met."

Wade snapped his fingers in front of the other man. "Could you *focus*? I mean, hell, do you just have a compulsion to hit on every beautiful woman you see? Is that one of *your* issues?"

Dr. North's mouth flopped a bit, rather like a fish. Then fury tightened his face. "I think I've answered quite enough of your questions. I don't know where Kennedy Lane is. I don't know what happened to her. And it's time for you to leave."

Victoria nodded curtly and headed for the door. She could feel the doctor's gaze following her—and she didn't like the weight of that stare.

I don't know him.

Or at least . . . she didn't think that she did.

"Innocent men don't hide," Wade said flatly behind her. "And they also don't stonewall when a woman is missing. They try to help." His voice was mocking as he added, "Thanks so much for your *help,* buddy." Then she heard his footsteps following her.

They exited the office and paused in the little lobby area. There was a reception desk to the side but no one was behind it. No one had been there when they arrived, either.

The door was shut—sharply—behind them.

"At least he didn't slam it," Victoria said as she gave Wade a weak smile. "But I'm thinking that interview didn't go so well."

His eyes glittered. "Do you know him?"

"No." She didn't think that was a lie.

"Then he was just trying to throw us off. Change the topic because he didn't want to answer any more questions about *her*. Nice technique, but it's not going to work for long."

Was that what it had been? The knot in her stomach eased a bit.

He put his hand at the small of her back. She tensed, and hated herself for that.

Wade leaned in close to her. His breath feathered over her ear as he said, "One day, you won't."

"I . . . won't?"

"You won't get nervous when I'm near. You'll like it when my hands are on you."

Actually, that was the problem. She already liked it when his hands were on her. Did he think that she tensed up because she was rejecting his touch? *No, far from that.* She liked it too much.

They headed toward the stairwell. She reached for the door—

But it flew open before she could grab the handle.

A man stood there, a guy with sun-bleached hair, a golden tan, and an expression carved with absolute rage. He wore a T-shirt and loose jeans, and he rushed right by her and Wade, almost as if he didn't even see them.

"What the hell . . ." Wade muttered as he pulled Victoria back.

Yes, that was what she'd been thinking.

She turned and saw that the guy—he appeared to be in his early twenties—hurrying toward Dr. North's door.

"Now this could be interesting," Wade said. And he followed.

"Uh, Wade?"

The blond man threw open the door. "Where the hell is she?" His booming voice seemed to echo through the building.

"*Very* interesting," Wade added as he picked up speed.

By then the blond man in a hurry was inside the office.

"What are you doing here?" Dr. North demanded. "Get out, you can't— *Ah!*" His words ended in a strangled cry.

Victoria ran toward the office and burst inside right after Wade. The younger man had Dr. North pinned against the back wall. Blood dripped down the doctor's face—probably from his newly broken nose. The blond attacker had his hand pulled back, ready to take another swing.

"*Where the fuck is she?*" he demanded.

"I don't know!" Dr. North yelled. He struggled in the guy's hold, reaching out desperately toward his desk.

"*Where is Melissa?*"

Victoria rushed toward the attacker, but Wade beat her to him. He grabbed the younger man and yanked him away from the doctor, but the guy came up swinging and drove his fist at Wade.

"Stop!" Victoria yelled.

No one stopped.

But Wade did duck. The fist missed him and he swung, punching the younger man in the stomach. There was a loud *ooof* as the air was driven from his lungs.

He fell to the floor, clutching his stomach.

Wade stood poised over him, his fists still at the ready. "How about don't attack before you *look* at who it is you're hitting," Wade advised, not even sounding a bit out of breath. "Might save your ass next time."

Dr. North had his hand to his nose—a definitely bleeding nose. He lurched forward and grabbed for his phone. "I'm calling security!"

Victoria figured that was probably a good idea.

The blond man looked up at Wade. "Who the hell are you?"

"I'd rather know who *you* are. No . . ." Wade glanced over at Dr. North. "I'd like to know why you're so pissed at him."

The young man rose—a little shakily. "Melissa is missing."

Victoria's blood iced at that one word. *Missing.*

"I need guards here, *now,*" Dr. North snapped into the phone.

"I know he slept with her," the blond raged. "I know it!"

The same way he'd slept with Kennedy?

"She didn't come back to the apartment last night. She didn't come home." The man glared at Dr. North. "I want to know where she is . . . *what did you do to her?*"

"Nothing," Dr. North said, his voice sharp. The phone was pressed to his ear.

Wade turned to confront the doctor. "I couldn't help but notice," he said, voice mild. "Your receptionist isn't here today—"

"*That's* Melissa!" the young man spat. "She's working as his assistant while she's in grad school!"

And she hadn't come home last night.

"I don't know where she is," Dr. North said quickly.

Victoria met Wade's hard stare. She nodded, then cleared her throat and noted, "You seem to say that an awful lot, *Doctor.*"

"Melissa is missing!" The young man sounded even more frantic. "She won't answer her phone. She didn't come home. And no one remembers seeing her after ten last night! She's *gone.*"

A chill slid over Victoria's spine. Maybe this Melissa had just spent the night with a friend. Maybe her phone was turned off.

Or maybe . . .

Maybe more was at work here. A serial abductor? Could it be possible? She didn't want to jump to any conclusions, not yet, but there were certain facts that couldn't be overlooked.

Two women, both with ties to Worthington University, both linked to Dr. North—those women were gone.

One look at Wade's clenched jaw and Victoria knew he was thinking the same thing that she was. Coincidences *didn't* happen. And if Melissa was truly missing, then LOST was needed in Savannah, needed desperately.

CHAPTER FOUR

THE CAMPUS SECURITY GUARDS ARRIVED AND hauled the young blond guy out of Dr. North's office. But, a bit surprisingly to Victoria, the psychology professor didn't demand that the fellow be arrested.

They'd just witnessed an assault, but Dr. North was shoving tissues at his nose. *Not* pressing charges.

"Take him off campus," he huffed. "Let him cool the hell down." He pointed at his attacker. "It's only because of Melissa that I'm doing this. You're her *friend*. And I know she'd be devastated if you lost that scholarship of yours because of this incident."

The other man paled.

Way to deliver a threat, Dr. North. Victoria didn't like that doc, and not just because he'd been staring at her so hard earlier. Something about him put her on edge, and she was desperately trying to remember . . . had they met? Surely she would have remembered him.

Right?

"Get your hands off me!" the blond man snarled. "I can take myself out of here!" He jerked free of the campus cops. "You guys are useless! I went to you earlier, and you did *nothing*! Melissa didn't come home! Why the hell am I the only one worried about that?"

He marched for the door, but before he could leave, Wade locked a hand on his shoulder. "I'm worried. My partner and I . . ." He glanced swiftly at Victoria. "We want to hear your story. So how about we leave campus, and you can tell us just what is happening?"

The kid's eyes narrowed in confusion. "Who the hell are you, man? And why would any of this matter to you?"

Wade pulled a card from his wallet. "Because my job is to find the missing."

Only they didn't normally handle a case as recent as this one. The girl had only been gone a few hours. Some law enforcement personnel wouldn't even characterize Melissa's disappearance as an official missing person's case yet, especially not if there was no sign of foul play.

But Wade was leading the now stunned-looking fellow from the office, so she turned to follow him.

"Wait."

That was Dr. North's cry. And he'd closed in on her.

He still held tissues to his nose, but his eyes were on her. "We have met."

She shook her head.

"Your father . . ." he said. "I remember now. I was a grad student, sitting in on his trial . . ."

A dull ringing filled her ears.

"Obsession can be a dangerous thing."

Her shoulders straightened. "Your nose is broken. You should take care of that." *And leave me the hell alone.*

Without another word, she turned and hurried from his office. The campus guards stood a bit awkwardly near the door, apparently not sure what they were supposed to do now. With the doctor not pressing charges, there wasn't much they *could* do. Especially since the attacker was willingly leaving the scene.

She quickened her stride to catch up with Wade. He glanced over at her, his eyes narrowed in suspicion. Had he heard Dr. North's words?

It wasn't as if her father was a big secret. Most people knew about him. They knew he'd been charged with her mother's death. They knew he'd been found innocent.

Then he'd died.

Simple facts. Cold.

And far, far from the real truth of the matter.

The sun felt warm on her skin when they finally cleared the ivory walls of Worthington University. There was a big park right across the street from the school, and Wade headed straight there. He pushed the blond man onto a beach and barked, "Your name. Now."

Instead of giving his name, the guy ran a shaking hand through his hair. "I punched the professor."

Yes, he had.

"Oh, jeez, I am in so much trouble." He hunched forward.

"The professor didn't press charges, so you're fine." No sympathy softened Wade's voice. "Now, your name." An order.

Victoria glanced back toward Worthington. She could just see the side of the Life Sciences building.

Actually, it was Dr. North's window that she noticed on the second floor. Was he watching them?

And still bleeding?

"M-My name's Jim Porter." Jim huffed out a breath. "And I just . . . I swear I just lost it when no one would listen to me about Melissa. But I know something is wrong. I know it."

Victoria eased onto the bench next to Jim. She made sure not to touch him. She bit her lip and tried to figure out what to say. *What would Sarah say?* "How do you know for certain? Maybe she just hooked up with someone last night."

Jim's head whipped up and snapped toward her. His dark brown eyes locked on her.

Crap. I did it again. Said the wrong thing.

"She wasn't looking for a hookup," he gritted out. "We were hanging out, dancing with friends. I went to the bathroom and when I came back she was just gone."

Right. Gone. Which means that she *could* have found a guy and left with him. Or maybe she'd connected with other friends and gone to check out another bar.

Lots of possibilities. Doesn't mean something bad happened.

Yet.

"She didn't answer her phone. She didn't call all night." Jim pushed his hand through his hair. "That's not like Melissa. She *always* checks in with me."

"Have you contacted her family?" Wade asked as he stood a few feet away, his arms loose at his sides.

"She doesn't have other family. Melissa was a foster kid, just like me. I *am* her family, and she wouldn't just vanish." His face hardened. "No one would listen when I started calling this morning. Cops told me that since she was over eighteen, there wasn't even a reason to look for her yet. *She's gone. That's a reason.*"

"Did you check the hospitals?" Wade asked.

Jim flinched. "No . . ."

"That will be our first order of business. We'll call all the hospitals and make sure no one fitting her description was brought in between last night and this morning."

Hope came and went on Jim's face. "LOST." He still held Wade's card in his hand. Though it had gotten a bit crumpled in his fist. "You . . . you really do this shit? You find the missing?"

They worked cold cases. Not something like this. If this Melissa actually turned out to be missing—and not just hanging with a friend or recovering in a hospital bed—then the local authorities would take over. LOST wouldn't have any sort of jurisdiction. They weren't a federal agency. They were the ones who came in when hope was lost.

Hope isn't lost here.

"We try to find them," Wade said carefully.

Jim sucked in a deep breath. "What do you need to know? What can I do?"

"First, I need her name. Full name."

"Melissa Hastings." He hesitated, then a brief smile curled his lips. "Melissa Margaret Hastings, though she's always hated her middle name."

"Tell me what she looks like."

"About five-foot-six, one hundred thirty-five pounds. Fit, cause she runs a lot."

Just like Kennedy had run? Victoria's stomach knotted.

"Blond hair, long, just to her shoulders. Blue eyes. Last night she was—she was wearing a blue shirt. White skirt. Heels."

"Good," Wade said. "That's good information."

Jim nodded and hurriedly said, "I can do you one better, man." He fumbled and pulled out his phone. He tapped on the screen a few times and then lifted the phone toward them. "This is her."

Victoria leaned in to see the picture of the pretty, smiling blonde. Dimples winked in her cheeks, and she had her arm wrapped around Jim's neck.

Wade took the phone. "Mind if I text this picture to my phone? It can help in the search."

"Anything man, anything." While Wade texted the photo, Jim mumbled, "I—I tried using that Find My Phone app, but it didn't work. I don't know if—if she disabled it or if . . ."

If someone else did? "Like I said," Wade said, his voice calm and easy as he handed the phone back to Jim. "First we check the hospitals . . ."

BUT MELISSA HASTINGS wasn't in any of the local hospitals, and an hour later Victoria found herself standing outside of a run-down little bar called Vintage. They were on the edge of the historic district in Savannah, and the area was bustling with tourists, even at that time of the day.

"The place was packed last night," Jim said. "It's always big at night. Melissa was dancing one moment, then gone the next."

Melissa Hastings, age twenty-three. A grad student in psychology who'd worked as an assistant for Dr. North so she could help pay the bills at the apartment she shared with Jim. Jim had been quick to point out that he and Melissa weren't involved in any relationship. He'd said they were more like family.

Sometimes, family can be your biggest danger.

Jim rocked forward on his heels. "I have to be at work soon, but, Jesus, I can't just walk away! She's out there. She needs me."

They'd learned more about Jim and Melissa in the last hour. The two had first met when they were fifteen and they wound up at the same foster home. They bounced around after that, but something had clicked for them, and when they'd been reunited at Wellington . . .

Jim had told Victoria that fate brought him back to Melissa.

Victoria hadn't been able to tell him that she didn't believe in fate.

"Go to work," Wade ordered him. "We'll look around here. See what we can find out."

There was no missing the relief on Jim's face. "Thank you!"

He shouldn't thank them. They hadn't done anything.

She paced away from the men as Jim rattled off his phone number and other contact information to Wade. Then the young guy was off—nearly running away. He seemed to do everything fast. Life passed at high speed for him.

She headed toward the alley on the side of the building. Long, narrow. Empty. Her gaze slid over the cobblestone path back there. The place appeared to have been freshly cleaned. There was a puddle of water, as if the area had been hosed off recently.

Footsteps sounded behind her. Victoria turned and saw Wade approaching. She bit her lower lip, then had to say, "You shouldn't have let him think we were taking this case."

Wade shrugged. "Don't know that there *is* a case yet. We're here. Why not look around a bit?"

Why not? "Because we're supposed to be searching for Kennedy Lane. That's what Lucas hired us to do."

His lips tightened. "Kennedy's been gone five years. We both know we aren't going to find her alive."

His words made her chest ache.

"But Melissa . . . there's hope with her."

She tore her gaze from his and looked back at the alley. "She could have hooked up with someone last night."

"You heard Jim. That wasn't her style."

Victoria's cheeks burned. *I just hooked up with you last night.* A hookup that she was very deliberately not talking about. "Sometimes, those close to you don't realize who you really are. They think they know . . ." She shook her head. "But they only see what you let them."

"Is that what you do?" His voice roughened. "You *let* the team at LOST see part of you and hold the rest back?"

"We aren't talking about me."

"Aren't we?"

Her shoulders straightened. "There isn't anything back here to see. Someone hosed off this area." She turned around and walked toward him. "We need to get back to the case we were brought in to cover." She started to skirt around him.

But Wade moved, deliberately blocking her path. "What if I told you . . . I want to learn about all the parts you hold back? That I want to know all of you?"

Won't ever happen. It couldn't happen. Not with Wade being the kind of man that he was. Oh, sure, he had a hard edge. He knew how to fight and play plenty dirty. But the man was an ex-cop, for goodness' sake. That kind of went hand in hand with being law *abiding*. And her past?

Her secrets?

Not so law abiding.

"I'd say too bad," Victoria told him quietly as her chin lifted the smallest bit. "Because that won't be happening."

He leaned toward her. "Into your bed, but not your head? Is that how it works?"

The breath she sucked in felt cold as it filled her lungs. She'd worried that sleeping with him had been a mistake, but at the time there was no way for her to pull back. In that moment, she'd just wanted him too much.

Now, her cheeks iced, matching that cold breath, and she pushed around him. Her steps were fast and hard, but he caught her at the edge of the building.

His fingers curled around her shoulder. "I'm sorry." She stilled.

"I'm fucking this up, and I don't know how to stop."

Breathe. Play the game. Act as if you have control. "Stopping is easy. You just walk away."

"That's not happening."

His words sounded like a threat. She opened her mouth to reply.

"Hey!" a sharp voice called out. "What's going on over there?"

She looked back.

A tall, broad-shouldered man with dark coffee skin rushed toward them. "There a problem here, ma'am?"

Wade stiffened. "No problem," he said, and a hard smile curved his lips.

"Yeah, well, I wasn't asking *you*, buddy," the guy fired back. "I was asking the lady. Because from what I just saw, she was trying to get away from you and *you* pulled her back." He edged closer, casting a suspicious glance Wade's way. "So I'll say again . . . is there a problem here?"

Victoria slid away from Wade. Some of her hair had come loose from her ponytail, and she tucked that lock behind her ear. "No problem. My partner and I—" Those words felt awkward. "We were just—just looking for a woman who didn't return home last night."

The man's dark eyes narrowed and he pointed to Wade. "He looks like a cop." Then his hand slid toward Victoria. "You don't."

"Me? No, no, I'm not."

"Then what are you? And how long do you plan to hang around *my* bar?"

His bar? She shot a swift glance back at Wade. Then she focused on the man, who still stared at both her and Wade suspiciously. "My name's Victoria Palmer, and this is Wade Monroe." She didn't tell the stranger he was right, and that Wade *had* once worked as a cop.

"We work for an organization called LOST. Our job . . . it's to find people who have gone missing."

The man seemed to absorb that detail for a moment. "And who is this missing woman?"

"Well, right now . . ." Wade stepped to Victoria's side. "We're looking for a woman named Melissa Hastings. She was at your bar last night. She left, and she never went home."

The bar owner laughed. "She's probably still sleeping it off! That stuff happens all the time. Don't worry. She'll show . . ." Then he turned and headed toward the entrance to Vintage.

Wade and Victoria followed him.

"Her roommate is worried," Wade said. "Apparently, it's not like Melissa to just vanish this way. We don't normally take cases like this one . . ."

They *hadn't* officially taken it, but Victoria didn't point out that fact.

"But we were in the area already," Wade added, "so we told the roommate we'd look around."

The owner paused at the club's door. "You want to come in my bar, don't you?"

Wade's smile was wide. "Well, since you offered."

The guy sighed. "Come in. Look around. You *aren't* going to find some woman hidden inside."

"Thank you, Mister—"

"Luther. Luther Warren." He pushed open the bar door. "Try not to spend all damn day inside, would you?"

They'd try.

Victoria and Wade slipped inside. Luther flipped on the lights as he made his way toward a door marked

PRIVATE and went in. Then they got busy searching. Nothing seemed undisturbed. It was easy enough to imagine the space packed at night, but during the day, the cavernous place seemed . . . hollow. Empty.

There were no security cameras inside. Just a stage. Chairs and tables. A long bar.

And, as Luther had said . . . no missing woman.

MELISSA'S HEAD FELT . . . funny. Aching and heavy. And she couldn't seem to think quite clearly. Her eyes opened and she squinted against the darkness around her, trying to figure out where she was.

But—she couldn't see anything. Just the dark. So heavy.

She wasn't in her bed. Melissa knew that with certainty. She didn't feel her soft mattress beneath her. Instead, she was lying on something harder, rougher. Thinner? Like a cot. Yes, she was on a cot—long, narrow, and hard. And her hands—they were tied to some kind of pole above her head. She could feel the pole with her fingertips. Her hands were tied, and so were her feet. Each foot was bound with rough rope, locked in place near the bottom of the cot.

All of these details sank in slowly for Melissa. So slowly. At first she just shook her head, certain that she was stuck in some kind of nightmare. Because she wasn't really waking up . . . not to this. She couldn't be waking up to this.

Her hands stretched and she felt the pull of the rough rope on her wrists.

Real rope that was scratching her skin.

She jerked then, hard, as fear spiked through her.

But the rope didn't give. Melissa screamed, as loud and as hard as she could. *"Help me! Someone help me!"*

Only there was no answer to her call.

So she screamed again.

And again.

Someone had to be close by. Someone had to hear her. Help would come. She'd get out of here . . . wherever the hell *here* was.

"Help me!"

She yanked at the ropes, pulling with all of her strength, and Melissa kept screaming.

"I TOLD YOU," Luther said about thirty minutes later, after Wade and Victoria had searched the entire bar, "no woman is in here."

No woman, no cell phone. Nothing. "Did you wash the back of your building?"

Luther blinked. "I pay a crew to come by every day. If the place smells like piss, it won't exactly attract a high-end clientele, now will it?"

The man had a point. Wade rubbed his chin. "So the folks who come in here . . ."

"They're college kids, tourists, folks with money to spend. This isn't some dump on the edge of town. I bring in great bands and the place is packed every night." Luther stood behind the bar now, his shoulders were ramrod straight. "I have a bouncer at the door—his name's Slater. He makes sure no trouble gets in here, and if someone had taken a woman out of this place—unwillingly—Slater would have noticed."

Victoria moved to stand near Wade. She'd been quiet while they searched the bar, but now her fingers were tapping against the bar's surface. Her gaze darted around, and he could practically feel the wheels turning in her head.

"Will the bouncer be back today?" Wade asked. "Because I'd like to talk to him." Then he took out his phone and pulled up the picture of Melissa that he'd gotten from Jim. He pushed the image of the smiling blonde across the bar. "I want to know if he saw her leave with anyone."

Luther frowned down at the picture. "Pretty girl." He glanced back up. "But I doubt Slater will remember her. Do you know how many girls come in and out this place every night? *Hundreds*. It's not like we can keep track of them all."

No, Wade had known it would be a long shot. But you never knew just what someone would remember . . . "Were you here last night?"

Luther nodded. "I'm here every night." His gaze slid back to the phone and the picture of Melissa. "This one . . . she doesn't stick out to me. I'm sorry. I really hope you find her."

"When will Slater be here?" Wade pushed. He wasn't ready to give up.

"An hour before the sun sets. We open early, you know, for the tourists. So come back then and you can talk to him."

Wade gave Luther his card. "If you remember anything else about her, you let me know, okay?"

Luther's fingers curled around the business card.

"She'll turn up. She isn't the first girl to come home late, you know."

She also isn't the first girl to never come home at all.

Wade nodded and turned away.

Victoria thanked Luther, her voice quiet, subdued, then followed Wade outside. When they were in front of the club, Wade lifted a brow and slanted a quick glance her way. "What are you holding back?"

She shook her head.

"Victoria . . ." Wade sighed out her name. "I get that you haven't worked with a partner before. So I'll clear up a few things for you. When you work with a partner, that means you're part of a team. It means you share things with your teammate, even if all you are sharing is a hunch."

"Roofie."

He blinked.

"In a crush like the one in a place like this, with so many people inside, it would be easy to roofie a drink. That's what I was thinking. That's what I always think in bars now. Because of LOST." She rubbed her arms. "You can't let your drink out of your sight. Just a few seconds is all it takes, and the drug can be in your drink. You won't see it. Won't smell it. Won't taste it. But it will hit you hard and knock you for a loop. Other people will just think you're drunk, not drugged, so they won't even notice if—" She broke off, clamping her lips together.

But he knew exactly what she'd been about to stay. "They don't notice if some kind asshole *helps* you out of the bar."

She nodded. "It could've happened. Or . . ." The wind caught the hair she'd tucked behind her ear and slid it over her face. "Or maybe Melissa is home now and this search of Vintage was a waste of time."

He looked back at the bar. Every instinct he had screamed that no, this wasn't a waste of time. He couldn't ignore this case. Not with his past.

Not with the shit that had gone down before in his life.

"We should get back to Kennedy's case," Victoria said. "She deserves to be found, too."

Right. He knew she did. All the victims out there deserved justice—and that was why he worked with LOST. He absolutely intended to continue working the case that had brought them to Savannah. "Let's go talk to the police detective who handled Kennedy's case."

Victoria blinked, seemingly startled by his quick agreement.

What? Had she really thought he would argue? No, he wanted to help Kennedy *and* Melissa. So while they were down at the PD doing recon work on Kennedy's disappearance, he could see just what else he could possibly discover about Melissa Hastings.

He and Victoria headed toward the SUV that Gabe had rented for them. They'd followed Jim to Vintage earlier, a fairly short drive from the university. He opened Victoria's door but she didn't slide inside. In-stead, she stood there, that light, sweet lavender scent sweeping up over him.

"I have . . . a hard time figuring you out." A faint furrow appeared between her eyes. When you looked deep enough—and he always did—there were flecks of gold hidden in those green depths.

He leaned toward her. "Ah, baby. I'm an open book. You're the one with layers." Layers he was dying to discover.

Her gaze held his a moment longer, then Victoria slid into the vehicle. Wade slammed the door shut and walked around to his side.

But before he climbed in, he glanced around the area once more. Melissa Hastings *had* been there before she vanished. Vintage had been her last known location.

So where the hell was she now?

BARELY DRAWING A breath, he watched as the black SUV headed down the street and away from Vintage.

Those two were going to be a problem. Asking questions that they shouldn't. Stirring up interest when everyone else would have just been oblivious to what the hell was going on in that town.

The man—he would be disposable. He was not anything particularly interesting. An alpha. Strong and aggressive, nothing more. The woman—*she* was different. One look into her eyes and he'd known that truth about HER.

She was just like him. Pretending. Lying to the world.

Because the world didn't accept monsters easily.

He'd make her reveal herself, though, before this was over. She'd show the world just who she was.

Just as he was about to show everyone . . .

Who I really am.

The world had better fucking be ready.

THE SAVANNAH POLICE Department was like a bee hive. Men and women in uniform bustled left and right, moving frantically as they tried to do their jobs. Witnesses were questioned, suspects were led off in handcuffs, and Detective Dace Black slowly led Victoria and Wade past the madness and into the relative quiet of his narrow office.

As soon as he closed the door behind them, Victoria did a quick visual sweep over the room. The desk looked as if it were about to sag beneath the weight of the manila folders on top of it. There was a framed picture of a woman, half hidden behind the files. No other photos were in the room. No other personal touches at all—except for the empty coffee mug that sat on the detective's desk. It was a mug that sported a pair of handcuffs on the front.

"I told the LOST rep who called me . . . there is *no* new evidence on that case." Detective Black pushed his fingers through his short brown hair. "I sure wish I had more to offer, but . . . there's just nothing."

"We read all the original case files," Wade said. "But I wanted to talk with *you*. What was your take on the abduction scene? On the crime itself? Was she taken? Or did Kennedy Lane walk away?"

"My partner thought she walked. I—I didn't." Dace looked a bit uncomfortable. "She never came back." His shoulders slumped a bit as he leaned against the side of his desk. "I listened to my partner back then and I didn't think there was much of a crime, not at first." He exhaled on a long sigh. "But time kept passing and she didn't turn up." A muscle flexed along his jaw. "When I got that call from LOST, hell, I was actually grateful. I'm supposed to be territorial and all that shit with my cases, right? I'm not. I want you to look into it. I *want* you to see if I missed something." His Adam's apple bobbed as he swallowed. "It's the five-year anniversary. Today's the big day. Five years, and never so much as a clue about what happened to her. That shit . . . it gets to me. It *changed* me."

"And your partner?" Wade pushed.

"Morrison died last year. Heart attack. He was a tough sonofabitch who never liked to admit he was wrong." Dace rolled back his shoulders. "But he was wrong on this one. He was wrong, and I was a green detective who didn't know enough to follow my own instincts."

"Where would those instincts have taken you?" Wade paused a beat. "Perhaps to Dr. Troy North?"

Dace's brows climbed. "The professor? He was—"

"Involved with Kennedy," Victoria said, because she'd stayed silent too long. She was in the field for a reason, and she'd do her part. No more hiding and watching. *Step up, Viki.* "We learned that today."

Dace whistled. "Then he is one lying piece of work . . . because I have it in my files . . ." And he started fumbling with the files on his desk. "I interviewed the guy—twice—and he denied being anything but her advisor and—" He stopped searching the files as his shoulders sagged. "I was so fucking green back then."

Silence.

He looked at Victoria, then at Wade. "Anything I can do to help you two, just say it, okay? Shit, you've been here only a few hours and you already know one witness lied to me. How many more probably did the same thing?" His cheeks flushed. "I just wish someone could bring Kennedy home."

There was a personal note in his voice when he said her name. His tone changed. Softened. For some reason, that change pulled at Victoria.

"But I guess . . . she doesn't have a home anymore, does she?" Dace said, shaking his head. "Her mother's dead. No other family left. No apartment. The world just kept right on spinning, even when she vanished from sight."

Just as the world was doing now . . . when Melissa Hastings was gone? The fact that it *was* the anniversary of Kennedy's disappearance made Victoria's stomach feel hollow. *Two abductions, two women from Worthington . . . exactly five years apart.* "There is something you can help us with," she said, even as Wade reached into his coat pocket and pulled out his phone. She knew he was pulling up the picture of Melissa.

"While we were at the Worthington campus today, we found out that this woman is missing," Wade announced. "Melissa Hastings. She disappeared last night around ten, and she hasn't been seen since then." He handed Dace his phone.

The detective's eyes locked on the photo. "She's close to Kennedy's age. But Kennedy was a brunette, and . . ." He exhaled. His gaze rose from the phone as he looked at Wade. "Last night at ten?" he murmured. "Not enough time has passed for an official investigation. You both know that."

"We do," Wade said, voice curt.

Dace's expression hardened. "The more time lost, the less chance we have of bringing her home."

He was absolutely right.

"Screw the official procedures." Dace headed for the door. "I'll see what I can do. I'll pull in some favors. I'll be damned if another woman just vanishes on my watch."

The door clicked shut behind him.

"I like that guy," Wade said.

Victoria nodded. "Yes, it's . . . nice to have a cop on our side." She'd met her share of hostile PD personnel before. As Dace had said, cases could become territorial. Real pissing matches.

Good to know this wasn't one of those instances.

"Maybe we'll get lucky," Wade added. "If they can search for Melissa's cell phone, we might be able to find out where she is."

But Victoria doubted it would be that easy, and, based on Wade's expression, she could tell that he felt the same way, too.

Curious now, she inched closer to him. "Is it because of . . . her?" She waited a beat, then pushed. "Amy?" *Gabe's sister. The woman who'd vanished and changed the lives of two men.*

Gabe.

And his best friend, Wade.

Wade's jaw clenched. "Be careful what you ask."

But she wasn't feeling careful. He'd said he wanted to pull back her layers. Well, she wanted to learn more about him, too. "I know you joined LOST because of what happened with Gabe's sister." A sister who'd vanished while Gabe had been away, fighting for his country as a SEAL. But while Gabe was gone, he'd asked his best friend to keep an eye out on his sister.

So the stories said.

"I thought Amy had gone off with her boyfriend," Wade said. "I should have dug deeper. Should have searched sooner." His voice roughened. "By the time I got my act together, hell . . . you know she was still alive until *two* days before Gabe and I found her? *Two fucking days.* Amy had a chance . . . If we'd just gotten to her sooner . . ."

There was emotion in his voice that couldn't be denied. *So that part of the story is true, too.* Maybe, Victoria reflected, she shouldn't have listened to gossip. But she had. "You cared about her." Maybe a whole lot more than *care.*

His gaze sharpened as he looked at her. "If you're going to dig up all the bloody parts of my past, does that mean I get to learn your secrets, too?"

She stepped back.

He swore. "Victoria, I meant—"

The door opened. Dace stood there, his expression grim. "Same freaking red tape," he muttered. "My captain won't authorize any sort of search, not yet. Not without any signs of foul play." His hands were fisted. "He is fucking old school on this. Every moment counts. Every single one. If she were a missing kid, he would have been all over this case. But because she's over eighteen . . . because we don't have any proof that she didn't go off on her own . . . he wants to wait. *Wait.*"

"Waiting is a huge mistake," Wade said. "Action needs to be taken. You are right—every single moment counts."

Dace shook his head, his disgust obvious. "Sometimes, I get so sick of the bureaucracy here. My job is to save lives, not . . ."

"Collect the dead?" Victoria finished quietly. *That's my job.*

Wade gave him a grim nod. "Don't worry, Detective. I'm not done on this investigation."

No, Victoria didn't think he was. Now she understood a lot more about him. Every case . . . every time he searched for the missing, was it some kind of atonement for Amy? Because Wade hadn't been able to save her, now he had to try and save everyone else?

She could have told him it was a mistake. There was no way to save the world. Some days you couldn't even save yourself.

CHAPTER FIVE

THE SUN WAS SETTING, AND VINTAGE WAS AL-
ready packed. A long line circled the entrance
to the bar. Wade headed straight for the front
doors, with Victoria at his side. They'd gone back to
their B&B—briefly—after leaving the police station.
He'd wanted to check in with Gabe and update him on
the changing situation in Savannah.

And now they were back at Vintage to see the
bouncer, Slater. Slumping on a stool out front, he had
long red hair and arms like tree trunks, and as far as
Wade was concerned, the fellow was looking at Victoria with way too much interest.

She still wore her glasses, perched lightly on the
end of her nose. Giving her what Wade thought of as
her smart and sexy look. Her hair was loose around
her shoulders, tumbling with a bit of wave, and she
wore jeans that hugged her awesome ass way too
well.

The bouncer waved her closer. "Irish?" There was a
note of hope in his voice.

Victoria looked a bit startled by the question. "My
mother was. Yes."

He smiled. "A beautiful Irish lass is always welcome in—"

Wade cleared his throat. "Hi there, Slater." An edge had entered his voice. Mostly because the steroid dick was flirting with Victoria *while I am standing right here*. "I'm not a beautiful Irish lass, but I have some questions for you."

Slater winked at Victoria. She flushed. "She can come in Vintage anytime. You can't." He jerked his thumb over his shoulder. "Get the hell out."

Asshole. "Yeah, I'm not going anywhere."

The bouncer stood. Was that supposed to be impressive? He was an inch shorter than Wade. So what if he had hulk muscles? *The bigger they are, the harder their asses will hit the ground*. That was a lesson he'd learned long ago.

But before he could start teaching him how *not* to gawk at a pretty lady, Victoria jumped between them. "We're looking for a woman who was here last night. She was seen around ten, but after that she seems to have vanished." She offered her hand to Wade and mouthed, *Give me the photo*.

Jaw locking, he handed her his phone.

She held it up so Slater could see the image. "Her name's Melissa Hastings. Your boss—Luther—said that you were working the door last night. Do you remember her?"

His eyes narrowed as he glanced down at the picture. "Actually . . . yeah, yeah, I do."

Hope pulsed inside of Wade. "Did you see her leave?"

Slater cut him a quick glance. "She looked drunk off her ass. I was worried because she was stumbling, but her boyfriend said she was okay. That he was taking her home."

Wade felt his muscles lock. "What did this boyfriend look like?"

"Didn't get a real good look at him. Just saw her because she stumbled." Two college-aged boys tried to slide past Slater, but he put up a hand. "Get your skinny asses back. Not your turn inside." Then he looked back at Victoria. "He had dark hair. I think."

"You . . . think?" Wade murmured.

"Not a lot of lights out there." Slater gestured behind him. "Maybe he had blond hair. Not like I could see that damn well."

Wade locked his back teeth. "Anything you can tell us for certain?" he growled.

"Yeah, he was about your size." He pointed to Wade. "I could see that well enough, even in the shadows. And he put her in some fancy new ride—a Jag. Sleek and sporty as shit."

"You're *sure* it was her?" Wade pushed.

"I think it was."

Again with the uncertain "think." Wade knew just how unreliable eyewitness testimony could be. When he'd been a detective, two witnesses who'd seen the exact same scene would often offer completely different accounts.

"Look, buddy . . ." Slater shook his head. "Nothing's sure in this world, now is it?" Then he turned his attention back to Victoria. "If you want to stay awhile, my break is coming up soon. Maybe you can help me remember a little more about that missing woman."

Wade closed his fingers around Victoria's wrist and

pulled her back. "This Irish is taken." *Go get your fucking own.*

He heard Victoria suck in a sharp breath, but she didn't speak. He was sure she'd have plenty to say to him later. But they had an agreement, didn't they? No ties. No strings. Partners, with benefits.

He squared his shoulders and faced off against the bouncer. "Melissa Hastings hasn't been seen since she left Vintage last night. The cops are—"

"Yeah, pegged you as a cop from the first glance."

Wade gave him a cold smile. "And you're wrong. I'm not a cop. I'm someone who is very, very interested in finding this missing woman, alive. So I need to know—did you get the tag number for the vehicle? Can you give us more details on the man? Can you give me *something* that might bring Melissa home?"

Some of the bravado left Slater's face. "Listen, man," his voice dropped, "like I said, I just saw her stumble, okay? That's why I remembered her. I glanced up, noticed her with the guy, but he got her in his ride and out of here before I saw any tag. Hell, I didn't even think about looking for one. It was just some dude, taking care of his lady."

Wade feared it was a whole lot more than that. "You said he talked to you, though." Wade forced his jaw to unclench. This guy was frustrating the hell out of him. "Did he have any accent? Anything odd about his voice that you noticed."

"Nah. No accent. Just . . . normal, you know? Nothing that stood out for me."

Right. *Not helpful.* "You should expect a visit from a Detective Dace Black soon."

Slater winced. "Boss isn't gonna like it if this place is crawling with cops."

"Yeah, well, I doubt Luther will like it more if he finds out that someone has been preying on women in *his* bar."

He kept his hand wrapped around Victoria's wrist as they headed back to the SUV. He could feel the tension in her body, practically rolling off her in waves. But she didn't speak. Not while he opened her door, not while he climbed inside and turned the ignition, and not afterward.

"Shit, Viki," he said, the shortened version of her name spilling from him. "Say something!"

He turned toward her. They were parked under a streetlight, and the faint illumination spilled into the vehicle.

"I think that if Melissa had just been spending the night with a lover, she would have contacted her friend Jim by now." Her words were hesitant. "The fact that she appeared drunk and this unknown man was so quick to lead her away, I'm suspecting more and more that she could have been roofied or—"

His hands tightened around the wheel. "You think she was abducted."

"Yes."

And almost twenty-four hours had passed. He'd be calling Dace and updating him on the news they had uncovered about the Jag, fucking ASAP. But first . . . "Aren't you going to rip into me because of what I said back there?"

Victoria's silence could say a whole lot. Too much.

That silence stretched and . . . "I agreed to your deal," she finally said.

It was hard to breathe. "Partners, with benefits." Just so they were both crystal clear.

"Since I agreed, you should know I'd tell you before I—"

"Decided to go fuck someone else? Hell, yeah, you'd better tell me that." He was about to rip the steering wheel out of the dash. He sucked in a deep breath and had to say, "Be careful."

"With what?"

Wade pulled away from the curb. "Me." *Be careful with me, sweetheart. Because I sure am not the sharing type.* And when he'd seen the redhead practically eating Victoria with his eyes, a jealous fury had burned within him.

He'd promised her no ties. No strings.

He'd lied.

He wanted her bound just as tightly as he was. One way or another, that would be happening.

THEIR BED AND breakfast was filled with antique furniture, heavy and dark. Victoria and Wade had been given a cottage to share—one in the very back of the historic Savannah property. One that promised them the utmost privacy. There were two bedrooms in that little cottage. One bathroom. A kitchen and even a den area.

So why did the space seem so incredibly small?

It was just after midnight before Victoria and Wade made it back to the cottage. They'd returned to the police station. Talked more with Dace. The detective had promised to retrieve traffic cameras from the area around Vintage. Hopefully, the cops would find a shot of the Jag on those cameras. Maybe an image of Melissa and the mystery man who'd been with her.

But the day had ended, and Melissa still hadn't come home.

And as for Kennedy . . .

Her five-year anniversary had passed. Vanished, gone without a trace. Victoria rubbed her arms as she paced toward the large stone fireplace. The fireplace wasn't lit. It wasn't cold at all in the room. Victoria's chill came from inside of her.

Life moved on and just left Kennedy behind.

Wade's footsteps sounded behind her. He had a heavy tread as he moved across the gleaming hardwood floor. She glanced back at him. Now that they were in the cottage, she was on edge. Actually, she seemed to constantly be on edge with him.

This Irish is taken.

His words kept ringing through her head. They weren't supposed to have ties between them. She *wouldn't* let herself have any ties with him.

Possessiveness, jealousy—obsession. No, that wasn't going to happen with her.

Wade lifted a brow and his golden eyes gleamed. "You don't need to be afraid."

She immediately shook her head in denial. "I'm not."

"Liar," he accused. "You think I can't read you?"

Dear God, I hope you can't.

"It's because I got all pissed that the bouncer was flirting with you, right? You didn't like that." He rubbed a hand over the back of his neck. "Am I supposed to apologize because I didn't like the way he was looking at you? 'Cause that's not happening. The asshole was lucky I didn't take a swing at him."

Victoria shook her head. "No, this is wrong. This isn't . . . you." He was the ex-cop. The good guy. He was supposed to be safe.

But Wade gave a low, rough laugh. One that sent a shiver over her. One that made her think of darkness and tangled sheets. Sex and pleasure. "It isn't?" His head cocked. "And just who is the real Victoria? The smart and reserved lady in glasses who pulls her hair back? Or the woman who puts on the short skirt and goes looking for a night of fun?"

She licked her lower lip. "They're both me."

He nodded. And his hand rose, his knuckles sliding over her cheek. She had to resist the urge to lean into him.

"And the jealous lover? The one who doesn't want anyone so much as looking at you?"

She flinched at his words.

His hands dropped. "That was me. Ex-cop, jealous lover—all me."

"W-We have a case to work here." She backed away from him. Fast.

But this time he followed her. He caged her between the wall and his body. Wade didn't touch her, though, just trapped her there. "I hate it when you do that," he said.

The pounding of her heartbeat filled her ears. A desperate drumming that seemed to shake her entire body.

"You don't need to back away from me. I might be a

tough asshole, but I swear, I would *never* do anything to hurt you."

Her breath felt cold as she pulled it into her lungs. Very carefully, his hands rose and he took off her glasses. She blinked, staring up at him as he put the glasses down on the nearby table. His body kept surrounding hers. Trapping her.

"Did another lover hurt you, Viki? Is that why you pull back from me?"

"No." A lover had never hurt her. "I'm always careful."

As soon as she said the words, she realized they were a mistake.

"Careful?" Wade pounced on that one word. "How so?"

I don't pick lovers who can hurt me. I don't look for ties. It's just sex. Pleasure. Bodies in the dark. Because anything more than that was dangerous. Anything more would be positively lethal.

Not just to her . . .

I won't be like him.

"I'm tired," Victoria said softly. "I'm going to bed."

But he didn't move back.

"I can see it," Wade said, his voice just as soft as hers had been, but . . . rougher. "When I look into your eyes, I can see the fear there."

"I'm tired," she said again.

"Want to know what scares me?"

The question caught her off-guard. She'd thought that he would push her more. But . . . "What?" She couldn't imagine anything frightening him.

"The idea of you being hurt."

His words stunned her.

"You think I didn't get a serious wake-up call when you were taken in Louisiana? When you were stabbed? When that bastard could have killed you?" His voice seemed to roughen even more with each word. "I couldn't help you. I couldn't *get* to you. And when I finally had you back, I had to stand there and watch the docs work on you. I had to see your blood and know that there was nothing I could do." He backed away.

She didn't move.

"So the *last* thing you ever need to worry about is me doing something to hurt you, Victoria. Because I can't. I would sooner cut off my own arm than do anything to you."

His words were so brutally honest and dark. Her gaze slid from his and she moved—woodenly—toward her room. At the door, she stopped. Without looking back—it was easier if she didn't have to look at him—Victoria allowed herself to confess, "I'm scared that I will hurt you."

"What? No, Viki—"

"I won't mean to do it. But it will happen. That's why no one gets close. Not because I'm afraid of them. But because I don't trust myself." What if she had a monster inside, one waiting to break out? She wasn't like Sarah. Sarah had confronted her demons, head on. She'd beaten them.

But Sarah . . .

Sarah hasn't committed my crimes. She doesn't know what I've done.

Or what I've already become.

Victoria opened her door, went inside, then shut it softly behind her.

WADE STARED AT her bedroom door.

Because I don't trust myself. What in the hell kind of bullshit was that? Victoria was one of the sweetest, gentlest people he'd ever met. He couldn't imagine her hurting anyone, but . . .

She has secrets.

Secrets he was more than ready to uncover.

He'd played nicely before. Never digging too deep, respecting her privacy. But now . . . he grabbed his laptop and headed into his room. Victoria was driving him mad. He needed to know as much about her as possible.

Because he wanted to make her pain stop, and he didn't know how.

He shut his door and a few moments later the laptop was booted up. A few clicks in the search engine and he had the stark facts of Victoria's life laid out in front of him. It wasn't as if he didn't know the general details. Everyone at LOST knew. Once upon a time, Victoria's life had been pretty big news.

The media had splashed her story far and wide when she'd been a teenager.

Young girl accuses famed geneticist father of murder.

Did Dr. Marcus Palmer kill his wife . . . and destroy her remains?

Wade hunched over the screen. He *knew* these details, but there was more to her story than just these headlines. So many secrets that Victoria was carrying with her.

When she was thirteen, Victoria's mother had disappeared. Just vanished.

Like so many at LOST.

He scrolled through the search results. Scanning the information. Five years later, Victoria had come forward with a shocking claim. She told the cops that she'd witnessed her father kill her mother in a jealous rage.

Fuck, I've got to watch my jealousy around her.

The last thing he wanted was for Victoria to ever think he was like her father . . .

He kept reading, looking for new information. During the trial, Victoria had described—in grim and grisly detail—how she witnessed the murder and how her father got rid of the body. Her father had been arrested. Tried . . .

And found innocent.

But less than a year later he was dead. Killed, by his own hand.

I know all of this already. I need to know what haunts her. What puts that sadness and fear in her eyes?

After her father's death, Victoria had packed up and moved across the country. She'd been given a full academic scholarship. The lady was a genius, no doubt. She'd got her M.D. and also received a doctorate in Biological Anthropology.

Facts. Simple. Cold.

But he wanted *more*. He wanted to understand why she'd been so driven, at such a young age. Why had she chosen to study the forensics of the dead?

She wasn't telling him her secrets, and Wade was desperate to understand them.

Just as he pulled up another newspaper account of

her father's trial, he heard the squeak of the hardwood floor, a soft sound, just beyond his door.

He froze.

Then he heard the squeak again. For one wild moment he thought it might be Victoria, coming to him. But the lady had been pretty damn adamant that she wasn't looking for a bed partner that night. When a woman walked away and *shut* her door pretty much in a guy's face, it was a hard hint to ignore.

But if it wasn't Victoria . . .

Then who the hell was tiptoeing around outside his room?

Silently, he rose and stalked to the door. He didn't have a weapon, but he wasn't about to let that fact slow him down. Because if someone *was* on the other side of that door, then Victoria could be in danger.

And that wasn't fucking happening.

He curled his hand around the doorknob and turned it silently. He'd shut off the lights in the outer room before heading into his bedroom, so darkness filled the area when he crept out of his room. His eyes adjusted quickly, and in seconds he could see the form standing there.

Halfway between his room and Victoria's.

He rushed forward, moving without a whisper of sound. He grabbed the shadowy form and—

Lavender.

Sweet, tempting lavender. Sweet, soft woman.

And he was holding her too hard. His hands were too rough. He needed to back the hell off—

Not hold her tighter.

"Victoria!"

He'd pulled her body against his. He should let her go. He didn't.

"Sweetheart, what the hell were you doing?" Walking in the dark? Sneaking around? She was—

"I was coming to you."

Wade shook his head. Hell, no. No, that made zero sense. Why would she turn him away and then seek him out?

"I needed you," she told him, her voice husky. He'd just grabbed her in the darkness, but she didn't sound afraid. Not at all.

Her hands were on his chest. "I don't want to hurt you," Victoria said.

He was the one who'd grabbed her so that now they were pressed—body-to-body—as intimately as lovers.

We are lovers.

"But I need you," she whispered. "Why do I need you so much? I was in my room, and I couldn't stop thinking about you. About the way you make me feel. About the way you make me forget everything else."

Wade locked his hands around her hips and lifted her up against him. He knew he held her far too tightly as he moved unerringly in the dark, but there was no way he could let her go. Her arms wrapped around his neck and he felt the faint whisper of her breath on his cheek. "I'm . . . using you," she said, the words hushed and ashamed. "It's not . . . right."

He carried her to the bed. Then he turned off the light. He knew she wouldn't want him seeing her scars, even though he didn't care about them.

She didn't want him seeing her scars or knowing her secrets.

But she wanted him.

And he . . . he couldn't remember wanting another woman the way he'd started to want her.

"Screw right and wrong," he said as he lowered her onto the mattress. "It's us. *Us*. That's all that matters." He stripped off his shirt. Tossed it aside. His laptop was still open, providing a faint glow in the room. Victoria wore a loose T-shirt, a silky pair of panties, and nothing else.

His fingers slid to the hem of her T-shirt. He pushed it up slowly, his callused fingertips trailing over her stomach, her ribs, then touching her tight nipples. She was gasping for him, moaning his name. Electrifying him with her need.

He anchored the shirt above her breasts and bent down, leaning over the bed and licking her nipples. She tasted so freaking good. And as he tasted her nipple, strumming her with his tongue, his hand slid between her legs. He stroked her through the panties. He felt her grow damp, wetting that soft silk. His fingers slid under the elastic edge of her underwear.

Then he pushed two fingers into her.

Her hips arched up to meet him even as her sex squeezed him tightly. Fucking perfectly.

Two bodies, coming together in the dark. No past. No promise for a future.

He'd take that. *Now*. Later . . . later, he'd take everything.

Wade yanked her panties down, pulling them over her hips and jerking them off her feet. Then he unzipped his jeans and had his protection on in seconds.

He didn't need long foreplay. He just needed her. But he had to make sure that Victoria was—

"Now, Wade, *now*."

Like he could tell her no. He had the uncomfortable feeling that he might just give her anything, everything, she wanted for the rest of his life.

He pulled her to the edge of the bed. Her legs locked around his hips, and he drove into her, one hard thrust that sank him in, balls deep.

For an instant he stilled. His hands caught hers. His fingers threaded with hers as he stared down at her.

She was so much more than a body in the dark to him. And he waited, needing her to say . . .

"Wade?"

Fuck, yes. *His* name. Because he was the one with her. The one who wanted to be with her through all the dark nights to come. *Fucking use me, baby. Use me until you're as far gone as I am.*

He withdrew, then plunged deep. Again and again. There was no more holding back. She felt too good. Too right. And then there was only pleasure. Her release. His. Blending together in a mad tangle that was the fucking best climax of his life.

When it was over, he ditched the condom and crawled into bed with her. He wrapped an arm around her stomach and held her there, close against his side. He figured she'd leave him soon enough. After all, the last time they had sex, she'd been quick enough to kick his ass out.

But for that moment he just held her.

Slowly, he heard her breathing become even and

deep. He kept his body still, not wanting to jar her. Victoria had gone to sleep. In his arms.

And she felt so good against him. Right. *Like she belongs.*

He pressed a soft kiss to her temple and his eyes closed.

"YOU AREN'T LEAVING me."

His voice boomed, seeming to echo through the house.

"You can't do this to me! You married me. You stay with me!"

Victoria tiptoed to the top of the stairs. Her parents were fighting again. Or rather, her father was. He'd been yelling so much lately. She thought he knew . . .

Her mother was seeing someone else.

Victoria knew. She'd begun to suspect weeks ago, when her mother started smiling and laughing more often. Her mother was *happy.* And Victoria hadn't realized just how sad her mom had been . . . not until the laughter started.

So that's what it sounds like. That had been her first thought. She liked her mom's laugh.

Only her mother wasn't laughing right then. Victoria peered over the banister. Her mother and father were below her. As she watched, her father grabbed her mother, holding her shoulders, and he shook her.

"Stop," Victoria said. Her father—he shouldn't be doing that. He yelled, but he never hurt her mother. He was a respected scientist. Brilliant. Everyone said how brilliant he was. And they also said . . .

Victoria is just like him. Just like her father. She's got his mind.

His mind, and her mother's face.

But her mother's face was now a mask of fear. She was trying to get away from her husband, but he was still shaking her.

"Stop!" Victoria said again. Her voice was louder. Her mother heard and her head tipped back, her long red hair trailing over her shoulders. When she saw her daughter, the fear on her face got even worse.

Victoria started running down the stairs.

"No, Victoria, no!" her mother cried. "Go back upstairs! I'm fine!"

Her father shoved her mom away and whirled toward the stairs. Toward Victoria. "She's not fine. She's leaving us. For some bastard she met at a bar."

Victoria felt tears on her cheeks. She knew her father was telling the truth. And she wanted so desperately to say . . . *Take me with you, Mom, please.*

Over her father's shoulder, she saw her mother's suitcase. Packed all nice and neat, and waiting right next to the door.

"I married her," Victoria's father said. His glasses glinted as he stared at Victoria. She was just a few steps above him. "She won't leave me. She won't do this to me. I gave her *everything*." Each word rose with fury. "The house. The cars. The cottage on the fucking lake. My money. My life. She won't do this to me!"

His rage was shocking. Horrifying. His cheeks had reddened and his eyes blazed with a fury she'd never seen before.

"She won't do this to us," he swore, then whirled back to her mother. Her mother was just standing there, staring up at Victoria, not with shock but with . . . .

Sorrow.

She knew he would do this.

This is why she was never happy. Never happy with him. She isn't shocked. She's seen this before.

But Victoria hadn't. She'd never seen this side of her dad before . . .

Her father hit her mother then. A sharp blow to the face. Her mom fell back, and Victoria raced down the stairs. *"No!"*

DARKNESS. THE DARK always hid so much. Lies, secrets . . . all were safe in the dark.

Most people had a natural fear of the darkness. They knew that bad things could wait in the shadows.

Very, very bad things.

He carried his precious burden through the dark. No one was at the spot—why would they be? It wasn't safe here, not in the dark.

But he wasn't afraid. Why would he be?

He put her down gently. Brushed back her hair. He couldn't see her well but he knew just how beautiful she was. She would always be beautiful. He'd made sure of that.

He put her down on the worn path. His gloved fingers slid over her cheek, a final good-bye.

He covered her up, wanting her snug and safe.

Then he walked away.

The darkness . . . it could hide so much.

Even the blackest of sins.

CHAPTER SIX

MATTHEW WALKER RAN DOWN THE OLD PATH, his pace steady, his heart drumming. The sun was starting to rise, an absolutely perfect freaking view, and it felt as if he had the whole morning to himself. He loved this part of the day, getting in the four-mile run was always a top priority for him, and this path—his path—was the best way to start any morning.

His feet pounded against the ground. The path snaked, heading deeper between the trees. His ear buds were in and the hard blast of music filled his ears. His gaze stayed focused up ahead and—

Shit. Something is in my way.

Someone had dumped, hell, *something,* right in the middle of the path. Seriously, this wasn't the place to dump crap.

His pace slowed as he approached what looked like a big black bag . . . and maybe a blanket. Yeah, a blanket because part of it was flapping in the breeze and—

That's not trash.

Matthew froze. He'd just caught sight of a—a hand? A hand, reaching out. Only the hand looked wrong.

Fuck, was that *bones*? He stumbled to a stop a few feet away from whatever in the hell was on that jogging path. But then, helpless, he inched forward.

Hair. There was hair blowing in the breeze.

And yes, *bones*. Dirt-covered bones that had once been a person. A person who was thrown away like trash right in the middle of his running path.

Bile rose in his throat as he stared, helplessly, at the person he'd just found.

A PHONE WAS ringing. A fast, hard beat of music. Rough rock. The sound jarred Victoria from her nightmare—a nightmare that she kept reliving, no matter how many times she tried to leave the past behind.

When her eyes opened, she saw the tall post on the bed—an antique four-poster bed. But not the bed she'd been assigned.

I stayed with him.

Her heart was pounding too fast because she'd been jerked awake by that jarring ring tone, and now she saw that she was still in bed—Wade's bed. It came back to her then. She'd gone to him last night. Had hot sex with him and then . . . fell asleep in his arms.

The bed dipped beside her as Wade swore, and then he was padding—naked—to grab his still ringing phone. Victoria sat up quickly, pulling the sheet with her. *Naked. Oh, crap. I'm still naked.*

She didn't know how to do the morning after routine—mostly because a morning after didn't happen for her. She spied her T-shirt, tossed on the floor. Were her panties close by? She sincerely hoped they were.

"Monroe," Wade barked into his phone. "This had better be good—"

He broke off and, as his face tensed, Victoria stopped worrying about her clothes.

Because, based on his expression, there was something far more serious for her to worry about.

"When? Where?" Each question shot from Wade with the impact of a bullet. "Yeah, yeah, I'll have her there as fast as possible." His gaze flickered to Victoria. "Damn straight she's the best."

She slid from the bed, keeping the sheet wrapped around her.

"You secure the scene, and we'll be there as fast as possible. And hell, yes, I'll want to talk with the guy who found the body."

Body.

He hung up the phone. Wade nodded as he stared at her. "We need to get dressed, fast."

She licked her too dry lips. "What body?"

His mouth tightened. "That was Detective Black. A jogger discovered . . . human remains this morning while making a run on Jupiter Trail."

"Jupiter Trail." She knew that name. "That's where Kennedy went missing."

"And the remains were found just feet from where the cops discovered her discarded ear buds five years ago."

No way that is chance.

"Since our visit yesterday, it seems that Detective Black has been researching us," Wade continued grimly. "He knows about you and your specialty—"

The dead.

"—and he wants you on scene to consult with the local M.E."

Right. She hurried for the door. But on her way out of his room, her hip bumped the table, sending his laptop into a wobble. She was often clumsy when her mind was focused on something else and her body decided to follow its own path.

Instinctively, Victoria reached out to grab his laptop before it could topple over and hit the floor. When she touched it, it woke up and the screen flickered to life.

"No, Victoria," Wade said quickly. "I'll get—"

A search engine popped up on the screen. It showed exactly what information Wade had recently been seeking. Her cheeks flushed red hot, then seemed to go ice cold. There were dozens of search results on his screen. Some were purple, not blue, indicating that Wade had already clicked the links to read all the sordid details.

Young girl accuses famed geneticist father of murder.

Did Dr. Marcus Palmer kill his wife . . . and destroy her remains?

"Victoria . . ." There was a rough edge to Wade's voice.

Carefully, she pushed down the screen until it clicked back in place. "I guess Detective Black wasn't the only one doing some research." And it hurt. Wade had been digging into her past moments before—

Before what? You went to him, a dark voice reminded her. *You wanted him. Don't get pissed because he gave you what he wanted.*

Too bad. She was pissed.

Her chin lifted as she marched for the door once more.

But, suddenly, he was there. Face grim, Wade said, "I just need to know more about you."

A broken bit of laughter escaped from her lips. "Oh, Wade. You should be so careful what you wish for." Her hand lifted and her fingers rasped over the early morning shadow that coated his hard jaw. "Because sometimes, you really might not like the end result." Then she skirted around him. "We have a job to do. Let's get it done." *Because that is what I have to focus on now. The job. Not my past. Not you.*

He didn't call out to her, and she didn't look back.

Victoria grabbed her glasses as she passed the table in the outer room—glasses that Wade had so carefully removed the night before—and she could feel her hands shaking. But she didn't know if they were shaking because she was angry.

Because she was scared . . .

Or because her careful control had totally been blown to hell and back.

JUPITER TRAIL. THE place had been deserted when Wade and Victoria investigated it just a day before . . . but now it was filled with activity. Police cars. Yellow tape. The M.E.'s van.

And onlookers. Wade didn't know where the people had come from, but a crowd of about fifteen had gathered just beyond the line of yellow police tape—tape at the entrance to the path.

He made a point of looking at all the people there.

He knew that sometimes killers came back to the scene and watched the discovery of a body. Certain perps got a real kick out of standing back and seeing their dirty work, up close and personal.

Victoria bent to go under the police tape.

"No, no, ma'am!" one of the uniformed officers called out. "You can't do that!"

She straightened. "I'm pretty sure I can," she muttered.

Before the young cop could argue with her, Detective Black was there. He rushed forward. "They're with me, officer. The team I said I'd be calling in." He lifted the tape and motioned Victoria and Wade forward. Victoria slid under the tape, but Wade hesitated.

He looked at the uniformed cop who'd stopped Victoria. "You need to get the name and address of every person here. Make sure your crime scene guys get pictures of the crowd."

The cop, a young guy who looked about twenty-one and was already sweating bullets, stammered, "Wh-Why?"

"Because you want to make sure your killer isn't hiding in plain sight."

The young cop backed up, then shot a questioning glance toward Detective Black.

"Do it," Dace said immediately, voice curt.

Damn straight the kid needed to do it.

Satisfied, for the moment, Wade followed Victoria under the tape and down the worn path. No birds called out this time, and the rising sun beat down on them with every step.

"When was the body discovered?" Victoria asked Dace, her voice devoid of emotion.

"Just after dawn this morning. A jogger thought he'd found trash on the path, but it . . . wasn't."

"We'll want to talk to the jogger," Wade said at once. He'd already told him on the phone. Hell, yes, he wanted to interview the man who'd found the remains.

Dace glanced back at him. "We don't know that this is related to your investigation yet." There was no missing the caution in his tone. "I called you in because I wanted Dr. Palmer's expertise, not because I thought—"

"That you'd found Kennedy Lane?" Wade finished. "Seriously, man, you don't need to bullshit me. This is the same place she vanished. *You* told me it was nearly the same spot where her ear buds were found. And on the five-year anniversary . . ."

Dace faced forward. A small huddle of three men and one woman were up ahead on the path. "I can't speculate. I need to know for certain."

And that was why he'd wanted Victoria.

She had worked for all the major universities at one point or another, lecturing, analyzing . . . and even the FBI had consulted her on numerous cases. When it came to identifying remains—especially remains that had been exposed to the elements for long periods of time—Victoria was the best, plain and simple.

"Dr. Palmer is here," Dace announced as they closed in on the little group on the path.

Two men immediately backed away. Wade saw the gleam of the badges clipped to their hips—*more detectives.* A woman was still bent over, a short distance away from what looked like a large black duffel bag. But at Dace's words she turned around, squinting up at them as the sunlight hit her face.

"That's our M.E., Dr. Eleanor Chambers," Dace said.

A few feet behind Dr. Chambers, a man was crouched, snapping pics of the remains. *Crime scene tech.* It was easy enough for Wade to place all the players at the scene.

Dr. Chambers rose and nodded toward Victoria and Wade. Her hands were covered in white gloves. "It's good to meet you, Dr. Palmer," she said, addressing Victoria. "I've been an admirer of your work for a long time." Eleanor Chambers was an African-American woman in her mid- to early forties. Her heart-shaped face and wide eyes were solemn as she stared at Victoria.

"I . . . um, thank you." Victoria tucked loose hair behind her ear. "What do you know so far?" The sunlight glinted off her glasses.

"I was waiting for you," Dr. Chambers said. "The bag hasn't been moved at all. The guy who discovered the remains—he said he didn't touch it. Swears it." Dr. Chambers motioned to the man with the camera, and he stopped taking his photos. He rushed forward and pulled another set of gloves out of a black supply box on the ground. "Thanks, Tommy," Dr. Chambers murmured.

Victoria pulled on the gloves while she stared down at the bag. "He covered her up," she murmured. "He left her face exposed but he brought in the blanket so that her lower body would be covered."

Wade could see what looked like human hair blowing in the faint breeze. Hair and bones. *Fuck.*

"We can use the hair for DNA analysis," Victoria said. "We can find out if it's . . . Kennedy or if it's someone else." She looked over her shoulder, glancing up at Wade. "She's been buried."

He blinked.

"The dirt. The decomposition. This body was put in the ground, then dug up and brought here." Her breath whispered out, "It's deliberate. A message." Her gaze said what she wasn't saying.

I think it's her. I think he brought her back because he wanted her body to be found on the anniversary of her disappearance.

Wade's gut clenched. One body returned . . . and a new woman missing. Was that why Melissa Hastings had vanished? Because the killer had decided it was time to go out and get a new toy?

"I want to talk to the man who found the body," Wade said again. Hell—body. There was hardly any *body* left. Just bones. And it fucking infuriated him. If he was staring down at Kennedy Lane, then some sick bastard had destroyed her.

And then he'd brought her back and dumped her body as if she didn't matter.

Dace motioned to him, and Wade moved with the detective back down the path. A final glance showed him that Victoria hadn't touched the remains. She was just staring at the bag and the bones, her shoulders hunched.

Does she even realize how much she gives away? When she worked her cases, Victoria tried to act as if the remains never bothered her, as if she were comfortable with them. But he knew the truth. Sadness always swept over Victoria with the discovery of each body.

Another one we didn't save.

"This is Matthew Walker," Dace said, pointing to a man who waited behind the yellow police tape, a man wearing black running shorts and tennis shoes. His phone was strapped to his arm, and ear buds hung loosely around his neck. The guy was pacing back and forth, nearly bouncing on his feet as he moved, but when Dace said his name, he immediately swung toward the detective. "He's the one who found the remains. Dr. Walker, this man is Wade Monroe. He's got a few more questions for you."

"I thought . . . I thought it was garbage." Matthew ran a hand over his face. Sweat gleamed on his forehead. "I was pissed that someone had dumped trash on the path, but then I realized I was staring at a freaking skeleton." His breath heaved out. "At first, I thought maybe it was a joke—maybe some frat boys had lifted a skeleton from one of the labs at the college and dumped it out here."

Wade didn't think this was any kind of joke. "You run this path often?"

"Three times a week." Matthew put his hands on his hips and rocked forward again, his body seemingly filled with nervous energy. "I try to get in the runs before my classes start at Worthington."

And they were right back to the university.

Wade slanted a quick glance toward Dace. The detective nodded.

"You work at Worthington?" Wade asked him carefully.

"Yeah, yeah. I teach computer programming."
He rose onto his toes, seemingly trying to look over
Wade's shoulders. "Who was that woman with you?
And what's she doing with the body?"

Wade didn't answer.

Matthew's gaze slowly slid back to him. He must
have read the suspicion on Wade's face because he
swallowed nervously and gave a little laugh. "What?
Why are you looking at me like that?"

"Did you see anyone else when you found the remains?" Wade asked him.

"No. The place was deserted. The bag was just waiting . . ."

Waiting to be found. In just the perfect spot.

Wade glanced back toward the path once more. He
saw Victoria walking toward him. Her face was pale,
her eyes so solemn.

He wanted to rush to her. To take her pain away, because he could all but feel that pain surrounding her.
But—Victoria might not want that. Not while they were
on a case. Working as a team. So he locked his muscles. He waited for her to come to him.

And when she was close, he caught the light scent of
lavender.

"You're the one who found her?" Victoria asked,
staring at Matthew.

He nodded. "Yeah, yeah, I'm Matthew Walker." He
offered his hand to her.

Victoria looked down and seemed to realize that she
was still wearing her gloves.

Matthew dropped his hand quickly.

"I'm Victoria Palmer."

"You're a cop."

"She's a doctor," Dace cut in. "She's consulting on this case."

Matthew looked confused. And still a little green.

Her gaze darted to Wade. "We're LOST."

"LOST? What the hell is that?" Matthew wanted to know.

She turned to look back down Jupiter Trail. "It means we were her last option. Only we didn't find her soon enough."

HER WRISTS WERE bleeding. So were her ankles. And she'd gone hoarse from screaming.

Melissa had screamed for hours and hours, but no one had come to help her. She'd heard no sounds at all.

Just her own broken voice. Then she was no longer able to speak.

Her throat was burning. She was so thirsty and she . . . needed a bathroom. Desperately. Shame had filled her the first time she lost control of her body. She'd vowed not to do it again but . . .

I'm trapped. Helpless.

How many hours had passed? What was happening? Why was she just being left there?

Locked away. Forgotten. I could starve to death in here. Is that what will happen? Is that going to be my end?

She remembered being at Vintage. Being with Jim. Then . . . nothing. Darkness. A big blank in her mind. She didn't know how she'd gotten here. *Wherever the hell here is.* She didn't know who'd brought her to this place.

Not Jim. She wouldn't believe that. Jim wouldn't do this to her. Jim loved her. Sure, his life had been hard. She knew about the abuse he'd suffered, but Jim hadn't let that get to him. He'd been stronger than the pain in his past, just as she had been stronger. He *wouldn't* do this.

Tears were drying on her cheeks. She tried to cry out again but only managed a weak rasp.

Screams weren't working. She had to get loose. Get out.

Her bloody wrists scraped against the rough rope once more. More tears slid down her cheeks at the pain but she kept pulling. Kept twisting her wrists as she tried to slide out of the rope. She *would* get out.

She had a life waiting.

"I HEARD ABOUT your work on the Lady Killer case," Eleanor said as Victoria made her way around the M.E.'s office. The remains had carefully been transported just an hour ago, and Victoria had traveled in with Eleanor to complete the exam. "I can't imagine what it was like, finding all those bodies buried in the sand."

The image of the dead flashed in Victoria's mind. For just an instant she could smell the salt air of the ocean and she was back on Dauphin Island. *The Lady Killer.* One of the darkest cases that LOST had handled . . . and one that brought closure to many families. "I'm just glad we were able to stop the man who'd hurt them all." *For so long.*

She had her gloves on as she headed toward the remains. There had been hair on the skeleton at the scene, and she stopped now to examine it. At this point of decomposition, the hair was no longer attached to the skull. Actually, there was very little left other than the bones and the teeth.

But the hair was still there, long, heavy locks that had been tucked behind the skull. The wind had taken those locks and seemingly blown them off the skull.

Blond locks. Only Kennedy Lane didn't have blond hair.

Carefully, she picked up the hair and put it in an evidence bag. She was aware of the weight of Eleanor's eyes. Victoria glanced over at her. "This is your city," she said carefully. "You can be lead on this—"

Eleanor held up her hands. "I know who you are and what you can do with the dead. I want to watch you and learn." She motioned toward the bones. "So, please, go right ahead."

Victoria nodded. "Fair enough." Then she said what she'd suspected from the moment she saw the skeleton. "That hair . . . it belongs to someone else." Bright blond hair. Clean hair—not dirty like the rest of the skeleton. *Staged.*

"Someone else?"

Yes, and all of the coincidences were adding up to a sickening total in Victoria's mind. "I think it would be a good idea to compare that hair to . . . to samples that belong to Melissa Hastings."

Eleanor just looked confused. "Who's Melissa Hastings?"

His new victim.

Eleanor took the evidence bag.

Victoria turned back to the remains. The body was

obviously that of a female. "You're a woman," she said, dropping into her old habit of speaking directly to the victim. She knew it was creepy to others, but since Eleanor worked with the dead, maybe she'd understand.

Maybe not.

But when Victoria worked, she couldn't distance herself. She couldn't just see *the dead*. She saw the victim instead. "Your pelvis and your head tell me you were a woman. Probably a very pretty one." Her gloved hands hovered over the skeleton's face. "Rounded chin bone, less developed brow ridges, small mastoid process . . ." She pointed behind the ear area and cleared her throat as she said to Eleanor, "All signs say she's female." *Of course, Eleanor would know that.* Her gaze strayed to the victim's mouth. "We'll need to pull in dental records for Kennedy Lane. Because I can tell you already, this victim was Kennedy's height." They were dealing with a completely intact skeleton. Care had obviously been taken with her.

He buried you. Kept your remains together. Safe.

That hadn't been the way Victoria's father had worked. He'd known how risky it would be to keep a victim's body close by.

No body, no crime.

So he'd made her vanish. But Victoria had known and she'd—

"Dr. Palmer?" Eleanor's voice sharpened. "Dr. Palmer, is everything all right?"

Victoria shook her head, sending those memories right back to the darkness of her mind. She wasn't going to deal with them. Not then. "Let's get the dental records. And let's figure out . . ." Her gaze was on the skeleton. At the sightless sockets where eyes had been. "Let's figure out what was done to you."

She leaned in closer. She could see dirt on the remains. Dirt and . . .

Spanish moss? Yes, yes, that was some Spanish moss, attached to the rib bones.

"Where were you?" Victoria whispered. "Where did he take you?"

What did he do?

Soon enough she would have answers.

Victoria took a deep, bracing breath. For an instant her gaze slid toward the black bag that the remains had been discovered in.

She remembered . . . *A body bag. Being inside. Fear. No, terror. Pain. Can't breathe. Can't—*

"How can I assist?" Eleanor asked.

And the horrible memory vanished. Victoria's heart was beating too fast. Her fingers held the faintest tremble. She clenched her gloved hands. She was *not* going to let her fear take over. That last case she'd worked in Louisiana—it had gone to hell. But she'd survived. She hadn't broken then and she wouldn't fall apart now.

Just a bag. That's all it is. Just a bag.

"Come over here," Victoria said, and her voice—amazingly—came out sounding cool. Calm. "Let's get a better look at these small indentions I can see on the bones . . ."

THERE WERE SHADOWS beneath Victoria's green eyes. Her skin seemed paler than before and faint lines bracketed her mouth.

Wade rose when he saw her approaching. He'd been

about to head into the M.E.'s office with Dace—they'd spent hours combing over Jupiter Trail and one hell of a lot of time talking with the people who'd been on the scene.

One look at Victoria's face and he could see the sadness that touched her. She was always like that after working with the dead. Every encounter seemed to take a new toll on her, and he hated that.

"It's her," Victoria said. "The victim discovered this morning is Kennedy Lane. He took her, and then, five years later, he . . . brought her back to the same spot."

Fuck.

The M.E.'s office door opened behind Victoria. Dr. Eleanor Chambers hurried out, moving to Victoria's side. She nodded quickly at him and Dace, then gave them both case files. "She works fast," Eleanor said, admiration in her tone. "And her hunches are dead on."

Wade didn't look down at the file. He couldn't take his gaze off Victoria's face. There was something going on . . .

"We've got samples of the soil that were found with the body," she said. "Soil and Spanish moss. I think she was . . . buried for the last two years. Based on the rate of decay and the condition of the bones, she's been in the ground and—"

"The last two years?" Dace said, frowning as he asked the question. "Where the hell was she before that?"

Victoria's lips pressed together and her gaze strayed to the report in his hand. "There were numerous signs of broken bones. Her scaphoid showed repeated fractures—"

Dace shook his head. "Okay, I'm gonna need a translation there."

"Her wrist was fractured," Eleanor supplied. "Both wrists, actually. It can be a fairly common break, right where the wrist bends . . ." Her words trailed away as she glanced back at Victoria.

"I suspect the injuries to her wrists occurred because she was restrained." Victoria's voice was soft and sad. "If she were tied up or—or handcuffed and she tried to get away, the fractures could have easily resulted."

Wade's back teeth clenched. "You're saying she was ready to break her own wrist if it meant she could get away."

"I'm saying she *did* exactly that."

Fuck.

Victoria cleared her throat. "Based on her other injuries, I believe she was tortured, rather extensively. There were nicks on her bones—very consistent with knife injuries. I counted . . ." She blew out a hard breath. "Over fifty-seven nicks on her bones. All in places where they would not cause fatal harm."

"Holy hell." Now Dace was looking a little green. "You're saying some whack job tortured that woman by stabbing her fifty-seven times?"

"Yes." She nodded. "That's exactly what I'm saying, and like I told you before, her name is Kennedy Lane. The dental records were a match. We know the victim on the table in there . . . is Kennedy." Her stare focused on Wade. "I guess LOST can consider this another found victim." But for an instant, anger—no, disgust?—entered her voice.

"How did she die?" Dace wanted to know. "Was it because of the knife wounds?"

Eleanor shook her head. "None of those wounds were designed to kill."

"Just to inflict maximum pain," Victoria said. "And I think the killer wanted us to know that—why else would he deliver the complete skeleton to us? He wanted us to see exactly what he'd done to her. All of the knife marks. All of the broken bones. Everything. He wanted us to know just what she endured . . . before he bashed in her head."

Dace swore.

"Sorry," Victoria said. Now her voice was going brittle. "That wasn't the clinical term. My apologies. The victim suffered a severe contusion to her head. A fatal blow. I doubt she died instantly from it, though. There would have been substantial brain swelling, as evidenced by the faint fractures in the skull itself. A fairly slow death, and one that could have been quite painful." Her lips thinned. "But maybe not. Maybe after that blow, she stopped feeling anything at all. I can't say for sure on that. Only Kennedy would know how those last few moments actually felt."

Victoria was too pale now. Too fragile. Wade wanted to pull her close. To shield her from what was hurting her. *The case. The case is doing this.* "Kennedy would have known," he said, his words a rumbling growl. "And so would the SOB who killed her."

Victoria's lashes fluttered. "Yes, yes, he would know." Then she squared her shoulders. "I think my timeline is accurate. You'll find the breakdown of decay listed in the file, but based on my findings . . . I would say that Kennedy died approximately twenty-four months ago."

Right, she'd said that Kennedy had been in the ground for two years and . . . *fucking sonofabitch.* "He tortured her for three years before killing her?" Wade demanded. "Three years?"

"I believe so." Her voice was barely a whisper now. "He kept her alive and he kept hurting her, until two years ago."

"Christ." Dace closed his eyes. "We gave up on her. We just *gave up on her.* And she was out there. All that time." He spun on his heel and walked away. He'd tucked the file under his arm as he took angry fast steps, and then he slammed his fist into the nearest wall.

Wade knew just how the guy felt. When he and Gabe had finally found Amy, when they realized that she'd been alive. *If we'd only fucking got to her sooner . . .* The guilt had nearly consumed him.

He saw Victoria blink quickly and look away from the detective. "There is more."

"I don't think I want to hear any *more* right now." Dace slapped his hand against the wall and leaned forward. "Alive. For three years. And we were barely searching for her. No one was looking while that sick prick took his time with her and he just—"

"He has another victim." Victoria's words were low but they seemed to echo like a scream in that hallway.

From the corner of his eye Wade saw Dace's head whip up. "Say again?"

But it was Eleanor who spoke. "I told you, her hunches are dead on."

Wrong choice of words there, Doc.

"The hair shouldn't have been there. Not after the body had been in the ground and exposed so much that—" Victoria sucked in a sharp breath. "The condition was too good. And the color was *wrong*. Kennedy's hair wasn't blond like that, it was much darker. Blond hair that shade—" Her gaze darted to Wade's.

Fuck me. "Melissa Hastings."

She nodded. "Eleanor pulled a lot of strings and got a rush comparison for us. It's still tentative, because there are more tests that have to be done and those tests take one hell of a lot of time. But the markers are there so far. They're matching. I think . . . I think that hair belongs to Melissa. I think the man who took her also took Kennedy, and . . . he wanted us to know. *That's* why he left the hair there. He wanted us to know exactly what he'd done."

He took another woman.

"If he kept Kennedy alive," Wade said, his muscles tightening, "then he'll keep Melissa alive, too." They just had to find her in time.

"Let's see if my captain stops us from putting out that full-scale search now," Dace said, then he ran down the hallway.

Victoria didn't move.

Neither did Wade, not yet.

"I'll, um, fax our results to his captain. That should help things along," Eleanor said as she backed into her office.

Then they were alone. Dace's pounding footsteps had faded away. Wade closed in on Victoria. He had the odd feeling that if he moved too fast, he'd spook her. "Are you okay?"

She blinked, three times, too fast. "Of course. I—I was just doing my job. An exam on remains, nothing more." A faint and ever-so-vacant smile curled her lips. One that didn't even come close to reaching her eyes. "I'd better go after Dace—I mean, Detective Black. I can talk to his captain and assure him that even though my findings on the hair are preliminary, they—"

"Don't bullshit with me."

Her smile wavered.

"She isn't remains. Not to you. None of them are. They are always more. They're people. They're victims. They matter."

Her long lashes swept down and a lone tear slid down her cheek. "She suffered so much, Wade. So much."

"We're going to get the bastard."

She shook her head. "That's not our job. We find the missing. We aren't supposed to hunt the killers."

"If you believe that, then I don't think you fully grasp the reason why Gabe brought me and Dean on board with LOST so early."

A faint furrow appeared between her brows.

"I was a homicide detective, love." The tender endearment slipped out. A tell he'd have to watch. "Dean was violent crimes with the FBI. Sure, Gabe might give some lip service to just finding the missing, but he wants *justice* for them. He wanted justice for his sister, and he got it, even though the price was fucking high." He clamped his lips together because the end for the bastard who'd taken Amy—that was one secret he'd carried for a long time. He'd backed Gabe up during those dark times and crossed a line that had made him turn in his badge.

Because when I lied—under oath—there was no going back for me.

"Justice." A shiver slid over her. "I want Kennedy to have justice."

So did he. "And Kennedy isn't the only victim. We can find Melissa. We can bring her back."

The faintest flicker of hope lit Victoria's gaze.

"We *will* bring her back," Wade said. Because he didn't want to lose another victim. And he sure as hell didn't want to think that Melissa Hastings would be trapped for years, used as a sick bastard's torture toy.

HER RIGHT WRIST slid out of the rope. At first Melissa was so stunned that she actually froze. Her fingers were nearly numb, there was so much blood, but—

My hand is out.

She started shaking her fingers, trying to get the feeling back into them, and then she reached for her left hand. She'd get the knot untied and then she'd get the hell out of there. She would not give up. She *would* escape.

She worked faster, harder, her fingers desperate on the ropes. She had to be free before he came inside. She didn't even know who *he* was but . . .

But I know he'll hurt me.

The knot slipped beneath her bloody fingers, loosening . . .

CHAPTER SEVEN

VICTORIA HURRIED TOWARD POLICE CAPTAIN Harry Vann's office. He was on board—fully now, according to Dace—with the search for Melissa. He wanted to put every available resource into her search. There was hope. And Victoria was both elated and terrified.

What if we can't find her? What if we just keep knowing she's out there and that he's hurting her? And the years pass right by . . .

The muscles in her back had knotted from spending so many long hours examining the remains. She'd wanted to be as thorough as possible, and the daylight hours had slipped away. A glance through the window showed her night loomed, and the sight of the darkness made her shiver.

Her phone rang, the sharp cry jarring her to a stop. Unlike Wade, she didn't have some cool, rough music ring tone that played when her phone rang. It was just a normal beep. High and long. She automatically yanked out the phone, but she didn't recognize the number on the screen. Victoria started to ignore the call, because she was so intent on going to talk with the captain, but some instinct nagged at her, and she put the phone to her ear. "Hello."

A rush of air—as if someone had just taken a sharp breath.

"Hello?" Victoria repeated again, her fingers tightening on the phone.

"You found her." The voice was low and rasping. She had to strain to hear the man's words. "You found Kennedy."

Goose bumps rose onto her flesh. "Who is this?" Her gaze darted around the hallway. Wade was up ahead, already in the captain's office. Dace was with him. She took a tentative step forward.

"I'm the man who knows . . . all your secrets."

Her goose bumps were getting worse. "I doubt that."

He laughed. "Death can be so cruel, can't it? Taking away beauty. Leaving only . . . bones in its place."

Now she wasn't creeping down that hallway. She was full-out running toward the captain's office. Wade saw her coming and surged forward, frowning.

With her eyes wide and—no doubt—desperate, she pointed to the phone. *Him.* Victoria mouthed her fear. Her certainty. *It's him.*

Wade's eyes narrowed. Behind him, the captain pushed to his feet. "What's going on?"

A killer. I think the killer just called me.

"Did you study her bones?" that rasping voice wanted to know. "Did you see the marks I left on her?"

Oh, Jesus. He'd just confirmed her fears. She was talking to the man who'd killed Kennedy Lane. *How has he gotten my number?* Her private line. "I saw the marks. All fifty-seven of them."

That laughter came again. "Is that all? For some reason . . . I thought I'd left more."

"We need to find out who the hell just called her," Wade said, his voice a lethal whisper. *"Now."*

Victoria stumbled forward. With her free hand she grabbed a piece of paper from the captain's desk and scribbled down the number that she'd seen on the screen moments before. Then beneath that number she wrote: *It's him.*

Dace raced out of the room. She knew that he could contact the cell phone company and get a location on that phone. LOST had even pulled some—somewhat shady—strings before and done the same type of search. Dace would need to demand real-time information about that cell phone—the company would need to ping the phone every minute or every few seconds so it would report back its location. So in order for Dace to do his job . . . *I can't let this guy off the phone.*

"Keep him talking," Wade said to Victoria, obviously thinking the same thing she was. His voice softer than she'd ever heard it before. "Keep him on the line."

Well, she knew one way to engage the guy. "Why did you take Melissa?"

Silence.

And fear swamped her. Maybe that had been the wrong thing to say. She wasn't the shrink. She didn't know killers. Sarah did. Sarah could get into their heads. She could always say the right thing. But her—

"I like to see . . . just what people can endure. How far they can be pushed."

Her heartbeat was so loud she almost couldn't hear his words as that frantic drumming filled her ears.

"Sometimes, though," he said—still in that rough voice, *disguising his voice*—"people have to be punished. Don't you agree?"

"I—it's not my place to punish."

"Liar, liar . . ." He taunted. "I know all about you, Victoria. All those dark secrets . . . are you ready for them to tumble out?"

Fear and rage beat through her. She thought of Kennedy. The pain she'd endured. And Melissa. "You know nothing about me. Or those women or—"

"I won't tell. Don't worry."

Her heart skipped a beat.

"I like you," he said. "More than the others. You and I . . . I think we're the same."

And she thought he was crazy. But Wade was staring at her, nodding encouragingly, and she was obviously supposed to keep talking to the madman on the phone.

This was out of her realm. She was going to say the wrong thing. She said the wrong thing all the time. Wade should know better. He should—

"Want to make a trade?" the rasping voice asked her.

"What?"

"We could do it. You can come to me, and I'll let Melissa go."

Her lips parted. She stared straight into Wade's eyes. "A trade," she repeated, needing Wade to understand what was happening.

"Speaker," Wade said, barely breathing the word. "Put it on—"

Speaker. Right. Shit. She should have done that sooner. Her fumbling fingers flew over the phone's screen. But there was only silence. She sucked in a deep breath and said, "You want me to trade myself for Melissa?"

At her words, Wade lunged forward and grabbed her wrist. He gave a hard, almost violent shake of his head.

But she wasn't just supposed to let a victim die, was she? If the guy was going to let Melissa go . . .

The caller asked her, "Can I trust you, Victoria?" Still disguising his voice. Still playing some game.

No, you can't trust me.

"Because if you betray me, the world will know what you did . . . that friend of yours . . . your LOST agent . . . he'll know, too."

What was going on? How had the guy learned so much about her? About Wade? Because he *had* to be talking about Wade.

"But then . . ." His sigh carried over the line. "You've always been the monster, hiding in the room."

He knows. He knows. Her gaze flew away from Wade's. She couldn't stare into his eyes right then. She was too afraid of what she might see. "Tell me where to go," she ordered, voice breaking a bit. "Tell me where to come for the trade."

"Jekyll Island." His voice was even lower now. "Always a good place for a hunt . . ."

He hung up. For an instant Victoria just stared down at her phone. No, no, that wasn't right. He needed to tell her more. He had to tell her *where* on that island to trade for Melissa. *When* to meet. She spun around and nearly ran right into Dace.

"Got the location," he said, voice excited. "Fucker actually used Melissa's phone—arrogant SOB. But we have an address on the bastard—let's go get him, *now*."

She took a step back. It all seemed so easy. The killer had just called them and basically handed over his location. *Too easy.* Nothing had ever been that easy before, and the situation made her nervous. But Dace and his captain were whirling and rushing into the hallway, already in hot pursuit.

What about the trade? Jekyll Island? The name was vaguely familiar, but she couldn't place it, not fully, and there was no time to stop and question anyone right then. Wade had her arm and he was hauling her with him down the hallway. Up ahead, Captain Vann was barking orders and uniformed cops were surging forward.

Just as they reached the glass doors that would take them outside, Victoria staggered to a stop. Her hand turned and she was the one grabbing Wade. "It doesn't work this way." He knew that. She knew that. It was never this easy.

"It can work this way if the perp is too damn cocky. Too sure of himself and he screws up with a small mistake."

Like a phone call that could be tracked. Maybe the guy hadn't realized how quickly they'd be able to lock on to his location. *Maybe.*

"Come on, Viki, we're following those cops."

And then they did. She and Wade jumped into their SUV and gave a fast and frantic chase behind the cop cars. Only those cars weren't rushing in with sirens blazing to the scene.

The cops went in with a silent attack. Because they didn't want the perp to know they'd found him? She figured they were trying to keep the element of surprise on their side. And a perp who wasn't alarmed . . . she knew that would be a perp who was more likely *not* to hurt his hostage in a moment of panic.

They stopped a block from their target. The cops quickly set up a perimeter at the scene, and then the captain marched toward her and Wade. "Appreciate all the help," he said with a curt nod. "But I'm sure you understand . . . my team has this now. You're civilians, so you have to stay back." He motioned to a spot *behind* the patrol cars.

Victoria had been wondering when that order would come in.

Wade's face tightened with anger but he didn't argue.

They stood behind the line of police cars as Dace led a team toward the house.

"They didn't get a warrant that fast," she murmured.

"Probable cause," Wade said, not looking at her because his gaze was focused on the scene unraveling before them. "They think Melissa is in that house, so they are sure as hell running in with guns blazing."

And, sure enough, the cops barely paused at the front door. She heard Dace give a loud shout and then he kicked in the door. The cops swarmed then, going in the front of the house. The back of the house.

She heard a woman scream.

Victoria tensed.

After that scream, the moments seemed to tick past in painful silence. Victoria realized she was actually holding her breath, and she forced herself to exhale and then suck in a deep gulp of oxygen.

Then she saw—

Dace, coming out, leading a man in front of him. A tall man with dark hair and wide shoulders.

"I didn't do anything!"

He was a *familiar* man.

Her mouth dropped open.

"Oh, shit," Wade said.

And then she saw the woman. A woman who was also in handcuffs. A woman with a tangle of long blond hair. A woman who was yelling, "You can't do this to us! *Why* are you doing this to us?"

More cops were running in and out of the house. The man and the woman were being led toward the patrol cars.

Just then the man glanced up—and his blue eyes locked on Wade and Victoria. There was fear in his gaze. Fear and desperation as he recognized them.

"What's happening?" Lucas Branson shouted at them. "Why are the cops doing this to me?"

Dace had a tight grip on Lucas's shoulder as he pushed the younger man forward. "We traced your call, Branson, though I sure as hell never expected to see you when I went into that house. I actually bought your act years ago. I thought you *cared* about Kennedy."

"I do care about Kennedy!" Lucas jerked against his cuffs while the blond woman with him started to cry.

Do care. He's using the present tense. For some reason those words pierced Victoria straight to her core.

"Dr. Palmer! Wade!" Lucas yelled their names. "Look, shit, will you two just tell this detective that I hired you? That you're working for me to *find* Kennedy?" Lucas demanded.

They hadn't even had a chance to tell him the news about her remains yet. Victoria had identified the body, they'd been going to the captain's office and—*the killer called me.* She had planned to deliver the news about Kennedy's remains to Lucas in person.

"Cut the act," Dace snarled. "We traced the call you just made to Dr. Palmer. We know what you did."

"I didn't just make any call!" Lucas was nearly screaming. The blond woman was still crying. "I just got here a few minutes ago. This is my fiancée's house. We were out, meeting with the caterer. I brought her back—and then you guys burst in the house with your freaking guns blazing!"

The woman looked over at them, her dark gaze tear-filled. "We didn't do anything," she cried. "I swear. We just got home. We just—"

"Found the phone!" one of the uniformed officers yelled as he ran from the house. He had an evidence bag in his hand. "It was on the kitchen counter, just waiting for us."

Dace shoved Lucas toward a patrol car. His lips twisted in disgust. "You sick sonofabitch. You used Melissa's own phone to make the call."

"Who is Melissa?" Lucas yelled.

Dace glared at Lucas. "The doc over there—she identified Kennedy's remains."

Lucas's eyes widened.

"Uh, detective . . ." Wade began, voice tense.

"K-Kennedy?" Lucas whispered.

"We know what you did to her. We know you kept her alive for years. You got off on torturing her, right?

You stabbed her. You broke her bones. You made her life hell—"

"Detective Black," Wade barked. He rushed toward the detective and his prisoner. And Victoria ran right after him.

"Then you bashed in her head and you buried her body. That wasn't enough, though, was it? 'Cause on the anniversary of her abduction, you had to bring her back. You dug her up and you dumped—"

Lucas vomited. Again and again.

"Fuck." Dace jumped back.

Wade grabbed his arm. "Lucas hired us to find her. This setup—it's not right."

The blond woman was staring at them all with dazed, horrified eyes. "Kennedy? Kennedy Lane? You . . . found her?"

Victoria stepped closer to the blonde. "Are you Connie?" Because she remembered that name. Lucas had told them that Connie didn't know he'd hired LOST. *He was going to move on, with Connie.*

The woman blinked. "Y-Yes, I'm Connie. Connie Sutherland." Then she very slowly turned her attention to the evidence bag that the uniformed officer had brought over to Dace. "That's not mine." Her voice was wooden. Too flat. *Is she in shock?* "We—We both have the newest models, the big screens, the—" She broke off, her lips clamping together. Her body rocked back and forth. *"What is going on? You—You all think Lucas killed Kennedy?"*

No, Victoria didn't think that. She also didn't think that Wade believed that, either.

Lucas had stopped vomiting. Now he was hunched on the ground, covered in filth, and he was—crying.

"Kennedy . . . he tortured Kennedy . . ." Lucas mumbled again and again.

Her chest ached as she listened to him.

No, she didn't have Sarah's expertise with killers, but every instinct she *did* have told her one thing. Lucas Branson wasn't the killer they were after.

"I think the cops know that isn't your phone," Victoria quietly told Connie. *It's Melissa. And I hope the cops can realize that Lucas isn't the man they're after.* But before Victoria could say anything else, a cop led the crying blonde away. But at least the guy's touch was more careful now, as if they'd all realized Connie and Lucas weren't the terrible criminals they'd suspected.

While Connie was secured in the back of a patrol car, Dace stared down at Lucas, and Victoria could see the uncertainty in his eyes.

"Branson." Dace's voice was softer now. "Can anyone verify that you just arrived at this house?"

Lucas nodded. "N-Neighbor. Over there . . ." He pointed to one of the neighbors who'd come out to gawk at the scene. "Mr. Morris saw me and Connie pull up. Stopped to talk to us . . . said he'd—" His head snapped back as he stared first at Wade, then Dace, with wide eyes. "Said he'd seen some guy in Connie's backyard."

Victoria's gaze shot to the neighbor even as Dace ordered a uniformed cop to bring Mr. Morris over for questioning.

"Lucas needs to get cleaned up," Victoria said, her heart still aching for him.

At her words, Lucas turned to focus on her. "You

found Kennedy." He'd risen to his full height, but his shoulders were hunched, his body wavering a bit unsteadily.

She nodded.

"He . . . hurt her?"

He already knew that truth, and she found she couldn't say it again. "She's not hurting anymore."

His eyes closed and tears tracked down his cheeks. Dace swore. She thought the detective had fully realized what she knew—that the killer had just played them all.

He planted that phone here. One last bit of torture for Lucas Branson. One big screw-you to the cops. The killer didn't make some overconfident mistake.

He played us like a pro.

"THE NEIGHBOR BACKED up the story," Dace said, his voice gruff. "He said Branson and his girl arrived just moments before we did. But the trace we got identified the call as coming *from* this location. It wasn't on the move, it was stationary."

Wade watched as uniformed cops continued to sweep the scene—Connie's house. "Did the neighbor get a good look at the man he saw in the backyard?"

"No, just said he was some guy wearing a black hoodie. He called out to him but the guy ran."

"He ran because he was done with his job." *Planting the phone. Throwing us off the trail.* And that worried Wade. He crossed his arms over his chest as he faced Dace. "The perp kept tabs on Branson over the years. He knew the guy had a fiancée, he knew where she lived, and he also knew when they'd both be gone."

The creep knew when they had an appointment with a caterer that would keep them out of the house—his perfect drop time. And that created a whole new problem. Wade wanted Sarah brought in on this case, ASAP. Because the guy they were after here—he was one twisted sonofabitch. "He wanted the cops to think that Branson had hurt Kennedy. He wanted this whole scene to go down exactly as it did."

But . . . something was nagging at him. The killer could have just called Dace directly. He could have just called the police station with his fucking taunts.

He hadn't. He'd called Victoria instead.

His gaze slid toward her. She was talking softly with Branson's fiancée. Victoria always said she wasn't good with the living, but she sure seemed to be doing a fine job of comforting Connie. She didn't give herself enough credit.

"Why the hell would the guy do this?" Dace wanted to know.

Wade didn't get into the minds of killers, not the way Sarah did, but he had his suspicions. "Torture. Pain. That's his thing." He nodded toward the patrol car. "He made sure that even at the end, when Kennedy finally was back, that her lover suffered more."

Dace swore. "*I* made him suffer. I did exactly what the asshole out there wanted."

"But it's not happening again. You're going to get him. *We're* going to get him."

Dace stepped closer. "You know my captain is going to fight having you on this case. Kennedy—yeah, that one he could let LOST cover. But Melissa? He's going to see her case as his domain from here on out."

"Let him." Wade shrugged. He *wanted* the cops involved. That didn't mean he was going to stop searching. "We were already hired by Jim Porter. He wanted us to find Melissa, and that's exactly what Victoria and I are going to do." He knew Gabe would back him up on this one. There was no way that his best friend would pull him off this case, especially not with the chance Melissa was still alive.

Oh, hell, no, there would be no backing down. And the more manpower they had on the search, the better.

He intended to see Jim Porter ASAP. The guy needed to be brought up to speed on all the tangled shit that was happening with this case. But first . . . "You aren't going to charge Branson with anything."

"What the hell *can* I charge him with? My captain wants an arrest, but I'm not taking in an innocent man." Dace jerked a hand through his already disheveled hair. "We're going to interview him. We're going to collect any evidence that the killer might have left in the house, but no, I'm not about to put Lucas Branson under arrest."

Wade's focus shifted back to the house. "Lucas and Connie need to be put up in a safe house, just for the next few days."

Dace's laugh was bitter. "No way will the captain go for that. Our budget is stretched enough as it is."

"LOST will foot the bill." Again, he had no doubt that Gabe would back him up. "But if the killer has been watching them," and Wade was sure he had, "they need a safe place. They need to get off his radar while we figure out what the SOB's next move is."

Victoria was heading toward them.

"His next move," Dace told him, voice only carrying to Wade's ears, "could be her."

"The hell it will be." His instant response. But . . . Wade was afraid the detective might be right, though it made no sense for the killer to contact Victoria. She should have barely been on his radar. They'd just arrived in town, but *something* had made the perp connect with her.

It was a connection Wade wanted to end.

Someone called out for Dace and the detective gave Wade a curt nod. "Look, I'll keep you updated and you do the same for me, got it? After all, we both have the same end goal here."

Bringing in the missing girl alive.

Stopping the killer.

"Will do," Wade said, and he watched as Dace hurried away.

Victoria eased closer to him. Her shoulder brushed against his arm. "I think the killer is playing with us."

He did, too.

"The killer—he wanted the cops to come storming up here. Calling me, staying on the line long enough for the cops to follow the signal from his phone . . . that wasn't a mistake."

"No." Wade agreed with her on that.

Her head tilted back as she studied him. "Why me?"

His back teeth ground together as he thought about just *why* the killer wanted her. Then he forced himself to say, "You were probably just convenient." *Don't scare her.* "You won't hear from him again."

She looked down at the ground. "I would have thought . . ." Her voice came slowly. ". . . that after everything else, all that I'd been through with LOST, you wouldn't try to hide the truth from me."

Dammit.

"I don't think there are any coincidences or any conveniences with this guy," she added.

Wade swallowed. "Then you tell me, baby. Why did he call you?"

Her lips parted. She was still looking at the ground, not him, and it took her a moment to say, "He told me that he knew things about me. Secrets."

Wade wanted to know her secrets.

"I think we should get to Jekyll Island," she said suddenly, as her gaze lifted. "He mentioned that place for a reason."

"Or he mentioned it to throw us off track. To send us running in the wrong direction." Just the mention of Jekyll Island made him tense. Shit, he knew that place—and he didn't exactly have fond memories of the island. He'd grown up in Atlanta, but a few times he'd come with his mother and his brother to Jekyll on holiday.

An image of his brother Adam flashed in his mind, and the pain hit him hard—just like the stab of a knife. He hadn't been back to Jekyll, not since that fucking day. What a cruel bitch fate was, to send this shit his way now.

Victoria gestured to the house. "This is the wrong direction. He said he wanted to trade. He said to go to Jekyll Island." She straightened her spine. "That's what I'm doing."

Then she turned away from him and started walking toward their SUV.

For a moment he just stared after her. No, no, she couldn't be serious.

But . . .

She was almost at the SUV.

I hate Jekyll. I'd be happy if I never saw that island again.

But he couldn't let Victoria go alone. Shit. *Shit.*

He rushed after her. He had the keys, dammit, so she couldn't just leave without him. Knowing Victoria and her secrets, the woman probably knew how to hot-wire a car. He caught her just before she reached for the door handle. His hand closed around her shoulder and he turned her back to face him. "No." That one word was all he could manage right then. Fury choked him too hard.

"Uh, *no*?" She blinked. "*No*, what?"

He took a deep breath. Another. He smelled lavender. He could feel her delicate shoulder beneath his touch. But in his mind . . . he saw a knife. Could almost hear a woman's screams.

Not Kennedy's screams. Not Melissa's.

Victoria's.

"There is *no* trade." It couldn't, *wouldn't* happen. The killer was focusing on Victoria, and Wade would figure out why the hell that was happening, but he wasn't just going to stand there while she offered herself up to him.

"If it saves Melissa . . ."

His hold tightened on her as he leaned in close, his body pressing to hers. "You don't risk your life, got it?" And he knew he sounded like a dick, but he couldn't help it. Too rough. Too angry. *Too scared* . . . scared that something would happen to her.

"Am I just supposed to let her die? Is that what *you* would do if he'd asked you to make the trade instead?"

"It isn't me." *It's you. You matter. You can't . . . I can't lose you.* But he didn't tell her any of that. Instead, Wade took another deep breath and made himself step back. "First thing we need to do . . . find Jim Porter. Let him know what's happening. Then, yes, we'll go to Jekyll Island. *Together.* You don't go off without me. I don't go off without you. We're partners, and we'll stay together every single moment."

She shook her head. "We need to get there *now*—"

"The killer was here in Savannah when he made that call to you. Jekyll Island is almost an hour from here. We check in with our client first, we call Gabe and update the rest of LOST, then we'll search Jekyll." They had to do this thing right.

Her jaw locked, but Victoria said, "Fine, we'll play it your way."

His way? His way would be to lock her up so she was far away from any danger, and that was not how he should be thinking. She was his partner, but they'd crossed a line when they became lovers, and keeping things professional, keeping his emotions out of the mix, was damn impossible. He wanted to protect her. Shield her from everyone and everything. But that wasn't the job.

Maybe it fucking should be.

He opened her door. He took out his phone and tried to call Jim. But the line just rang and rang, and finally his voice mail picked up. Wade left Jim a terse message, explaining that he needed to call, ASAP. Then he climbed into the SUV and dialed Gabe. He wasn't surprised that his friend picked up on the second ring.

"Tell me you've got news," Gabe said immediately.

"Not the kind you're going to like." Wade's fingers tapped on the steering wheel. "We found Kennedy Lane."

"That *is* the news I—"

"The perp kept her alive for three years, torturing her."

Silence. Then, "Son of a fucking bitch."

"And he's taken another woman . . ."

THE DOOR OPENED. Light spilled into the little room where she'd been kept, but Melissa didn't move.

She was standing behind that door, her body frozen. She'd gotten free moments before, and now he was coming—whoever the hell *he* was. The door inched open, so slowly, and soon she knew the light would spill on the cot. He'd see that she wasn't there.

I only have a moment. I have to act fast.

Her hands were linked together, forming one big fist. She had them lifted over her head. She was going to hit him as hard as she could. She would knock him down and run. Run fast and never look back.

"Melissa . . ." His voice was low, raspy. And . . . familiar?

She saw his back as he stepped into the room. Broad. Strong. The light hit his blond hair.

And the light also fell on the empty cot.

"Melissa!" he roared.

Betrayal burned through her, so painful and hard, tearing her apart. Not him. *Not him. Not him.* It was a terrible chant in her head because this couldn't be happening.

Yet . . . it was.

And he was starting to turn. Had she made a sound? A whimper of pain? A gasp of denial?

It didn't matter. She surged forward and slammed her hands into him as hard as she could. She hit his back with her fists and he fell forward, caught off guard by her attack.

There was a hard *thunk,* and she realized he'd hit his head on the edge of the cot. He was sprawled on the floor, and she didn't hesitate. She ran out the open doorway, her heart about to burst out of her chest. She had to get away.

Not him. Not him.

The terrible echo wouldn't stop in her mind. She raced through—a house? Yes, it was a house, with sparse furnishings, heavy curtains. She stopped for a moment and spun around, trying to figure out which way to go. Where was the door? How did she get *out*? "Melissa?"

He was calling for her. Coming after her.

"Help . . . you . . ."

No, he didn't want to help her. He just wanted to hurt her. Damn him. That was all he wanted.

To destroy her.

She found another door. Yanked it open, and fresh air hit her. She gasped, nearly choking on that air as she stood in the doorway. Her wrists burned. Had she broken one of them? Both? She didn't know. Maybe . . .

she'd struggled so long and hard to get out of those ropes.

She ran forward, into the night. It was so dark. So terribly, terribly dark. No moon, no stars. No light at all. She was being swallowed right up by the darkness. But she had to keep going. Had to get away.

Before he found her.

And killed her.

CHAPTER EIGHT

VICTORIA'S PHONE RANG, VIBRATING IN HER pocket. She yanked it out, her nerves on edge as Wade drove down the long dark interstate.

The screen lit up, and she frowned when she saw the words *Unknown Caller*. Not hesitating, she immediately answered—and also immediately put the call on speaker. "Hello?"

Wade kept driving fast, not slowing at all.

"Hello?" Victoria repeated. "Who is this?"

"Trade."

That low, rough rasp had her sucking in a sharp breath. *It was him.* And since they'd just left Lucas—in the company of nearly a dozen cops—this was solid proof that he wasn't the man who'd called her before.

The man who'd killed Kennedy.

"You're still offering a trade?" Victoria said carefully, but she knew fear had slipped into her voice. "I'm coming to Jekyll Island right now, I—"

"You told the police." A cold accusation.

Carefully, she responded, "I was at the station when you called me. I'm not now. I'm coming to Jekyll."

But he laughed. Grating, rough laughter. And he said, "Don't worry. Someone else made the trade."

Her heart stopped. "What? No!" Now her heart beat in a furious, triple-time rhythm. "Who?"

"If he's there . . . she lives . . ."

He was making no sense to her and—

"But he dies."

"Who dies? Who? Tell me!" Her voice was nearly a scream and she tried to pull back the emotion, but it was too late. She was on edge and far too desperate.

Wade didn't speak, but she felt the acceleration of the SUV as he sped up.

"I'll tell you . . ." Now that rasp almost sounded like a caress. "But you have to tell me first . . . when did you know you were going to kill him?"

An icy sensation slid around her body. "I—I don't know what you're talking about."

"That isn't how the game works." Now he was angry. Snarling. "Better luck next time." He hung up. Just—

When did you know you were going to kill him?

Her fingers fumbled as she called Dace. She wanted to tell him what had just happened and see if he could get some kind of trace going on that call—or her damn phone. *If he calls again, maybe they can get him.* Her voice stuttered as she talked to him, and no matter how many times she cleared her throat, she couldn't get rid of the heavy lump that had lodged there.

He knows. He knows what I did. But it should have been impossible. No one knew.

Because she'd been far better at covering her tracks than her father was.

"Victoria?"

She jumped at Wade's voice.

"We're going to be there soon," he said. "Twenty more minutes and we'll be at Jekyll."

"Melissa is there . . ."

"We're going to find her. Keep believing that. We will *find* her."

"Who else would have made the trade?" Victoria asked. "Who else would do it?"

Wade didn't answer. Her fingers fisted in her lap and she stared straight at the road ahead of them.

MELISSA COULD HEAR the sound of water, rough waves lapping at a shore. She stumbled out onto the beach, not realizing where she was until she felt the sand beneath her toes. Dark, so dark out there, she could barely see anything. No matter how many times she blinked, her eyes just couldn't seem to adjust to the darkness.

She rushed forward and slammed into something—something hard and rough. A tree? It felt like one, so sturdy and big. Only there were no leaves on the tree. Her fumbling fingers ran over its surface. She'd hit the tree too hard because she'd been running as fast as she could.

Her side ached at the impact, and she took a moment, trying to desperately gulp in air. Then she heard . . .

Footsteps? Yes, yes, that was the rustle of footsteps. Because there had been a section of earth before she'd stumbled onto the beach and the softness of the sand.

She slid down, kneeling in the sand as she crouched next to the old tree. She wanted to just put her hands up over her head, hide like a child, pretending that if she couldn't see, then the monster that was coming couldn't see her, either.

Why was this happening? Why had he done this to her?

She just wanted to get away. She began to crawl, moving silently in the sand, creeping along because she didn't want him to hear her.

The moments ticked past in silence. There was no other sound of footsteps. Had she imagined him before? Or—Or had he gone off the rough path that she'd first been on and stumbled into the sand? When he walked on the sand, he wouldn't make a sound, and the waves were so rough, pounding hard and frantically against the beach. She couldn't hear anything but those waves.

The waves.

That was what she needed to do. She needed to get in the water. She was a good swimmer. She'd swim away. He wouldn't be able to get her if she could just reach the water.

So she stood. She turned toward the water—that crashing of waves—and ran toward the sound. The scent of the saltwater reached out to her, and she stumbled forward, fast and sloppy. But she didn't hit the water. Her feet sank in mud. Heavy, thick mud. She tried to trudge forward. The waves had to be there. She was close, surely—

She fell. The heavy mud had tripped her and it seemed to be sucking her down. The waves were so close—the water was close. She could feel the spray on her face.

But the mud held her captive. A sob escaped from

her, burning her aching throat, and she crawled, so desperate to get forward. So desperate for freedom. Her hands were in front of her, sinking into that mud as she pulled herself, inch by inch, forward.

Inch by—

Her grasping hands didn't touch the sand.

She touched—a leg? Pants?

He's been here the whole time.

"No," she said, a broken whisper.

A shadow seemed to loom over her. And she felt the prick of a knife slide under her neck. "Yes . . ."

The knife sliced deeper. Harder. Even if she'd still had her voice, there was never a chance to scream.

WADE'S FINGERS WERE too tight around the steering wheel. He knew he needed to ease up, but the tension pouring through his body was unrelenting.

The bastard had called her again. The killer was fixating on Victoria, and Wade knew just how dangerous that fixation was.

"Where do we go?" Victoria asked, voice hushed. "Where do we start searching?"

They eased off the bridge that led to Jekyll Island. He knew the place well, having spent those summers here as a kid. The island was usually pretty empty, which would make it the perfect spot for the killer to use.

It's a pretty place. Everyone always thinks so.

But when I see it, I just remember death.

"Wade?" Victoria sounded worried. "Is everything okay?"

Not even fucking close. But this wasn't the time to go into his nightmare of a past. He had a job to do on

Jekyll. They'd do it and then get the hell out of there. He didn't want to face his ghosts, not then.

He wanted to find the girl. "Everything's fine." *Lying to her feels wrong.*

"Why is it so dark here?" Victoria leaned forward to peer through the windshield.

"Because of the turtles." He remembered this from his youth. "Nesting season. They keep the lights off or dimmed on the island so the turtles can follow the moonlight to the beach." His brother Adam had loved those damn turtles. Every year that they came to the island, Adam had volunteered, helping out with them. But that had been Adam—good, kind.

Such a waste. I miss the hell out of him.

"There isn't any moonlight tonight."

No, there wasn't any light at all. During their drive, they'd passed through a rough storm, and though the rain was gone now, heavy clouds still blocked the night sky.

Wade's phone rang then, and he tensed at the sound. Freaking phone calls were starting to drive him mad. His phone was connected through the car's speakers via Bluetooth, so he just hit the button near the steering wheel to take the call. "Monroe."

"W-Wade?" a hesitant voice asked. A voice that he knew.

"Jim." Good. Relief swept through him. "Jim, we've got news on Melissa. We think she's alive and on—"

"Jekyll Island."

Wade pulled the SUV to the side of the road. "What?"

"H-He told me to come to Jekyll Island. Gave me

the address. Said to come alone." Jim's words were tumbling out, too fast. "My life for hers. Of course, I'd make the trade."

"Oh, my God," Victoria whispered.

The perp is going to kill Jim. "Where are you?" Wade demanded. "Give me a specific address, *now*."

"She's not here." Jim sounded confused. "I—I think she was . . . but she's not here now. Where is she?"

"Look, I want you to get in your car. Lock your doors. Got it? The bastard is out here, and he's hunting."

Jim didn't speak. His ragged breath carried easily over the Bluetooth connection.

"An address!" Victoria cried out. "Tell us where you are! We can come to you!"

Jim mumbled an address, then said, "Cottage . . . at the end of the road. All alone. Almost didn't see it. Trees were so thick. Climbing all over it . . ."

"Get the hell back in your car," Wade ordered. "Right now, do you hear me?"

"I—I need to find Melissa."

"He's *there,*" Wade snarled. "He will kill you." How much clearer could he be? "Get in your car. Get the hell in and lock the doors, do you understand me? Better yet, get the fuck out of there. Come meet me at the bridge or—"

"I won't leave this place!" Now Jim was angry. "She's here! I know she's here! I won't leave her!"

"Then just get your ass in that car! Lock the doors. Stay there until you see me!"

There was a rush of footsteps in the background, and then the line went dead. Wade immediately plugged the address into his GPS. *Opposite side of the damn island*. Figured. He just needed Jim to stay alive until he got there.

Then he heard Victoria on her phone, updating Dace on what was happening. He already knew Dace was trying to coordinate with the local authorities and get a search team out to the Island.

Jim made the trade. The kid should have called him first. He should have told him what the hell he was planning and not gone off on his own.

Wade drove down the bay side of the island, his gaze straining to see in the darkness. He knew the old Jekyll Island Club Hotel was nearby. Once upon a time the island had been a hunting getaway for the rich and famous. Rockefeller. Pulitzer. The big names had all spent time there. Back in the day, it had been their perfect place to hunt.

Now he's hunting here. A killer who liked to play games.

Wade headed past the historic district on the island then went farther. Past the remains of an old house, one that he'd been told was haunted when he was thirteen. He'd even been dared to spend the night out there.

He'd always taken up dares. Adam hadn't. Adam hadn't cared about dares. But his brother stayed with him that night . . .

To make sure I was safe.

Wade hadn't realized how much this fucking island would haunt him. Why the hell had the killer picked this spot?

He rounded the curve and started heading toward the Atlantic side of the island. His GPS told him to turn, and he headed down a snake-sized road. Down, down . . .

His headlights cut through that pitch-black darkness. The beam hit a battered-looking truck parked on the edge of the pavement. He saw the silhouette of a man in the truck.

Wade killed the SUV's engine, but before jumping out, he took his gun from the glove box. He had a concealed carry permit in Georgia, and the way this killer was jerking them all around—hell, no, he wasn't about to rush out unarmed.

When he and Victoria hurried out of the SUV, he made sure to stay in front of her. Victoria didn't like guns. They'd talked about that—once, a lifetime ago. She never carried a weapon that he knew of, and Wade thought that was some dangerous shit. Considering the way their cases had gone lately, the woman definitely needed to be armed if she was going to work in the field.

When he approached the truck, Jim shoved open the door. Then he climbed out, staggering a bit. Victoria hurried toward him and wrapped her arms around his torso to steady him. "What happened to you?"

"Melissa . . . I—I think it was her. I went to get her out. He'd said she was locked inside . . ."

Wade looked over at the old cottage. He could see light glowing from the interior.

"But when I got in there, the back room . . . there were ropes and blood."

Hell.

"No Melissa." Jim's voice was hoarse. "An empty cot. That blood. Not her. Then . . . then someone hit me from behind. I went down, hit something . . . and I—I thought I saw her running away." His words were heavy with confusion. "I think . . . maybe she was hiding behind the door?" Jim shook his head. "Why would she hide from me?"

Wade's fingers were curled around the gun. The weight of the weapon was a familiar comfort in his hand. "We're going inside." He wanted to search the place and figure out what the hell had happened. But he was determined that they would go in together. Until backup arrived, their little group would be going everywhere together. There would be no Scooby-Doo separating shit, not until he knew just where the killer was.

Not with his fixation on Victoria. I'm not leaving her until I know she is safe.

Victoria kept her arm around Jim as they climbed the front steps that led to the old house. The door was unlocked, hanging open a bit. Wade opened it more with the tip of his weapon. "Don't touch anything," he whispered. The warning was for Jim, not Victoria. She knew better than to contaminate a crime scene.

He inched forward, studying the place. Light blazed, but he wondered if Jim had turned the light on when he rushed inside, running to Melissa's rescue. The place had the heavy closed odor that told him it probably hadn't been used in a long time.

Two years? Did you use this place before, when you kept Kennedy hidden away?

The furniture was dusty, another sign that no one had been using the house in a while. He walked down the tight hallway, the old wood squeaking beneath his feet. He pushed open the first door on the right, needing to do a thorough sweep and make certain the house was empty.

This room was empty. No furniture. Nothing in it at all. No clothes in the closet. No toiletries in the bathroom.

He eased out. Victoria and Jim were right behind him. "There . . ." Jim pointed down the hallway. Wade noticed the blood dripping from a gash on Jim's forehead. "I went in . . . there . . ."

The door Jim indicated was partially open. As Wade continued down the narrow hallway, he was aware of a cold tension in his body. Battle-ready tension. He'd felt this way before, right before confronting perps when he'd been a detective with the Atlanta PD. He knew scenes could go to hell in a heartbeat. There had been times—times he didn't like to remember but could never really forget—when he was forced to pull the trigger. In order to defend himself, his partner, and even to protect other victims, he'd had to shoot.

He'd done what was necessary. Hadn't hesitated.

And he wouldn't hesitate now.

As he approached the room, his footsteps slowed. He could see what looked like a narrow cot. Thick rope had been tossed on it, the ends still tied to metal pipes that seemed to come straight from the walls. And Jim had been right. There was blood in there. Blood near the top of the mattress, where a person's head would be. Blood near the bottom ropes.

You tied her here, didn't you?

"That's not enough blood for a mortal wound," Victoria said, voice hushed.

He'd figured the same thing. He leaned over the cot,

careful not to touch anything there. "There's a lot of blood on the rope." And he knew what Melissa had done. "She got loose."

"Where is she?" Jim asked. "Why did she run?"

"Probably because she's scared out of her mind." He turned back toward Jim and Victoria. The house was empty. No killer. No victim. "We have to start a search of the island." Because Melissa could be out there, running blind or . . .

She could be out there, and the killer could be hunting her.

Victoria nodded as she gazed at Wade. "Every inch," she agreed.

Melissa needed them, and every moment was important. The problem? Getting a team organized and getting the hell out there. Each second that passed without a search was too much of a waste. Dace and his cop buddies were rushing in, but how long would it take them to mobilize there?

Wade hurried back outside, with Victoria and Jim close by. Victoria made Jim sit on the steps while she examined his wound.

"How'd you get the gash?" she asked him.

"I—I fell forward when she hit me. Must have . . . slammed into the floor. Or the cot. Something . . ."

Wade paced the scene, trying to imagine where Melissa would go. She would have been terrified when she went outside. So desperate.

It would have been pitch-black out there . . .

He stilled, listening. He could just make out the roar of the surf. That roar meant . . . waves. The beach. In Melissa's desperate mind, had that roar equaled some kind of safety? *If you couldn't see anything, then maybe you'd run toward what you could hear.*

He wanted to run toward that sound, searching for her, but . . .

Victoria.

He didn't know where the killer was. He *did* know that the guy was already too fixated on her. *Can't leave my partner on her own.*

Then he saw the flash of lights rounding the corner. Local cops, coming to help on the scene. Hell, yes.

Victoria would be safe. He could hunt.

"Talk to them," he ordered her as the cars drew closer. "Get the search going." She knew how to organize a search task force—at LOST, that was day fucking one material.

Victoria grabbed his arm. "Where are you going?"

The pounding of the surf called to him like a lifeline, the way he thought it might have called to Melissa. "The water. I'm going to the beach. Starting the search there. Get boots on the ground, Viki. Get her help! Call in the K-9 unit!" They needed every single asset they could get on this case.

And they didn't have time to waste. Because Melissa was running out there, desperate, and the perp could be, too.

"I—I TRIED TO find her," Jim confessed, anguish heavy in his words. "I wanted to help her."

The local authorities had swarmed the scene. Unfortunately, Dace hadn't been with them. It had taken far too much time to organize the local authorities. They'd wanted to focus on the house, on collecting evidence, when Victoria kept telling them that the missing woman was *out there. Focus on the island—start looking for her!*

No wonder Wade had run when he saw the cop cars. He'd known that the scene was safe with the authorities so close by, and she realized he hadn't wanted to be slowed down by a million and one questions. He'd wanted to search.

So he'd left her with the million and one questions.

But the men and women there . . . they meant well. They were just in far, far over their heads.

"Never had something like this happened here," one of the guys said.

Victoria thought he had come over from the mainland. He seemed so hesitant as he stood next to the patrol car.

"You really think some guy . . . he's been torturing women out here?"

"It wouldn't be the first time a killer has used an island," she said. Her mind drifted back to the Lady Killer case and the victims she'd found on Dauphin Island. "Sometimes, the proximity to the ocean and the seclusion—they work to a killer's advantage." Especially when it came to body disposal. Talk about easy. Just jump on a boat, weigh down your victim, and drive away . . .

But Kennedy's body wasn't dumped in the water. She was buried.

Buried . . . and Victoria had found Spanish moss in that black bag with her.

Her gaze darted around the scene. Heavy trees twisted and turned around the little house—trees that were all weighed down by Spanish moss that blew in the breeze. Thanks to the cop cars, the scene had been illuminated enough for her to easily see the moss.

Did you bury Kennedy here? Instead of sending her out to the ocean?

Maybe the killer had wanted to keep her close.

Maybe he hadn't been able to let go . . .

Not until he took someone else.

"We can have a K-9 unit here in an hour!" a woman called out.

An hour . . . that wasn't going to cut it.

Victoria's gaze tracked back to the darkness. She hadn't seen Wade since he'd run off. Where was he? He needed backup.

I'm his backup. I'm his partner. I should be out there with him.

Jim was in the back of an ambulance. An EMT was treating him, examining the heavy gash on his head. He was safe. She'd talked to the cops in charge. Given them as much information as she had. Now she was just standing there, playing a waiting game, while Wade was out there, alone.

Every instinct she possessed screamed for her to go after him.

"Captain!" She grabbed the arm of the man who was leading that group. "We need to start that search!"

"My men are almost ready to go, ma'am. We'll start a full-island sweep, heading to Driftwood Beach and combing from the north end of the island on down." He gave her a brisk nod. "We've got this, ma'am. We will find her."

She wanted to have his confidence.

Her head tilted back and she glanced up at the night sky. The heavy clouds that had covered the island were starting to pass. She could see the glitter of stars and almost make out the glow of the moon. If they could get just a little more light, it would help the search so much.

"You coming with us?" the captain asked.

As if she would be left behind. "Let's do this." *Please, Melissa. Just hold on. We're coming.*

TREES WERE TOSSED onto the beach, stripped of leaves, battered by the waves and shaped by the tide.

Wade knew exactly where he was—Driftwood Beach. A place that had been whispered about so much when he was thirteen. A beach of ghosts.

The trees were scattered all over that long stretch of beach. Getting through them was like navigating a maze. But the moonlight and starlight had finally started to spill onto him, and he could see better as he made his way through the obstacles.

"Melissa!" He yelled her name as he headed down the beach. He'd been calling out to her, again and again, during his search, but she hadn't called back to him.

Maybe he was in the wrong place. Maybe she'd gone south. Or, hell, maybe she'd even gone into the water, so desperate to get away from her abductor.

For an instant Wade stilled. His gaze turned to the ocean and those rushing waves.

Jekyll Island. He really hadn't wanted to come back to this fucking place. It held too many memories for him. Mostly bad ones.

The water . . . it taught me about loss.

He fucking hated boats and water now. Hated them.

If Melissa had gone into the water, they'd have to get the Coast Guard out there, ASAP. She could be weak, confused, and the waves out there were already rough because of the storm that had come through earlier. If she wasn't careful, the water would take her away.

Just as it took my brother.

"Melissa!" Wade shouted again. "I'm here to help you!" He continued moving deeper down the beach. The driftwood trees were slanted, left and right, across the sand. He climbed over one. "I'm with a group called LOST! The cops are here, too! It's time to go home!"

He stepped forward. Maneuvered past more driftwood and—

There was a faint sound behind him. A rasp. Could have been nothing. A crab moving across the sand. But . . .

He swung back around with his weapon drawn.

That was when he saw her.

Her arms were tied to the driftwood. One anchored on her left side, one on her right. Her head sagged forward and she was on her knees, all but hidden behind a massive tree.

Fuck. He rushed toward her, dropping to his knees in the sand. He put the gun down beside him when he reached to touch her chin. "Melissa? Melissa, it's all right . . ."

But it wasn't.

He tipped back her head, and her hair—hair that had been cropped to barely hit her jaw—slid away from her face. Even in the faint moonlight, he could see the blood that covered her—blood that poured from her neck. Wade realized that she hadn't been able to call out for help because that bastard had sliced her throat.

A faint rasp came from her, a rough gurgle—probably the only sound she could make right then. But it told him that she was still alive.

Not too late. Not—

He grabbed at the ropes holding her and wrenched the one at her right wrist free. He could feel her blood there, too. Blood that just seemed to surround her whole wrist.

"It's going to be all right," he told her. "You're safe now. I won't let anyone hurt you."

She made that pitiful, painful rasp again.

"No, don't try to talk. It's okay." Talking was the last thing she needed to try doing at that moment. "Save your strength." He put his hand on her throat, trying to stem that terrible blood flow. He could feel the blood seeping through his fingers. *A fresh wound.* The killer had been close—no doubt was *still* close. They needed backup out there, and they needed it fast.

He couldn't tell how deep her wound was. He didn't know if she'd last five more minutes or an hour. He just knew he had to get her help.

He pulled out his phone, ready to call Victoria and get the cavalry on that beach but—

No fucking signal.

Just his luck.

He dropped the phone, letting it fall into the sand. Then he kept one hand at Melissa's throat, keeping up the pressure. With his right hand, he fumbled with the ropes that still held her other wrist captive. The damn knots there wouldn't give and he yanked and yanked—

The rope broke. Her arm fell.

"It's okay," Wade said again. He grabbed his gun and tucked it into his waistband. Then he picked her up. "We're getting out of here."

The killer is close.

Was the SOB watching him even then? Hiding in the dark?

Wade half expected to feel a bullet lodge into his back as he rushed to make his way off the driftwood-covered beach. But maybe all those trees—tossed and broken as if a giant had thrown them aside, scattering them here—maybe those trees were actually helping him as he fled with Melissa. Providing cover.

She was so still in his arms. Not holding onto him at all. Just limp. "Stay with me," Wade told her. "You hear me? Stay. Fight. You have to fight."

He tightened his hold on her and rushed into the darkness.

THE LOST AGENT had found Melissa. She hadn't been given a chance to bleed out. Not yet.

He'd found her too soon.

Now he was rushing away with her, talking to her, telling her that everything would be all right.

The agent was a very good liar.

Nothing would be all right again for Melissa. He'd made sure of it.

He waited until Wade Monroe was well down the beach, then slid from the cover of another broad driftwood tree. He'd been less than ten feet away from Melissa the whole time. He thought she'd known that. He thought she'd actually been trying to warn Wade about him.

Pity she hadn't been able to talk.

His foot brushed against the sand, and he knelt near the discarded ropes. His gloved fingers reached out but he didn't touch the rope.

Instead, he touched . . . a phone. One that the agent had just dropped and forgotten. He slipped it into his pocket. It would come in handy. Ever so handy. Very soon.

Then he backed away. After all, he had a promise to keep. A trade had been offered.

But that trade hadn't been made.

He'd see Melissa again. Just as he would be seeing Wade Monroe again. First, though, he had other prey to seek out.

Waves crashed against the beach as he slipped away.

CHAPTER NINE

THE SEARCH TEAMS HEADED INTO THE WOODS that surrounded the cottage. Victoria could hear the rush of the surf just beyond the woods. She could smell the ocean air.

"Melissa!" the cop beside her yelled out. "Melissa Hastings!"

But Melissa wasn't answering them. And even though she'd tried to call him on her phone, Victoria hadn't been able to reach Wade, either.

The cops had lights with them. They shone them to the left and right as they tried to see in the darkness. Victoria followed, moving as quickly as she could. There were so many places to hide in those woods.

The ground rose up, cresting, and the rough dirt slowly gave way to the cushion of sand—she could feel it beneath her shoes. The lights turned to the left—

A stark white tree lay on its side, nearly covering the whole beach.

She blinked at the sight. All of the bark, the leaves—everything was gone from the tree. It appeared almost otherworldly with its stark white body and—

"Driftwood Beach," the cop to her right said. "Watch your step."

She moved forward cautiously and saw more trees. Dozens of them. Tossed left and right on the beach. Massive, giant trees.

"Help!"

Victoria froze at the cry. So did the cop—Jacob—who'd been searching with her. "Did you hear that?" she asked him.

Jacob immediately swung his light in the direction of that cry.

"Wade?" Victoria shouted. "Wade, is that—"

"Help her!"

It was Wade's voice. She took off running, grabbing out to latch onto Jacob's arm and haul him with her. They shot across the sand and she tripped over a thick chunk of stone. *Why is there stone on this beach?* But then she hurtled around another ghostly tree and Jacob's light fell on Wade.

She wouldn't forget that sight, not as long as she lived.

Wade stood there, his arms wrapped tightly around a woman's body. The woman was slumped forward in his arms, but the light shone on her clothes—blood-covered clothes—and Victoria saw the blood pouring from her throat.

"She's alive!" Wade shouted. "She needs help! She—"

Victoria leapt toward him. Behind her, she heard Jacob on his radio, calling for help. Demanding a life flight to the island.

When she touched the woman, Melissa's head tipped back. Sagged brokenly.

"Wade . . ." Victoria began, her voice husky.

"We have to get her to a hospital! The bastard slit her throat!"

Victoria's chest burned. "I have to check her trachea." It wasn't just about the blood—it was about getting air to Melissa. And Victoria was very, very afraid of that wound—*it's too deep. Too wide and long. He didn't just cut her carotid. He hit her trachea.*

Wade lowered her so Victoria could better examine the woman.

Melissa didn't move.

"She was making a rasping sound when I first found her," Wade said. "Just a few minutes ago. She was alive! She—"

She wasn't breathing. And when Victoria tried to find a pulse, she couldn't.

There was no rustle as if she were trying to get air. There was no rise and fall of her chest that Victoria could see at all.

"Life flight is coming!" Jacob shouted, his voice breaking. "EMTs are rushing through the woods to meet us, and the airlift will come for her right here—they'll land on the beach."

Wade put Melissa to the ground. And it *was* Melissa. With Jacob's light, Victoria could clearly see her face. Her still face. The woman's lashes were closed. Blood was everywhere.

"She's alive," Wade said. "We got to her in time."

He was breaking her heart. Gutting Victoria because there was such desperate hope in his voice.

So she went to work, even though she feared—even

though everything she saw—told her that, no, Wade was wrong.

Melissa wasn't alive. At least not anymore, she wasn't.

THE HELICOPTER ROSE into the air. The *whoop-whoop-whoop* of the chopper's blades filled the night and sand blew toward Wade and Victoria. He turned, trying to shield her body with his as that helicopter rose ever higher.

Then . . .

It was gone.

His hands—blood covered—had wrapped around Victoria's shoulders. They fell now as she glanced back at him. She hadn't said anything during those long painful moments while they waited for Life Flight to arrive. She'd just worked on Melissa with a desperate focus.

He'd heard the whispers from the cops, though. He knew what they all believed . . .

She's already gone.

Rage burned within him, a fierce, deep fury because he knew they were right. Even as she'd been loaded into that chopper, Wade had known the truth.

He hadn't saved Melissa Hastings. He'd arrived too fucking late.

Another one I lost. I should have searched the area sooner. Should have forgotten about that fucking house and run straight out to search.

No, he should have gone to Jekyll Island first, not followed the cops to Connie's house. He should have done a million damn things differently.

Instead . . .

"Wade . . ." Victoria's whisper held such pain. "I'm sorry."

He spun away from her and started walking. Blindly. Just straight damn ahead. The cops were combing the beach, but it was still so dark—what the hell did they think they would find? The killer? Hell, no. He wasn't just going to walk right up to them. He was too smart for that.

He'd taken his prey. He'd killed her. And he'd gotten away.

The waves brushed over Wade's feet. He stilled, realizing now that he'd walked to one of the things that he hated most.

Fucking ocean.

The waves battered at him.

"Wade . . ." Victoria had followed him. Beautiful Victoria, with all of her secrets. Secrets that she wouldn't share with him. Secrets that he'd tried to figure out on his own.

When I wasn't even sharing my past with her.

Was that right? Hell, no. But *right* wasn't always in his vocabulary, despite what Victoria thought of him. She believed he was the good guy. The stand-up one.

She had no clue.

Growing up, he'd been the rebel. The one most likely to sneak out and look for trouble. The one who'd taken dares. The one who'd been pissed that his old man skipped out, and he'd run wild.

His brother, Adam, had been the good one. Always looking out for him. Watching over their mom.

The water hit him again, reminding Wade too much

of the past. This island. Why did it have to be this place? Fate was a cold and cruel bitch, that was for sure. He hated this place, and if he'd had his way, he would have never set foot on Jekyll again.

But I came back. And someone else died. Freaking story of my life.

"I think . . . I think Detective Black is here now." Her voice was hesitant.

Wade stared into the darkness of the ocean. He knew he needed to pull his shit together. *Melissa's blood is still on me.* "I wanted to save her." His voice was stark.

"I know."

He spun to face her. "When did you *know* she was gone?"

He couldn't see her face, but he heard the sadness in her voice when she said, "When I—I touched her. She was too still."

"She bled out."

Victoria didn't speak.

"Fuck, *what*? What is it?" He could feel her holding back.

"It was more like . . . you don't really want to hear this, okay? Not now. Let's just go talk to Dace. Let's see if the crime scene team can find anything in that house."

She was trying to protect him? He got that. But he wasn't in the mood for protection. "What the hell happened to her?"

"He didn't want her to live, Wade." Her hand rose. Curled around his arm and squeezed. "Isn't that enough? Why do you want more pain in your mind?

Don't you think . . . there's already enough there as it is?"

"Tell me." She was the doctor. She knew . . .

Her hand pulled away. "He cut her carotid. Her . . . trachea. The wound was deep and long. That rasping you heard? I—I believe she was . . . Wade, look, we don't have to—"

Now he was the one to grab her and hold tight. "She was in my arms. I put pressure on her wound. I tried to help—"

"She was choking and drowning on her own blood. You tried, but there just wasn't anything you could do by then."

Something . . . shut down in him. Shut off.

Another victim. *She died in my arms and I didn't even realize it.* He'd been so intent on rushing her to safety. He hadn't felt it when she'd slipped away.

"Wade?"

He walked past Victoria, heading back toward the little cottage. Away from the ocean and away from the memories. Part of him just wanted to keep walking.

He'd joined LOST to make a difference. And in the last twenty-four hours, instead of saving the missing . . . he'd just added to the list of the dead.

Would it ever end? Would he ever make any sort of difference? Seemed like his life was just about the dead. About being too late. Again and again.

Just like I was too late to help my own fucking brother. I jumped in the water too late. Didn't find him fast enough.

And then he was just gone.

VICTORIA BLINKED THE tears from her eyes. She didn't follow behind Wade. Not right then. She just . . . she needed a minute.

Yes, yes, they had to go talk with Dace. Had to talk to all the cops. Had to see just what they could do to help the investigation.

But for a moment Victoria just stood there. She wrapped her arms around her stomach and drew in a deep, shuddering breath.

She'd wanted to save Melissa, too. The woman had been so young and she'd obviously suffered so much. Why couldn't there have been a happy ending for her?

Wade was beaten up, no doubt about it, but did he feel the same gut-wrenching guilt that she did? Because as she'd tried so frantically to help Melissa, the perp's words had been replaying through her mind, again and again . . .

You can come to me, and I'll let Melissa go.

She hadn't gone to him, and now . . . now Melissa Hastings was dead.

Tears were on her cheeks, and Victoria didn't care. So what if she cried while on the case? So what if others saw her? She hurt—hurt for what Melissa had been through with that sick freak.

She hurt for Kennedy.

And she hurt . . . for the next victim. Because Victoria knew, beyond any shadow of a doubt, that there would be another victim. With a guy like this, there always would be. He wouldn't stop, not until someone stopped *him*.

"Are you all right?"

She sucked in a sharp breath at the question. A question that had been asked by a deep, male voice.

Not Wade, though.

Victoria glanced to the left. Dace stood there, his body mostly in the shadows. "No, I'm not, but that doesn't really matter, does it?"

"You think we should have come here first." He edged closer to her.

She cast a quick glance around. Wade was nowhere to be seen, but a few other cops were on the beach.

"You think we made a mistake in following that phone to Connie's place, don't you?"

"It was your captain's call," she said, swiping at the tears on her cheeks. "He—"

"You wanted to come here."

Yes. Her hands fell to her sides. "If I'd made the trade, Melissa wouldn't be on that helicopter right now."

"I know she was dead when she left the beach."

She shivered. "They'll still work on her. I've seen . . . there are miracles out there." She'd stopped herself because, no, she hadn't always *seen* them. But she'd heard stories. Some people were brought back. Amazing things could happen.

"I'm not Wade. You don't have to bullshit with me."

His words pulled her gaze back to him. Cautious now, she said, "I don't lie to Wade. He's my partner."

"He may be, but that still doesn't mean you tell him everything, now does it?"

Where is this going?

He advanced toward her. "I'm glad you didn't make the trade."

Instinctively, she shook her head. *Melissa was dead—*

Dace grabbed her arm. "If you had, then you would've been on that helicopter. Or hell, maybe you'd be in the ground someplace, just like Kennedy."

Maybe. Or maybe she and Wade could have caught the killer. Maybe they would have been able to stop him *and* save the girl.

"Sacrificing yourself won't help the victims," Dace said, nearly growling the words. "It won't—"

"Victoria." Now *that* was Wade's voice. Hard and sharp, cutting right through the night. "What's going on?"

Dace stepped back. "Just talking to your partner."

She'd thought that Wade had left. He could move so silently, but with the rush of the surf, hell, maybe everyone was moving silently. The surf smothered so many sounds.

Did that pounding surf help the killer escape?

"My captain wants Victoria to keep consulting on this case," Dace said, his words abrupt. "He thinks she can help us . . . especially if this cottage has been the perp's prison for his girls."

His girls.

Victoria cleared her throat. "Kennedy's . . . Her grave may be close. The Spanish moss that I found in her bag, it could easily have come from this area."

"And if he kept Kennedy here . . ." Dace mused darkly. "Kennedy *and* Melissa . . . hell, my captain is worried there might be even more bodies on this island. He's requested your help, Victoria."

It wasn't the first time she'd been brought in for consulting by local law enforcement. She nodded. "Of— Of course. If there is any way that I can help, I will."

"Thank you." Dace backed away. "I need to go interview Jim Porter. That guy is a freaking mess."

Because he *had* traded himself for Melissa.

Only the trade hadn't worked out.

Dace disappeared into the darkness. Victoria could feel Wade's stare on her. "I thought you'd gone."

"Not without you." But he didn't reach out to touch her. And she wanted him to—wanted him to take her hand.

She pulled in a deep breath. The helicopter was long gone. The cops had fully taken over the scene. There wasn't much left for her and Wade to do, not just then. "We should report in to Gabe. Let him and the others at LOST know what happened."

"Don't consult."

Her eyes widened. "What?"

"This case . . . the way it's going . . . the way that perp *called* you. I don't like it, Viki. Not one damn bit. There is nothing good happening here. I think you need to go back to Atlanta. Our work is done."

She stiffened. "You don't think I should be in the field." She hadn't thought so, either, not when Gabe had first given that order. Jeez, had it just been days ago? But things had changed. *She* had changed. And she didn't want to let this case go. She couldn't.

"I think you could be in danger. I think the perp gets fixated on women, and all signs are pointing to him being fixated on *you*." He was so close, but still not touching her. "I hate the setup. I hate this fucking place. And I want you out of here."

Her chin notched up. "I'm not leaving. Not until I see what's been found here. Because if I can help catch this guy, I *will* do it." If there were bodies buried near that cabin, then hell yes, she would stay. She could learn secrets from the dead. She'd learn those secrets and maybe they'd find evidence that would point to the killer's identity.

She knew that Dace hadn't been able to turn up anything usable on those traffic cameras near Vintage. Apparently, they'd gone on the fritz weeks ago, and the city hadn't gotten around to footing the bill and getting them fixed. So there was no footage of the mystery man in the Jag who'd taken Melissa.

Taken her. Killed her.

She brushed by Wade. She'd wanted him close a moment before, but now—

He caught her arm. His grip was too tight. "I keep thinking . . . what if you had been in my arms?"

"Wade?" She strained to read his expression.

"What if you'd died while I held you and I didn't even fucking realize it? Do you have any idea what that would do to me?"

Hesitant now, she shook her head.

"Sometimes, people are far more dangerous than we think." His hold loosened on her, but Wade didn't let her go. His fingers began to stroke the inside of her wrist. "Then something happens and a person . . . he just snaps."

He was making her nervous. "You aren't the type to snap."

"Don't be too sure. If that bastard came for you, if he tried to hurt *you*, believe me, there is nothing I wouldn't do to keep you safe."

He was warning her, and she didn't know what to say

in response. This was a Wade she hadn't seen before. Dark and hard and with a stark, deadly determination that chilled her.

"Do you ever wonder," he asked her softly, "why I turned in my badge?"

"B-Because Gabe asked you to join him at LOST. He wanted your help to get the organization off the ground—"

"No. I quit the force before LOST. There are some lines that, if you cross them once, they haunt you forever."

What did you do? But she couldn't get those words out. Because if she asked him about the darkness of his past, then wouldn't she have to share her own secrets, too? And that wasn't something she was ready to do. Not by a long shot.

So she didn't say anything. They left that beach together. Not touching now, but bodies still close. Bodies tense. The waves crashed behind them, and the darkness hid so much.

His sins.

And hers.

THEY'D BEEN AT that scene all night long. Sunlight finally rose across the water, rising ever so slowly, a ball of red that turned the water to fire.

The cops had searched and searched. They'd even locked down the island at one point. Not letting anyone else on, not letting anyone else off.

Like that had done any good.

The cops had just shut off the main road, but boats kept coming and going.

And the killer . . . well, Victoria suspected he could be hiding in plain sight and they wouldn't know.

She walked slowly down Driftwood Beach. The beach was a crime scene now, but she had access. Curious bystanders had gathered—bystanders held back by two police officers and a thin strand of yellow plastic tape. In the rising sun, the beach was even more of a stark, almost sad place.

She could see now that all of the trees there were white—they'd been bleached by the sea and the sun. Massive trees. With dead roots and no leaves. Crisscrossed all over that sandy stretch of beach.

A camera flashed and she blinked. The crime scene tech was in front of Melissa's tree. At least, that was how Victoria thought of it . . . a white tree that was streaked with red blood. The waves rose, sliding over her toes. She knew the techs had been working against the tide the whole time, but Mother Nature seemed determined to make their job as difficult as possible.

The ropes had been taken away. Bagged and tagged. As had so many of the items in that little cottage. The cops were still trying to track the owner of the cottage.

She knew Dace had one idea . . . *Find the owner, find the killer.*

But she doubted things would be that easy, despite what Dace wanted. Just like with the phone trace before, she suspected their perp was too smart to have made an obvious mistake. *And having your name listed on the property where you torture and murder innocent women?* That would definitely qualify as an obvious mistake.

Her gaze lingered on the blood. Melissa must have

been so afraid at the end. When she'd seen Wade, had hope pushed that fear away?

Victoria prayed that it had. Because no one's last moments should just be all about fear. And maybe, maybe, Melissa *had* been able to hope, for a little while.

Victoria squared her shoulders and headed back up the beach. She climbed the small incline that led to the woods and slipped beneath the yellow police tape. As soon as she cleared the tape, her phone vibrated. She pulled the phone from her pocket and saw the text from Wade.

I miss you.

The text made her pause. And . . . warmth bloomed in her chest. She'd barely seen Wade in the last few mad hours. He'd been working with the cops, making certain that evidence didn't get contaminated. And she'd been on the phone, trying to call in as many favors as possible. If more bodies *were* buried out there, they'd need corpse-sniffing dogs on the scene as well as ground-penetrating radar. They couldn't just start digging. They needed the tools to do the search right. She'd tried to get them those tools.

I miss you.

Her fingers slid over the screen. She typed back . . .

I know you worry. I will stay safe. Promise.

Then she kept walking up the trail. Half a dozen people were gathered there, watching. Whispering. Gossip had spread fast, and Victoria knew that it was only a matter of time before news crews showed up. This story was going to be everywhere. It was too horrific not to make headlines.

Her phone vibrated again.

Don't make a promise you can't keep.

The warmth she'd felt faded. Wade seemed so certain that she was in danger. But cops were all around. She was perfectly safe.

WADE LEANED AGAINST his rented SUV as he stared at the little cottage. Such a small place, to hide such hell. He'd watched as crime scene techs swarmed the house. If the perp had once held Kennedy Lane in that cottage, the techs would find proof. He'd made damn sure those guys were as thorough as possible.

Day had come. Fucking finally knocking out the night.

Melissa was dead. Not a big surprise, considering what Victoria had told him, but they'd received official word less than forty-five minutes after the chopper lifted off from the island.

"This is a such a freaking shame," Dace said as he stalked toward Wade.

Yes, it was.

"We've got a hit, though, on the burial site." Dace's lips thinned. "Two cops found a spot, about one mile back from the house, buried deep in the woods. The cadaver dogs that Victoria got for us . . . they led the team there. There's a big hole . . . a hole that I'm betting once contained Kennedy's body."

Wade's eyes were still on the cottage. "So he kept her here, too."

"For three years? I don't buy that shit. Someone would have known. Someone would have seen *something*."

Wade shook his head. "Not if he didn't let her out. If he kept her locked inside, if she never escaped from him, then how would anyone know? He soundproofed the place—you and I both saw that." Smart SOB. "So the women could scream as long as they wanted, and no help would be coming to them."

"Why the hell would someone do this? What does he get from it?"

"Power." Wade knew that with certainty. "This freak likes being in control. He likes knowing that his victims are helpless."

At his mercy.

Only Wade didn't think the guy had much mercy in him.

Dace grunted. "I've got men tracking down the owner of this place—once we get him, we'll have—"

"What? The killer?" Wade wasn't so sure of that.

"If he's not the killer, then the owner can damn well give us some clues. If some sick prick has been using this place as his personal torture grounds for years, you can bet the owner *should* have known."

Maybe. Maybe not. Wade glanced around, trying to find Victoria. He knew she would be working with the ground-penetrating radar equipment soon, and if the dogs had indeed found the site of Kennedy's burial . . . yeah, she'd be staying there for a while.

He intended to stay with her.

He hadn't been bullshitting her before. Victoria didn't get just how important she was to him. And the fact that the freak doing the killing had contacted her directly—

"Do you think he's going to take someone else?" Dace asked.

Wade had just caught sight of Victoria's red hair,

glinting in the sunlight. She stared at him a moment, her expression tense. Her phone was cradled in her hand.

"Yeah," he said, voice gruff, unable to tear his gaze from her. "I think he is. Freaks like him—they don't stop. They don't just wake up one morning and say, 'Fuck me, I'm done with killing.' It's a compulsion. They can't stop. They won't." Wade paused. "*He* won't. And the bastard probably already has his next victim in mind . . ."

Victoria pushed her phone into her pocket and hurried toward him.

"We have to stop him," Wade said, voice soft, "before he has the chance to attack."

Then Victoria was in front of him. She looked too pale, and dark shadows slid under her beautiful eyes. They'd both been up all night long and he knew they should crash, but it wasn't about to happen.

At least, not anytime soon.

He exhaled and said, "Dace thinks the dogs have found Kennedy's burial site."

Her eyes widened.

A van pulled up, its tires slowly rolling to a stop.

Victoria glanced at it then back at him and Dace. "That's the equipment we've been waiting for. If bodies are buried near the cottage, we'll find them."

So the ground-penetrating radar had arrived.

Dace hurried off to go talk to the personnel who'd arrived with the van. Victoria started to follow him, but Wade blocked her path.

She tensed. He didn't like that. Hadn't they gone further than that shit? But he'd let his control crack on the beach, and now maybe she was seeing him for the man that he truly was.

Not so good.

Far too much bad.

"I'll tell you my secrets," Wade told her. "Every single fucking one when we're alone. But I need you to promise me something—"

"My past—"

He shook his head. "Promise me that you won't go off alone. That you stay with me or another cop. You stay protected until we figure out what the hell is happening here." Because he didn't want her to become the killer's next victim.

Not her.

Never her.

"Do I get the same promise from you?" Her head was cocked as she stared up at him.

"I'll be fucking glad to stay by your side." He couldn't think of any other place he'd rather be, but she didn't get that. Not yet.

She would.

"Then . . . yes, I promise." Her voice had softened.

"Thank you." He was finally able to take a deep breath. "Now let's go see if the bastard left any other bodies here."

CHAPTER TEN

WHAT IN THE HELL ARE ALL YOU PEOPLE doing on my property?" The loud, barking voice drew Victoria's attention.

She'd been searching with the ground radar team for most of the morning. Sweat dampened her clothes, and she'd yanked her hair back into a ponytail. So far they'd had no luck finding any other bodies.

Was that a good thing?

Or a bad one?

Her gaze turned at the sharp voice and she saw an older man pushing against two uniformed police officers. A grizzled white beard covered his jaw and his clothes were far too loose, hanging on his lean frame. "You people—get out of here!" he yelled. "You can't be here!"

"And I think we just found the owner," Wade murmured from his spot beside Victoria.

Like her, he was also covered with a light sheen of sweat. The sun had glared down on them as they kept working with the team, determined to search as thoroughly as possible.

She saw Dace approach the older man at a fast

clip. Wade inclined his head. She immediately understood—he wanted to get over there and listen to whatever conversation was about to go down. She felt the same way.

"You better have some kind of warrant!" the man yelled. "You can't just—"

"Are you Jeremiah Jennings?" Dace fired at him. "Because if so, our officers have been trying to reach you for the last four hours. Ever since the property clerk told us that *you* owned this land."

Jeremiah straightened and jutted out his chin. "Been in my family for thirty years . . . and *you* shouldn't be here! What the hell are all those dogs doing here?"

"They're searching for bodies," Dace said flatly.

Jeremiah's dark eyes widened. "What? Why the hell are they doing that?"

Dace's gaze held suspicion as he studied the older man. "Because a young woman was kidnapped recently. She was brought here, held in *your* house against her will, and then she was killed—her throat sliced open—right out on Driftwood Beach."

Jeremiah stumbled back. "No . . . no . . . that's not—"

"It's absolutely true," Dace said, voice biting. "And know what else is true? We found evidence that suggests another woman was buried in the back part of *your* property. That's why so many people are running around. We're trying to find all the bodies *you* buried, Mr. Jennings." He motioned to the nearby uniformed cops. "Get this guy in the back of a patrol car and get his ass taken into custody, *now*." He flashed a hard tiger's smile at Jeremiah. "So fucking glad you showed up here. Saved us the trouble of hunting you down like the sick bastard that you are." Disgust flashed on his face.

Two uniformed cops grabbed Jeremiah and held him tightly when he tried to break free. "No!" Jeremiah shouted. "You're wrong! This isn't—*that didn't happen!*"

"He sure looks clueless," Wade muttered to Victoria.

She had to agree. Shock had slackened the man's face. And if he was the killer—just why would he have walked straight up to the crime scene? Too dumb a move to make.

"It happened," Dace snapped back at Jeremiah. "And I'm the one who has to talk to the friends of the victims—I'm the one who has to tell them what the hell happened to those poor girls on *your* property."

Jeremiah shuddered. "I didn't—I didn't know!"

"Bullshit," Dace said, giving a rough shake of his head. "Here you are, bright and early, just waltzing right up to the place—"

"Because I got a call from my tenant!"

Wade stiffened.

"He said . . . said folks were running all over the place. That I needed to get out here." Jeremiah's gaze flew to the left, the right, and he tried hard to yank away from the cops once more.

He didn't get free.

"Your tenant?" Dace asked.

"Yeah, yeah . . . guy who has been renting the place for the last five years."

Five years. Victoria and Wade shared a long look, then inched closer to Jeremiah.

"Pays in cash. Always on time. First of the month, just like clockwork."

"A name," Dace ordered him. "Give me a name, right the hell now so I can check out this story."

"M-Matthew Walker."

The name rolled through Victoria.

"He's a professor at Worthington University!" Now the words were tumbling fast and frantically from Jeremiah's mouth. "The guy just wanted a place to escape, you know? Get away from the grind. So he started renting my cottage here. Paying me double what it was worth. Never caused any trouble . . ."

Because he'd been too busy torturing women.

"Matthew Walker," Wade whispered. "The guy who just *happened* to find Kennedy Lane's body on the jogging trail."

"Take Jeremiah in for questioning," Dace directed the cops.

"Wait! I didn't do anything!" Jeremiah yelled.

Dace spun away from him and confronted Wade and Victoria. "That fucking professor," he said, words low and lethal. "He stood right in front of me, acting like he felt sick after coming across her body. Kept saying he'd thought it was 'trash.'"

Matthew Walker. His image flashed in Victoria's mind. She remembered seeing him as she stumbled away from Jupiter Trail. The jogger who'd found Kennedy's remains. Tall, fit, with dark hair. He'd asked her if she was a cop . . .

"I'm bringing that bastard in," Dace said, nodding. "Right the hell now. He isn't getting away from me!"

But he could have already skipped town, she thought. He could be far, far away by now. Matthew could have killed Melissa, then left the island.

Guilty men ran.

"I want an APB on Matthew Walker!" Dace yelled, drawing the attention of the cops nearby. "We've got a suspect, and I want him brought in . . . *now*!"

BY THE TIME Victoria walked into their B&B at Savannah that night, exhaustion pulled at her. She was covered with sweat and grime, and she'd spent the day looking for the dead.

But there were no other bodies for her to discover on that little stretch of land. Maybe the killer *had* taken other women, but they weren't buried near the cottage. They could have been hidden on one of the little islands near Jekyll. They could have been dumped and forgotten at hundreds of other wooded sites along the interstate.

Only the killer knew for sure.

"I'm going to get LOST to pull all the missing persons' reports from NamUs," Victoria said. The list from the National Missing and Unidentified Persons system would be their best bet. If anyone else in that system matched up with a victim profile similar to Kennedy or Melissa—or other college-age women who'd vanished in the Savannah area—then they could be looking at more victims taken by the same perp.

Wade shut the door behind them. Then he propped his back against the wood. "Do you think there *are* more?"

"I hope not."

"I sure as hell do, too." He grabbed at the hem of his shirt and yanked it over his head.

She blinked, a little surprised that—

Wade gave a rough rumble of laughter. "Are you blushing? After what we've shared, I didn't think you'd blush with me any longer."

He stalked toward her.

Victoria's shoulders tensed.

"Relax," Wade murmured when he was just inches away. "I'm just going to shower."

Right. Shower.

"Want to join me?"

Actually . . . she wanted more than just a shower. She wanted him. They'd driven back in silence, but there had been a thick, heavy tension between them. Death could do that—wring you out and twist you up. She was exhausted, yes, but she also felt as if she were literally about to jump out of her skin.

She wanted to forget all the blood and death. She just wanted—

Victoria cleared her throat and said, "I'll join you after I make my call." Why deny what she wanted? What they both wanted? It seemed so pointless.

Life was short, hard, and brutal. People should grab tight to their pleasures. Take what they wanted.

Before life was ripped away.

His fingers slid under the edge of her jaw. No blood was on his hands now. He'd cleaned up as best he could and been given borrowed clothes after Melissa had been taken away. His other clothes had been taken in as evidence.

So much evidence on that island. Evidence of hell

and torture. His touch sent goose bumps rising over her skin. Not because she was afraid of him.

"One day," he said, "you'll tell me your secrets."

"Wade—"

"Until then, I'll just take what you fucking give me." His mouth closed over hers. He kissed her hard and deep and her fingers rose to curl around his arms as she held him tight.

Desire beat in her blood. A need that he stirred so effortlessly. She should be collapsing, sleeping off the last terrible twenty-four hours.

But she wanted to be with him.

He eased away. "Don't make me wait long."

Then he headed for the bathroom.

She could still taste him. Fumbling, Victoria put in the call to LOST and got Gabe to promise he'd contact NamUs. Any matches would be sent to her immediately.

The call to her boss lasted less than five minutes. She briefed him, assured him that she and Gabe were safe, then ended the call. Her fingers curled around the phone as her gaze slid toward the darkened hallway.

She took a step forward.

Her phone vibrated in her hand.

Victoria glanced down.

I want you . . . Come to me.

Talk about being impatient. Smiling, she texted back. *On my way. Stay in control until I get to you.*

She hurried to the hallway. Her phone vibrated again.

I'll lose my control, with you.

Her heart raced faster. This time she didn't stop to type out a response to him. She went into her bedroom and stripped as quickly as she could. Then, naked, she headed for the bathroom that they shared. As she approached, she heard the roar of water in the shower.

Time to see just how long Wade's control would last.

She pushed open the bathroom door. The shower was big—easily wide enough to accommodate two. The shower door was made of glass, so she could see Wade standing there, his broad back flexing beneath the pelting stream of water.

Steam slowly rose around him.

For a moment Victoria just stood there, staring at him. Admiring him. Big and strong and sexy. There was so much power in his body.

Wade glanced over his shoulder. When he saw her through the steam, his face hardened with desire.

Swallowing, she crept forward. Her feet slid over his discarded clothes. Her nipples were already tight, aching. Butterflies seemed to dance in her stomach as she opened the shower door.

He reached out and his hand curled around hers. She could see his stomach now. His chest. Those strong muscles and rock-hard abs.

He pulled her closer and her head tipped back as she rose onto her toes. His lips were wet when she kissed him. The water slid over her, pouring over her body as she pressed ever closer to him.

She didn't want to think about the nightmare they'd been through. Didn't want to think about the victim they hadn't been able to save.

She didn't want to—

Wade lifted her up. Holding her easily with that powerful strength of his. He pressed her back against the cold tile of the shower. Her legs locked around his hips. His cock pushed against her sex.

"Fuck—condom—" Wade gritted.

"I'm on birth control, and I'm clean." Stark words. She'd never gone without a condom with another lover. Never even thought about it before. But right now she wanted him to come into her just as he was. Sex-to-sex. She wanted wild. She wanted rough. She wanted every single bit of him.

A muscle jerked in his jaw. "I'm clean, too, baby."

"Then let your . . . control go . . ." She pushed her hips against him. "Just like you said . . . *let go.*"

He drove into her, full and thick, filling her so completely, and her head tipped back against the tile wall as she gasped out his name. The water kept pouring onto them, streaming down as he thrust into her. Her nails dug into his arms and she held onto him as tight as she could. Again and again he sank into her, sliding his cock right over her clit and increasing the frenzy of her desire.

Her gaze lifted to his face. So brutal in his need. So sexy. Her mouth moved to his shoulder and she pressed a kiss there. Then she bit him, a quick, light bite as the lust beat within her blood.

He growled, and she loved that animalistic sound. Basic. Primal. That was how she felt in that moment, with him. The drive for pleasure was all that mattered. No past, no future. Nothing beyond that instant, nothing beyond their need.

Her lips feathered over him. She pushed her hips against him. Harder. He had swelled even more inside of her, and when his hand came between their bodies . . . when he put his fingers on her clit and stroked her—

Victoria came with a scream. One that was, hopefully, drowned out by the pounding rush of the water.

He caught her hands, pinned them above her head, and her knuckles pressed to the cold wall. Her breath was heaving out as she peered up at him, and with that one look, Victoria knew . . . *His control was gone.*

Wade moved so that only one of his hands locked around her wrists, caging them easily above her head. His right hand came down. Stroked her breast. Already sensitive, her nipples were still pebbled and tight and his touch made her shiver.

"My turn," Wade said. Then he put his mouth on her neck, right there in the spot where her neck curved to meet her shoulder, and he bit her.

Sensual. Wild.

His hips drove against her, slamming deep, and she could only take the pleasure he gave her. Her climax was still rolling through her, making her sex contract, and the way he was moving, the wild plunge of his hips, the way his mouth slid over her shoulder then her neck—he was just building up her desire again. Making her want so—

She came again.

Came, just as he did. He groaned out her name as his body completely surrounded her. The pleasure ripped through her, so powerful that she struggled to breathe, and then . . . there was just the rushing sound of the water. Their ragged breaths.

Her drumming heartbeat.

Her eyes were closed, and Victoria slowly blinked

them open. Her hands were still above her head, anchored by his hand. He was still in her, still caging her there against the wall.

Slowly, his bent head lifted. He stared down at her, his gaze utterly unreadable.

Then he kissed her. Lightly. Softly.

A few moments later Wade turned off the shower. He dried her off and even carried her back to her room. Victoria found that she couldn't say anything.

She didn't know what to say.

The passion had swept through her so completely, and now, in the aftermath, her body was limp. The exhaustion she'd held at bay all day swept through her.

She slid beneath her covers.

He turned to leave.

"Stay."

Wade paused.

So maybe there had been one thing that she knew to say. Victoria lifted her hand toward him. "You can stay . . ."

"And still have no strings?" Wade asked, voice low.

She didn't want to think that far ahead, not then. "Just stay."

His lips curled. "Baby, when will you realize? For you, I'd do anything." Wade slid beneath the covers. He pulled her close, held her right against his heart.

And she slipped right into her dreams.

HER FATHER WAS smiling.

She crept down the stairs. He didn't usually smile, not like that. Not a smile that stretched from ear to ear.

"Things are going to be different now, Victoria." He

gave a firm nod. "We will make everything better."

The house was so quiet. Where was her mother? Where had she gone?

"I've always been so proud of you," her father said. "People are right, you know. You really are just like me." His hand lifted as he moved to brush a lock of her hair behind her ear.

When his hand lifted, she saw—his fingers were red. No, not red—there was . . . there was blood on his fingers.

A tremor swept over her body. "Where is Mom?"

Behind the lens of his glasses, he blinked. Once. Twice. His smile dimmed.

She edged back a step.

His blood-covered fingers fell back to his side. "I don't know, darling. She wasn't here when I woke up this morning."

Liar, liar, liar . . .

"I'm sure she'll turn up later." He nodded briskly once more. "Now, I must go shower. Don't worry, I'm sure your mother just went out on a walk. Perhaps a morning jog. She'll be back soon . . ."

He hurried toward the bathroom and didn't look back. A moment later she heard the rush of water in the shower.

She tiptoed toward her parents' room. She saw her mother's bag, the bag that had been near the front door—it was still there. Her mother's purse was there. Her clothes. All still there.

She turned around, confused.

Maybe her father was right. Maybe . . . maybe she would be back . . .

And then she saw the knife, gleaming on the dresser. Blood was on its blade. Her hand lifted toward it even as horror rose in her throat, nearly choking her.

"Victoria!"

"VICTORIA!" WADE SHOOK her, because she was seriously scaring the hell out of him. She'd started jerking in her sleep and making a faint moan. She'd sounded terrified, and that shit wasn't going to work. She wouldn't be terrified while she was in his arms. "Victoria, wake up!"

Her eyes flew open. He'd already turned on the lamp at the bedside, and the glow spilled onto her, showing the tears on her cheeks and the terror in her gaze.

"Baby?"

"I'm . . . not like him."

His muscles tensed. Wade wondered . . . would she tell him now? Would this be the moment when she finally started to trust him?

"He said . . . I was just like him, and I don't want to be."

She'd sat straight up in bed, and Wade wanted to pull her back into his arms. He also didn't want to scare her. If she was talking, he would listen to her all night long.

"Your father." He just put that piece right out there. After all, they both knew who she had to mean. But he wanted to learn more. *Tell me, baby. Tell me everything.*

Victoria gave a jerky nod. She pulled the bedcovers up to her chest, shielding her body. Her head turned and her gaze focused on him. "Have you ever been in love?"

Not what he'd expected from her. "Viki—"

"I heard the rumors at LOST. Some people think you were in love with Gabe's sister, Amy, but then . . . she went missing."

He'd thought they were talking about Victoria's past, not his own. But if she wanted him to share, fuck, he would. He'd bleed for her if that was what the woman wanted. "I cared for Amy. A lot." He wouldn't lie. "But she was my best friend's little sister, so I kept my distance." He swallowed as the memories stirred in his mind. "And I watched her go to another. A jackass who didn't deserve her. He didn't treat her well enough, and I wanted to get Amy away from him." Wade shook his head. "But it was her life, her decision, and I'd given up any rights I might've had . . ."

"You . . . never told her how you felt?"

"There wasn't time. Because one day she was just gone." His hands had fisted around the sheets, and he made himself ease his too tight grip. "We were friends, never more than that . . . *because I held back.*" He wasn't making that same mistake with Victoria. He wanted her to know just how much he wanted her. "I looked for her. Searched fucking desperately because I had promised Gabe I would take care of his sister. I swore I would look out for her." He gave a grim shake of his head. "But I let him down. I let her die and—"

"You blame yourself for what happened."

"A sick freak at her hospital—he became fixated on her," Wade said. "She was his nurse. He took her, he kept her, and he killed her."

"Just like our perp did with Kennedy and Melissa?" Her question was little more than a whisper.

"Pretty damn close, yes." But Amy's abductor hadn't kept her alive as long as Kennedy had lived. She'd died . . . and he'd watched Gabe splinter apart.

"I'm sorry," she said. Her hand curled around his and she squeezed, ever so gently.

His head tilted toward her. How had this become about him? About her giving comfort to *him*? Wade shook his head and decided to ask her the same question she'd posed to him. "Have you ever been in love?"

"I . . . can't be."

That wasn't the answer he'd expected.

"It's too dangerous." Victoria said the words in a rush. "Because what if he was right? What if I am just like him?"

"You *aren't* like your father."

"He was a brilliant man," she said, voice gone flat in an instant. "Respected, admired. Maybe that's why it took so long for the police to believe me. They bought the story that my mother had left on her own. That she'd just turned and walked out on her family. When the months turned into years, they *finally* listed her as missing, when she never contacted anyone. Not me. Not her cousins. Not her friends. It took that long for the cops to believe that something might have happened to her, and it took them even longer . . . to understand that my dad—my father—*he* was the bad thing that had taken her away."

Wade's fingers curled around hers so that he was now holding her hand. Trying to give her some comfort.

"Turn out the light," Victoria said. "It's . . . easier for me to say this in the dark."

He kept his hold on her fingers, but Wade's other

hand reached out and turned off the lamp, plunging the room into darkness.

He heard her suck in a quick, sharp breath. Then Victoria said, "Love can go bad."

Such sad, stark words.

"In the beginning, I do think my father loved her. And she loved him. But something changed, and it—it wasn't enough. She wasn't happy. She . . . I know she found someone else. I knew because she'd started to smile again."

Each word that she said pierced him to the core. There was so much pain in Victoria's voice, and Wade wished that he could take it away.

"She was going to leave my father. He . . . he didn't want to let her go. She was *his*. Like a possession." Her fingers squeezed his. A quick, hard squeeze. "No, an obsession. That's what she'd become to him. He couldn't let her go. I saw it on his face. So much darker than love—so much harder. Evil . . . I knew, *I knew,* he wasn't going to let her go to another man. If she wasn't with him, then she wasn't going to be with anyone."

Christ. Reading details of her mother's murder online was one thing, but hearing the pain and desolation in Victoria's voice was something totally different. Screw just holding her hand. He pulled her against him, cradling her as close as he could get. But she was so stiff in his arms.

"There are no strings," Victoria said. "There are never any strings because I won't . . . I won't become obsessed. I won't do that to someone."

"You *aren't* your father—"

"I've never been in love because I am too scared to be. Too scared of what I will become."

"Victoria . . ."

"I saw the blood on his fingers. I saw the knife. I knew what he'd done. I went to the police. I *ran* from my house, just in my gown, and I went to the cops. They didn't believe me. My mother was missing for years before anyone would believe me."

Fuck, fuck, fuck.

"And all that time, I was with him. He chided me for telling stories. But he said he forgave me. After all, how could he not? I was . . . *just like him.*"

"He was wrong, okay? Fucking *wrong*. The guy was a killer. You aren't. You are *not* like him—"

"I am."

He barely caught those murmured words.

"You don't understand," Victoria continued softly. "Because you . . . you *are* good, Wade. You go after the criminals. That's always been what you did. You never became one."

His heart thudded dully in his chest. "I'm not a cop anymore."

"My father was found innocent. A jury listened to my story, and they didn't believe me. Or maybe . . . maybe it was like the D.A. told me. There just wasn't enough evidence. She'd been in the ground for so long, there was too much decomposition. They couldn't find a strong enough tie to link my father to the murder. And me seeing blood when I was thirteen . . . it could have just come from him accidentally cutting himself. That was what he said, you see. That he'd sliced himself on a knife while he was cutting apples for me. *For me*." Her laughter was bitter and mocking. "But the bloody knife was in his bedroom. I saw it there. And I even think my mother was still there . . . when I saw that knife. I think he hadn't moved her yet, but the cops wouldn't listen. *No one would listen to me.* And they didn't search the house that day."

"And that's why you speak for the dead." Everything clicked into place for him. "Why you went on to focus in forensic anthropology—you *want* to work on the bodies that have been lost for so long, don't you? Because you want to find a way to help them."

She was silent.

"Viki?"

"I'm more like him than you realize. Proving his guilt became my obsession. *Punishing* him was an obsession."

"He's dead, too, baby. He can't hurt anyone any longer."

The sheets rustled as she pulled away from his arms. "You're right, of course. He can't." Her voice was so cold. She'd moved away from him, lying down once again. "We should both get some sleep. I—I'm sorry for waking you. I won't do it again."

What. The. Hell? "Wake me up a thousand times, I don't care." He reached for her in the dark, curled his fingers around her shoulder. He hated that she'd turned from him. "And don't pull away, okay? Because I want you. Your secrets, your past? That shit doesn't matter. You matter."

"He couldn't let her go," Victoria whispered. "He killed her because he wasn't going to let her live without him."

"That isn't *you*." Why couldn't she see that?

"Oh, Wade . . ." Now sadness slipped into her voice. "If only that were true."

"It is true." He knew it with certainty. So why didn't she?

He pulled her close. Kept her right against his heart. Victoria didn't speak again, and after a while he felt her breath ease into the deeper pattern of sleep. Her nightmares didn't come back.

And he *didn't* let her go.

"I DIDN'T KIDNAP anyone!" Matthew Walker yelled. He was in an interrogation room, a freaking *interrogation room,* at the police station. Cops had arrived at his door and they pulled him out—right in front of his neighbors! He'd been escorted to the station and left in this damn interrogation room for far too long, with only the briefest of explanations.

He stared at his reflection. Matthew knew he was looking into a one-way mirror, and cops were probably on the other side of that glass. Cops who thought he was some kind of killer.

"This is a mistake," he said, giving a firm nod. "I'm a professor at Worthington! I am a respected member of the community. I. Am. Not. A. Killer!" He was sweating, though, because one of the cops had told him that Melissa Hastings was dead.

The door opened behind him. In the mirror, he saw the dark-haired detective who'd been in before—Dace Black—heading his way. Matthew whirled to confront him. "If I'm not being let go, right the hell away, then I want my lawyer in here. This is *bullshit*. I haven't hurt anyone and—"

"Are you familiar with Jeremiah Jennings?"

"Who? What?"

"Jeremiah owns a cottage on Jekyll Island."

Matthew yanked a hand through his already tousled hair. "Great. Wonderful for him, but—"

"According to Mr. Jennings, you've been renting his cottage on Jekyll Island for the last five years."

Matthew's jaw dropped. Then he scrambled, saying, "The hell I have! I don't know any Jeremiah Jones—"

"Jennings," the detective corrected quietly.

"Jennings. Jones. Who-the-hell-ever. I don't know him, and I certainly haven't been renting a cottage from the guy! I haven't even *been* to Jekyll Island in years!"

Detective Black stared back at him. He really didn't like the way the detective was eying him.

Like he thinks I'm guilty.

"Melissa Hastings was killed on Jekyll Island. She was abducted and held prisoner in your cottage . . ."

It was hard to breathe. "Not my cottage!" He nearly yelled. "I don't care what BS that guy told you, I haven't been renting from him."

Detective Black placed a manila file on the small table that rested in the middle of the interrogation room. He flipped open the file. "Then why is your name signed on the rental agreement?"

Impossible. Matthew inched closer and saw—"That's my name." Shock ripped through him. "But that is *not* my signature!" His gaze flew up to the cop. "I don't know—someone is setting me up! That's what's happening. Because that is *not my signature!*"

The detective's face remained impassive. "Jennings has been receiving monthly cash payments from his tenant for the last five years. First of the month, just like clockwork. The guy lives in the middle of fucking nowhere, and the payments just show up on his doorstep. He deposits the payment into his bank account—and Jennings gave us his bank records to prove those transactions occurred."

"Who the fuck pays in cash?" Matthew swiped his hand over his face. "Someone trying to frame me, that's who! Someone who wanted me to look guilty—some jerk who was trying not to leave a paper trail." His breath heaved out and he started to sweat. "This can't be happening."

Detective Black pulled out a chair at the table and sat down, as if he didn't have a care in the world.

He doesn't. He isn't being set up!

"Jennings said he saw a black Jag leave his house one day, after a drop-off payment was made." Detective Black made that statement, then waited a beat and asked. "Do *you* own a black Jag?"

He already knows I do. I bet the guy pulled my tag and registration. "Yes," Matthew gritted out. "But I wasn't making any payments for a place on Jekyll! That's bull!"

"Did you know the victim?"

Matthew backed up a step. "You . . . you already know that I did." What was up with these questions—questions the detective already knew the answers to? Was the guy trying to trip him up?

"She was in one of your classes. No . . . two of them, correct?"

Was the room getting hotter? It felt as if it was. "Melissa was a . . . a very bright student."

"Is that all she was?"

He knows. "I didn't abduct Melissa! Okay? I didn't—"

"It's an odd coincidence, you see . . . a bouncer at Vintage—that's the club Melissa was at right before she vanished—he remembered seeing Melissa get into a black Jag."

Oh, hell. "I wasn't at Vintage." His voice had gone hollow.

"Ummm . . ."

What in the hell was *ummm* supposed to mean?

"You began teaching at Worthington University just over five years ago." Detective Black nodded. "Two weeks after your employment began, Kennedy Lane went missing . . . and then, what a twist of fate . . . *you* were the one to find her body—what was left of it—on the same trail that she vanished from so long ago."

It *was* hotter in there. Had the detective turned off the air? Was that some kind of interrogation trick? Matthew licked his lips. "I didn't know Kennedy."

"Didn't you?"

Matthew started pacing. "I *didn't* know her." He threw a glance toward the mirror. How many cops were watching him right then?

"Did you . . . want to know her? Is that why you abducted her? Why you kept her?"

"*Kept* her?" Matthew repeated. "Hell, no! I didn't do this! Not any of it!" He gave a frantic shake of his head.

"Someone is setting me up! Don't you see that? I didn't rent the cottage! I didn't hurt those women!"

"But you *did* have a relationship with Melissa, didn't you? Because I saw the way you flinched when I said her name. Saw your eyes widen and—"

"I want my lawyer." The words flew out of his mouth. He was in way, way over his head. "I want my lawyer *now,* and I am not saying another word until he gets here." Because this was a nightmare. An absolute freaking nightmare. And there had to be a way out of it . . .

"Have it your way," Detective Black said as he rose, collecting the manila file. "The guilty always lawyer up fast."

Matthew clamped his lips shut. The guy was just taunting him. A smart man would get a lawyer.

"Just so you know," Detective Black added. "We've got warrants to search your home and your work office. We're going to tear apart your life and all the dirty little secrets that you've been keeping. They *will* come out. They always do."

"My lawyer," Matthew gritted.

"I'll make sure you get to call him." The detective gave him a hard smile. "By the way . . . you didn't even ask . . . *How did Melissa die?* I mean, aren't you curious?"

"I—I—"

"Seems like, if you were innocent, you *would* have asked that, right? But then . . . if you killed her, then I guess you already know . . . she choked to death on her own blood, and there wasn't a damn thing we could do to save her."

Matthew didn't move. *Melissa* . . .

"I don't like it when women die on my watch," Detective Black said, jaw clenching. "So believe me when I say . . . I am going to fucking nail your ass to the wall on this one."

Then the detective turned and strode out of the interrogation room.

The door shut behind him with a loud click, sealing Matthew inside once again. Slowly, he turned to look back at the one-way mirror.

When he saw his reflection, Matthew hardly recognized the pale man with the desperate gaze who stared back at him.

CHAPTER ELEVEN

WHEN VICTORIA OPENED HER EYES AGAIN, Wade wasn't there. Her hand reached out and she touched his pillow.

Still warm.

For a moment she didn't move. Had she really bared her soul to him in the middle of the night? The nightmare had come too swiftly, and she'd been too tired to think clearly. She'd almost revealed too much.

If Wade learned the full truth about what she'd done, what would he do?

Sighing, she pushed herself up in bed. A glance at the bedside table showed her that he had brought her phone to her. Thoughtful. She probably should check in with LOST and see if Gabe had turned up any search hits on NamUs.

Just as she reached for the phone, it vibrated, telling her a text had just come through.

She lifted the phone up and stared at the text from Wade. When she saw the words there, it became very, very hard to breathe.

I know all your secrets. There won't be any hiding.

He didn't know them. Her fingers tapped on the screen. *I shared too much last night.* She'd been too open with him. More open than she'd ever been with anyone else in her life.

Her head lifted as she looked around. Was Wade in his room? Maybe she should just go talk to him, but—

Her phone vibrated. Her gaze slid back to the screen so she could read the message. *Before I'm done, you'll share everything with me.*

Victoria shook her head and started typing back a response. *I can't, I—*

Her bedroom door opened. Wade stood there. Startled, no, *stunned,* she sent that half-written text.

Wade smiled at her. "Morning, baby." He strolled toward her. His hair was wet. Fresh from the shower? And a towel curled around his hips.

Yes, yes, he'd been in the shower. Because his broad shoulders still gleamed with droplets of water.

He bent and kissed her. Victoria's phone vibrated in her hand once more. Wade's lips were gentle, so careful, against hers.

She pulled away from him, staring down at the screen of her phone in growing horror.

The message was short. Terrifying: *You will. And I will own you, body and soul.*

"Who's texting you?" Wade asked her, voice rumbling. "Is it Gabe? Did he—"

"It's you." Her cheeks felt cold. She was too cold. "You've been texting me." She forced her gaze away from that text and back up to his face. *I thought it was you.*

A furrow appeared between his brows. "What?"

"You texted me." Her hand slowly turned and she showed him the screen.

Fury came then, washing across his face as he took that phone from her with a quick jerk. "What the fuck?"

"It's your number," she said, pulling the covers tighter. "You—"

"I left my phone on the damn beach." His eyes were slits of rage. "I dropped it there when I bent to pick up Melissa. *Sonofabitch.* It's—"

"Him." She knew it, absolutely, and felt sick as she thought of the texts she'd exchanged with the killer. "He must have still been on the beach. Melissa—her wounds were fresh. He must have been there, watching . . ." *Watching her die.* "And he took your phone."

Wade was scrolling through her texts now, and the fury on his face just deepened. "*Fucking bastard.* He wants you."

"No, he's just playing with me." She climbed from the bed and wrapped the sheet around her body. Her guts were knotting but a cold rage burned within her, too. "Now let's play with him." Play with him. Trap him. Whatever worked. "Let's track your phone. I know you have the app. Let's do this."

He gave a grim nod. When he whirled to leave her bedroom—*he's going to get his iPad, he'll log in and check to find the location of his missing phone*—another text came through. She glanced down at the screen. The bastard was busy. Taunting her and—

How did it feel when you killed your father?

Her gaze shot up from the phone and locked on Wade's back. He was in the doorway, rushing out of the room so fast.

She had to delete the text. He couldn't see it.

The phone vibrated again. Helplessly, her attention turned back to the screen.

He deserved what you did. I understand. I understand so much about you now.

Victoria shook her head. He understood nothing.

Her fingers tapped on the screen, though, because she wanted to keep him talking to her. *I want to understand you.*

She sent the text. Held her breath. He didn't write back, not right away. The seconds seemed to pass by so slowly. Each moment lingered and her heart raced. That fast drumbeat filled her ears.

The phone shook in her fingers as the text came through to her. *You will.*

"Sonofabitch!" Wade burst back into the room. He had on his jeans and a T-shirt, and his eyes blazed. "The bastard is in the alley right behind this building. He's right outside!"

Had he been watching her room? Watching her, all that time? Just waiting?

Then she realized that Wade had a gun in his hand. She knew that he usually kept the weapon close, but right then—

"You aren't going out there, not without me," Victoria told him as she started grabbing her clothes. She dressed in record time, jerking on her underwear, shirt, and jeans, and then nearly tripping as she fought to get her shoes on her feet before tumbling toward the door—and Wade.

"We should call the cops," Victoria said. "Get Dace over here."

"After we get the bastard, we will." His face was tight with a hard fury, his eyes deep and cold. "He was coming for you. *You* were his next target. That shit isn't happening. I won't let it happen again."

Wait? *Again?* Yes, he'd said again but—*I'm not Amy.* Her chest ached as she stared up at him.

"Stay with me, every single moment, got that? Every—"

Her phone vibrated again. *See you soon.* Oh, hell.

"Wade—"

He'd read the text, too. He swore, then said, "Let's go, *now.*"

Right. They rushed outside together. She saw that Wade made a point of hiding his weapon. The better not to scare any of the pedestrians milling on the street. But they didn't head out to the main street. She and Wade immediately ducked around back, into the alley. It was a long, narrow passage, one that stretched behind the historic homes.

They pressed close to the alley's walls, staying covered as much as possible. Wade went first, checking the scene and—

"Bastard."

She saw a phone, positioned very carefully in the middle of the alley.

Wade kept searching, but the alley was empty.

See you soon.

Victoria ran past Wade and toward the mouth of the

alley. She rushed out and looked to the left, then to the right. People were all over the place. So many cars—even a horse-drawn carriage—filled the street.

Men. Women. Children.

A killer?

Yes, she thought he was there. Damn him, he was there, hiding in plain sight.

Victoria took a step back and she bumped into—

She whirled around.

"Easy," Wade told her softly.

No, no, there was nothing easy about the situation. The killer had been jerking her around. He'd been right outside their B&B. Now he was gone.

See you soon. "He had access to all your contacts, Wade. Your e-mails. Any data you had on your phone." She shivered. "He had you." For hours, and she hadn't even known it.

Worse, though . . . *he'd had me.* The conversations flashed in her mind and shame washed through her. A killer had been toying with her. She was supposed to be a professional. She should have known—

I didn't know. But he knows me. He knows what I did.

"I want to see those texts, every single one of them," Wade said. "We're pulling Dace in. Whatever the perp is planning, we will stop him, I swear it."

Her gaze darted to the busy street once more.

And the crowd just kept walking right past her.

SHE HADN'T SEEN him. It had been a very near thing.

Luckily for him, she'd given away the game. *I want to understand you.*

As soon as she'd written those words, he realized that Victoria knew she wasn't texting Wade Monroe. She'd realized the truth. She'd thought to play *him*.

She wasn't at his level, not even close.

He pulled up his collar as he walked away. He'd rather enjoyed that little dalliance with Victoria, and the phone he'd collected from the beach had certainly proved useful. He'd obtained all sorts of helpful pieces of information from Wade.

He'd use that information soon enough. But first, he had another man to visit. Someone who'd offered to make a trade, but then tried to change the rules.

A trade is a trade. Jim Porter had been told exactly what to do. He should have waited in the little cottage. Stayed there. Instead, he let Melissa run, and then *he'd* gone out, too.

A violation that would be punished.

He kept his steps slow and easy. After all, he didn't want it to look as if he were rushing away from the scene. And it was so hard not to look back. He really wanted to glance over his shoulder and see Victoria once more. But . . .

Soon enough.

He'd see her again, when the time was right. When Wade Monroe wasn't at her side. When she was alone and waiting.

The perfect prey.

"Let me get this shit straight," Dace said as he paced in his office. The guy looked tired—the seriously rough kind of tired that a man appears when he hasn't had sleep for twenty-four hours. "You're telling me that the killer . . . he's been texting you for hours? Sending you all kinds of notes?"

Her hands twisted in front of her. "Yes, that's exactly what we're saying. And we found the phone he used—Wade's phone—right behind our B&B less than thirty minutes ago."

Dace stopped pacing. "Impossible."

"No." Wade shook his head. "That bastard was still on the scene when I untied Melissa. I left my phone there, and he took it. I just—hell, I just forgot about it during the search. Didn't even give the thing a damn thought."

"No, no, I'm saying he *couldn't* have been texting her. He couldn't have been in that alley . . ." Dace exhaled on a rough breath. "Because I've got my suspect—Matthew Walker—in custody! He's been in my custody for hours. There is no way he's been texting you. I let him make one phone call. *One.* To his lawyer. He isn't—"

"Then he isn't the killer we're looking for," Wade said, cutting through his words. "Because I'm telling you—that guy had my phone. He was making contact with Victoria. The bastard was stalking her."

She didn't flinch at those words, but she feared Wade was right.

Dace looked at Wade's phone, which had been sealed in a clear plastic bag. Wade had been trying to protect the evidence as much as possible. "I want to read the texts," Dace said.

Victoria hesitated, then offered her phone to him. Wade's phone would only be touched again by crime techs, so no more contamination could occur. But Dace could easily read the texts on her phone. She kept her face expressionless as he scrolled through them.

"These times—*shit,* the times listed for the texts are when Matthew Walker was in custody!"

"Then I think you have the wrong man in custody," Wade said quietly.

"He owns a damn Jag! He *rented* the cottage! His name was on the rental contract. Okay, yeah, so the guy was blowing smoke and saying the signature was a forgery and that he'd never been to the cottage, but I know he was involved with Melissa Hastings. He was sleeping with her." A muscle jerked in his jaw. "The same way you're sleeping with Victoria."

"Watch it," Wade advised, voice curt.

Dace's gaze snapped between them when Wade took an aggressive step forward. "Easy there, buddy. *Easy.* Hell, I mean, come on, if she thought *you* were the one sending these messages, then it's obvious you two are lovers." His gaze went back to the messages. He scrolled. "And it's obvious that—" He broke off, stiffening.

Victoria knew exactly which text he'd just read. She steeled herself. She'd known this would be coming. She'd debated deleting the text, but . . . even if she deleted it from her phone, it would still be on Wade's. The crime analysis guys would see it. No, better not to hide it. Better to just—

"What is he talking about, Victoria?" Dace's face showed his shock. "'How did it feel when you killed your father'?" he read.

She didn't speak.

"'He deserved what you did.'" Dace's voice sharpened as he kept reading. "'I understand. I understand so much about you now.'" He shook his head. "What the hell? He's saying you killed your father!"

"Yes," Victoria said. She cleared her throat. "That's exactly what he's saying."

Dace's lips parted. She could see him struggling to find words.

She was struggling herself. *Time to admit the truth. I can't hide any longer. The killer knows. He's going to make sure my past comes out. Everyone will know what I did.*

"Did you?" Dace finally asked. "Did you kill your father?"

Yes, yes I did. "I—"

"Fuck, no," Wade said, stepping in front of Victoria. "You are *not* seriously asking her that, are you?"

His broad back blocked her view of Dace. Victoria sucked in a few quick, desperately needed breaths. She balled her shaking fingers into fists.

"The perp is just playing some mind game," Wade continued. "You should get that shit. And, hell no, you *don't* get to ask her if she killed her father. I mean, come on! She's Victoria fucking Palmer. The woman has worked with the FBI on some of their biggest cases. She's the go-to-girl that the cops use when they need help with their dead. *You* certainly were using her services. She spent her life trying to help people, and you're going to stand there and *ask* her if she killed her father?"

Um, yes, that was what Dace had done.

Because that is exactly what I did.

"No," Wade snapped before Dace could say anything else. "She did *not* kill him. Good enough for you?"

She craned her neck and looked around Wade's body. She saw Dace run a hand over his face. "Right. Sorry. Shit, I know you can't believe a word guys like him say. I just—why did he send *that* message?"

"Because he is trying to screw with her head," Wade said flatly. "The guy gets off on tormenting people, but he is not going to hurt Victoria." He looked back at her. "I'll be damned if that shit goes down on my watch."

There was such a dark intensity in his golden gaze.

"If the killer is the one who sent these texts," Dace said, "then if Matthew Walker is innocent—"

Before he could finish his statement, a sharp knock sounded on his office door. Seconds later the door was opened and a female officer poked her head inside. "Detective Black," she called. "Wanted to let you know that Walker's lawyer is here."

He swore.

The female cop lifted a brow. "You ready for him?"

"Hell, no." But he nodded. "I'll be right out."

The cop vanished.

"Shit," Dace said. "Now what the hell am I supposed to do? I've barely got enough to hold him. Jeremiah never actually saw him face-to-face, so he can't ID the guy. There are damn *hundreds* of Jags in this city. Smoke and fucking mirrors . . . that is all this damn case is."

The door shut behind the detective. Victoria slowly

exhaled. She hadn't even realized she'd been holding her breath.

Wade turned to face her. His gaze met hers.

"Thank you," she told him. "For coming to my defense that way."

His lips hitched into a half smile. "Like it was hard, baby. I know you aren't a killer."

You're wrong.

She glanced toward the door. They were alone. She didn't know how long they'd have before the detective came back inside. "What if I were?" As soon as the words slipped out, Victoria wished that she could pull them back.

Wade blinked. Then his brows climbed. "What?"

"Gabe . . ." She pressed her lips together, and then continued. "Gabe killed the man who took his sister. You were there when that happened." Her heart was beating too fast.

"Yes . . ."

"Self-defense, right?"

His gaze slid away from hers.

She straightened her shoulders and kept going. "Is that the only time you think it's okay to kill? If you're defending yourself? Because then it's kill or be killed, isn't it? There isn't really a choice. I mean, if you've actually seen what he can do." *He.* Oh, crap, that had been a slip-up. "If you . . . if you know the guy will really kill, that he won't stop, what are you supposed to do?"

He wasn't smiling any longer. "Victoria . . ."

Her breath came faster. So much faster. She couldn't

do this. Couldn't let Wade lie for her. No, no, he didn't even realize that he was lying. Because Wade was good. The cop. The stand-up agent. And when she said this, when she crossed this line . . .

It would be over for her.

Her hand lifted. Touched his cheek. "I'm sorry." And she really, truly was.

Because she'd enjoyed being with him. No strings, that had been their rule. She'd started to break that rule. So maybe it was good, that the truth was coming out. Maybe it was long past time for her to pay for her crimes.

THE FOOL HADN'T even locked his front door. Talk about being easy prey.

He curled his gloved hands around the doorknob and swung it open, and the door's hinges barely groaned. He slipped inside the little apartment. He'd been there before, of course, with Melissa.

Jim hadn't been home, not then. He'd been at one of his night classes, and never even knew about the little visit.

So he moved carefully, avoiding the area of the floor that would squeak too loudly, and headed toward Jim's room. Though he really didn't have to worry too much about a squeak of sound. Jim had his music on, and the pounding beat drifted through the apartment.

Jim's bedroom door was ajar, but a glance inside showed him that Jim wasn't in the room. The music was pumping in there, but . . .

No Jim.

He turned without even a rustle of sound and headed

for Melissa's room. Poor Melissa. She'd always been looking for love. Wanting someone to adore her so completely—thinking that if she just found the right man, she'd fill the emptiness inside.

Nothing would fill that.

Her bedroom door was open, too. Jim was inside her room, standing at the foot of her bed, his shoulders slumped as he stared at the quilt that covered the mattress. He knew all about that quilt. Melissa's grandmother had made it for her. The one thing she'd kept from the screwed-up mess that had been her home life. She'd said her grandmother had always loved her.

Such a blind girl. *You never realized how much he loved you, did you?* Melissa had died not knowing.

His fingers slid toward the knife that he'd tucked inside his coat. Jim never even looked back at him. He was too lost to his grief.

And then . . .

Got you. Just like that, he had the blade pressed to Jim's throat. "You were supposed to make a trade," he whispered. "Your life for hers. She died . . . so that doesn't sound like a fair trade to me."

Jim stiffened but didn't fight back. How could he? One move and the man's throat would be slit open.

Just like Melissa's.

"Not fair at all," he said, and he let the knife cut across Jim's throat.

CHAPTER TWELVE

VICTORIA HAD TEARS IN HER EYES. No, no, he couldn't handle that. He hated to see her cry. She couldn't be in pain. When a tear spilled over and slid down her cheek, Wade caught it with his thumb. "Baby, it's okay, whatever—"

But she shook her head. "You're wrong, Wade. It's not okay." She licked her lips. "I—I did it."

For an instant his heart stilled. "Viki—"

"I did it," she said again. "The perp—he isn't just playing a game. He's found out what I did. He knows that I—"

Wade kissed her. He just had to stop the tumble of her words. This was the wrong place, and the wrong sort of people—cops—were too damn close by.

But Victoria pushed against him. "Stop it! Stop!"

He needed to get her out of there.

"Wade . . ." She pulled away from him. "Didn't you hear me? I just told you that I—"

"No." His growl cut off her words. "Not another word here, understand?" He caught her hand in his. "Let's go outside. We'll find out if Dace gets any evidence from my phone later. You and I—we're getting out of this station." And he was getting a drink. A really big one. And giving her one, too. "Then we'll talk, and you'll see that—"

"I'm a killer, Wade."

Fuck. Did the woman want to get tossed behind bars? He cast a desperate glance toward the door.

"And . . . you're a cop." Now she sounded confused.

"Ex-cop," he gritted out. There was a real big difference there. "We aren't talking about this now. Come on, let's go." He locked his hand around her elbow and steered her to the door.

"Wade. Didn't you hear me? I just told you—"

"Baby, please, I'm begging here. Don't say another word about it. Not until we're out of the cop station, got it?"

Her eyes had never seemed bigger. She blinked, appeared a bit confused, but nodded.

Good. He yanked open the door even as he kept a grip on her with his right hand. The bullpen was full of cops, and the last thing he wanted was for one of those uniformed men or women to overhear Victoria's confession.

She killed her father. She killed him. Shit. He should have realized it sooner. Put all the pieces together.

"Wade . . ."

He kept walking. He could see the door. They were almost there.

And—

Matthew Walker was marching out of the room to the right. A bald guy in a suit was at his side, a guy who was speaking with a bellowing voice as he pointed at Detective Black.

Hell. Now it's a party.

"My client will not sit through any more of your badgering!" the guy in the suit blustered. *Has to be Walker's lawyer.* "So either you charge my client or he is walking out of this place right now!"

Dace didn't have enough to charge Walker. Wade already knew that. He tightened his hold on Victoria and—

She stopped. Froze.

For an instant his eyes squeezed closed. *Don't confess, baby. Not here. Not now. I have to think of a way to cover that sweet ass of yours and a confession now will blow everything to hell.*

"I'm getting another text," Victoria said.

He shook his head. "What?"

Her face had gone stark white. She was staring down at the screen of her phone. "My God . . . I think . . . I think it's Jim." Her hand was shaking as she shoved the phone toward Wade.

She hadn't just gotten a text this time. She'd gotten a picture. A picture of yes, dammit, Jim Porter. Jim was on the floor, holding a hand over his bloody throat.

"Fuck!" His roar had every eye in the station coming to him.

In the silence that followed, Wade ran toward Dace. "Get your men—we need people over at Jim Porter's place right now!" He pushed the phone toward Dace and saw the other man pale.

Melissa hadn't died right away. She'd survived for precious moments. Perhaps—maybe Jim Porter could survive, too.

But only if he had help. Right fucking *then.*

THE AMBULANCE BEAT them to the scene. Dace had sent cops and EMTs rushing to Jim Porter's apartment. And they *knew* the photo had been taken from Jim's place because they'd downloaded the picture and taken the GPS coordinates right off the damn thing. A little trick most folks didn't realize . . . unless you turned off the settings on your smart phone, the longitude and latitude coordinates of every photo you took were stored—all you had to do was check the properties on that file, and bam, you had a perfect address.

So the ambulance rushed to the scene. The cops went in with sirens blazing.

Wade and Victoria stayed back, watching from a distance because they'd been told not to interfere. Wade saw the EMTs burst out of the building's front door. Jim was on the stretcher, blood soaking him.

Just like Melissa.

He didn't seem to be moving. The techs were working frantically on him. A crowd had gathered near the street, watching in horror.

"We're too late," Victoria said. "I think we always were. The perp—he could have waited before he sent that photo. Jim could already have been dead before I ever got it."

Sonofabitch.

Dace marched down the front steps. He didn't even look at the ambulance as it sped away. Instead, his gaze was fixed solely on Wade and Victoria.

When he was right in front of them, Dace finally stopped. "The killer took that picture with Jim's own phone. Cocky sonofabitch. He took the picture, then he sent it to *you*." His eyes narrowed as they swept over Victoria. "Why the fixation on you?"

"I—I don't know."

Wade hated the fearful stutter in her voice. He hated for her to feel any fear at all.

The ambulance had left. Cops were still there, interviewing neighbors. Trying to find witnesses.

"No sign of forced entry," Dace said. "No signs of struggle at all. Hell, from the looks of things, the guy just stood there and let the bastard slice him open."

"I—I want to see the scene," Victoria said, still with that tremble in her voice. "Can we come into the apartment now?"

Wade locked his jaw. What *he* wanted was for Victoria to get as far away from that place as possible. They needed to leave town, right the hell then, and he was sure that Gabe would back him up on that decision.

But Victoria . . . she was moving forward because Dace had given a grim nod.

Hell. Wade hurried to follow even as his suspicious gaze swept over the crowd once more. Was the killer out there, watching again? He'd watched while Melissa died, so it sure stood to reason that the guy would be close this time, too.

Once inside the building, he and Victoria were given gloves. They were also given soft covers for their shoes so they wouldn't track in debris. They crept into the apartment, moving carefully.

Wade noted the front door—the lock didn't have so much as a scratch on it.

Uniformed cops were scattered through the apartment. Wade and Victoria walked carefully inside, and

Wade's gaze swept the scene as thoroughly as possible. They were on the third floor of the building, so the killer must have gone in and out through that front apartment door. Maybe they'd get lucky. Maybe someone in the building *had* seen him . . .

They walked into a bedroom. One with white furniture and black and white photos on the walls. Photos of waterfalls and beaches.

A bed sat in the middle of the room. A bed that was covered by what looked to be a hand-sewn quilt . . . and a spray of red.

"The perp came up from behind him," Victoria said. "Based on that spray . . . Jim had to be facing forward. The guy came up, sliced his throat . . ."

"And then sent you a pic," Dace muttered. "So you'd be in on his fun."

Yeah, that is fucking what it was like. The guy wanted to share with Victoria. Because he thinks they are so damn alike.

He was wrong.

"I—I'll need to see Jim's body." Her voice was wooden.

She's already talking as if he's dead. No, baby, no. Have hope.

"If I look at the angle of the cut, I can give you an idea of the perp's height. Tell you if he was right-handed or left and—"

Dace's phone rang. Frowning, he stepped back and took the call. "What?" he barked into the phone. "Is he dead?"

Victoria's gaze swung to meet Wade's. Her gaze seemed so sad. Desolate. His chest burned as he stared at her. There was no hope—none at all—in her green eyes.

"You're going to have to wait on seeing the body," Dace said, voice sharp.

Victoria glanced at him.

"He made it," Dace said, a wide smile splitting his face. "That kid made it to the hospital! EMTs say the knife missed his trachea, the cut wasn't that deep, and the guy—hell, he's lost a shitload of blood, but he's in surgery. He might just pull through!"

Victoria's eyes lit up.

Thank Christ.

"He can identify the killer." Dace gave a quick nod. "When that kid comes out of surgery, he'll tell us who did this to him! We'll have that perp locked up before he can *ever* think of hurting anyone else!"

Wade's gaze slid back to the blood-covered bed. A survivor. Hell, yes. That was exactly what they needed. The perp probably thought he was free and clear.

Think again.

The kid was a fighter, and they *were* going to find the man who'd attacked him. No more victims. No more games.

It was over.

WADE LOCKED THE B&B door.

"How long do you think the cops are going to keep my phone?" Victoria asked as she paced in front of him.

"Permanently." He leaned back against the door and his gaze slowly slid over her as she turned toward him.

She rubbed the back of her neck. "I was afraid you'd say that."

"If any more texts or even calls come in from the killer, the cops want to trace them. They're taking over the case now." Dace's captain had been clear on that. They'd barely had time to leave the apartment before Captain Harry Vann arrived, saying they had to surrender Victoria's phone and needed to step the hell back from *his* case.

His case . . . like they hadn't busted ass helping the PD. But now that the news crews were closing in, Vann had tightened ranks. They were out. Only the cops were in.

Vann had told them to stay away from the hospital. Yeah, reporters were already swarming, and Wade knew exactly what the captain had been thinking . . .

You don't want it looking as if LOST is in charge. This is your city, your people . . . I get it, man. You want to be the one running the show.

But a pissing contest mattered for less than shit when lives were on the line.

"So what do we do?" Victoria bit her lower lip. "Stay and see what Jim has to say? Do we help the cops to—"

"We go home."

She shook her head. "The killer is still out there. We can't just walk away!"

They could. They would. They fucking should.

He rolled his shoulders back as he walked forward. Yeah, he was closing in on her. They were alone, and it was finally time to clear the air.

"Wade?"

"Why didn't you tell me sooner?"

Her lashes fell, shielding her gaze from him.

"No, that won't work," he said curtly. His fingers

curled under her chin and he tilted her head back, making her look at him. "Tell me everything. I want to hear it."

But she pulled away from him and stumbled back. "This isn't right. I—I . . . you *can't* just stand there and act all calm when you know that I killed my own father!"

Her grief was tearing straight into him.

"This isn't you." Victoria gave a hard shake of her head. "You should be sending me to jail. Locking me away. I killed a man. And I covered it up. For years. I'm . . . still covering it up."

He locked his muscles so he wouldn't follow her. She was running scared, and the wrong move from him— hell, he did *not* want to make any more mistakes with her. "I don't think you know me as well as you believe."

"What?" Her laughter held a sharp edge. "You're going to cover for me? Is that it?"

"Tell me what happened. Everything. Then we'll go forward from there, okay?"

Her hands fisted at her sides. "It's not pretty. It's not—not right. I knew what he'd done to my mother. For years, I knew. I had to live in the same house with him, and no one would believe me. Even when the cops finally started searching for her . . . even when she was declared missing, no one would listen to me."

He wanted to touch her so badly. "You finally made them listen. You got him arrested. You—"

"Only because they found her body. But it was a paper thin case, and I knew it. I went in that court, I told my story, and he sat at the defense table, just smiling at me. A sad, patronizing kind of smile." She swiped at her cheek.

Hell. She was crying again. Her tears gutted him, did she realize that?

"I knew the jury would find him not guilty even before the verdict was read, but I still went back into that courtroom. I guess . . . I guess I still hoped."

He took a step closer to her, helpless now to stay away.

"Do you know what he said to me, right after he finished his press conference? A conference he held right on those courthouse steps?"

Wade shook his head. He had no clue.

"I stood there and watched him, and then he turned to take me back home." Her smile was absolutely broken. "Because I did have to go home with him. He was my father, and I was a minor. What else was there for me to do? No one was going to help me."

"What did he say?" Wade whispered.

"I forgive you." Her voice was totally flat. "And he kissed my cheek." Wade's hand rose once more and she touched her cheek, only this time she wasn't wiping away a tear. "Later that night, when we were alone, he broke that cheekbone."

Rage burst through him, so sharp and hard that he lunged forward.

"Stop!" She held up her hands, as if warding him off. "If you touch me again, I won't be able to finish this and I *have* to finish it!" She sucked in a ragged breath. "It was one blow. Just one. One that sent me right to the floor. He said that I'd turned on him. After everything he'd done. After all he'd given to me. I was on the floor, looking up at him, and he was yelling about how I couldn't make it without him. How I needed him to survive . . ." Her lashes flickered and she stared at Wade. "I knew then that I couldn't need anyone."

No, baby, that isn't how life works.

"I had to rely on myself. Only myself. Because he was yelling the same crap at me that I'd heard him yell at my mother, right before he killed her."

"You were afraid." His voice came out as an angry growl because he was pissed. Pissed at her psychopath of a father. Pissed that someone hadn't helped her. Pissed that no one had listened to her when she'd tried so desperately to get the cops to hear her.

"After that night, he started trying to control me more. Wanting to know where I was going. Watching me, all the time. If I did anything that upset him . . ." She shook her head. "I heard the whispers from everyone. People thought *I* was the crazy one. That I'd gone over the edge when my mom vanished and I'd just latched onto the idea of him killing her. I knew the truth, though." She paused. "The truth is that he killed her, and he was going to kill me."

"Victoria . . ."

"He was a brilliant man. He knew so much about science. Medicine. About the human body." Her hand rose and she pressed it to her heart. "He knew just where to cut, so that death could be fast or so it could be slow."

You think I'm going to blame you for stopping that bastard?

"I know . . . because he told me. He told me that he made my mother's death slow because she needed to suffer. But for me . . . He told me one night while I was in bed . . . he sat there, right beside me, stroking the hair away from my forehead, and he said that he'd make it fast for me. Because I was his daughter, you see. I was part of him. So he was going to be kind and he'd make it fast."

He took another step toward her.

She lurched back. "He said . . . no one would find me. They'd think I ran away. He'd learned from my mom's death. He was going to be better this time. No one would ever find me. I was just going to vanish, and he—he doubted anyone would ever even look for me. I'd be a troubled teen . . . the world already knew just how troubled I was. I'd vanish, and that . . . that would be the end of me."

Her father was a fucking bastard. "But you didn't die." *You didn't vanish.*

Her lashes lowered, shielding her gaze again.

"Victoria . . ." He needed her to look at him. "You didn't die."

Her lashes rose once more. She stared at him. "No, I didn't. But he did."

"I know. I read the files, a heart attack—"

She shook her head. "The perp who has been texting me. He was right, Wade. I am a killer. I *killed* my father. I couldn't just wait for him to come after me, and I knew he was . . . he was going to wait for the perfect moment. He was going to take his knife and kill me, and no one would ever find my body. I—I couldn't let him do that."

Jesus. "No, you couldn't."

"I went to the cops again. That next morning. I got

up and I ran there. I told them what he had planned for me, but . . . they didn't believe me." Her laugh was bitter. "Or if they did, they didn't do anything. I mean, what could they do? It was my word against his, and the jury had believed him before, not me, so . . ." Her words trailed away. "I had an option. I could run or I could stay and die."

"You ran." This hadn't been in the files he'd read. He just knew—she'd run.

"I didn't go back home that night. I was too afraid. I didn't want to die, but I didn't have any other place to go. I—I just stayed on the streets. Slept near the bus stop. When I woke up, a cop was shaking my shoulder. He . . ." She gave him a sad smile. "He took me back home."

Hell, no. "You didn't have anyone you could turn to?"

"There was no other family, and my friends—they'd pulled away during the trial. Not that I had a whole lot of them to begin with. I was always the quiet girl. The shy one." Her gaze hardened. "But I wasn't going to be the dead one. Right after that cop left, my father smiled."

"Smiled? Why—"

"He really was a brilliant man, you see. And I'd just played right into his hands by running away. By letting a cop find me. Now there was proof that I was a runaway. So if I vanished again . . ."

Sonofabitch.

"Everyone would be more likely to buy his story. He . . . thanked me, for being so helpful."

Talk about a twisted bastard.

"So that evening, I wanted to thank him, too. I made him dinner. Used my mother's favorite flower."

Okay, now he was lost.

"She loved oleanders, you see," Victoria said, a brief smile curving her lips. "She always thought they were so beautiful, and even though she'd been gone for years, the oleanders still grew in our backyard. Gorgeous, white flowers, but quite poisonous."

He could only shake his head.

"He didn't even know that he was being poisoned. He thought he was having a heart attack. I heard him, later that day, yelling for me. I found him on the floor, trying to crawl toward the phone. He was holding his chest, saying I had to get help." Her gaze held his. "He didn't get any help for my mother, did he? *He* killed her, just as he was going to kill me. So I closed his office door and went up to my room. I covered my ears, and I cried and I cried, and I didn't go down the stairs again until the next morning."

Wade couldn't move.

"I am a killer. I poisoned him, and even when I had the chance to change my mind, to save him, I didn't." Victoria shook her head. "I went down the next morning, and when I found his body, I called the police then. *Then.* No one even tested his blood. It looked like a heart attack, so that's how it went down. I . . . I asked them to cremate his body. That way—"

"No one would ever be able to prove what you'd done."

"Not without a confession." Her smile was heartbreaking. "But I just confessed to you. You know my darkest secret now. You know that *I'm* one of the monsters out there. He was always right when he talked about it . . . I am just like my father."

He didn't know what in the hell he was supposed to say to her. "You were defending yourself."

"You know that doesn't fly. He wasn't coming at me with a knife when I gave him that poison—"

"But he said . . . *he was going to kill you.* If you hadn't stopped him . . ."

"Then I would have vanished." She nodded. "I absolutely believe that. But that doesn't make what I did right. I took a life. My own father's life, and when he was gone, I just felt free. I could live my life then, and I did—I went off to college. I got my M.D. I thought I could help people, could make a difference. But . . ." Her gaze fell. "The guilt would come back to me. Sliding in late at night. I couldn't escape what I'd done. What I was."

"That's when you turned to the dead."

She nodded. "I was spending all my time studying anyway, so I just piled on more courses. I started wondering if I could have just proved his guilt. If I'd studied my mother's body, if the M.E. had just found more clues . . . and suddenly I found myself being called in as an expert on different cases. I'd find small details that others had overlooked." She laughed, a hollow sound. "I was even working with the FBI. I was absolutely terrified the first time I worked with an agent. I thought . . . *what if he finds out?* He's working with a killer, and he doesn't even know it. But he didn't find out. And I helped him. I identified the remains. I gave him a cause of death, and for a little while the guilt I felt . . . it eased."

"That's why you joined LOST."

"I didn't vanish," she said quietly. "So I thought maybe I could help those who had."

So much about her was clear now. So damn much. What he'd thought was her careful reserve was actually a shield she had in place—one designed to protect her from pain. Guilt still ate at her, he could see that now. No wonder she threw herself into the work so much. Victoria was trying to atone. Trying to balance scales that he knew—in her mind—would never equal up.

No strings. And he understood that part, too. She was too afraid of proving her father right. Of being just like him—of needing someone so much, so badly, that she couldn't let go.

So instead of reaching out, of connecting with others, Victoria kept holding herself back.

"That shit isn't going to work any longer," Wade said.

Alarm flashed on her face. "What do you mean?"

"You aren't holding back with me anymore."

"I—I'm not holding back. I just told you everything!" No secrets. No lies.

"Now what are *you* going to do? Because I can't— I'm sorry," she said, and the tears came then, trickling unchecked down her face. The wall she'd built crumpled as he stared at her. "I'm so sorry . . . I did it, I killed him. I didn't . . . *I didn't want to die!*" And she was about to fall right before his eyes.

Wade surged forward and caught her in his arms. He held her tightly and could feel the tremors that shook her. She'd carried this weight around, for this damn long? And she thought he was going to judge her? That he was going to turn her in?

If I could, I'd kill the bastard myself.

She obviously didn't understand who he was—or rather, she didn't realize just how much she mattered to him. Her life—her. He'd do anything to keep her safe.

So while she cried, Wade just held her tight. After a while he lifted her into his arms and carried her back to his bedroom. She didn't say a word when he put her in the bed or when he crawled in beside her.

But she did reach out to him again. She wrapped her arms around him and fit against him.

So very perfectly.

"SO . . . I'M CLEAR?" Matthew Walker demanded as he turned to face his lawyer, Bob Moore. He'd just exited the lawyer's car. Moore had brought him back home after Matthew finally left the hell of that police station.

Bob gave him a broad smile. "Dr. Walker . . . there are no charges against you."

"But—But I heard what was going down at the station. The killer attacked someone else, right? While I was in custody. So now the cops know, absolutely know, that I'm innocent."

Bob nodded. "You're clear. They'd be fools to bring you in, and the PD doesn't want the kind of media firestorm I'd bring their way if they so much as *hinted* they were still trying to link you to this mess."

Good. Matthew exhaled and inclined his head toward the lawyer. "Thanks, Bob. I owe you."

"Oh, don't worry, you'll be getting my bill." Moore

gave him a little wave. "Now try to get some sleep. After today, you deserve some time to crash." Then he drove away, zipping down the road in his red Ferrari. *If any car yelled mid-life crisis . . .*

Matthew shook his head and headed toward his gate. He punched in the security code and the wrought-iron gate swung open. His steps were slow as he headed across the sidewalk that led up to his house, and for a moment he tipped back his head, glancing up at the historic home.

Tall, with red brick and big white columns. Surrounded by blooming flowers. A gorgeous house. And his Jag sat waiting in the drive.

He'd always wanted to live in a big house. He'd grown up with nothing and had vowed to have everything.

Now I do. But today, in that cop station, he'd nearly lost it all. If he hadn't been able to prove his innocence, his life would have come crashing down.

Matthew unlocked the door and flipped on the lights. He made his way into his study and poured some of his twenty-year-old bourbon in a glass. He downed the dark amber liquid fast and—

"Are you going to say thanks?" a mocking voice asked.

He'd known the guy was there, of course. That was why he'd made sure not to invite his lawyer in for a thank-you drink. Figured the guy would come by. *Arrogant asshole. Just have to let me know how much I owe you, right?*

"Told you the cottage would come back and bite you in the ass," he continued.

Matthew didn't turn to look at him. "It only bit me

in the ass because *you* screwed things up. You led the cops right out there and *you* killed Melissa." Fucking hell. He'd had so many fine plans with her. "Want to tell me why you did this? I thought we'd planned this all out. I take her, we keep her, and—" His voice was rising. He took a long, low breath as he tried to get his control back. "You changed everything. Why? For shits and giggles?"

"No . . . I did it for a very real reason."

Those words just pissed him off. Matthew slammed down the glass and whirled to face him. "Your *real* reason caused me to be hauled off to jail! And what the *fuck* did you mean, digging up Kennedy's body? That wasn't part of any damn plan! I didn't even realize what the hell I'd found at first when I was on that freaking trail. She was mine! She should have—"

"I needed her. She served her purpose."

The bastard just sat there, in his favorite chair, looking all smug and cocky. He'd screwed everything to hell and back. Nearly destroyed his life. *I hate this asshole.*

"The cops won't be looking at you anymore. An attack was committed—one that they *know* Melissa's killer committed—while you were in custody."

"I wasn't done with her! You shouldn't have killed her!"

"You were sloppy during her abduction. The bouncer saw your car. He told the LOST agents that, and then I got him to tell me the same thing. She wasn't going to disappear like Kennedy. Not with them here. I was just cleaning up your mess."

Bullshit. He didn't believe that, not at all. "What did

I miss?" Matthew asked. "Shit, were you sleeping with her, *too*?" Had to be. It was the only thing that made sense.

"We enjoyed each other. She made the mistake of thinking she controlled me *and* you. In the end, I think she learned a very valuable lesson."

His temples were throbbing. He needed more bourbon. So he poured another glass. Even got one for the cocky bastard in his chair.

"Maybe I was a bit . . . reckless taking her from Vintage. But she'd tried to ditch me. *Me*." He exhaled. "Now the cops know all about my fucking cottage, you dick."

Regret tainted the other man's words as he said, "Yes, well, it was a very good kill sight."

True. But he'd found another place. For next time.

Matthew handed him the glass. "You got a problem. I heard—at the station—they were saying that kid you attacked, he made it to the hospital."

But the guy just nodded. "Of course he did. I wasn't trying to kill Jim. Just hurt him. He needed to bleed for what he'd done."

"Uh, you're missing the big picture here."

"And that would be?"

"He *saw* you. He lived so he can tell the cops all about you—"

"He never saw my face. He won't be able to tell them anything. Well, except, of course, that *you* weren't the killer. Because you were in police custody." He took a sip of his drink. Frowned. "This tastes like piss."

Offended, Matthew blasted, "It's twenty years old! Freaking classic!"

The bastard smiled. "You just can't appreciate what's really good, can you? That's why you don't see just what we've got in our hands."

"Right now, we don't have anything in our hands," Matthew muttered. "We're clear, and we need to just lay low. So when you leave tonight, don't come back around, got it? Not until those agents from LOST are out of town. They're the ones pushing things."

"Yes, they are." But he sounded . . . pleased.

Hell. "*Don't*. Whatever it is you're thinking . . . just don't. We need to back off for a time." Even he could see that, and he was pissed as all hell that he hadn't been given the chance to truly enjoy Melissa. *I'll find someone else. But . . . I have to wait.* They both did.

The bastard murmured, "We've been . . . friends . . . for a long time now."

Friends? Is that what they were? Five years ago the guy had spotted him taking Kennedy away, but he'd kept quiet. He'd covered that secret. Did a past of blood and death and torture make two men friends?

Hell, maybe it did.

But . . . *I don't think he feels friendship. He doesn't feel guilt. He doesn't feel anything that I can see.* The bastard watched him the whole time, seeming to study him as if . . . *as if I were some new experiment for him.*

"I saved your ass tonight."

"*You* are the one who got me in that interrogation room! You—"

He sighed. "You did that. You killed Kennedy, remember?"

Fuck.

"It was my turn."

Matthew took a long gulp of his drink.

"And it's still my turn . . ." The bastard smiled his perfect grin. One that always made him look harmless. *He's not.* "Don't worry. I have everything planned out perfectly. No one will tie anything to you. Or to me. The cops can't catch us. They're too dumb."

"What about LOST?"

That smile stretched, and a knot formed in Matthew's stomach.

"I'll handle them."

"None of this comes back to me." It was a warning.

"Trust me, I've got this covered . . ."

Trust him? Hah. Hell, no. He didn't trust anyone. *I have to protect myself.* And that was exactly what he would do.

CHAPTER THIRTEEN

S OMEONE WAS KNOCKING AT THE DOOR.
Victoria cracked open one eye when she heard
the distant pounding—and saw Wade lying in bed
right beside her.

Awareness came flooding back through her—and her
second eye snapped open, too.

Wade was still asleep. His features were a bit softer,
his eyes closed, his long lashes casting shadows over
his cheeks.

He was on his stomach, with one arm wrapped
around her. His face was turned toward her, and the
sun poured through the blinds, falling over his broad,
tanned back, and—

The pounding came again.

"I don't want any," Wade muttered, sounding so
sleepy and disgruntled that a quick smile came to Victoria's lips.

*Is this what it's like? To just let go and be held by a
lover? To wake in his arms?*

The pounding came once more.

His eyes flew open.

"I think we have company," Victoria murmured.

"Hell." He pressed a quick kiss to her lips, surprising her, then rolled from the bed. He grabbed his jeans—when had he taken those off?—and strode from the room.

For a moment she didn't move at all. *He kissed me. He held me. He knows my darkest crimes and he still . . . wants me?*

It didn't make any sense to her. It just didn't fit, not with the kind of man that she knew Wade to be.

When she heard voices, Victoria hurriedly climbed from the bed. She was still wearing her shirt and jeans, and even though she probably looked rumpled as all hell, she hurried out of the bedroom.

Then she saw who their visitor was.

Lucas Branson.

He stood just inside the doorway, glancing nervously at Wade and then back over his shoulder.

His fiancée. Connie stood a few feet behind him.

"I, um, I needed to come by and see you. I tried calling you," Lucas said, "but some cops—they had your phone."

Wade stepped back. He'd put on a shirt but his feet were bare. "Come inside."

"Sorry to come by so early, but . . . but reporters have already been calling me. They know about Kennedy." Lucas reached back and caught Connie's hand in his. He pulled her inside after him. "And now with that other woman dead, too . . . one creep even asked me if *I* had taken her as well."

"Lucas never hurt anyone," Connie whispered.

"The killer set him up," Wade said flatly. "The same way he set up Matthew Walker for Melissa's murder—"

"Professor Walker?" Connie said, eyes widening. "The cops think he did it? I—I didn't realize . . ." Her words trailed away.

Victoria stepped forward quickly. "You know Dr. Walker?"

"He was my systems development professor when I was an undergrad. He's really brilliant with computers."

"Connie and Kennedy were both in his class," Lucas said quietly.

Victoria schooled her expression as she focused on Connie. "I didn't realize that you and Kennedy knew each other."

"Ships in the night," Connie said with a weak smile. "Kennedy was the star student—every class she took— and I just struggled to make C's. We only had that one class together, so, no, I didn't really know her . . ."

She saw Lucas squeeze Connie's hand.

"I told Connie everything," Lucas said. "About me hiring you. About needing to get some . . . some closure on Kennedy."

They had her body. Did that count as closure for him?

"The police are searching for her killer," Wade assured him.

"Right. Especially now that they know I'm *not* that killer." Lucas exhaled. "But they had five years to look, and all they found was jack shit. After all this time . . . I don't have much faith that they'll catch him now."

"He . . . he stabbed someone else last night," Connie said. Fear made her voice tremble. "He's just running around out there, hurting people, and no one is stopping him. What if . . . what if he comes after Lucas next?"

Her hand rose to her throat. "He was in my house. *In my house.* What if he comes back?"

"The police are sending extra patrols to your house," Wade said. "I talked to Detective Black, and he assured me that the police presence would be stepped up. And you were given a safe house to use—"

Connie shook her head. "That isn't good enough! We can't just hide in some police house forever. We need to get out of this town."

Victoria understood the other woman's pain.

"He got in before." Connie's voice lowered. "I'm so afraid he'll get to us again." Her eyes were stark. "I don't want to end up like Kennedy."

Kidnapped. Tortured. Killed. Victoria swallowed. Right. She certainly didn't blame Connie.

"We're leaving," Connie announced, lifting her chin. "My mom . . . she has an extra room at her place in Charleston, and we're heading up there. There are plenty of jobs in Charleston and it's just . . . it's time for us both to have a new start. Kennedy's ghost is always going to be here, and I can't live with that anymore. I just—I won't."

Lucas's face was stoic. "I asked you to find her. To tell me what happened so I could move on with my life."

Only they hadn't found her. Not really. Her killer had just dumped Kennedy's body because *he* wanted the world to know what he'd done.

Lucas's gaze reflected his pain. "Now it's time for me to focus on my future. I don't want that sick freak anywhere near me or Connie. I just . . . I can't go through that again." His voice broke. "So I came to say that I'm done. Thank you for coming here. Thank you for . . . for what you did."

We didn't do anything.

They hadn't helped. Hadn't brought Kennedy or Melissa home alive. And the man out there—the killer was still loose.

Wade offered his hand to Lucas. "I understand, and I wish you luck. If you ever need us, you know where we are."

Lucas shook his hand. "Thank you." Then he glanced at Victoria. "You . . . you worked on Kennedy."

She didn't want him to ever see Kennedy, not as she was now. Because she knew that Lucas had loved her very, very much.

"I want to bury her," Lucas said. "But her body isn't being released yet."

"It's going to take time," Victoria told him, her heart hurting for him.

"I don't want her just . . . left. She deserves a proper funeral. The cops said they'd contact me and let me know when to make arrangements."

Victoria nodded. She didn't want to tell him just how long it could be before he got that call from the cops.

Lucas held her gaze. "You found where he took her. You learned . . . what he did to her."

She wanted to comfort him but she didn't know how.

"Thank you," Lucas said with a quick nod. "For letting Kennedy talk one more time."

She had to glance away from Lucas and blink quickly because his words had pierced straight through to her.

"We should go now," Connie said. "My mother is waiting in Charleston . . ."

"Right." Lucas turned back to Connie and gave her a quick smile. "You go back to the car. I'll be right behind you."

Connie hesitated but then turned and hurried out.

Don't blame her for being in a hurry. She just wants to put this nightmare behind her.

Lucas followed her outside. Victoria noticed that he kept his gaze on Connie as she walked toward the car.

Victoria and Wade stood on the narrow porch with him.

"I have this urge," Lucas said, speaking quietly, "to watch her all the time. To make sure that she's always safe." He gave a rough laugh. "I know that's not normal, but I can't seem to stop myself. Not while knowing *he's* out there."

"Normal can be overrated," Wade murmured.

Lucas glanced over at him. "LOST finds the missing."

"Yes . . ."

"The killer *is* missing. No one can find him." Lucas licked his lips. "Could I hire you to do that? To find the bastard and stop him?"

Wade glanced at Victoria, then back at Lucas. "The cops are handling the investigation. They've actually . . . the captain told us not to overstep. With Melissa's death—he's closing ranks. Her body was found in another jurisdiction and the cops are drawing their line in the sand."

A line that had said: *no more outsiders.* Victoria knew Captain Vann was teaming up with the authorities in Jekyll. She wanted to help more, but . . .

That help wasn't wanted, not right then.

"Captain Harry Vann." Lucas said the name with disgust. "I remember him. He was the one who did nothing when Kennedy first vanished. I went to him directly. I *begged* the guy to put more manpower in the hunt." His hands went to his hips. "You know what it's like to have the cops do nothing? To have no one believe you?"

I know too well.

"LOST believed me. You helped me." He turned his attention to Connie once more. "I wish you could find that bastard. Because I don't think the cops will." Then he hunched his shoulders and headed toward the waiting car.

Victoria wrapped her arms around her stomach as she watched him walk away. Lucas seemed to carry so much pain.

Kennedy hadn't been the only one to suffer during all those years. Lucas hadn't been with her, but he'd been in agony, too. Always looking, always searching.

But now he knew she wouldn't be coming back to him.

He climbed into the little car and drove away.

"It's not what we do," Victoria said. "I mean, it isn't supposed to be what we do." She turned to look at Wade. "But we have managed to stop killers. On Dauphin Island—"

"The Lady Killer nearly took out Gabe. That was no easy scene, and you know it—blood and death and hell, baby."

But in the end the serial killer had been the one to perish.

"And don't even get me started on the shit that went

down in New Orleans recently." A muscle flexed in Wade's jaw. "You carry the scars that prove just how close to death you came."

"Walking away doesn't feel right," Victoria said. Because the killer was still out there. He'd gone after Jim, and who would be next? "He's making contact with me. We can *use* that."

He caught her arm and pulled her close. "You're not going to be bait."

"Someone needs to be. Or are you really fine with letting another innocent woman be taken and killed?"

"You wound up in a freaking body bag the last time a killer got hold of you." He growled out the words. "Do you really want that same thing happening again? Only this time, you won't be left alive . . ."

For an instant she saw the darkness all around her and remembered just what it was like to be in that bag. *Kennedy was in a bag. I was in a bag.* "I—I want to help."

"You want to atone." He kept his hold on her arm and pulled her back inside the little cottage they shared. "But there's nothing for you to atone for." He shut the door behind them. "Your father was a bastard, and you did what you had to do in order to survive."

The breath she sucked in seemed to chill her lungs. "What are you going to do about that?"

"Do?" His brows shot up. "You actually still think I'd turn you in to the cops?"

She didn't know what to think.

His hand curled under her chin and he tipped her head back. "Trust, baby. It has to start." His lips took hers. Carefully at first, gently. *"Trust me."* The kiss became harder after those words. He wasn't just caressing her, he was . . . taking? Staking a claim?

Her fingers wrapped around his shoulders and she held onto him. She might have also risen to her toes to better meet his kiss.

Too soon, his mouth lifted from hers. "Trust me to protect you. Trust me not to let you the fuck down."

She wanted to trust him. She wanted to open herself totally to him. "It's not you," Victoria whispered. "I don't trust myself."

"Stop letting your father's ghost control you. You aren't him. You can need and want and love just like anyone else."

His words pierced straight to her core.

"You're stronger than he is. You're better. So much better. You have to see that."

"You don't . . . you're not turning me in." She was having trouble getting past that fact.

He pulled back, just a bit, but he didn't let her go. "No." He spoke with absolute finality. "I'll keep your secret, you don't have to worry about that."

She didn't understand him. "In the police station, when Dace first read the text, you immediately stepped to my defense."

He waited.

"You . . . knew, didn't you?"

"I suspected."

Her eyes widened. He'd suspected, but said nothing?

"And I wasn't about to have you making a big confession there."

"Wade?"

"You don't get it yet, do you?" He gave her a little

smile. "You will, soon enough. Because I'm tying up those strings . . ."

But they'd said no strings . . .

"No secrets. No lies. Just trust."

Trust. It seemed like such a simple thing to give. For most people, it probably was. She wasn't most people.

But for Wade . . . she'd try.

VICTORIA COULDN'T LEAVE town.

He watched the little B&B, keeping his gaze focused. Lucas Branson had come and gone, keeping the simpering blonde with him.

That woman was *nothing* compared to Kennedy. So weak. So bland. A woman like her would never hold a candle to Kennedy. Did he realize that?

No matter.

Kennedy was gone now. So was Melissa.

Melissa was my warm-up. One he'd been building up to for so long. He'd watched Matthew. Learned. Grown.

There was no more standing in Matthew's shadow. He thought he'd proved that. Now it was *his* time, and he was ready for a much better target. A target he could understand. One who could understand him.

But he couldn't let her leave town. And he was sure that was the plan. After all, there were no more missing in Savannah. No one out there for sweet Victoria to find.

You'll be the one missing soon.

He just had to separate her from the asshole who seemed to shadow her every move. The man who touched her far too much. Her *partner.* Wade Monroe. Monroe needed to be removed from the equation.

Then Victoria would be his to enjoy. Oh, but he couldn't wait to hear all of her secrets. He even had the perfect place to take her, a spot already picked out. They could be alone for so very long.

The cops had her phone. He couldn't reach her that way. No more texts. He'd made her a promise in those texts. She wanted him to lose his control. *I will.*

But she might not like it when he did . . .

He put his phone to his ear. Matthew answered on the second ring.

"This is fucking insane," Matthew muttered. "We *aren't*—"

"All I need is for you to distract him." A distraction that they'd talked about last night. "Do what I said, and leave everything else to me."

Matthew's long sigh filled the line. Matthew was too hesitant. He'd saved the guy's ass, and now he wanted to play cautious in return? No, playing cautious wouldn't work.

Not while she was close.

You started it for me. And you don't even realize it . . .

"Fine," Matthew said. "I'll do it, but then we're even, got it? No more games. No more *favors.* I'm going to get out of this town, and I really never want to see your ass again."

There was a stark pause.

"No offense," Matthew muttered, as if he realized that he'd overstepped.

He smiled. "No offense taken. I think separating is very wise for us." He'd learned quite a bit from Matthew. But he wasn't a student any longer.

I'm the fucking professor now.

Matthew had become too predictable. He had a narcissistic personality. From a young age, Matthew had enjoyed watching women. Following them.

Controlling them.

Kennedy had been a tipping point for him. His obsession had consumed him too much. By the time he realized what he'd done . . .

It's a good thing I managed to convince him that she needed to stay alive. Otherwise, the last few years would have really been a waste.

Instead, he'd got to see Matthew evolve. A beautiful thing.

Even if Matthew could be an ass.

He ended the call. Put the phone back in his pocket. And knew that it was time to act. Victoria Palmer would be disappearing soon, and even her LOST buddies would not be able to find her.

Once he took her, no one would ever see her again.

THE PHONE RANG, jarring Victoria as she stared up at Wade. The ring was so old-fashioned—a long, shaking blare, when she was used to her smart phone— that she sat up and glanced at the landline on the table.

"Could be Gabe," she said. "He ran that NamUs check for us . . ."

Wade nodded curtly and hurried toward the phone. When he moved away from her, Victoria's shoulders relaxed. She hadn't realized she was tense until that moment.

He picked up the phone. "Monroe." His gaze sharpened. "Right. Now? . . . Yeah, yeah, we can make it. Okay. Thanks."

That had certainly been a fast call. Wade put down the handset and surveyed her with a faint scowl on his face.

The news must not be good.

"What is it?"

"That was Gabe. Our plane is here. It's time to go."

She backed up a step. "What?"

"He sent the company plane to pick us up. It's waiting at the airport. Let's get our clothes together and—"

"You called him." It was the only thing that made sense. No way would the plane just suddenly appear for a pickup. "Last night, when I was asleep, you called Gabe."

His shoulders rolled back. "I needed to update him on—"

"Did you tell him what I did?"

Anger flashed in his eyes. "That trust we talked about isn't going to be easy with you, is it, baby?" Then, before she could respond, he said, "No, I didn't tell him that. I did tell him that the perp has an obsession with you and that I wanted us both out of here."

"We can find the killer!"

"Not if the cost is you." He gave a grim shake of his head. "That cost is far too high. So I talked to Gabe last night. Yeah, I called him after you went to sleep. Because I was worried about you. The killer has only been contacting you. *You,* Victoria. You're the one he's interested in. He's lost his other prey, so who the hell do you think he will focus on next?"

"You can't—"

"I made the decision to call Gabe. Be pissed at me, but you'll be alive. LOST agents have been put at risk too much on recent cases. You almost *died* the last time a killer caught you in his trap. I wasn't going to let that happen again." He gave a hard shake of his head. "Our job here is done. Captain Vann wants us gone. Kennedy has been recovered. So has Melissa—there is no more work for us here."

She rushed toward him, hands clenched at her sides. "And when the next woman is taken? How will you feel then?"

"The cops are working on—"

"I can draw him out!"

His cheeks flushed. "No, you can get killed. It was Gabe's decision. He doesn't want to risk you." He lowered his voice. "Neither the fuck do I. It's time we packed it in and got out of the area."

This wasn't what she wanted. They could do something here. They had the chance to make a real difference.

"I can't lose another woman I—" Wade broke off. "I can't do this."

"I'm not Amy." Time to be very clear on that.

He shook his head.

"I'm not going to vanish. I'm here, and my job—it's to help people."

"We don't have a job here. No client, not anymore. Gabe has the plane waiting."

So they were just supposed to walk away? It seemed so wrong. A killer, still out there, hunting. And them—what, running away?

"There were no other hits in NamUs that matched

up with this guy," Wade continued. "Gabe had Sarah create a victim profile, and she didn't find anyone else in the system. He isn't following any kind of pattern—"

"Kennedy and Melissa were both Worthington students."

"Yes."

"*That's* a pattern right there. And Kennedy's body was found on the running path near the school. The missing women both link back to Worthington." And suddenly she knew what she was going to do. "The plane can wait. I want to go back to that school." She turned on her heel and headed toward her bedroom.

"What in the hell do you think you'll find there?" Wade called after her. "The killer? He isn't just going to walk up to you and confess! It doesn't work that way! We need to leave."

Victoria's shoulders stiffened. "*I* need to do this." It was almost a compulsion for her. "I'm not ready to leave, not just yet. And so what if the plane waits a few hours? It will be there when I'm done." There was one more person she wanted to see before she boarded the plane. One person who interested her in this tangled investigation.

One man who might be holding secrets back.

"Viki . . ."

Her hand rose and curled around the door frame. "Dr. North recognized me that first day. He knew me. He was in the courtroom when my father was on trial." She looked over her shoulder. "Then, ever so conveniently, the killer knew about my past. That's not a coincidence."

"You think North is the perp?" He'd shot forward at her words.

"I think . . . I want to see him again." She wished that she could read people the way Sarah did. That she could look at a killer and figure out all of his secrets.

But those were Sarah's talents. Not hers.

"You can come with me, or I can go alone. But one way or another, I am going back to Worthington." Because that was where their investigation had begun.

And she was convinced it was where it would end, too.

WADE DIDN'T LIKE this setup. Not at all.

They were back at Worthington University. Back in that pompous ass North's office. He was seated behind his desk, his nose still swollen and his eyes now black. *Yeah, that's what happens when you get punched in the fucking face.*

And just how convenient was it that the man who'd hit North . . . well, Jim Porter was now in the hospital, currently hooked up to a dozen tubes as he struggled to live.

"I understand that . . . Melissa was found." Troy North's voice had just the right degree of sadness. "I'm very sorry. The story was on the news and . . ." His gaze turned distant. "It's horrible to realize that humans can commit such terrible crimes."

"Yeah," Wade muttered. "Really fucking horrible."

North's gaze became less distant as he focused on Wade once more. "Why did you come back here?" he asked.

"Because I needed to see you," Victoria said.

At her words, he straightened.

Settle down, asshole.

North's hands flattened on his desk. "What can I do?"

Wade cleared his throat. At the sound, North's gaze jerked back toward him. *That's right. Eyes over here, jerkoff.* If this guy was the killer . . . "You know Dr. Matthew Walker, don't you?"

"Vaguely." North lifted one hand, waved it a bit. "I've seen him at school functions. Around campus. I hardly know him well." He leaned forward. "But I did hear about what happened. How the police thought he was involved in all that madness with Melissa Hastings." The faint lines near his mouth tightened. "Terrible, terrible business."

Wade slanted a fast glance toward Victoria, curious to see what she was thinking of this guy. But her gaze wasn't on North. It was on the wall of diplomas behind him.

"You know so much about human psychology," she murmured. "About what motivates people. What drives them . . ."

"Yes." There was pride in that word. "I try to be a student of the human mind."

Victoria's attention slid back to him. "My friend, Sarah, is like you. She studies the mind. Only with Sarah, she likes to figure out what motivates killers. She's not interested in the average person. It's the monsters that call to Sarah."

North licked his lips. "You mean Sarah Jacobs."

Victoria inclined her head toward him. "So you *do* know the LOST group."

"I—I did some research. After the first day when you were in my office." His gaze darted between Victoria and Wade. "But most people in the profession know about Dr. Jacobs." His laughter was high-pitched, nervous. "I mean, when the daughter of a serial killer becomes a profiler, people take note! What I wouldn't give to look into her mind . . ."

A heavy silence followed his words. The really uncomfortable kind of silence.

Yeah, okay, this guy could be a killer. Not only is he pissing me off, but he is freaking me the hell out, too.

"I bet Sarah would enjoy looking into your mind," Victoria said quietly.

A furrow deepened between North's brows. "My mind?" He gave another light, nervous-sounding laugh. "Why would she? I'm quite dull, I assure you."

Victoria shook her head. "I'm not so sure that you are." Her gaze slid to the wall of diplomas behind him once more. "Why did you become a psychiatrist?"

He shrugged. "Because the mind fascinates me. People fascinate me. What they'll do, their drives, their secrets . . ."

Wade wanted to drive his fist into the guy's face. There was just something about the way he was looking at Victoria. *Eyes the fuck over here, jerk.* But this was why they had come here. Because Victoria wanted to get a read on this joker. Wade cleared his throat. "Do you know a lot about secrets?" he asked him.

The doctor hesitated. "I can usually read people pretty well." His shoulders straightened and that arrogant air kept right on clinging to him. "You, for example, you're an open book."

Think again. "Am I?"

"Ex-cop," North said, giving a deep nod, one that led with his chin, then took his whole head forward. "Probably got tired of all the red tape that came with the job. So you went independent, thinking you could make a difference, but it's not that easy, is it? The dead keep coming, and you can't seem to ever get ahead of the killers."

"Don't be so sure about that," Wade murmured.

"You lost someone, obviously." Now, North really seemed to be getting into his profile of Wade. "That was the tipping point for you. You followed the law, always did what was right, but the blood was too much. So you left the job, but you keep following that thin line—the line between right and wrong. You can't cross that line. And you can't allow others to do it, either. It's just . . . not who you are."

You don't know me. Wade gave him a grim smile. "Dead on." *In your fucking dreams.*

Victoria glanced toward Wade, a swift, worried stare.

Just keep him talking, baby. It's bullshit. But let the guy feel confident. Because he had seen this routine dozens of times in interrogation rooms. Jackasses would get too confident, too cocky, and they'd spill all that they tried so hard to keep hidden.

"You can profile me, no problem." Wade jerked his thumb toward Victoria. "What about her? What do you see when you look at her?"

Avid interest filled North's eyes as his stare fixed on Victoria again. She stared back at him, looking nervous.

That look will work to our advantage. Good old Troy, he likes to feel in control.

"Always wanting to prove yourself," North murmured. "You've been driven by that need your entire adult life, haven't you? No one would believe you when you were younger, so you made sure they *have* to believe you now. You were the best one in your classes, you *are* the best in your field, and it's all about proving your worth. Proving that others can believe you. But deep inside you always think . . . you're still not good enough. Still the young girl who sat on that witness stand, with tears streaming down her cheeks as she swore her father had killed her mother. Only there was no evidence to back up your story. There was just you. And no one believed you." He leaned forward. "That must have devastated you. I can't imagine what it was like, going back to that house, with *him,* after you'd gone against him like that in court. It must have taken all that you had . . ."

I fucking hate this guy. It pretty much took all the self-control Wade had not to jump up and attack him. The shrink was practically salivating over Victoria. *No, over her pain. This freak likes it.*

Victoria had paled and her gaze dropped to her lap. *Keep pushing him, baby.* Because if she believed this was their guy, their chance to act was right the hell then.

"I knew living with him wasn't going to be an option," she said quietly.

"No, it wouldn't be. All that rage he must have felt toward you." North licked his lips. "Did he threaten to kill you? Because I'm thinking he did. I bet that he said you'd pay for turning on him. After all, you belonged to him, and then you went against him. You would need to be punished and—"

His stare slid to Wade.

The shrink stopped talking. His body jerked back and he swallowed nervously, his Adam's apple bobbing.

Shit. He saw . . . Wade knew the guy had just realized how much he wanted to rip him apart. So much for keeping his control. Victoria had been the one to play things perfectly but . . . *I can't play when it comes to her. Not anymore. Not even close.*

North gave another of his high-pitched nervous laughs. "How'd I do?" His smile was too big and fake. "Think I'd make it at LOST? Maybe I could work with Dr. Jacobs. I could profile the victims while she took care of the perpetrators."

Victoria was still looking down at her hands. "I don't think you're right for LOST."

North's nervous gaze darted to Wade.

Wade gave a slow, negative shake of his head. "Hell, no." Then he was the one to lean toward the guy. "And you got a few things wrong, just so you know."

"Wr-Wrong?"

"Yeah, things aren't always black and white. Right and wrong . . . they can shift. Especially when someone you love is put into the equation." Wade rose to his feet. He moved to the desk and leaned forward, slapping his hands against the wood as he towered his head over North. "Take me, for example. When I'm pushed far enough, by the wrong bastard, I forget all about what I'm *supposed* to do. And I just act out. I attack."

North shot to his feet. "I—"

"Do you do that, Dr. North?" Victoria had risen, too. Behind the lenses of her glasses, her stare seemed so very solemn. "Do you ever just . . . act? Or do you simply stay in the shadows, watching others? Learning their secrets and lies?"

He started to smile. A telling movement . . . one that sent more fury spiraling through Wade. "How about," Wade snapped, "I tell you what I see . . . when I look at you . . ."

"You're hardly qualified to—"

"I don't have a wall full of degrees, no. Sure don't. Because I was in the military, then I went straight to the police academy. I spent years tracking criminals, so that hands-on experience? It sure taught me a few things. First up . . . killers can be arrogant, cocky bastards."

North's jaw locked. "If you're saying—"

"I'm saying that they always think they're so much smarter than the cops. And you with all your degrees—I mean, how many fucking ones are on the wall?—you must think you're incredibly clever."

The doctor didn't speak.

"Criminals . . . well, there are certain types. There are those who value control more than they value anything else. They like to be the ones pulling the strings. Dishing out pain. They can't take the pain, you see. Just give it." His gaze slid over North's bruised features. "I noticed the first day how you freaked the hell out when you got hit. Never been hit before, huh? Bet that was an eye opener. Bet it pissed you off."

North just stood there. Glaring.

"I bet . . . you wanted payback against the guy who'd dared to hit *you*. And isn't it funny . . . he *was* attacked and had his throat slit open? Now poor Jim is unconscious in a hospital bed, connected to a dozen tubes as he fights for his life."

"It's not funny," North said, voice sharp. "It's tragic. For him to lose the woman he loved, then to be in this condition—"

"'The woman he loved'?" Wade pounced. "I thought they were just roommates. Old friends . . ."

"No, it was more. I could tell by the way Melissa talked about him and he—he was always standing too close to her. Touching her too much. When you're in love with a woman, a man's body language changes. *He* changes. He becomes protective. Possessive. Territorial." The doctor's lips curved, just the smallest bit. "The way you are with Dr. Palmer here. In so deep that you can't see anything else . . ."

Clever bastard. And Wade knew this prick wasn't going to screw up, there wouldn't be any rushed confession from him. Victoria had been hoping for just that—Wade knew it, but North was slick.

And I'm also thinking she's right . . . he could be the bastard we are looking for.

"I have classes, so I really must be going," he said, giving a curt nod. "Though if you want to schedule an appointment later to talk more, I can certainly do that."

"No." Wade's voice was flat. "We're leaving town. Another appointment won't be possible for us."

Alarm flared in North's eyes. "But . . . but the killer is still loose."

Now isn't this interesting . . .

"As I've been told . . . our job isn't to catch killers," Victoria said, all emotion gone from her voice. "We help victims. They're the ones that matter."

Keep talking, baby. Because the shrink is looking confused now. Huh. Guess he didn't see this shit coming. What had the guy thought? That Victoria would hang around forever?

Victoria gave a brisk nod. "Good day, Doctor—"

"What if others are taken? How can you just leave, knowing he's still out there?" North's eyes had narrowed on her. "*You* can't. You have to want to find him. Because he's just like your father, isn't he? Still loose, still capable of hurting someone else. Unless you stop him. Unless you step in—" He broke off. Shook his head. "Your job isn't done here, and you know it."

And you just convinced me you were the fucker calling Victoria, because you know what she did. "We aren't cops," Wade said. "Detective Black will find this guy." He caught Victoria's arm in his hand and steered her toward the door. *Make him follow us, baby. Make him.*

"Before or after another woman is taken?" There was a shrill edge in North's voice. "How can you risk that? I thought you—you would keep looking. *You* would understand."

Wade and Victoria were at the office door.

"I understand plenty," Victoria said. She looked over her shoulder at North. "Just how long have you known what I did?"

Wade glanced back, too. He saw the shrink's lips part on a quick, sharp breath. He also saw the flash of victory in the man's eyes. Sick fuck—the guy thought this was all some kind of game. It wasn't. Not even close.

But he won't confess. We need proof. Fucking proof. Detective Black can't get a search warrant on this guy because we don't have enough evidence to sway a judge. Right now, we've got our gut instinct—and the knowledge that this prick knows Victoria killed her father.

They sure as shit couldn't go to the cops with that.

And he realizes it.

Wade jerked the door open. He wanted Victoria away from Troy North. He wanted her *out*—

Someone was at the reception desk. Melissa's desk. A man sat there, his dark head bent forward, his shoulders slumped. He looked up, very slowly, and Wade saw that the guy's hands weren't empty.

Matthew Walker sat in Melissa's chair, and he had a gun in his hands. A gun that he lifted and pointed—right at Wade and Victoria.

CHAPTER FOURTEEN

VICTORIA SAW THE GUN, DARK AND DEADLY, IN Matthew's hands. His fingers were shaking that gun as he lifted it.

And pointed it at her.

Wade jumped in front of Victoria, shielding her. Her hands grabbed his back because she wanted to shove him out of the way. He couldn't do this. He couldn't risk his life for her.

But he was an unmovable block before her. His hands were fisted at his sides and his attention seemed totally on the man with the gun.

A man the police had released hours before . . .

"Wh-What's happening?" Troy demanded. Victoria heard the fast scuttle of his footsteps. He wouldn't be able to see Matthew, not with Wade blocking the door.

He can't do this! He can't risk himself this way!

But he was.

"I . . . cared about her." Matthew's gruff voice drifted toward them.

Behind her, Victoria heard Troy's shocked gasp.

"She shouldn't have been killed. Too fast. Too quick. That wasn't the way." Matthew sounded a bit lost.

"That wasn't the way it should happen. You don't . . . you don't learn anything that way."

"Put the gun down," Wade said, his voice calm. Almost easy. "Put it down, and we'll all talk."

Troy's fingers closed over Victoria's shoulders. They tightened, digging into her skin. "What is he doing?" His words were a hiss in her ears.

"That's all that asshole in there ever does," Matthew called out. "Talk and talk and talk. He thinks he's so fucking smart. Like he's the only one who can get a degree."

Wade's shoulders were tense before Victoria. She could practically feel him gathering his energy for an attack. Then she heard . . .

The squeak of a chair. Wheels, rolling back. She knew Matthew had stood up.

"I'm pretty smart, too," Matthew said. "So I figured things out. You're here, that means you figured them out, too, huh? You know what I know . . . that the bastard behind you, he killed Melissa."

At those words, Troy jerked Victoria back against him. His arms wrapped around her and he held her so tightly she could barely breathe. She gave a short, involuntary cry at his movement, and Wade whipped around toward her. He took one look at her, trapped in Troy's arms, and his face—

It iced.

All emotion vanished. His eyes even seemed to go dead.

That's not Wade.

She wondered just what he was preparing to do.

"What's happening here?" Troy demanded as he

stumbled back, pulling her with him. "What is going on?"

"Let her go," Wade said flatly.

And then . . . then she saw Matthew closing from behind on Wade.

"No!" Victoria yelled. "Stop!"

Wade swung back around. He struck out with hard, vicious force. He slammed his fist into Matthew's jaw, and in the next second Wade's other hand flew out and chopped Matthew's wrist. The gun fell from Matthew's fingers as he cried out and stumbled back.

Wade grabbed the gun in an instant. He brought it up and aimed it right at Troy. "Don't even *think* of moving again!"

Matthew was on his hands and knees. He'd tried to scramble for the gun. He'd missed it, by inches.

"Not me!" Troy yelled. "I didn't kill Melissa! It was him! *Him! Shoot him!*" Troy had one arm around Victoria's neck. The other was around her waist. Was he trying to use her as a human shield or—

"Don't listen to North! *Shoot him!*" Matthew yelled as he lunged to his feet. "He's the killer! He's going to kill *her*!"

"Let me go," Victoria said at the same time, her voice low and hard. "Wade has the gun. *Let me go.*" They all needed to calm the hell down. Fast. Before this scene went too far.

But Troy didn't let her go. He took another step back, pulling her with him. He seemed to be pulling her toward his desk.

"Walker, stay the hell back," Wade snapped out. "Get your ass under control!"

"It has to be him!" Matthew yelled right back. "He knew—he knew how I felt about her! He saw us together—I picked her up for lunch one day, *right here*. I kissed her and he opened the door. Freaking smug bastard . . . smiling the whole time! He took Melissa! He wanted her and he took her!"

Troy wasn't saying anything. But . . . he took his arm away from her neck. He was just holding Victoria now by the waist. His grip was so tight.

"Victoria." Wade's voice was clear in the storm around them. "It's okay."

How was this okay?

"Let her go, Dr. North. *Now*." Wade was advancing on her and Troy. One step. Another.

And Troy was—reaching for his desk. For the top drawer. He could almost touch it.

What was in the drawer?

"He won't do this to me," Troy said, his words a frantic whisper. "I won't let him. I won't let him!"

Matthew was inching toward Wade once again.

Wade—with Matthew at his back and Troy in front of him. His attention was too divided. This couldn't work. Wade was too focused on her. Helping *her*.

When danger was all around him . . .

"No," Victoria said, voice fierce. "Stop him, Wade! Behind you. *Stop him*."

Wade whirled. Matthew had grabbed a letter opener off Melissa's desk. He was screaming and rushing forward.

Wade fired the gun. The boom of the shot seemed deafening, and Victoria felt Troy jerk behind her. She seized that moment. He was so intent on the drawer—so shocked by the thundering gunfire—she drove her elbow back into his side as hard as she could.

He let her go. She lunged forward, her momentum sending her falling to the floor as she stumbled.

"Drop it!" Wade roared.

She looked back.

Troy had fully opened the desk drawer. And he'd taken out the weapon inside. A gun. One that he now held with shaking fingers.

"Have to protect . . ." Troy muttered. "Won't let him do this . . . *I won't!*"

And Matthew was still on his feet, just a small distance away. His shoulder was bleeding and the letter opener had fallen from his fingers.

She glanced back and forth between Matthew and Troy, her eyes wide.

"Put it down," Wade ordered.

Matthew smiled. *Smiled* as he stared down Troy's gun barrel.

Then, with no weapon in his hand, with blood pouring from his shoulder wound, Matthew surged into Troy's office.

"Victoria, stay down!" Wade roared.

Troy fired.

So did Wade.

The blasts happened so close together—the retort just seemed like one big explosion.

Her ears rang and she shook her head. She crawled back—

Wade grabbed her hand. He pulled her up, holding her close to his side. His right hand still gripped the gun. A gun that was trained on Troy.

Troy was on his feet, but blood bloomed on his chest. The gun trembled in his hand and he seemed to be struggling to raise the weapon once more.

"Drop it," Wade ordered. "Drop the damn thing *now*!"

"Shoot him!" Matthew yelled at the same instant. "He's crazy! He'll kill us all—*shoot him*!"

Troy's gaze jerked to Matthew. Rage and pain burned in his eyes, and he swung the weapon toward Matthew. Victoria had no doubt in her mind . . . he was going to kill Matthew Walker.

"Drop it!" Wade roared again. He hadn't shot to kill before. Victoria knew he was a good marksman. If he wanted Troy stopped . . .

Troy smiled as he lifted his gun.

"Shoot him!" Matthew screamed. "Help me, *help*—"

Troy's shaking fingers were tightening around the trigger.

But Wade fired before the psychology professor could. The bullet blasted right into Troy's chest this time. He stumbled back, ramming into the wall. His hand seemed to spasm around the gun and the bullet erupted, flying through the air to slam into the wall inches from Matthew's head.

Troy dropped the gun. He fell to the floor.

Wade had a death grip on Victoria.

She was pretty sure Matthew was crying from his perch on the ground.

"Why the hell . . ." Matthew whimpered as he clutched his shoulder. ". . . did you shoot . . . *me*? He was the one . . . wanted people . . . dead."

Troy was gasping and shuddering. Victoria tried to pull free in order to check on him, but Wade's grip was unbreakable.

She stared up at him, and the fury in his eyes—it stole her breath.

"He had you," Wade whispered. "The sonofabitch had you."

Footsteps thundered out in the reception area and uniformed security guards stumbled inside. Victoria recognized those men. They were the same men Troy North had called the very first time she and Wade had come to his office . . . when Jim had attacked him.

Now they stood there, faces slack with shock, as they stared at the brutal scene in front of them.

Two men shot. One man still armed.

So much blood.

The security guards grabbed for the Tasers on their belts as they stared at Wade with rising horror.

"Easy." Wade put the gun down. "Call the cops, right the hell now. Get Detective Black here. This isn't what it looks like . . ."

"You shot two men!" the red-haired guard shouted. He appeared to be about two seconds away from Tasering Wade.

"It's not even my weapon. Dr. Walker came to the scene with the gun." Wade had his hands up. "I can explain it all, but first . . . *get the cops. Get an ambulance.* Because I think Dr. North is dying."

That last shot—Victoria knew there had been no choice. He'd had to shoot . . . to kill.

The older guard grabbed for his radio.

"Get me help," Matthew gasped out. "I need . . . help, too. And . . . North . . . Troy North . . . *he's crazy* . . . make sure he's . . . down . . ."

The red-haired guard gulped and glanced over at Troy. Then he made sure to kick Troy's gun farther away. "He's still alive," the guard said. "But he's bad." He looked green as he muttered, "That blood is pumping out of him so hard."

Victoria could taste the bitterness of fear on her tongue. Troy had been holding her, grabbing for that gun in his desk, and she *knew* he'd been ready to shoot Matthew.

And Wade?

But now Troy North was lying in a pool of his own blood. A big, growing pool. Troy was bleeding from his shoulder, and it looked as if another bullet had grazed his side.

"I'm a doctor," she whispered. "Please, let me try to help." Because she couldn't just stand there and watch him die. It just . . . *I can't.*

The older guard had knelt next to Troy.

The red-haired guard kept his Taser up and his wary gaze on Wade, but he motioned for Victoria to go ahead.

"Be careful," Wade told her. "Even a dying man can try taking you to hell with him."

She swallowed at that stark warning, fear heavy in her gut. But when she knelt next to Troy, his eyes—so wild and desperate—locked onto hers with a frantic intensity.

"D-Don't . . ." He rasped.

"I'm just checking your wounds." And they were bad. So bad. She put her hands on his chest, and his blood soaked her fingers as she tried to staunch that wild flow. Victoria was very afraid that Wade's bullet had come too close to Troy's heart.

He'd had to stop Troy.

And he had.

She put more pressure on his wound, trying to help, but—

It's too late. I can see it now. His breath was too ragged, his skin color already changing. His pupils were pinpricks as he stared up at her.

"Don't . . . t-trust . . ."

She had to lean closer in order to hear him. "Who? Who shouldn't I trust?"

Troy's gaze darted over her shoulder. His lips parted. But he didn't say anything else. He couldn't.

He was gone.

She tried to bring him back, pumping on his heart, desperate because she didn't want him dying there, not like that—not even with the horrible things he'd done.

I don't want to be anyone's judge and jury. Not ever again. I can't be.

But . . . but there was nothing. No hope. His body was limp beneath her hands. She tried and tried—and she was still trying when the EMTs rushed into the office.

They pulled her back, but she knelt there, body slumped, chilled, as they checked him—and shook their heads.

Gone.

And his words kept replaying in her mind. A record that wouldn't end. *Don't . . . t-trust . . .* She glanced over her shoulder. Wade stared back at her, his expression carved from stone. Beside him, another EMT was trying to patch up Matthew Walker.

"It was him," Matthew murmured. "All along . . . *it was him.*"

A shiver slid over her, and she wished that she'd been able to make a dead man talk, just a little bit longer.

THE AMBULANCE PULLED away from the scene, its lights blazing. Matthew Walker was in that vehicle, strapped down on a stretcher. He'd live. And he'd have plenty to talk about with the cops . . .

The crazy bastard brought a gun onto a college campus. Wade still couldn't quite wrap his mind around that shit. The computer professor had sent the whole scene crashing straight to hell.

But Walker hadn't been the only one there with a gun . . .

"You're saying that Dr. North had a weapon stashed in his desk drawer? A gun?" Detective Black asked.

Wade turned toward him. "Yeah, that's what I'm saying. What I said five times already." Troy North was a dead man. Wade figured the guy's body would be wheeled out any moment, and plenty of the student body had gathered to see the event. "I had disarmed Walker, I took his gun . . . but North grabbed Victoria. He backed her up to the desk and reached for his weapon—"

"And that's when she got away from him," Dace Black cut in.

Wade nodded.

"But he didn't stop," Dace continued, reading his notes. "He was firing, and you had to shoot back."

"My first shot wasn't meant to kill." And he hadn't, dammit. He'd wanted that bastard to go in alive. If North was the twisted freak they'd been seeking, then he wanted him in a cage. They needed to question him, to learn . . . had more women been taken? Were their more victims who needed closure?

We won't know. Wade sighed. "But then things escalated. Troy was about to shoot Matthew, he was going to kill him." Wade was certain of this. "I had to stop him."

Because he'd suspected Matthew would have just been Troy's first victim in that little shootout. *I would have been the second.* And then Victoria . . . Wade feared she would have been killed last. *The better to enjoy her pain.*

His gaze slid around the perimeter. He and Victoria had been separated as soon as the cops arrived. Wade knew that was standard operating procedure, the better for the cops to be able to question them separately— and then compare the statements they provided.

"Why the hell," Dace wanted to know, "was Matthew so convinced Troy was the killer? How did he know?"

"You'd have to ask him that," Wade said flatly.

"Yeah, but you and Victoria were here, too, talking with the psych doctor. So you must have been suspicious. What tipped you off?"

Wade had just caught sight of Victoria's red hair, gleaming beneath the sunlight. "She knew," he finally said. "Victoria is the one who convinced me to come by here. Said something about the guy was nagging at her. Something he'd said the first time they met."

"And what would that be?"

She thought he knew that she'd killed her father.

Wade gave him a tired smile. "He was involved with both women who'd gone missing. Too much of a co-incidence, right? So we didn't head to the plane that's waiting for us. We came here, to see if we could rattle his cage a bit."

The doors to the Life Sciences building opened then and a black body bag was wheeled out.

"Oh, I'd say his cage was rattled," Dace murmured.

Wade clenched his jaw. "You think I liked shooting him? That I wanted to take a life?"

Dace lifted his brows. "I think you'd do anything, if it meant that Dr. Palmer was safe."

He wasn't going to deny that very basic truth.

"I'd like to know more about that 'hunch' of hers," Dace said. "Wonder . . . would it have anything to do with the fact that Dr. North was at her father's trial? See, I did a little digging on my own . . . that text she got on her phone about her father . . . it made me curious."

Wade held his gaze. "Nothing to be curious about there. The killer was jerking her around."

"Ah . . ." Dace's smile was grim. "There it is again. You'd do *anything,* wouldn't you? Kill? Fight? Even lie to protect her?"

Hell, yes.

"Detective Black!" The cry cut through the hum of voices filling the courtyard area.

Dace's head jerked toward it. A uniformed cop stood just outside the Life Sciences building. "We found—" The cop cut himself off and ran toward Dace. When he reached him and Wade he staggered to a stop. His breath heaved out and his cheeks were flushed bright red. "Sir, there was a . . . a file in the bottom of Dr. North's desk."

"What kind of file?"

"Pictures . . . so many pictures . . ." The cop looked sick. "Of a woman, with dark hair. She was . . . she was tied to a bed. I—I think . . . the photos look like the missing persons' poster of Kennedy Lane. You know, before she—"

Became nothing but bones.

"It was him," the cop said, giving a firm shake of his head. "It was that professor all along."

Dace looked toward the M.E.'s van. "He was the first person I interviewed when I got the case . . ."

The M.E. slammed the back door of the van.

"I could've stopped him," Dace said. "Fucking hell."

THE CHILL WOULDN'T leave her body. No matter what Victoria did, she just couldn't seem to feel warm. She was at the police station—in Dace's office, and Wade was with her.

The cops had talked to Matthew Walker—he'd backed up their story. She didn't know if the guy would be charged with anything—*He brought a loaded gun onto that college campus*—but she knew Wade was in the clear.

"Yeah, yeah, Gabe, I know . . . we were supposed to be on the damned plane." Wade slanted a fast glance at her as he talked on the phone. "But we hit a snag. Yeah, I'd call a guy trying to kill us both a bit of a snag."

A shiver shook her. It was hot in the office. Hot enough to sweat, so why did she feel so cold? Victoria glanced down at her hands. No blood was on them. Not now.

"Backup?" Wade's voice floated to her. "I don't know if we need it right now. Hell, that would have been good to know a few hours ago."

Her eyes closed as she leaned back in her chair.

"We're waiting to hear from the detective in charge. Dace Black . . . Yeah, he's a good guy. Once he gives us the all-clear, we can head back to Atlanta . . . Sure. I'll meet the fellow at the B&B . . . Asher Young. I got it. Thanks." There was a long pause, and Wade's voice turned gruff as he said, "No. I'd do it again in a heartbeat. Forget that shit, man. Just forget it."

Her eyes opened. She saw Wade put the phone down on Dace's desk. His back was to her and his broad shoulders seemed tense.

"What happened to the plane?" She cleared her throat because her voice had come out husky. "Is it . . . you told him we weren't leaving today, right?" They couldn't. Not in the middle of an active investigation like this one. *The guilty run.* And they had to prove that the shooting had been justified.

Don't . . . t-trust him . . .

"The pilot took care of it. The plane is going to be waiting for us when we have the all-clear to return home." He turned to face her, propping his hips against the desk. "Seems we've got a new LOST member. Asher Young. He's a former SEAL, a guy Gabe worked with during his time for Uncle Sam. Gabe vouches for him. Says he's the kind of man you can count on." He inclined his head toward her. "And he happens to be our pilot. He'll be taking a room at the B&B while we get the last of this case sorted out."

"Another SEAL?" She was surprised. "Why—" Victoria broke off, not really sure how to word her question. The people who worked at LOST were so diverse—a detective, a psychiatrist, a former FBI agent, but . . .

"Gabe thinks our last few missions have been on the dangerous side. He wants more backup for the agents in the field, and he wanted someone who was used to . . . being in the shit."

She blinked.

"Gabe wants the guy to stay close, just in case . . ." His words trailed off.

"In case of what? Troy isn't going to hurt anyone else." Not any longer. It was hard for the dead to hurt others. *Unless you let them.*

The door opened. Dace stood there. The lines on his face were deeper than she'd seen before. "Found your phone, Wade." He had an evidence bag in his hand. "It was at Troy North's house."

Victoria's breath expelled in a rush. *Another nail in Troy's coffin.*

"And I talked more with Matthew Walker. He said that North knew about Walker's affair with Melissa Hastings, and that he thought Troy was jealous. No, 'obsessed' with the woman."

An obsession that led to death.

"It looks pretty open and shut," Dace said as he strode to his desk. But he didn't sit. He ran a hand through his hair and peered out the small window on the right. "The killer's dead. My boss . . . hell, the captain doesn't want any charges pressed against Walker. Says we'll come across as bullies if we do, and he thinks the press will have a field day, especially seeing as how we thought *that* guy was the killer."

Wade regarded him with a guarded stare. "What about my shooting?"

"You're clear. Self-defense is hard to argue with in this case, not when you've got two witnesses who corroborate your story." Dace's hand sawed over his jaw and the heavy shadow that was growing there. "Jim Porter woke up. Couldn't talk, but he wrote down some answers to my questions. He didn't remember who'd attacked him. Never saw the guy's face but . . . but he *did* say that Melissa had been worried about Troy North. She'd mentioned a few times that he made her nervous."

He'd made Victoria feel nervous that first day, too. "He was so interested in secrets."

Dace's hand fell as he glanced over at Wade. "Yeah, well, considering how many dark secrets that guy was dragging around, makes sense, doesn't it?"

The case was over. Closed. "Are there more dead?" Victoria asked. That question had been haunting her. Were there more victims out there?

"Don't know yet. My crime team is tearing apart North's home and his office. If I find anything . . ." Dace exhaled and his shoulders dropped. ". . . you can bet I'll call you."

Wade offered his hand to the detective.

Dace took it and gave a hard shake.

"You didn't know," Wade said. "When you interviewed him . . . you don't always know when you're staring at a monster."

Dace backed up a step. "You should know, though. Someone that evil, you should be able to see it in them. I interviewed him three times after Kennedy Lane went missing. Never knew the truth . . . three times," he muttered, a faint furrow between his brows.

Victoria stepped forward. "Sometimes, evil is too good at hiding."

He glanced at her.

"And no matter how hard you look, you just *can't* see it." The cops sure hadn't seen the truth about her father. Victoria offered him her hand. His fingers—slightly callused—closed around hers. "Thank you for giving those women justice."

He held her hand. Stared into her eyes. "Thank *you* for that," he murmured.

She pulled her hand free. It was time to go home.

Wade opened the door, held it for her. She turned away from Dace.

"Dr. Palmer . . ."

Victoria looked back at the detective. His head was cocked as he studied her.

"You know . . . I think I would have believed you. If you'd come to me and told me about your father, *I* would have helped you."

Her heart was suddenly beating far too fast.

"Bet it was incredibly hard," he murmured. "Living with a monster like that."

Harder than you can imagine.

"You would have to do whatever was necessary," Dace continued, voice quiet, almost sad, "in order to survive."

He knows.

"Good-bye, Dr. Palmer," Dace said. "I wish you well."

She tried not to run from that little office. Her pounding heartbeat echoed in her ears. She didn't speak to Wade, not until they were out of the police station and back inside their rented SUV. As soon as the doors closed, sealing them inside, she turned to him. "Wade—"

He leaned across the seat and kissed her. The kiss stole her breath. Her hands lifted and locked around his shoulders. She meant to push him back. Instead, she pulled him closer. She kissed him—her mouth open and almost desperate in an instant. Fear still rode her—fear for what the detective knew, fear for what she could have lost because of Troy North and blasting gunfire.

So much fear.

She was ready for that fear to vanish.

Wade kissed her with a hungry, complete focus. As if nothing else mattered. Almost as if nothing else even existed. Tears stung her eyes as she held onto him.

She'd tried to avoid strings with him. That had been her rule, from the very beginning, but she knew the truth now. She was bound to him so tightly, she wasn't sure she'd ever be able to let go.

How could she?

Very slowly, Wade's lips pulled away from hers. He stared down at her. "I can't lose you."

She shook her head. "That isn't happening."

"As soon as I saw his arms around you—I saw North's eyes, they were so desperate—I would have done anything to stop him. I was looking at a dead man the minute he grabbed you." His breath rasped out and he let her go. "What the hell does that say about me?"

He turned away, his hands curling around the steering wheel.

Victoria reached out to him. "Do you think I'm not the same?"

His arm tensed beneath her touch.

"Do you truly think . . ." Victoria continued, "that I wouldn't kill to keep you safe?"

His head angled toward her.

"You've changed things for me," Victoria said. And, yes, this vehicle—in front of the police station—probably wasn't the spot to have this little talk, but she wasn't going to hold back. Not any longer. "I want to be with you. I'm scared of myself—yes, I still am. I won't lie. Scared of what I might become. But I'm more afraid of not being with you." Because she had more hope when she was with him. She was . . . happier.

Even if they were facing monsters.

"Baby, giving you up wasn't ever an option for me." He cranked the car.

"It's not an option for me, either," Victoria whispered.

They pulled away from the curb. And as they drove away, she saw that Dace had walked out of the station. He stood on the sidewalk, watching them as they left.

"ARE YOU IN any pain?" the pretty little blond nurse asked him, her brows pulling together. She'd just adjusted his medication—giving him another wonderful dose of morphine, so pain was the last thing Matthew felt.

"No," he said, making sure that his voice came out weak and a little slurred. "I can handle it."

Admiration filled her blue eyes. Wide blue eyes. "You caught that killer today, didn't you?"

Matthew almost smiled. "Just . . . tried to stop some-one . . . from hurting others . . ."

Her hand lingered on his arm. "You did a good thing. A brave thing." She gave him a sad smile. "That poor fellow he attacked . . . he's on the same floor with you."

Is he? What a coincidence.

"He's not in very good condition." She gave a little sad shake of her head. "Someone needed to catch his attacker. And to think . . . it was another professor at the college." She sighed softly. "I guess you can never know people."

No, you couldn't. Not who they really were, beneath the skin.

She gave his arm a gentle squeeze. "If you need anything, just hit that button on your right. I'll come straight in for you."

He was sure she would.

Matthew watched her as she hurried from the room. Nice ass. Firm and high. He bet she was a runner. With those long legs, she'd be a great runner.

He liked runners. Loved to watch them move ahead of him. Loved to chase them.

Loved to catch them.

He lay in bed as the morphine slipped through his veins. It was cold, and he could imagine it as ice slid-ing through him, moving ever so slowly until it covered him completely.

His injuries weren't that bad. It pissed him off, certainly, because he didn't like being hurt. He'd never expected old Troy to put up such a fight. He'd known Troy kept that gun in his desk drawer. The guy was always so paranoid about his safety. Probably because he'd spent too much time with criminals during his early days as a psychiatrist.

The drawer had been open once, when Matthew paid a little visit to see Melissa. He'd remembered that gun and thought . . .

All I have to do is show up, armed. He'll react. He'll grab for the weapon.

And North had. So perfectly. Acting as if on cue.

He glanced at the big round clock on the wall and figured the pretty nurse must be back at her station. Matthew eased from the bed. He stood for a moment, swaying a little. Then he smiled. His hand grabbed for the IV machine. He was sure it had some other technical name, but he didn't give a fuck what it was. He grabbed it and pulled it along with him. The wheels rolled with a soft squeak. The stitches in his shoulder pulled a bit as he walked. Maybe he'd get some more morphine for that pull when he got back. He'd call in that sweet runner of a nurse.

He opened his door. Looked left and looked right. The linoleum gleamed beneath his feet. So . . . Jim Porter was on this floor. Wonderfully convenient. But which room was his?

Matthew started walking. The wheels squeaked again, and the noise seemed too damn loud. He took his time, though. If someone spotted him, if a nurse appeared, he'd just act confused.

Morphine could do that to a person. Make him all disoriented.

His gaze slid toward the doors. Names were written on them—just last names. Oh, that made things easy.

He just kept walking, looking for the right door.

A janitor headed toward him. The guy barely even glanced his way.

A young man in scrubs followed behind him. Again, not even a second look.

Hospitals. *Got to love them.*

Then Matthew found the door he needed. *Porter.* He opened it and pulled his squeaking buddy along with him. Maybe he should have taken out the IV before this little trip, but—nah, why bother?

The curtain was pulled around the bed. His left hand rose and pushed it back. The man in the bed had his eyes closed. Monitors beeped beside him. Heavy white bandages covered his throat.

Matthew crept closer to the bed.

The wheels squeaked again.

And Jim Porter's eyes flew open, locking on him.

Matthew smiled. "Hello, there . . ."

CHAPTER FIFTEEN

CLOSURE. VICTORIA NEEDED IT BEFORE SHE could get on the plane and leave Savannah. So she and Wade didn't go straight back to their B&B. They went to Mercy Hospital, and when the elevator doors opened on the third floor, a nurses' station waited right in front of them.

They asked about Jim Porter's room and a blond nurse pointed to a hallway. She didn't ask for IDs, didn't even ask if they were family. Just pointed and got back to work.

The hospital floors were gleaming, and they passed a janitor swinging his mop. Doctors were buzzing around, nurses going in and out of rooms.

"This is it," Wade said, stopping before the door at the very end of the hallway. A whiteboard hung near the door, *Porter* written on it with blue marker. The door was slightly ajar and Wade rapped lightly with his knuckles.

There was no response from inside.

"Jim?" Wade said.

Victoria shook his head. "He isn't going to be able

to talk, Wade." She pushed open the door and headed inside. "Jim?" She called. "It's Victoria and—"

Jim wasn't alone.

Matthew Walker stood beside his bed, his body swaying, one hand gripping an intravenous infusion pole. He wore a green hospital gown and he blinked a bit dazedly at her.

"What are you doing?" Wade demanded as he closed in on Matthew. "Why are you in here?"

Jim's eyes were open. His gaze slid from Victoria to Wade to Matthew, and he looked so confused. And scared.

Victoria reached out and her fingers closed around Jim's. He was connected to half a dozen machines, and beeping filled the room. "It's all right," Victoria said. "We just wanted to check on you."

That's what we wanted . . . but why is Matthew Walker here?

Some of the panic faded from Jim's gaze.

"The nurse . . . she told me he was in here," Matthew said, his voice sounding groggy. "After everything . . . I wanted to see him . . . tell him how sorry I was . . . about Melissa . . ."

Jim's gaze cut toward him. His stare seemed to harden.

Victoria pulled her hand away from Jim's. There was a notepad on the bedside table. She reached for it—and the pen attached to it—and handed it to Jim.

He gave her a quick nod of thanks.

Then he scribbled on the pad. *Dr. North? Dead? Saw . . . on TV.* She read his notes out loud as he wrote them so the others would know what he had to say.

"Yes," Matthew said on a long sigh. "He's gone. He won't hurt anyone, not any longer. I just wish . . ." His grip on the intravenous pole tightened. "Wish we could have stopped him . . . before he took . . . Melissa."

"Melissa and Kennedy," Wade said. "Two women. Two victims."

Matthew's eyes lowered to the bed. "Right. Two . . . He took them both."

Jim wrote on the pad. *Did she . . . suffer?*

Victoria swallowed. There was nothing to be gained from him knowing the truth. "She isn't suffering now. And Troy North won't ever hurt anyone else."

Jim's gaze met hers. She hadn't wanted to tell him the truth but . . .

When tears clouded his eyes, Victoria realized that he'd already known. "I'm sorry," she said. "I wish . . . I wish we could have found her sooner."

Jim's lips parted.

"So do I," Matthew mumbled.

Footsteps padded into the room and a blond nurse popped her head around the curtain. When she saw them all, her blue eyes flared, but she seemed to focus specifically on Matthew. "Dr. Walker!" She hurried to his side. "You should be resting! Especially after that dose of morphine, you should *not* be wandering around."

He wrapped an arm around her shoulder. "Just . . . needed to see for myself . . . young Jim was okay . . ."

"I'll help you get him back to the room," Wade said.

Jim watched as Matthew was led out. Victoria kept her gaze on Jim, not the others as they filed out. There was something about the way he was watching Matthew . . .

Jim glanced back at her.

"Is everything okay?" Victoria asked him.

He motioned to his throat. Right. Getting your throat sliced was hardly okay.

"I wish things could have ended differently." It was odd. She'd once felt so uncomfortable with the victims—the live ones anyway. But she'd needed to come to the hospital and see Jim. To tell him good-bye. So what if Captain Vann hadn't wanted them there? She couldn't leave town without seeing Jim one more time.

He picked up the pen again. *Me, too.*

She put her card on the bedside table. She felt so helpless. "If you ever need anything, please let me know." LOST was taking care of his medical bills. Just a small thing, but . . .

He was writing again.

Melissa always . . . hated that guy.

Victoria's eyes narrowed on the text. "Dr. North?"

Jim gave a hard shake of his head, then winced. He wrote, *Walker.*

"I thought they were involved," she said, voice careful.

Jim's brows shot up.

"That's what he said."

Anger flashed on his face. He wrote, *She never told me.*

"Sometimes people keep secrets."

The machines beeped around them. Sadness had slid over his face.

She wanted to comfort him. "Melissa loved you. And you loved her."

He nodded.

"Isn't that all that really matters? Maybe any secrets she kept . . . she kept them because she didn't want to hurt you."

He put down his pen.

"Everything seems hard now," Victoria continued, aware that her voice had gone ragged. "You probably don't believe this . . . but I truly do understand. Just *breathing* seems hard, and the idea of going back out into the world with everyone else, acting as if life is normal when you know it's not, when everything has been ripped away from you—that idea terrifies you."

Jim watched her. His eyes—they looked dead. *I know that expression. I saw it in the mirror after my mother's trial.*

"But the world can only scare you if you let it. Take it one day, one minute, at a time. Small steps, no big leaps. One day you'll decide to take a walk in the park, and the sunshine won't seem so glaring to you . . ."

Tellingly, his gaze slid to the shut blinds in his room.

"Another day, you'll join friends for dinner, and the conversation—it won't seem so empty to you."

His stare came back and doubted her.

"It won't," she said again, giving a determined nod. "You'll go through bad days and good days, but you *will* get through them all. And then . . . when you think that life is just—just there, that you're only going through the motions . . . it will change."

Jim shook his head.

"It *will* change. And you'll stop wondering why you didn't die. You'll stop thinking about how much easier death would have been." She knew. She'd been there.

"And you'll find that you're living." Her laughter held a bitter edge. "None of that will be easy. None of it will be quick, but it will happen."

And it was there. The faintest flicker of hope in his eyes.

"If you ever want to talk to someone who's been there . . ." Her gaze slid to the card she'd put down for him. "Give me a call."

This time, Jim nodded.

"Right." She exhaled and blinked quickly. "I'll be expecting my phone to ring." And *not* to get any texts from a dead man. Victoria moved briskly away from the bed, and she found Wade staring at her.

She hadn't even heard him come back into the room. His gaze was so intent and focused on her. Emotions were burning in that golden stare. Emotions that stole her breath. But Wade didn't speak, not until they were in the elevator, heading back down to the ground floor.

"You never told me . . ." Wade's voice was gruff. "That you thought it would have been easier if you died."

"Guilt is hard to carry. And what I did . . . it wasn't an easy choice." Taking a life. But . . . Wade would know that. Wade would understand. Her fingers curled around his. *Fit* his. "I'm glad you followed me that first night. I'm glad that Gabe made us partners."

He lifted their locked fingers and pressed a kiss to her hand. "Guess this is where I confess . . ." The elevator doors opened. They walked out of the hospital and toward the parking lot.

"What do you have to confess?"

"I asked Gabe to partner us."

Now she stopped, truly surprised.

"Ah, baby, you really didn't see it, did you?" He cocked his head as he studied her. The sunlight poured down on them. And it wasn't so glaring. Just bright. "After that case in New Orleans . . . when I almost fucking *lost* you, everything changed for me. There was no more playing around. No more denying. There was only you."

Her heart was beating too fast in her chest.

"Only you," he said again, "and that's how it's been for me since that day. I asked Gabe to put us together because I wanted to be close to you. I wanted us to have a chance."

And they did.

A real chance. One that wouldn't be haunted by ghosts or monsters. One that was just open for them.

She didn't know if she loved Wade. Didn't know if she could surrender just yet to that overwhelming emotion, but . . . she couldn't imagine her life without him. She wanted him close. She was happy when he was near.

One day. Another . . .

And the words she'd spoken to Jim came back to her. *And you'll find that you're living.*

With Wade, she was living. Not just going through the motions. He'd brought her back, and she wouldn't give that up—wouldn't give him up.

She rose onto her toes and pressed her lips to his. "I think you're the best partner that I've ever had."

When he laughed softly, the last bit of cold she'd felt slipped away.

MATTHEW WATCHED THEM from his window. Lovers, had to be.

Wade and Victoria. He'd suspected as much, considering the way the guy had done a full-on freak-out when her life was threatened. A man would do anything for the woman he loved.

Lie.

Cheat.

Steal.

Kill.

Been there, done that.

Matthew picked up his phone. He dialed quickly. The sweet nurse had given him more morphine, and the drug was slipping through his veins, but he had to make this call before he gave in to that dark oblivion.

The call was answered on the second ring.

"Case closed," Matthew murmured. *Debt paid.* "Do whatever the hell you want now."

VICTORIA WASN'T SURE what to make of Asher Young. He was waiting at the B&B when they returned, and his dark brown eyes held no emotion as they seemed to assess her and Wade.

Judging.

She straightened her shoulders and lifted her chin. After all she'd been through that week, she wasn't in the mood for anyone's judgment.

"You were a SEAL with Gabe," Wade said, nodding at the other man. "If Gabe trusts you, that's more than good enough for me." He offered Asher Young his hand. "Welcome to the team."

No smile curved Asher's face. *Quiet. Intense.* His

hair was nearly jet-black, and a thin, white scar slid under his chin. "Gabe said you were one of the good guys," Asher murmured, his voice deep and tinted with the faintest Texas drawl.

Wade gave a hard laugh. "Then it looks as if Gabe might have lied to you."

No, he hadn't.

Wade released the guy's hand and glanced over at Victoria. Did Asher see the shadows in Wade's eyes? The pain?

He'd taken a man's life, and she knew that wasn't sitting easy on him. She wanted to wrap her arms around him. Hold him tight. But they weren't alone. Asher had followed them into their little cottage so they could all make plans for their departure tomorrow morning.

Time to head back to the reality that waited in Atlanta.

"Gabe also spoke very highly of you, Dr. Palmer," Asher told her with a nod. His voice had . . . softened when he talked to her. Gentled.

She caught the narrowing of Wade's eyes behind him.

"He said you're the best when it comes to the dead. But then, I'd already heard about your reputation."

"Thank you."

He offered his hand to her. Right. She should shake it. Her hand was immediately swallowed by his bigger grip. She figured that Asher was close to Wade's size, maybe an inch taller, and built along the same hard, dangerous lines.

Wade moved behind her. His body brushed against hers.

"Got it," Asher murmured. He immediately let her

go. "Sorry I wasn't any help on this case. Didn't realize shit was going down so fast. I was pissing away time at the airport when I could've been giving backup to you." He gave a hard nod. "Don't worry. I won't be making that mistake again."

"Wade handled it," Victoria said. She glanced back at him. "He did what was necessary."

"Doesn't mean it was easy," Asher responded. "I know. Next time, man, you can count on me."

She focused her attention on Asher once more. "Why did you decide to join LOST?" She got why Gabe had hired him. Extra muscle could only be a good thing. Especially the way their cases were going lately, but . . .

"Not just me," Asher murmured. "My twin sister will be working for the team, too. Gabe hired her first. I was just the tagalong. Story of our lives. "

She was surprised.

"Ana was the best bounty hunter in the Southeast," he said, more than a hint of pride entering his voice as he rolled back his shoulders. "When it comes to tracking, she's the best."

"I look forward to meeting her," Victoria said, and she meant just that. She wasn't worried any longer, not terrified that someone new would see the secrets she carried. Maybe—finally—she'd put her past behind her.

"She'll be there when we land." He gave them a brisk nod. "So enjoy your sleep. We'll be taking off at 0600 tomorrow."

Right. Sounded good to her.

Asher headed for the door. When it closed behind him, Victoria was aware of the silence.

And of Wade.

She took off her glasses and smoothed a lock of hair behind her ear.

"You don't move as much anymore."

She blinked at those words, not understanding what he meant.

"It used to seem like you were all energy, always moving, always . . . going."

"Maybe I don't want to go anymore." She faced him fully. "Maybe I'm exactly where I want to be now." And he was right—her nervous energy had faded. She wasn't on edge, worried about a discovery of what she'd done.

She was . . .

I'm me.

Her hand lifted and stroked over his cheek. His five o'clock shadow pricked her palm. "I'm so sorry that you had to pull the trigger."

His head turned and he pressed a hard kiss to her hand. "For you, I'd do it again, without even hesitating."

She knew that. But she didn't want him carrying that burden on his soul. If there had been another way . . .

His gaze slid back to her. "I need you, Viki."

Primal. Honest. Deep.

She nodded. "I need you, too." They were alone. The darkness had come. There would be no holding back. So she took his hand and she led him to the bedroom. She stripped in front of him, saw him toss his clothes away.

Maybe this should have been the time for gentle touches. Pretty promises. Sweet words.

But . . . it wasn't.

He put her on the bed, spread her legs and put his mouth on her. His touch was rough, hard, and he feasted. Wild and hot and hard, and she came—erupting with a sharp cry.

Fast. Desperate—that was what she felt.

Blood and death . . . *no more. Life. Wade.*

His cock was heavy and long, full, and she reached for him eagerly, stroking and pumping his erect length. Then he was positioning his cock at the entrance to her body. He stood at the edge of the bed, and his hands wrapped around her hips, lifting her up.

He sank into her, driving deep in that first plunge. Her hands fisted around the sheets.

He withdrew. Plunged again. Again.

Deeper. Harder.

Her back arched off the bed. The only sounds she could hear—the panting of her breath, the wild thunder of her heartbeat.

Again and again.

Deeper, harder, and—

She came, a wave of release that swept through her, not stopping, an orgasm so powerful that she nearly jerked off the bed.

But it wasn't enough.

Because he pulled her up. Held her in his arms. Moved fast—and pinned her there against the wall. In and out, over and over, he drove into her. She was slick and hot and so ready for him. There was no restraint, no holding back. Their bodies hit, and he drove frantically for his pleasure.

When he came, she felt the release deep inside. She

turned her head and pressed an open-mouthed kiss to his neck. She squeezed him, loving the feel of him inside her, outside, all around.

She—

"I love you, Victoria."

Her eyes closed. She locked her arms around him and held on tight. He carried her back to the bed. Put her under the covers.

She should say something back to him. She knew that she should. A man had just said he loved her. No other lover had ever done that. But . . .

"I'm not going to stop." He settled in beside her and curled an arm around her stomach. "But there are a few things you still need to know about me."

She knew everything.

"I tried to tell you before, I'm not the guy you think I am." He gave a bitter laugh. "I'm not the guy Gabe tells people I am, either. I'm the guy who hunted with him. I'm the guy who helped him track down the bastard who'd taken his sister, and I'm the guy . . ." His hold on her tightened. "I'm the guy who didn't stop Gabe from killing the man."

Now she stirred. "That was self—"

"Self-defense. Right. Because he was armed and attacking, but Gabe and I—we could have stopped him. Could have let him live. Could have taken him down another way . . ."

And she remembered. When he'd shot Matthew—he'd gone for a hit in the shoulder. And even when he'd fired at Troy, the first hit hadn't been a kill shot.

She swallowed and listened. She wanted to hear everything he had to say.

"I was just as angry as Gabe. Just as fucking furious because I saw what he'd done to her. Amy was good. Always a good person. And I cared about her."

A tear slid down her cheek because there was so much grief in his voice. She hated for Wade to be in pain.

"And I let her the fuck down. I should've found her sooner. I should have done something. When I saw that prick, when I saw him laughing at what he'd done to her—crazy asshole—something snapped in me. I wanted to stop him. Gabe just beat me to the punch."

Her heartbeat was slowing. His arms were so warm around her.

"I didn't grow up easy. My dad died when I was young. It was just me, my mom, and my . . . brother."

Silence. She barely breathed.

"Adam *was* the good one, baby. I was the rebel. The troublemaker. I was the one who took the risks. Not him. He was sixteen and he'd always looked after me. He looked after everyone. Adam was the fucking hero . . ." His breath roughed. "Until the very end . . ."

"Will you tell me what happened?" They'd both revealed so much. He'd helped to heal her pain. She wanted to heal his.

"A kid went out too far. Some little guy—maybe around six. He got caught in an undertow. I didn't even notice—too busy with my own shit. But Adam noticed. He ran out there, didn't even hesitate. He got that kid out and he was coming back. When he was coming back . . ." His breath rasped out. "I saw him then. I was on the beach, watching. Why the fuck was I still on the beach? I should have already been in the water, but I'd just been screwing around and I saw him with that kid and—a wave hit."

Goose bumps covered her arms.

"It was a big wave, and when it cleared I didn't see him. Didn't see him or the kid."

Another tear slid down her cheek.

"I ran into the water. Other people were running then. Trying to help. My mom was screaming. I—I was a good swimmer and I got out there first. I grabbed and I touched someone."

She waited.

"It was the kid. He was choking and crying and he held onto me so tightly."

"Wade . . ."

"I—I swam back to shore—just close enough that I could give him to one of the other people out there, then I went straight back out. By then half a dozen people were in the water. We were all looking for Adam. Searching so hard. But he was . . ." Wade's words trailed away.

She knew what he'd been going to say.

Lost.

She pressed closer to him. All she wanted was to comfort him. To take away that pain.

"He must have gotten swept back into the undertow," Wade murmured. "I fucking hate the water."

She knew that he did, and now she understood why.

"Three days. It took three days of searching on boats, of getting the Coast Guard and divers out there, before they found my brother."

"I'm so sorry." She held him as tightly as she could. "So sorry . . ."

"My mother just . . . she broke for a time after that. It was like I heard you say to Jim. She was just . . . there. Going through the motions. I could see it. Nothing I could do seemed to get through to her. She didn't laugh. She didn't smile. She was like a ghost, one being forced to hang around the living." His voice was so sad.

He's breaking my heart.

"I couldn't make her want to fight. I couldn't help her. And when I was nineteen, she passed away. Just . . . got sick. Pneumonia. She withered away right before my eyes."

He'd carried all of this? This pain? And she hadn't known. He'd always seemed so confident. Strong. Happy.

And . . .

Victoria kissed his jaw. His cheek. His lips. She just had to kiss him. To let him know—

Wade, I'm sorry. Wade, I care. Wade, I—

Love you?

She eased back, stunned by the force of her own emotions.

"I joined the military. I swore that I would be as good a person as Adam had been. I would help people. I would make a difference. I would do my best to make him proud."

"I'm sure he would be very proud of you."

She felt him tense against her. "Adam was the good one. I think I just went through the motions."

"No." Victoria snapped out that denial. "That is absolutely not true. You are the best man I've known, Wade. You're strong and brave and you—"

"We both know I have a dark side, Viki."

"That doesn't make you a bad person!" she threw right back, desperate for him to understand. "You are good, Wade. I know it. I've always known it. You do help people. You help me. You help so many at LOST. You make a difference." He'd changed everything for her.

"You make a difference, too." His voice was so solemn. "I hope you know that, baby. You make a big difference for me. Because I'm not going through the motions any longer."

It was hard for her to breathe. He'd heard so much of her talk with Jim, but she'd never even thought Wade—

All this time, he was in as much pain as I was.

"I'm living," he whispered. His lips pressed to hers. Did he taste the salt of her tears? She thought that he did. In the darkness, they just held each other. And, maybe, maybe they both healed.

"I love you," he said, voice growing a bit husky, sleepy. "That's not going to change. We'll go day by day, and one day, you will trust me enough."

"Enough?" She could barely whisper that one word.

"Enough to love me back. Enough to know that you can count on me, through good times and fucking bad times. Enough to know that I will always have your back, and that, for me, you will always be the one who comes first."

She wanted to have a future with him. A life. Could they do that? Go for kids? The whole picket fence? Knowing what they did—having seen the violence out there, could they really do all that?

"One day at a time," Wade whispered. "Because we have plenty of days ahead of us."

He bent his head and pressed a kiss to her lips.

WHEN THE PRIVATE plane touched down in Atlanta, Ana Young was there to greet them. Petite and delicate, physically she seemed the very opposite of her brother.

But she had Asher's dark, almost pitch-black hair. And her eyes were the same deep brown—though flecked more with gold.

And they shared scars.

Ana's scar wasn't on her chin. It was a faint slash that slid over her top lip.

She greeted them with a cautious smile and a quick handshake. "It's a pleasure to be working with you," Ana said. "I've, um, got a van waiting and I'll take you both home so you can get some much-needed rest."

Home. Odd, when Ana said that one word, Wade's image flashed in Victoria's mind. She glanced over at him—and found his stare on her.

"Great to see you, sis," Asher murmured. He scooped his sister up in a massive bear hug. "Nightmares?"

It was the faintest of whispers, but Victoria was standing so close to Ana that she heard the question.

She also saw Ana's nearly imperceptible shake of her head . . . and the way Asher's shoulders seemed to relax.

The twins had secrets. But Victoria wasn't about to pry. Why would she?

"It's a pleasure to be working with you, too," she told Ana, and the smile she gave the other woman was real. "Your ears should have been burning because your brother was telling us how amazing you are during the flight. I know you'll be an asset to LOST."

Relief swept across Ana's pretty face. "I just want to help." The words seemed blurted out. "Just help."

"You will," Victoria said with certainty. That was what LOST did, after all.

And they were growing. Getting stronger and bigger every single day.

As promised, Ana had a van waiting for them out front. They climbed in and soon they were sweeping past the familiar streets of Atlanta. The buildings passed in a blur. Wade was the first one to be dropped off at his place, but before he climbed out, he gave Victoria a long, lingering kiss. "See you soon, baby," he said.

Yes, he would.

She watched him walk away.

Asher cleared his throat. "Gabe was a bit, um, worried, that you two might not have gotten along so well in the field."

She smiled. "Don't worry, we got along just fine."

"Yes, ma'am. Definitely see that."

They headed to her place. When she climbed out of the van and stared up at her building, it almost seemed foreign to her. Cold and empty.

"Are you all right?"

She glanced back at Ana's question. "I'm fine." She would be, from now on. Her hands tightened around her bag.

"You sure you don't want me to get that?" Asher asked her.

Victoria laughed. "Trust me. I've got this. But thanks." She gave them a little wave. "See you in the office soon."

Because it was time to get back into her normal routine. Life at the office. A home here.

She took the elevator up to her floor, dropped her bag near the front door and walked toward her windows. She looked out at the city below. She'd always felt so safe up there, but now . . .

She felt alone.

WADE'S PHONE RANG. He heard its echoing cry when he stepped out of the shower. He'd crashed for hours after he got home, and when the sun set, he'd finally managed to wake up enough to wash the hell of travel off his back.

He knew his machine would pick up the call, so he didn't hurry too fast toward the hallway, not until he heard Victoria's voice.

"Wade?"

He nearly fell, rushing with his wet feet and slipping over the tile.

She gave a little laugh, the sound transmitting easily from the speaker on his answering machine. "I know I just saw you but . . . I miss you. That's crazy isn't it? But . . . but I was thinking . . . want to grab a drink? That's what normal couples do, right? They get a drink? How about we meet up tonight? At the place where you pretty much changed everything for me."

He was surging for the phone.

"If you want to come, I'll see you there in an hour. If not . . . then I'll see you soon."

He swiped for the machine.

But she'd already hung up. He started to call her back but . . .

Baby, I'm coming for you.

CHAPTER SIXTEEN

THE BAR WAS TOO CROWDED. THE BODIES TOO sweaty. The music was too loud. The laughter too fake. Victoria had noticed all of that before when she'd gone to Wild Jokers, but none of that had bothered her. She'd just wanted to get lost in the throng of people.

To escape.

She wasn't looking for escape this time. She was looking for him.

Victoria settled in at the bar. She waved to the bartender and he nodded, indicating he'd be her way soon. Then she glanced over her shoulder, looking toward the entrance. It had been almost an hour since she'd left that message for Wade. She needed him to walk through that door. Excitement bloomed inside her as she waited.

The bartender came back, took her order, and when she sipped her apple martini a few minutes later, the sweet taste rolled right over her tongue.

Again she looked back toward the door.

Warm hands settled around her waist, making her

jump and sending some of that apple martini spilling over her chin and down the front of her top.

"Welcome home."

The hands were a heavy, possessive weight on her hips, and she spun in her chair because the voice wasn't Wade's.

"Flynn," she said, her eyes widening as she took in the blond male before her. The man she'd left the bar with just days before. They'd gone into the back alley . . .

And Wade had changed everything.

"Hey there, gorgeous." Flynn flashed her a wide smile, one that made his green eyes gleam and his dimples wink at her. "Missed you while you were in Savannah."

She and Flynn . . . they'd been lovers. Once. No commitment, no—

Strings.

Her gaze darted over his shoulder and to the door. "How did you even know I'd gone to Savannah?" She hadn't mentioned that to him, had she? Hadn't she just said that she was leaving for a case?

He laughed. A rich, deep rumble. "You told me. When we ran into each other on my morning jog." He took a seat on the bar stool next to her, but he leaned in close, crowding her with his body. "Though you didn't give me any more details. You and your mysterious cases . . ." His hand reached out and his thumb gently slid over her chin.

Victoria jerked away from his touch.

His brows shot up. "Easy. You just had a little bit of

drink on you." He brought his thumb to his mouth and licked away the moisture.

She shot off her stool. "No, Flynn, it's not happening."

He laughed again. "What's not?"

Flynn had always been so easygoing. No pressure. And he was fine with no strings. She wasn't.

"I'm meeting someone tonight. The guy—the guy from the alley."

"Your *partner.*" His face darkened. "I didn't like the look of him, Vik. Too intense. Dangerous."

No, Wade wasn't dangerous, not to her. "We're together," she said flatly. She wasn't going to play around with some other guy while Wade was on his way.

Flynn nodded. "Fine, Vik, fine. As long as you're happy . . ." He took a bottle of beer and saluted her with it. "Good for you."

Her shoulders relaxed.

Then Flynn glanced around the bar. "But if you're so together . . . why isn't he here?"

WADE RAN OUT of his apartment. He was running too damn tight on time. Gabe had called, wanting a full update because Dace had contacted him . . . trying to tie up loose ends.

The call with Gabe had gone long. And now he was rushing to get over to that bar and meet Victoria. No other bozos had better even think of moving in on her—

What the hell?

Wade stopped right next to his motorcycle. A motorcycle with very flat tires. Tires that hadn't just deflated—close examination showed that they'd clearly been slashed.

His bike had been fine earlier. He'd checked it out briefly right after he got home. *Then* he'd crashed.

Now, though . . .

I can't get to Victoria this way.

Sonofabitch. He jogged toward the main street and saw not a single fucking taxi. He needed to call Victoria but—

The cops in Savannah kept her phone. She'd contacted him from her landline before, he'd seen her number on the caller ID. When he'd talked with Gabe before, Gabe told him that he was taking care of replacing both his and Victoria's smart phones. That replacement really needed to hurry the hell along.

He started jogging down the road. There had to be a taxi somewhere. This was Atlanta, for shit's sake. He'd find a ride, and he *would* get to Victoria.

VICTORIA GLANCED DOWN at her watch. "It's only been an hour."

"What?" Now Flynn sounded shocked. "You've been waiting on the jerk for an hour?" He hopped off his stool and reached for her hand. "No way. Absolutely not. You don't wait for some fool. Come on, dance with me."

So meeting at Wild Jokers hadn't been her best idea ever. At the time, everything had seemed to start for her and Wade right there . . . and it seemed like—maybe a fitting place to meet. She'd thought they could dance, get a drink, and then go back to her place.

"Dance with me," he said again, flashing his dimples.

His dimples were cute, but he wasn't Wade and she was far past the point of being interested. "No." She pulled her hand away. "He's not late. This is when he should be arriving, and I know he'll be walking in that door any moment." She gave him a weak smile. "I am sure there are plenty of other women who would love to dance with you, Flynn. They're probably already lining up." She put down her money on the bar top. There was a booth close to the door. She'd go wait over there. Victoria pushed her way through the crowd. She was wearing heels—ones that were a bit higher than normal, and she'd dressed as sexy as possible.

For Wade.

For herself.

She wanted to look good for him. She wanted to let go, with him.

"Here you go."

And Flynn was back. Only this time he held up a martini glass—one filled with green liquid. "Your favorite," he said, and he put it on the table in front of her. "My way of saying sorry for spilling your drink before."

Her shirt was already drying.

"When Prince Charming gets here," Flynn continued, "I hope you two have a great night. Really." He gave a quick nod. "You deserve some happiness after the rough times you've had."

Then he slipped away, vanishing into the crowd.

Her fingers rose and curled around the long stem of the martini drink. She stared into the liquid and wondered . . .

How did Flynn know about my hard times?

Her breath sucked in on a quick inhale as she glanced around, but he was gone. Long gone. Had he dug into her past, researched her the same way that she'd caught Wade doing that one night?

Or . . .

I don't remember telling him that I was going to Savannah.

She stood up quickly, suddenly ready to leave that too loud club. Her hand brushed against the martini, sending it falling across the table. A second spill in one night. She was certainly on a roll. Now her hands were sticky, covered in the drink. She hurried toward the bathroom, zigging and zagging around the crowd. She'd clean up and then she'd wait outside for Wade because something . . . it was off.

With Flynn.

With the way . . . he acted.

Did I tell him I was going to Savannah?

She didn't remember telling him, just as she hadn't told him about any hard times. They hadn't exactly been into deep conversations. She'd met him, they clicked, and yes, okay, so maybe she'd done a little research on the guy before they hooked up.

I wasn't going to walk away with a stranger.

She'd run his records at LOST. Flynn Marshall, age thirty-three. A pharmaceutical sales rep who traveled frequently, had never been married, and had attended . . .

Northwestern University.

That one detail clicked in her mind.

He'd attended Northwestern, just like Troy North. They were around the same age. They even looked a bit alike, with that blond hair and similar height. Had they attended college together?

Why does that matter? Why?

Victoria pushed the bathroom door open. The fluorescent lights flickered overhead. Her high heels clattered as she made her way to the sink. No one else was in the bathroom as she yanked on the water and soaped up her hands.

Victoria felt as if there were a puzzle right in front of her and she was just missing a piece.

The water thundered into the sink.

Flynn . . . I told him I was leaving town, going on a case, but not where . . .

The first time they'd met, it was right outside her building. He'd been jogging and she didn't see him. He collided with her, and, right before she would have fallen to the ground, his hands had risen and he caught her. Then, that night, she'd gone to Wild Jokers, just wanting to escape from the darkness that seemed to surround her.

He'd been there. At the time, she just thought it was chance. A coincidence. Nothing more.

Now . . .

What if it wasn't chance? What if none of it was?

The lights flickered again.

The door began to creep open—she heard the groan of the hinges.

In the mirror she saw a man's hand reach through that opening. A tan, strong hand. The hand went straight to the light switch on the wall.

And the bathroom plunged into darkness.

A JEEP SLOWED at the corner. Wade glanced over at it with a glare—

Asher Young gave him a wide-eyed look. "Uh, yeah, man, Gabe sent me over to deliver a new phone to you—"

"I need a ride."

Asher shrugged and motioned to the seat beside him. "I can do phone delivery. I can do rides, too."

Hell, yes. Wade jumped into the Jeep's passenger seat.

Asher cleared his throat. "Just where are we headed?"

"Victoria." Saying her name made his body tense.

"Right, Victoria's place. She's not there, though, just so you know. I tried to deliver her phone first and the place was shut down."

"That's because she's at Wild Jokers, waiting for me." And his ass wasn't there. "Someone slit the tires on my motorcycle, and I didn't have a way to contact her. I need to get there, now." Because he didn't like this whole setup. No way to reach her. His tires fucking slashed.

Why slash my tires unless you didn't want me leaving?

And he'd only been going to one place . . .

To find Victoria.

But no one else had known that.

Right?

"Okay, okay, calm down . . ." Asher shifted gears and had the Jeep spinning around in the road moments later. "I'll get you there." But his jaw was grim as he drove. "Slashed tires?" Asher asked, voice thoughtful.

"Yeah. And they were fine when I went into my place earlier. But I got a message from Victoria, asking to meet, and when I went out—"

"Interesting."

No, it fucking wasn't. "Drive faster." Because the knot in his gut wasn't going away, not until he saw Victoria.

THE LIGHTS WENT off and the last piece of the puzzle fell into place for Victoria—too late.

She immediately tried to move to the left but—

He's blocking the door. I know he is.

"Victoria . . ." Flynn's voice called out to her, sounding worried. Concerned. "Something's wrong with the lights . . ."

No, nothing was wrong with the lights. She'd glanced up in time to actually *see* his hand turn them off.

"I'm worried about you. I—I saw you come in here, and you were weaving a bit on your feet."

Only because I was trying to shove my way through a packed dance crowd.

But . . . she needed that crowd right then. She needed to get back outside to them. Screaming wasn't going to do her any good—no one would hear her. She could hear the wild pounding of the music. Outside that bathroom, there was chaos. Enough chaos to muffle any scream she made.

"I think you had too much to drink . . ." he continued in that same, soft voice. "I saw your empty glass on the table. I know . . . you don't always like to drink too much."

Empty glass. No, she'd knocked that glass over. She hadn't drank from it. He thought she had, though. And he thought that she'd been weaving . . .

Pharmaceutical rep. Dammit, he had access to so many drugs! He'd probably put something in her drink. *Not just mine.*

"Victoria?" Now his voice was sharp. "Shit, have you already passed out?"

He hadn't seen her standing in front of the mirror. He'd put only his hand inside the bathroom when he turned out the lights. So he hadn't seen that she'd been standing there, perfectly aware.

She heard the rustle of his footsteps. He was coming toward her. Probably about to search the place for her unconscious form. The guy had tried to drug her, and she knew he wanted to take her away from the bar. She couldn't let that happen.

She had to think of a way out of this mess.

Unfortunately, there were only two stalls in that bathroom. One large sink. And one exit.

An exit that he still blocked.

"Victoria . . ." Now anger roughened his voice.

She had to answer. Had to say something or he'd know that she wasn't drugged. "F-Flynn?" She made her voice stutter. "Something feels . . . wrong with me . . ."

His sigh swept toward her. "Too much to drink," he said, voice back to being concerned. Friendly. "I suspected as much when I saw you stagger in."

You were watching me. How long have you been watching me?

"Good thing I followed you."

For how long? Nausea twisted within her. "I feel sick." She wasn't lying. She'd slept with him. She felt like vomiting.

"It's okay," he assured her. "I'm here. I'll take care of you."

Like you took care of other women? No way was this his first shot at drugging his victims. *And he knew I went to Savannah . . .*

"Walk toward my voice," he told her. "I'll get you out of here. My car's out back. I'll take you home."

"Home . . . n-not far," she mumbled. "I can walk . . . there . . ." Anything to get away from him.

There was the rustle of sound again. And then he grabbed her arm. But his hold wasn't rough. It was ever so careful. "Not in this condition. I'll help you."

No, he wouldn't.

But as soon as she got out of that bathroom, she'd be home free. Others would be out there. She'd break away from him. She'd get help.

He thought she was drugged.

He was so very wrong.

Flynn slid his arm around her, pulling her close against his body. "Did you think . . ." His breath blew against her ear. ". . . that we were done? Just because *you* said we were through?"

They'd never been together—just a few hookups. That wasn't a damn life commitment.

"I'm here to love you," he said, his voice a rasp in her ear as they shuffled back toward the bathroom door. "And you *are* going to love me."

The hell she would.

"I've seen it happen before," Flynn murmured. "I knew just what to do with you. I learned."

Learned? He was terrifying her.

Victoria figured they were almost at the door. Now that he wasn't blocking it—she shot out of his arms, lunging hard and fast to escape the bathroom. To escape him.

"Victoria!" He roared her name, but she'd grabbed the handle of the door. He was just seconds behind her. Seconds. She rushed into the narrow hallway. She could see the crush of people up ahead. Bodies dancing, hands in the air, music pumping—

He grabbed her.

"Help me!" she screamed, desperate, even though she knew the music was too loud.

Flynn spun her back around and pinned her to the wall. Then he put his knife to her throat.

An image of Melissa flashed before her eyes. Melissa . . . Jim . . . their throats . . . blood.

One slice, that's all it would take. Because she could feel the sharp blade already cutting into her skin.

"You didn't finish that drink, did you?"

The bright light in that hallway glared down on them. He was surrounding her so completely. If anyone came up behind him, they wouldn't even see the weapon. They'd just see two lovers, pressed tightly together.

They'd see what Flynn wanted them to see.

She stared up at him. Handsome Flynn. Still smiling the wide grin that flashed his dimples. But it was a grin that didn't reach the coldness of his eyes.

"The drink would have made things easier, but I can

still work with this." He gave a nod. "Come with me. Don't make a fucking sound. Or I will slit your throat right here and now."

"Dr. Palmer is full of surprises," Asher murmured as he glanced over at the packed bar and the line of women in their tight skirts. "You are *so* lucky you met her first. I've really got a thing for smart women . . . and if they like to wear short skirts . . . my kryptonite."

"Fuck off," Wade said as he jumped out of the Jeep.

"You're welcome for the ride," Asher called after him.

Wade waved him away with his middle finger and he headed right for the main door. The bouncer there put up a hand, and Wade shoved a fifty at him.

Then he was inside. The music was blaring. Bodies were slammed together on the dance floor. Pressed way too close.

His gaze scanned the booths. He didn't see Victoria. Not in the booths, not on the dance floor, and not even at the bar.

Am I too late?

He pushed his way to the bar. The same bartender he'd met a few nights back—*hell, just a few nights?*—turned toward him.

"I'm looking for a woman," Wade said.

The guy's brows climbed, then beetled down low. "I know you . . ."

"Gorgeous redhead," Wade continued. He lifted his hand. "This tall. Green eyes, curvy, and—"

"I remember you . . . and her, from before." The bartender put his hands down on the bar top. "Look, I keep hating to be the one to tell you this, but she went off with him again."

"Him?" The noise around Wade seemed to dim.

"Yeah, him, you know, the blond she was with the first night you came hopping in here, searching for her." The bartender's gaze held pity. "The guy even brought her a drink a few minutes ago. Disappeared with it, and I haven't seen him—or her—since."

No, that didn't make sense. Victoria was there to meet him. She wouldn't just go out and hook up with some other guy. They were together.

Wade shook his head. That wasn't right.

"Sorry, buddy," the bartender said. "But there are plenty of other women here. Go find one of them." He turned away.

Wade didn't want to find anyone else. Victoria was it for him. She'd called him. She wouldn't have ditched him for some other guy. That just didn't fit.

He turned away from the bar, his gaze sweeping over the crowd once again. But there was no sign of a familiar figure with dark red hair. No sign of her at all.

Eyes narrowing, Wade headed back toward the entrance. He walked outside, his gaze sweeping over the crowd that waited to pass inside. Definitely no Victoria in that line.

Had she gone back to her place? Because he'd been late?

He moved right, heading in the direction of her building. But then . . . his gaze slid toward the alleyway. And he found himself turning. He'd been behind Wild Jokers once before, when he discovered Victoria,

locked in an embrace with Flynn. No way would he
find that scene now.

He trusted Victoria completely.

His steps quickened as he neared the back of the
building. He turned and—

Victoria was there. Held tightly by Flynn.

Only there was nothing loverlike about the embrace.
The bastard had a knife to her throat and he was trying
to drag her away from Wild Jokers.

But when Flynn saw him, the guy froze.

Victoria didn't speak at all. That knife was digging
into her throat. Wade was afraid that—was blood sliding down her neck? Faint light spilled from the club
onto the alley.

"Well, well," Flynn called out. "I guess Prince
Charming *did* decide to join the party."

Fucking bastard.

"So very late, though." Flynn put his mouth close
to Victoria's ear. "If he'd been here earlier, if he'd just
cared more, none of this would've happened."

"You cut my tires," Wade snarled as he lunged forward.

"Stop!" Flynn's order cut through the night. "Another step and I will slice her from ear to ear. She will
be dead long before help can arrive. Another woman,
choking to death on her own blood while you hold her
so tightly in your arms."

Fuck me. That bastard had not just said . . . "You
were there," Wade realized, stunned. The bastard *must*
have been on that beach. How the hell was that possible?

Troy North had been the killer. North had taken Wade's phone.

Hadn't he?

Or . . .

Or had North been set up?

If he had, then Wade knew he'd shot an innocent man. A man who'd been pushed too far.

Pushed by . . . by Matthew Walker? By—

"I said stop!" Flynn bellowed.

Wade stopped inching forward. He also stopped trying to figure out what the hell had gone down in Savannah. Right then all he could afford to think about was Victoria. Saving her. Stopping that SOB with the knife.

Wade didn't take another step forward, but his gaze darted around the alley.

Had he just seen a shadow move behind Flynn? Was someone else out there?

Flynn laughed. "Your phone was real damn helpful, by the way. Lots of good info. Especially about your security system. Thanks to it, I was able to get in your home and tap your phone, no problem. Though I did need to haul ass back. Lucky for me, though, you decided to make that pit stop at the hospital and stay in Savannah longer."

Sonofabitch. *That's how you knew to slash my tires. You heard Victoria ask me to meet her here.*

And if Flynn had taken his phone—*he is the bastard who killed Melissa Hastings. Him, not Troy North.*

What in the hell?

How did he know about the hospital visit, though? If he'd already gone . . .

"So this is how the night is going down." Flynn's voice roughened. "You're in my fucking way. You're going to turn around and walk out of this alley. I'm going to take Victoria and we'll leave."

Wade didn't move. "Not happening." Because he would never see Victoria again. He knew it. If she left the alley . . . if Flynn took her away . . .

She's dead.

"I wasn't giving you options," Flynn snarled. "I was telling you what would go down. Either get the fuck out of here or I will slit her throat right now!" He yanked her head back and let the blade cut into her skin.

Wade heard Victoria's cry of pain, but she quickly clamped her lips together.

Again, a shadow seemed to move just behind Flynn.

Keep him talking. Keep him focused. "Why the hell are you doing this?"

"Because I can." Flynn laughed. "Because I've seen how very easy it is for others to get away with such terrible crimes. You think you're looking at a fucking stand-up member of society, like *her* dad, right? But you're not. Everyone has secrets. You look into the darkness long enough, and you'll finally see those secrets."

Victoria's hands had risen. She was clawing against Flynn's hold. He just laughed. "I know her secret."

Every muscle in Wade's body had locked down. That bastard was not getting out of the alley with Victoria.

"She wants me, you know. She told me so. Sent me messages . . ."

"Victoria thought she was talking to *me*," Wade yelled. He wanted to make his voice as loud as possible.

Maybe someone in that line outside Wild Jokers would hear him. A bystander who would have enough sense to call the cops.

"Did she? Is that what you tell yourself?" Flynn pressed a kiss to Victoria's temple. "I don't think so. There's been a connection between us from the beginning."

"A connection . . ." Wade nodded. "Like the connection between you and Melissa Hastings?"

"Melissa . . . she was really his, not mine."

His?

Shit, there were two killers. *Two.* Now it made more sense. Because Melissa had been taken before he and Victoria even arrived in Savannah. And Flynn had been in Atlanta then. So who had his partner been?

North?

Or . . .

"Though I have to confess," Flynn added darkly, "I did enjoy playing with her—and killing her. That was quite a rush."

So someone else kidnapped her—and you killed her? Bastard.

"I'm going to give you ten seconds," Flynn called, "to get the fuck out of my way. Or she dies right here."

Wade glanced over his shoulder. The alley behind him was empty. People were focused on getting into the bar, not on what was happening in the shadows. No one ever looked too closely at shadows. They walked past them, moving as fast as they could to avoid the darkness.

"Five seconds left . . ."

"You won't do it," Wade yelled back.

"Four."

"You kill her, you lose your shield." He was sweating.

"Three."

"You kill her, then I will kill *you* with my bare hands." An absolute promise. *Think, think!*

"Two . . ."

There was no fucking choice.

Wade spun away from them as if he were leaving the alley, giving Flynn just what he'd wanted.

Flynn's mocking laughter filled the air. *Keep laughing, asshole. You aren't getting out of here. You—*

There was a thud behind Wade. The slam of flesh hitting flesh. Wade whirled back around. He saw Victoria on the ground, lying facedown. Flynn was fighting someone—the shadowy figure that he had glimpsed creeping up behind the other man. Flynn was swinging his arm out, slashing down with the knife.

Wade lunged forward—and went straight to Victoria. He rolled her over and saw that she had her hand to her throat. Was blood on her fingers? It was so damn dark, he couldn't see clearly enough and his heart fucking stopped right then. Just stopped because she couldn't die. He couldn't lose her. This shit could not hap—

"Help . . . Asher . . ." Victoria rasped.

He looked back over his shoulder and saw Flynn slash the man who'd attacked him—*Asher.*

Asher was on the ground now. Flynn's attention was completely on him. The bastard lifted his knife up high, and Wade leapt at him. Before Flynn could sink that knife into Asher again, Wade had slammed into his back. He and Flynn fell to the cement in a tangle and the knife clattered from Flynn's hand.

Wade drove his fist into Flynn's face and he heard the crunch of cartilage, but Flynn fought back, lifting his feet and driving them into Wade's stomach. The wind was knocked from Wade as he flew back, but he didn't even pause as he lunged right back at the SOB.

Flynn was on his feet now, circling around Wade. "You think you're gonna win, Prince Charming? Think the hell again."

"You don't have your knife. I like my odds," Wade fired right back. "Your ass isn't getting away. You're going to be locked in a jail cell for what you've done."

Flynn laughed at him. His hands were fisted at his sides. "And Victoria will be with me. Because I'll tell them what she did. *I know.*"

"You don't know shit."

"She killed her father. She confessed . . . confessed all to me."

He didn't believe that.

"She talks so much in bed," Flynn taunted him. "Doesn't she?"

Wade lunged at him. He caught Flynn and they went barreling back. Back and—

Flynn drove a knife into Wade's stomach.

"Didn't think that was my only one, did you?" Flynn whispered to him. "Bet you didn't even see me pull it from my boot. Fatal mistake, letting that rage take over." He twisted the blade. "Now you're going to die, that fool hero wanna-be on the ground will die, and Victoria—"

He broke off, choking. Gasping.

Wade wrenched his body away from Flynn, feeling the slide of the blade as it cut him on its damn way out.

He staggered back and blood pumped from him. Then he braced his body, ready to attack that bastard again.

But Flynn stumbled forward. The knife fell to the ground as he lifted his hands and swatted at his back. He made a drunken circle as he tried to look behind him . . .

Victoria was behind him. Standing there, with her hands still up.

And when Wade saw Flynn's back, he realized just why the other man had stopped his attack. Victoria had driven a knife into Flynn's back, one that was buried hilt-deep.

"I never *slept* when we were together," Victoria rasped out. "You didn't matter enough for me to stay. So I know I didn't talk to you."

She'd had nightmares—she'd spoken in her sleep to him, Wade thought. *Not to you, asshole.*

"You bugged my place, didn't you?" Victoria continued. Red had streamed down her shirtfront, a red that terrified him when she stepped forward into the faint light cast from the club. But her voice grew stronger with every word. "*That's* how you knew my secrets. You've been watching me all this time, stalking me, and I didn't know it."

Wade wrenched forward and grabbed the knife that Flynn had dropped. The bastard was still alive, and that meant he was still a threat.

"You don't know me," Victoria said as Flynn fell to his knees before her. "You know nothing . . ."

Flynn was still trying to swat at his back in a vain effort to pull out that knife.

A groan came from Wade's right. He looked over

to see Asher rising—a bit wobbly—to his feet. "Told you . . ." Asher muttered. "Got your . . . back . . . for now on . . . Said you could . . . count on me."

Asher Young had sure as hell been a man of his word.

Wade ignored the burning pain in his belly and closed in on Flynn. He put the knife to the asshole's throat.

Flynn's hand dropped. His head tilted back as he stared up at Wade.

Wade's fingers were trembling. He'd never wanted to take another man's life more . . . Never wanted to yank that knife so hard and cut so deep . . .

"Do it," Flynn taunted, breath heaving out. "Show her . . . who you . . . are . . ."

His hold tightened on the knife. This freak had wanted to kidnap Victoria. He would have hurt her, again and again, and then, when he was done . . . he would have killed her.

"How many others?" Wade demanded.

Flynn's eyes closed. "Just one. Melissa . . . she was fun. Buddy of mine introduced me . . ." He swayed. "But she was no . . . Viki . . . So dark and twisted up inside . . . perfect out, evil in . . . made for me . . ."

"No, she wasn't." The SOB truly knew nothing about Victoria.

"We should call the police," Victoria said. "Get help . . . an ambulance . . ."

Wade pulled the knife away from Flynn's throat. "They're going to . . . lock you up. If there are more missing, we'll . . . find them. You'll . . . never be free."

"Neither will she . . ." Flynn gave a gruff laugh. "I'll make sure . . . neither . . . will . . . *she* . . ."

And he lunged up. He came at Wade with a desperate heave of strength.

Wade didn't hesitate. The knife went straight into Flynn's chest. Slid in like cutting into butter . . .

Flynn's eyes were open and . . . satisfied.

"Now . . . she sees," he whispered.

Someone screamed. Wade's head snapped to the right and he saw that—finally—someone else had come into the alley. A woman and man stood there. The woman screamed again—even louder as Flynn's body fell to the ground.

"Call the police!" Wade shouted. He took a step, wanting to get to Victoria, needing to help her—and Asher. "Call—"

He fell. Why had he fallen?

Wade tried to get up, but his hands weren't working right. He couldn't push himself up. And that wound that had burned so badly before? It was cold. Ice cold. Numbing him. He tried to roll over because he needed Victoria. Needed to see her and touch her . . .

"Lie still." Victoria was above him and he was flat on his back now. No, no, she was crouched next to him, not over him. When had she moved? When had she come so close? He tried to lift his hand because he wanted to touch her.

But he was too weak.

Then her hands were touching him. Pressing down hard on him. "I'm not letting you go," Victoria told him.

She was bleeding. She was hurt.

She was—crying?

"I'm not letting you go," Victoria said again. "You stay with me, understand?"

He nodded, his head sliding against the cement. He wasn't going anywhere. Didn't she get that? He was in it for the long haul with Victoria. When he pictured the rest of his life, she was right by his side. Time would slip past, and they'd be together.

Maybe they'd move to the 'burbs. Get a house with lots of room, in case she wanted to have kids. A kid with her red hair would be a beautiful little princess.

Or if she just wanted to stay right there in the city, they could do that. They could make anything work.

"Wade! Don't you do this!"

He wasn't doing anything. Just staring up at her. Loving her. His Victoria. Did she even realize how perfect she was to him?

"Wade, please . . ."

"Love . . . you . . ."

"No! Do not pull some 'I love you' line that is going to be the last thing you say to me, do you understand? You do *not* do that. You keep fighting. I've got the artery, and I'm not letting go."

He didn't understand.

"We'll get blood for you. The doctors will patch you up. Just *stay with me*. Wade, you understand? You stay!" Her breath heaved out. Victoria was crying. No, he didn't want her to cry. He wanted her to laugh and smile and to be happy . . . forever.

"You stay—" Victoria seemed to choke out the words. "You—"

He couldn't see her any longer. His eyes had sagged closed.

"You stay!" Victoria screamed. "Please." A desperate whisper. "Please stay with me . . ."

And he tried to nod once more. There was no way he'd leave her. They'd found each other, and he didn't intend to let go.

So death could just screw off.

CHAPTER SEVENTEEN

"VICTORIA!" WADE'S EYES FLEW OPEN AND HE glanced frantically around.

White stared back at him—white walls, white ceiling, white floor and—

"I'm right here."

His head jerked to the right. Victoria sat in the chair next to . . . to his bed? Yeah, yeah, he was in a hospital bed. Tubes ran to his body. Machines beeped. And Victoria held his hand.

She smiled at him. Dark shadows slid under her eyes. "I see what you meant about hospitals."

He had no clue what she was talking about. "What . . . happened?" His voice sounded rusty to his own ears and something was pulling low in his stomach.

"Are you back this time? Not just doing some drunk drug talk to me?"

A furrow pulled down his brows. "I get that . . . I'm in a hospital." He tried to remember what the hell had happened. He'd gone to Wild Jokers, looking for her. She hadn't been there. She'd been out back, with that guy Flynn—

The machines went wild.

"Bastard," Wade snarled.

Victoria squeezed his fingers. "Easy. Don't want that blood pressure sky-rocketing." Then she paused and muttered, "Or bottoming out, the way it did before."

"Victoria."

She smiled at him. "You *are* back. Good. Because you kept drifting in and out, and most of the time you weren't making any sense to me."

With his free hand, he lifted the sheets. He saw that he was wearing a loose pair of pajamas and that a big white bandage covered half of his stomach.

"The pajamas were my idea," she said quickly. "I just . . . a regular gown wouldn't cut it because of where your wound was positioned. I wanted you to be comfortable, and I didn't want the nurses seeing your—um, seeing you every time they came in, so it seemed like a good idea to go with the pj's."

He lowered the sheet. "The bastard twisted the knife." Flynn had been trying to go for maximum damage. *He'd been trying to kill me.*

She nodded.

And he saw— *"Baby, your neck."*

Her hand rose and pressed to the small white bandage there. "It's nothing. Probably won't even scar."

Her voice had notched up, so he thought she was lying to him. His eyes turned to slits as he gazed at her bandage.

"Nothing," Victoria said again. "A flesh wound. He didn't cut me deep enough for permanent damage. I don't think Flynn wanted to kill me in the alley. He had other plans for me."

His gaze shot to the door. "Is he in this damn hospital?"

"He's in the morgue."

Wade didn't move.

"My knife attack killed him. *Mine*. I just—I don't want you carrying that around on you, too. I knew when I drove that knife in him, I knew *where* to put it in. He wasn't going to recover. He only had seconds left. So by the time you got to him . . . he was just a walking dead man."

"I would have killed him a dozen times if it meant you were safe." She needed to know that brutal truth.

Victoria sucked in a sharp breath.

"Does that . . . scare you?" His voice still sounded rusty as all hell.

Victoria pulled her hand from his and picked up a pitcher on the side table. She poured water into a plastic cup, her fingers trembling. "Nothing about you scares me." She put a straw into the cup, then used the remote to lift him up in the bed. When the straw touched his lips and the water rolled down his parched throat—paradise.

"But like I said before," Victoria murmured, "I see what you meant about hospitals."

He slid back against the pillows. Slowly, she put down the cup. Then her gaze came back to him. It sure looked as if there were tears in her beautiful eyes. "When I was in here, watching you . . . when you were so pale and still, I was terrified."

The machines kept beeping. He lay there, frozen. Wade couldn't look away from her gaze.

A tear spilled from the corner of her eye. "You were bleeding out at the scene, do you know that? I had to—I had to stop the blood. I had to hold—" Victoria broke off, shaking her head. "Promise me you won't ever do that again. Promise me that you won't make me think my entire world is ending . . . because you're trying to leave it."

"Baby . . ."

"I was scared." A hushed confession. "From the very beginning. No strings . . . no strings because *I* was scared. I didn't want to open myself up. But I did—to you. With you. Then I was so afraid—every time we touched—because I needed you, too much. Was that natural? Or was I being like my father?"

"You're *not*."

She swallowed. "But none of that fear compared to the way I felt when you were on the ground in that alley. And when I was in this hospital, and I was praying for you to wake up, I swore that if you came back to me, I wouldn't be afraid any longer."

The machines beeped a bit faster.

Her lips rose in a wobbly smile. "I love you."

Hell, *yes*.

"I'm not saying things will be easy between us. Nothing is perfect, no one is. But I want to try. I want to try being with you because I *don't* want to live without you. You make me happier, you make me feel . . . free. And I know that's crazy, but when I'm with you, I don't have to hold back. I can just be . . ." Her voice dropped to a whisper. ". . . me."

He caught her hand. Pulled her onto the mattress beside him. His thumb brushed away her tears. Then he kissed her wet cheeks. Her soft lashes. Her sweet mouth.

"Wade? Please, say something."

"Marry me."

"Wh-What?"

"Tomorrow or a year from now. Whenever you're ready . . ." He kissed her again. "You'd make me the happiest—and damn luckiest man—alive, if you'd marry me." He pulled back, just enough so that he could stare up at her. "I want you to be my partner, baby. Forever. Only you. You fit me. You make me happy. You make every damn thing in my life seem worthwhile. If I have you . . ." It was simple for him. ". . . I have everything."

Her breath choked out. Ever so carefully, she wrapped her arms around his neck. "I have everything, too," Victoria whispered. Then she kissed him. He could taste the salt of her tears in that kiss, but he could also taste so much more.

Hope.

Love.

Darkness hadn't won this time. They'd survived. Two lost souls . . . found.

One week later . . .

"I DON'T UNDERSTAND why I have to come into the police station," Matthew Walker said as he straightened his tie and glanced over at Bob Moore, his lawyer. "I mean, I'm recovering from my injuries. I should still be at home. On bed rest."

"What a dick," Wade muttered from bedside Victoria.

She, Wade, and Asher Young were in the Savannah police station's observation room, separated from the interrogation room by a thin one-way mirror. Detective Dace Black had just followed Matthew and Moore into interrogation, and the real show was about to begin.

"Hmmm," Asher murmured as he moved in for a better look. "He does look like a dick, I agree."

He looked like a killer to Victoria, and LOST was about to prove just that.

"Why don't you have a seat?" Dace waved toward the chairs that waited on the opposite side of the small table. "I just have a few questions that need clarifying."

"I could have 'clarified' things over the phone," Matthew huffed as he sat down, his lawyer sitting next to him. Victoria thought Matthew made an extreme show of struggling to sit. Painful injuries, her ass. Wade and Asher were both up and walking again just fine. And this guy?

We are going to nail you to the wall.

Dace pulled out his first piece of evidence, and sat the gun—bagged and tagged as evidence—onto the table next to Matthew. "This is the weapon you brought to Worthington University, correct?"

Matthew glanced down at the gun, then at his lawyer.

Moore gave a short, negative shake of his head.

Victoria saw Matthew's eyes narrow. *He doesn't like being told what to do.*

Matthew's stare cut back to Dace. "Looks like it."

"Right. Well, your prints were all over it, and it *was* recovered at the scene." Dace gave a wide smile. "But what I don't get is why would you bring an unregistered weapon to a college campus to begin with?"

"Because I was out of my mind with grief!" Matthew threw out his hand. "I'd just figured out—before any of you cops did—that Troy North was a sadistic killer! I just wanted to stop him—"

"With an unregistered gun."

The lawyer leaned forward. "The gun was a gift to my client. He had no idea it wasn't registered."

Dace's eyelids flickered. "Want to tell me who . . . gifted that gun to you?"

Matthew smiled. "Melissa did. Fitting, isn't it? That the woman Troy killed would have a hand in his death."

"He is so fucking confident," Asher mused behind the one-way mirror. "The bigger they are . . ."

"The faster they become someone's bitch in prison," Wade finished.

Victoria kept her gaze on the scene in the interrogation room. It was almost showtime.

"Why would Melissa give you anything?" Dace asked Matthew. He opened a manila file. Pulled out a stack of papers. "According to this sworn statement, her roommate, Jim, said Melissa was never involved with you—"

"She just didn't tell him—"

"Melissa told him that you'd made advances to her. Advances she rejected. You'd followed her on her jogging path twice—"

"That was *my* path, I ran it all the time!"

Moore tugged on his sleeve. Matthew just jerked away from the lawyer. "No, no, this is bull! Melissa and I were involved. Okay, it just started as sex, but it was going to be—"

"Jim actually *did* see Melissa's lover," Dace interrupted. "He saw him from the back one day, and the guy's build is very similar to Troy North's and he had blond hair, so I could see where Jim would've initially thought it was the psychology professor she was involved with, but . . ." He pulled a photo out of his file. "I believe Jim actually saw this man. Flynn Marshall."

Matthew didn't look at the photo. "I don't know him."

"I didn't ask if you knew him."

The lawyer rose. "Okay, this has gone on long enough. We came here as a courtesy and—"

"If you happen to follow Atlanta news," Dace continued smoothly, "you probably already know that Flynn Marshall is dead. He was killed when he attempted to abduct LOST agent Victoria Palmer."

Matthew was starting to sweat. Just a bit.

Wade's hand slid over her back. "You ready?"

She thought of Kennedy. Of Melissa. "Absolutely." Victoria squared her shoulders and left their observation area. Moments later she opened the door to the interrogation room.

"I don't follow Atlanta news—" Matthew blustered. But when he saw Victoria, his words jerked to a halt.

She inclined her head toward him. "Are you sure about that? Because according to your credit card statements, you make pretty frequent trips to Atlanta. It certainly looked as if . . . you were consistently visiting a friend in the Atlanta area."

His face became a blank mask.

"Why would you access my client's private financial reports?" The lawyer demanded. "This is outrageous, outrageous!"

Victoria didn't look at Moore. She kept her gaze focused on the prey that mattered. "Before he died, I was in that back alley with Flynn for a long time. Too long. He'd tried to slip me a drugged drink—I suspect it's a technique he used before. Seeing as how he was a pharmaceutical rep, I bet he had all kinds of tricks he liked to use with his drugs . . ."

"I'm sorry you were attacked," Matthew said flatly. "But I don't see what I am—"

"He thought I'd been drugged, but I hadn't. So maybe that's why he spoke so freely with me. Or maybe he just figured I'd die soon, so what he said—or who he incriminated—didn't matter so much."

Matthew's gaze slid down to her throat. And to the red mark still there.

For an instant it almost looked as if he smiled.

They were right. You are a dick.

"He told me about his friend in Savannah," she said. "Interesting, the things he revealed to me . . ."

Matthew pushed to his feet. "I'm done with this—"

"Dr. Troy North wasn't involved in any murders. He was just the perfect fall guy, wasn't he? Serve him up, plant evidence in his office, and bam—all the focus is off you. And the LOST agents—well, we left town. We lowered our guards. We were distracted."

The lawyer, Bob Moore, was standing now, too, as if ready to leave. The light gleamed off his bald head. She'd known the attorney would be difficult. She just had to play Matthew the right way . . .

I'm not Sarah, but I can do this. I will do this.

And, lucky for her, Sarah had given her some advice on just how to handle this particular monster.

"Troy and Flynn Marshall went to school together," Victoria said. "Northwestern University."

Matthew smirked at her. "Well, there you go. More proof that Troy was the killer. He and that Flynn guy must have teamed up to—"

"They didn't team up for anything. But five years ago Flynn *did* come to Savannah for a visit with Troy. He was catching up with his old college roommate. And it was during that visit that Flynn found a guy who he could *really* understand . . ."

Matthew just shook his head and gave her a confused glance. "I'm certain I have no clue about Flynn or his visit or anyone who *understood* him . . ."

"Liar." She called him out on it.

His eyes narrowed.

"The police searched Flynn's house. It seemed he liked to keep mementos of things that interested him. He had . . . a scrapbook, of sorts. Clippings—old newspaper accounts of my father's trial."

"Guess that's why he was obsessed with you."

"*That's* why he came up here to visit Troy, actually. To learn more about my father. He interviewed Troy on and off over the years. Seems they even talked about doing some kind of book on my dad. 'The Monster Next Door,'" she murmured.

That had been the title the cops found scribbled in Flynn's scrapbook.

"We need to leave," the lawyer ordered.

But Matthew wasn't leaving. Arrogant, cocky Matthew. "All I'm hearing," he said, "are links between Troy and that Flynn guy."

"There were a lot of links there," she agreed quickly.

"They were both psych majors, back in the day. But Flynn couldn't handle the master's program. He flunked out. Troy didn't. He excelled. Because he was doing so well, Troy was the one who got to attend my father's trial, not Flynn." She lowered her voice. "Between you and me . . . I think that really pissed off Flynn. He didn't like thinking he was second best, and his college roommate proved—every single time—that he was better than Flynn."

A flicker of worry passed over Matthew's face. Just for the barest moment, and then it was gone.

But I saw it.

"A scrapbook?" Matthew asked.

"Matthew," the lawyer called. *"Now."*

She nodded. "Very interesting photos were in there, too." Now she lifted the file that she had carried into the room. "Photos of Kennedy, before her death. Photos of her being taken off a jogging trail . . . photos of her abductor."

Matthew brushed past her. "Well, her abductor is dead, so that's one case that is closed." He stalked past his lawyer and grabbed for the door.

Victoria glanced over her shoulder. When the door opened, she saw Wade and Asher standing there outside the room, perfect shields blocking Matthew's exit.

"Get out of my way," Matthew muttered.

They didn't move.

Even Moore looked nervous.

"Don't you want to look at this picture?" Victoria asked him softly. "It's a rather good picture. Gets the abductor's face so well . . . *your* face so well."

Matthew's shoulders stiffened. "I'm not in that picture."

"Flynn saw you, didn't he? Such a chance encounter. But *he* was an avid jogger, too, and he happened to be on that trail the morning you took Kennedy. And that was the moment everything changed. For you. For him. He knew what you'd done, but he didn't go to the cops. Somehow—you and Flynn connected. Monster to monster, I guess. Which one of you had the idea to keep Kennedy alive so long?"

He glared at her.

"Was it you?" Victoria asked.

His jaw hardened. "Do your fucking job, Bob!" he yelled at his lawyer.

His lawyer's mouth opened as if he was about to start to argue. Sarah didn't give him the chance, as she fired out, "Or was it Flynn?"

Moore reached for the photos. "I need to see—" He broke off as his gaze scanned the images. "Ph-Photos can be faked." He began thumbing through them.

Victoria knew exactly what he'd see in all those terrible images. Kennedy—being tortured. Kennedy—being held captive. Kennedy—and her abductor.

Matthew Walker.

"Flynn took the pictures. You did the crime." *No, both men were just as guilty. Both sick, twisted men.* "Do you think they'll hurt you?" Victoria asked him, cocking her head to the side.

"Who?"

"The men in prison."

He lunged forward and grabbed her. "You cunt, I'm

not going to prison! Flynn was the sick bastard who dug her up! I didn't even *know* he was doing that shit! He did it because he knew *you* were coming to town. Wanted your fucking LOST self to *find* her. But he couldn't have you leaving town too soon. No, no, he liked the game. Thought it was his turn. I'd taken Melissa. I'd waited, I'd planned, then he swooped in and he fucking *killed* her! After he'd taught me the value of keeping prey alive—he killed Melissa! He took her away before I—"

Still gripping her shoulders, Matthew broke off, but she knew what he'd been going to say. "Before you had any fun?" she finished, feeling sick.

"Get your hands off her." Wade's voice was low and lethal. "Or I will fucking break them right now."

Matthew blinked. He shook his head. "I—" His hands fell away.

"My client is confused!" the lawyer sputtered. "His attack and his pain medications have made him . . . they've made him . . ."

For the first time since Victoria entered the room, Dace spoke. "They didn't make him anything. He's a murdering bastard who just confessed to his crimes, and I'm going to see to it that he rots in jail."

He had confessed. He'd *confessed.*

Matthew stared at her—stared. Glared. And she knew he was going to attack even before the snarl ripped across his face. He lunged at her.

She punched him in the face. His lip busted under her fist and he howled.

In the next instant, Wade had grabbed Matthew's

hands. Wade twisted hard, and Victoria knew that Matthew's bones had just snapped.

He fell to the floor, screaming.

"You can't do that!" Moore yelled. "Police brutality! You can't—"

"We're not cops," Victoria said.

"And from where the *cop* sits," Dace added, "that was self-defense."

Matthew was on the floor in a fetal position.

A grim smile curved Wade's lips. "They are going to love you in prison."

Matthew whimpered. "My hands . . . my hands . . ."

The hands that had brutalized Kennedy . . .

"Matthew Walker," Dace said, voice sharp and hard. "You're under arrest for the abduction and murder of Kennedy Lane."

Victoria took a deep breath. Her racing heartbeat eased.

"You have the right to remain silent."

Matthew was crying.

"Anything you say can and will be used against you . . ."

He'd already said plenty.

Enough to seal his fate.

"Let's see how you like being prisoner," Victoria said. And a cold smile curved her lips. Justice, finally.

Maybe both Kennedy and Melissa would be able to rest in peace.

"THANK YOU," DACE said as he offered his hand, first to Victoria, then to Wade. "The case just wasn't sitting right with me. I *knew* I was missing something, but my captain was yanking back. Telling me to close that shit down."

"The case is closed now," Victoria said, giving a quick nod.

Dace glanced toward the interrogation room. Matthew had already been taken out. "Sometimes, I wonder if I'm in the right place . . ."

Asher joined their little group. "Plane will be ready to leave within the hour."

Dace's brows rose. "Another case?"

Asher slanted a quick glance at Victoria and Wade. "According to the boss, those two get a vacation. Maybe a honeymoon."

Because I said yes.

"But my sister and I are about to get a crash course on all things LOST," Asher added. "Time for us to jump in with both feet."

Dace shook Asher's hand. "Good luck to you."

The case was closed. The plane waited. Time to go, but . . .

"We could always use another good team member," Victoria said to Dace. Because he hadn't given up on Kennedy. Or Melissa.

And he hadn't revealed my secrets, either.

Surprise flashed in the detective's eyes.

"If you ever think about getting into the private sector," Wade added, "you should give us a call."

Dace laughed, but his gaze held speculation. "I'm not a freaking Navy SEAL. I doubt I'm the kind of guy your boss would want to hire—"

"Actually," Wade told him, "you're exactly the kind of guy LOST needs. Think it over."

Dace's head tilted down and he stared at the floor as he said, "Don't see how I'd be any good. I didn't find Kennedy. Didn't help her—"

"You didn't give up on her," Victoria said. "That's what matters. And maybe next time, you *will* bring the missing home."

She felt Wade's gaze on her.

"Hope," Victoria explained simply. "That's what this is about. Not just closing a case, but finding those victims. Giving the family hope." Hope could be such a beautiful thing.

Wade had taught her that.

It was a lesson that she would never forget.

Her fingers curled with his and they walked out of the police station. Asher was right. They had a vacation coming. Maybe someplace tropical. And maybe . . . maybe while they were there, they'd even get married on a sunny beach.

Life was full of hope now. She saw it—everywhere she looked.

Wade squeezed her fingers, and she knew, finally, that there would be no more desperate searching for her. No more fighting to keep her secrets hidden. She was safe. She was loved.

She was home . . . with Wade.

Exactly where she was supposed to be.

Are you addicted to the sexy and suspenseful novels

from *New York Times* best-selling author

CYNTHIA EDEN?

Then you won't want to miss the next LOST novel!

TAKEN

Coming soon from Avon Books!

Read on for a sneak peek . . .

PROLOGUE

BAILEY JONES DIDN'T WANT TO DIE. NOT TIED UP, tortured, and all alone in that damn little shack.

She couldn't feel her fingers. That should have scared her—that terrible numbness—but she was long past the point of being afraid. She was mad now. So fucking angry—why had this happened? Why her? And, why, *why* wouldn't the jerk who held her just let her go?

Her face slid over the rough wooden floor of the cabin. She jerked at the rope that held her wrists, but it wouldn't give. She was sure she'd been bleeding from her wrists earlier, but had that stopped? Or maybe she was still bleeding—from her wrists or from the slashes on her body. Bailey didn't know if the wounds still trickled blood.

She only knew . . . she'd been in that cabin for nearly three days. Light had come and gone, spilling through the window. Her lips were busted and raw, and her throat was sore—scratched from screaming and bone dry because the bastard who'd taken her had only given her the tiniest sips of water. And no food, no food at all. No bathroom.

Just pain.

She inched across the floor, moving like a worm. If she could just get across the room, she'd be able to get out of the door. If she could get to that door, she could escape.

Her captor had made a mistake. After his last time using that knife on her . . . he'd thought that she passed out. Bailey had learned fast with that freak. He only liked to hurt her if she was awake. If she was unconscious . . . well, there must not be any damn fun in the act for him. He liked to see her suffer. Liked to make her beg.

Eleven slices of his knife . . . he'd been counting. He'd stopped after eleven, his breathing heaving, his body shaking. And when he stopped . . .

I just pretended to pass out. And that freak in the ski mask stormed out of the room. In his haste, he'd left the door open. Oh, hell, yes, he'd left the door open. She'd gotten off the bed, fallen onto the floor—and now—she *was* getting out of this place. Her rage gave her the energy to keep moving. She'd get to the door. Get out and . . .

Her shirt snagged on a nail. Bailey froze. She hadn't even seen that nail but when she moved her body, she felt the head of that nail—round and big—sticking up from the floor. Her breath heaved in and out of her lungs as excitement pumped through her blood. Bailey twisted her body and put the ropes that bound her wrists against that nail top. She jerked and sawed, moving as frantically as she could. Her breath keep rushing out in too hard pants, burning her lips and making her tongue feel even more swollen in her mouth.

I'll get out. I'll get away.

For the first twenty-four hours, she'd thought she was trapped in a nightmare. That there was some mistake. She couldn't have woken up, tied and gagged in a dirty cabin. There couldn't have been some sick freak in a black ski mask who kept coming at her, slicing with his knife and laughing while she screamed. *None* of that could be happening, not to her.

Not . . . her.

She'd seen the stories on TV in the last few weeks. About women who'd vanished in the mountains of North Carolina. Their stories had been tragic. Their families pitiful as they begged for clues. She'd watched them and felt sympathy. Sorrow. But . . .

Those women had been strangers. Because things like *this* . . . stuff like this only happened to people you didn't know. Unfortunate people you saw on the news.

Not me. This can't happen to me.

But it had.

And I don't have any family to beg for me. No desperate parents to plead for my return . . . I lost them long ago.

Bailey was very much afraid she'd be losing her own life in that small cabin.

One minute, she'd been heading out of her Wednesday night freshman history class at the local college. It had been the last class she had to teach before spring break. She'd been at her car, her keys gripped tightly in her hand, and then—

Then he hit me. Took me. I woke up in hell.

The ropes around her wrists gave way. Bailey choked out a sob as feeling surged back to her fingers—pain.

Burning, white hot pain. But as soon as that sob slipped from her mouth, she immediately bit her lower lip, terror clawing at her. Blood dripped down her chin from that busted lip.

Had he heard her cry?

Would he come back?

Bailey's whole body went tense as she waited. Waited. She heard the creak of footsteps, a sound that had her heart squeezing.

He's coming. He heard me. He's . . .

A scream seemed to echo all around Bailey. A woman's scream. Loud and long and desperate. Full of pain.

Bailey bit down harder on her bottom lip. She wasn't the one making that scream. Someone else was. Dear God, that freak in the ski mask had someone else in the cabin.

I'm not alone. He took another victim.

And when he'd stopped having his fun with Bailey, when she'd played possum with him, he'd turned his attention to that someone else.

Bailey jerked upright. Her fingers were slow and fumbling as she fought to free her ankles from the rope that bound them.

The scream died away.

She broke her nails on the rope. Jammed fingers that weren't working right.

Another scream—

And the rope gave way. Bailey immediately jumped to her feet and tried to stride forward, but her legs collapsed beneath her. She crawled then, dragging herself toward the door. She had to get to that other woman. Had to help her. Bailey grabbed the door, prying it open a little more with her right hand. Every breath she took seemed incredibly loud to her, and she was afraid he would hear her.

I guess I'm not over the fear after all. Maybe I'll never be over it.

A peek in the hallway showed two other doors. One was shut. One open.

The screams were coming from behind the shut door. *He's in there with her.*

Bailey rose again, shakily. She kept a hand on the wall as she inched toward that closed door. She had to find a weapon. Had to get something to use against that bastard.

Another scream had her wanting to cover her ears. It was so loud.

"Help me! Please, help me!" the woman yelled. Begged. Pleaded. *"Please, dear God, someone help me!"*

And then Bailey heard the laughter. That taunting, snickering laughter that the bastard had made when he drove his knife into her. At that sickening sound, Bailey stopped thinking—a primitive instinct took over her body. She lurched forward and threw open the door. "Leave her alone!" Bailey bellowed.

His back was to her. A woman was on the bed in front of him. A knife was in his hand. A bloody knife. The same knife he'd so gleefully used on Bailey.

"Coming to save her?" he whispered, his back still to Bailey. When he spoke, he always whispered. "Ah, Bailey . . . is that what you're doing? Coming to help her?"

The woman on the bed didn't move.

Bailey lunged at him. She didn't have a weapon, and there was nothing in that room to use. No lamps. No tables. The only furniture was that old bed—the woman was on that bed. So Bailey attacked with her body. She went straight for him with a guttural cry.

He turned toward her, slicing with his knife, but Bailey didn't stop. The slice went right across her left arm. She barreled into him, crashing hard and they both hit the floor.

The knife slid from his hand, sliding across the wooden floor.

"Beautiful bitch," he rasped at her. "I'll make you pay . . ."

She was on top of him, and Bailey kneed him, as hard as she could. When he howled, she smiled, stretching her bloody lips. She was so glad he was the one who got to enjoy some pain.

But then he hit her, driving his fist right at her cheek. She fell back, her body rolling across the floor.

And footsteps thudded in that little room. The woman on the bed—she'd gotten up and she was running for the door. She hadn't been tied up like Bailey. She moved quickly, easily. Bailey saw her long, dark hair, her pale limbs, the blue of her shirt as it flashed by—

"Wait," Bailey gasped out, the word a weak croak. "Don't—"

Leave me.

For an instant, the woman turned back toward her. Hope burst inside Bailey. Yes—

The woman ran out of the room. Didn't look back again.

He was laughing again. Her abductor. Her killer?

"Trying to stop me . . ." he whispered. "Oh, sweet Bailey, I'll teach you . . ."

His hands went around her neck. Glove-covered hands. She felt the leather against her skin. Oddly soft. So soft as he began to choke her.

"I can do this until you pass out . . ."

"H-h . . ." She was trying to say *help,* trying to call that woman back, but she couldn't get the word out. Not with his hands so tight around her.

"Then I'll tie you up again. I'll sharpen my knife . . . get it so that it can slice right through your skin . . ."

From the corner of her eye, Bailey saw the glint of the knife he'd dropped. Her right hand stretched for it. The knife was close. So very close . . .

"Still glad you tried to save her? Was she worth *your* life?"

The other woman had gotten away. Bailey couldn't hear her footsteps any longer.

"I'll take care of you," he promised as black dots danced in front of her eyes. *"And her."*

The knife. It was right there. She just had to reach it . . .

He squeezed harder. No air. No hope. No damn knife.

She couldn't reach it. But Bailey's right flew up toward him, and with the last of her strength, she ripped that mask off his face.

He stared down at her, as shock widened his eyes.

"No, Bailey . . . *no* . . ." And he almost seemed sad . . . as he kept choking the life right out of her.

BAILEY'S EYES FLEW open. She sucked in a desper-

ate gulp of air, one, then another. Another. Her lungs
burned and she coughed and choked.

I'm alive. I'm still alive.

Her hands flew out, and she touched—dirt. The scent
of dank earth filled her nostrils and she sat up fast, feeling pain cut through her—her arms, her stomach and—

Dirt is all around me. Her grabbing hands closed
around soft dirt and when Bailey looked up, she saw
the glitter of stars above her. A thousand freaking stars.
I'm not in the cabin any longer.

But she didn't remember escaping. Didn't remember getting away from that bastard. He'd been choking
her. The other woman had run, but Bailey hadn't. He'd
caught her.

And . . . he'd tossed her into a hole? She sat up, but
couldn't reach the top of that hole. Too deep. Bailey
tried to stand, but her legs wouldn't hold her up, and
when she grabbed at the sides of that hole again, the
dirt just rained down on her.

Dogs were barking. She heard the sound distantly,
and fear pulsed through her. Were those his dogs? Was
this another game? Were the dogs going to attack her?

Bailey put her hand over her mouth so she wouldn't
make a sound. She tasted the dirt that was on her fingers. Her tongue was so thick and swollen in her mouth.
The nightmare wouldn't stop. Everything just kept getting worse and worse.

The barking was louder. Closer. The dogs were going
to get her. Would they rip her apart? Bite and tear into
her skin?

She curled into a ball in the middle of that hole, trying
to make herself as small as possible. If she didn't move,

if she didn't make a sound, maybe the dogs would leave her alone. They'd go away, and then she'd find some way out of there. She'd escape.

The other woman . . . where did she go? What happened to her?

But the dogs weren't going away. They were getting louder and louder. So close.

"Something's over here!" a man shouted. "Dirt. Oh, hell! A pile of it! Could be a body!"

Her head lifted.

"Get the lights!" Another voice. Another man. "Follow the dogs!"

The dogs . . .

Maybe they weren't there to hurt her. Maybe they were there to find her. Maybe the other woman . . . maybe she'd gotten away and sent help back to Bailey.

"H-help . . ." she whispered.

No . . . no sound had come from her lips. She'd tried to whisper but couldn't. Her throat was too raw. Her mouth too dry.

The lights were flashing over her hole. Not *in* the hole, but flying over the top of it. People were up there. She needed them to look down at her.

"*H-help . . .*" Another voiceless whisper. Inside, she was screaming. Roaring for help. But she couldn't talk. She tried to stand up again, but her body wasn't listening to her, not anymore. Too long without water? Without food? Too much blood loss?

Her hands curled around fists of dirt. *Look down here. Look at me. Look!*

A bright light hit her, falling straight into her face. It blinded her and she turned away.

"She's—she's alive! We've got a live one here!" Excitement burned in that voice—a voice with a heavy southern accent—and then a man was there before her. He'd jumped into the hole, and he was reaching for her.

She flinched away.

"It's okay," he told her quickly. "I'm a deputy. Deputy Wyatt Bliss. You're safe . . . we're gonna take care of you."

Bailey wanted to believe him.

More lights fell on her. So bright. She looked up and she saw the shadowy figures of other people—men and women. They surrounded the top of her hole now.

"Can you tell me your name?" He took his coat off, held it out to her. Was it cold? Was she supposed to take the coat?

Her teeth were chattering, but she hadn't noticed the cold, not until then.

She didn't take the coat. She didn't think her fingers would work and just keeping her eyes open was a serious effort.

"Your name, miss," he continued, that drawling voice of his careful now, sympathetic. "Can you tell it to me?"

"B—B . . ." *Bailey.* But she couldn't talk. Just that sad croak was all she could manage.

His flashlight fell to her neck. Whatever he saw there made him swearing.

But then others were jumping down into the hole. More men with flashlights. They were in the hole with her and they lifted her out. Someone carried her a few steps forward and then—then she was on some kind of gurney. Bailey craned her head and looked back. There were so many lights out there then, and the dogs were nearby, whining.

She saw her hole. Big and wide and deep. And a giant pile of dirt was beside it. A shovel lay forgotten on the ground.

Was that my grave?

"It's okay." It was a woman's voice. Bailey jerked at that voice and at the soft hand that touched her shoulder. "You're safe."

She didn't feel safe.

"I'm an EMT," the woman continued. "And I'll . . . I'll get you taken care of just . . ." The woman's voice trailed away. "Is all that blood yours?"

Bailey looked down at her body. Her shirt was soaked. Stained red, she saw in the light. Red and dirty. But was all the blood hers? *I think so.* Bailey nodded.

The scent of ash drifted to her. Ash and fire. *What's burning?* Her head turned as she was loaded into the back of an ambulance. She saw the fire in that instant, big and red as it burned so hot and bright. But . . . was that the cabin? Her prison? Was that what burned like hell right then?

"The fire brought the deputies in," the woman said, her blond hair in a bun near her nape, "it helped us find you." The ambulance's back doors slammed closed. "We found the other bodies first . . ."

No, no . . .

"And then you."

A man was in the back of the ambulance, too. Another EMT. He had red hair and freckles across his nose. He gave her a reassuring smile. "You're safe."

So she kept being told. *But I'm not. I'm not safe.* She needed to tell them about the other woman. They had to find her.

She grabbed for the redheaded man's hand. Held tight.

"What is it?" he asked, frowning at her. "Tell me where it hurts."

Bailey hurt everywhere, but this wasn't about her pain. "Wo . . . man . . ." She mouthed the words because she just couldn't speak.

His blue eyes narrowed on her lips.

"Wo . . . man . . ." She mouthed them again as her whole body began to shake. "Another . . . vic . . . vic . . . tim . . ."

His eyes became saucers. "Another victim was alive?"

She nodded.

"He had another victim with you?"

Once more, she nodded.

"Christ!" He lunged away from her and shoved open the ambulance's back door. "Keep those dogs searching! There's another woman out there!"

Bailey's head sagged back and her eyes closed. She'd done it. They would find the other woman. She'd be safe, too.

They'd find her.

The ambulance's sirens screamed.

And Bailey closed her eyes.

HARLEQUIN

I N T R I G U E

NEW YORK TIMES bestselling author

CYNTHIA EDEN

Brings you her 6 book edge-of-your seat mini-series

THE BATTLING MCGUIRE BOYS!

CONFESSIONS

SECRETS

SUSPICIONS

RECKONINGS

DECEPTIONS

ALLEGIANCES

Available wherever books are sold!

Connect with us on Harlequin.com for info on our
new releases, access to exclusive offers, free online
reads and much more!

Other ways to keep in touch:

Harlequin.com/newsletters

Facebook.com/HarlequinBooks

Twitter.com/HarlequinBooks

HarlequinBlog.com

AVON BOOKS

The Diamond Standard
of Romance

Visit AVONROMANCE.COM

Come celebrate 75 years of Avon Books
as each month we look toward the future
and celebrate the past!

Join us online for more information about our
75th anniversary e-book promotions,
author events and reader activities.
A full year of new voices and classic stories.
All created by the very best writers of romantic fiction.

Diamonds Always
Sparkle, Shimmer, and Shine!